continued . . .

Hard Time

"Gritty and compelling. Cara McKenna is a master at capturing realistic situations and characters."
—#1 *New York Times* bestselling author Maya Banks

"A lovely, heartfelt romance.... The letters, the sweetness, the tender eroticism made this book a recommended read for me." —Dear Author (recommended read)

"McKenna has crafted an intense, at times dark, heated romance." —*RT Book Reviews* (4½ stars)

"It's different and sexy, and I love that Cara McKenna explores protagonists that . . . have more real, grittier lives."
—Smexy Books

"*Hard Time* has gripping, emotional sections paired with some serious sexy times.... Fans of McKenna will be happy with her latest offering." —Fiction Vixen

Unbound

"Beautifully written and brilliant.... If you're looking for nuanced portrayals of complicated characters, I can't recommend it enough." —Dear Author

"I've said this countless times . . . but I love Cara McKenna's voice." —Smexy Books

"It's a very happy day for me when I get to read a new Cara McKenna novel . . . a very emotional, tug-at-your-heartstrings type of book . . . so very good." —Fiction Vixen

"I appreciated the depth in this story and the raw emotion that McKenna brought to her characters. She treated the subject matter with great respect and allowed her characters to fully explore their sexuality in a way that sizzled the pages. I think my e-reader needs a cooldown period."
—The Book Pushers

After Hours

"Intense, funny, and perfectly dirty all at the same time. *After Hours* is a new favorite."
> —Victoria Dahl, *USA Today* bestselling author of *Fanning the Flames*

"After reading *After Hours*, I went on a Cara McKenna glom and read seven books in a row. This book is that good!"
> —Fiction Vixen

"Exceptionally evocative writing . . . fascinating."
> —Smart Bitches Trashy Books

"A well-done, real-life, gritty erotic romance with a bossy, bossy hero and a heroine who can fight back."
> —Smexy Books

ALSO BY CARA McKENNA

BURN IT UP

A DESERT DOGS NOVEL

Cara McKenna

A SIGNET ECLIPSE BOOK

SIGNET ECLIPSE
Published by New American Library,
an imprint of Penguin Random House LLC
375 Hudson Street, New York, New York 10014

This book is an original publication of New American Library.

First Printing, November 2015

For more information about Penguin Random House, visit penguin.com.

ISBN 978-0-451-47660-9

Printed in the United States of America
10 9 8 7 6 5 4 3 2 1

Penguin
Random
House

With thanks to Christina, Claire, and Laura. Gestating two books and a baby at the same time wasn't easy, but you gals got me through.

Chapter 1

James Ware strolled into the prison yard alongside a couple hundred fellow inmates, welcoming the weak February sunshine on his shoulders and scalp. Normally the sensation would amount to a tease, a mere hour's escape from the cinder block and noise of the inside, but this afternoon it felt different. Felt manageable.

"Two days," came a voice from behind him. It was the young guy everybody called Tugs, for reasons James didn't care to know. He was skinny, hyper, a little too wide-eyed and loudmouthed for this place where bluster required muscle to command any respect. James didn't mind him, though. They worked in the kitchen together, and the kid was all right.

"Two fucking days," James agreed, slowing until Tugs was at his side, the both of them heading to the far corner of the yard.

"Lookit that wall, man." Tugs pointed to the fourteen feet of concertina-capped brick that penned them. "Two days from right now, you'll be on the other side. That's gotta feel good."

"No doubt." They reached the corner known as the gym—though a couple weight benches and a rusty collection of barbells weren't exactly worth a membership. James snagged a bench and Tugs stood by, always eager to spot. Kid was like one of those little fish that stuck close by a shark, grateful for scraps and a taste of protection.

"What'll you do, first thing after they let you out?" he asked James.

"Pray to God my sister remembers to pick my ass up." James hefted a thirty-pound dumbbell and began to curl. "Then eat a hot meal off an actual plate and get a decent cup of coffee." No more plastic trays, no more brown sludge-water.

"Bet you're gonna get so shitfaced on Tuesday," Tugs said wistfully.

"Sure." James didn't drink, but neither did he go into details about his personal life. He didn't need to drink, he thought, feeling the chemicals moving through his blood as his muscles woke up. His temper was a thrashing, snapping dog while he was stone-cold sober, and he kept it on a short leash. Get him drunk and that tether got real slippery, real quick. He hadn't had so much as a beer in two years or more. And he hadn't been as pissed as he was now in almost too long to remember.

"Bet you got a girl waiting for you," Tugs said. "Get wasted, get laid—that's what I'm gonna do the second I get out of here."

James didn't reply.

Yeah, he had a girl waiting for him. Two of them. An ex and a daughter. A four-month-old daughter he'd never met, and hadn't even known about until recently. He aimed to see her, as soon as he could track her down. And his ex . . . well, time would tell how difficult she might decide to make that for him. If the girl knew one thing, it was how to run.

The last time he'd seen her . . .

The last time, things had gotten out of control.

The two of them had always been out of control, but that afternoon it had all boiled over. Their relationship had only ever been a messy, staggered succession of fucking and fighting. Normally James prided himself on resisting other people's bait, but that girl could tempt his anger like nobody he'd ever known. She could rouse his softer side, too, and they'd had some good times. But that last blowout had rasped all the shine right off what they'd briefly had together in a roof-rattler of a fight that must've left them sounding like a pair of feral rednecks to the neighbors.

She'd wanted that fight, too. She'd goaded him until he'd lost control enough to clasp her shoulders and shake her. She had poison inside her. Other people had put it there, but she knew just how to strike out and weaponize that shit. She'd also had their baby inside her, during that fight. Neither of them had known it then, but it had already been growing. Just a tiny little speck, invisible to the eye, yet since James had found out about it, it had grown big enough to eclipse the whole of his world.

He'd never known a woman like Abilene. A seeming kitten, except catch her on a bad day, pet her wrong—she'd scratch and bite you like a fucking wolverine. She'd been all claws when they'd met, all claws when they'd parted less than three months later. In between there'd been good times, but stress had never brought out the best in her, and if a baby was one thing, it was stressful. If there were claws drawn now, he needed to know. Needed to see for himself that his kid was in safe hands.

As his muscles worked and his blood thundered in his temples, anger flared with every pulse. He wasn't a good man—there was no doubting that—but she was no saint herself. And if she decided he needed to be blocked out of his own daughter's life, that *he* was the one that child needed protecting from . . .

You've got a fucking nerve, you little bitch.

And in two days' time, he'd find her. In two days' time he'd see his kid, come hell or high water, and he'd decide precisely what needed to be done about it all.

Chapter 2

"Motherfuck—"

Casey froze, eyeing the baby asleep in his lap.

"You didn't hear that. Just keep sleeping. *Sleeee-pinnng,*" he pleaded, rising gingerly from the couch to reach for his ringing phone. He shifted Mercy's weight to one arm and checked his screen.

Unlisted—no shock there. He hit TALK. "Hello?"

"Grossier?"

"Yeah."

"It's Emily. Why are you whispering?"

"It's three a.m., man."

"And this has been a problematic hour for talking business since when, exactly? Oh, wait." He could hear a smile in her voice now. "You got a girl next to you?"

Casey glanced down. "Sort of."

"I'll keep it quick, but you'll want to hear this—I've got *the* perfect job for you."

"I'm not taking any more contracts, Em. I told you that in October."

"There's some policy bullshit on this one," she went on, ignoring him. "Has to go down by March fifteenth."

"Em—"

"Which is soon, I know, but it's *so* fucking easy. Commercial, super remote, no neighbors for half a mile. You're in and out and it's all over before the good guys even get the call. You could do this in your sleep."

"No, I can't—"

"Your slice would be twenty, *minimum.*"

Twenty thousand bucks? Casey wasn't broke, but a payday like that would certainly make his life a hell of a lot easier . . . He felt sweat break out under his arms and at the small of his back. He eyed the mounted antelope head on the wall above the fireplace, feeling as frozen as that poor bastard.

"Mi-ni-mum," Emily repeated.

Casey took a deep breath, glanced at Mercy, and screwed his head on straight. "I can't. I'm in Nevada, for one."

"Vegas? That's not far."

"No, fu—frigging way up near Idaho."

"Okay, so what? Get in your car and drive. You're the best, but four weeks is tight, even for a cake job like this."

"Shit's changed." He eyed the baby again. *Not shit— crap. Crap's changed.* "I have responsibilities now."

A pause. "You? Have responsibilities? What kind of responsibilities?"

"I own a bar, for one."

"A bar? Do tell."

"Don't even think about it. I'm not laundering a penny for you."

"Spoilsport."

The baby began to fuss. "No, no, no . . ."

"Are you talking to someone else?"

"No, I— Listen, I *can't.* We had a great run, but I'm out. I can't be doing that shit anymore. I've got a business partner to think about. I go down and it's not just my ass on the line now."

"This doesn't sound like the Casey Grossier I know. Plus you won't go down—you're too good."

"You've got other guys."

"None like you. Bunch of dumb-ass punks. But you— you're a fucking artist, Case. Just this one job. Come on, please? For old times' sake?"

"I'm telling you," he said, gently bouncing the now-pissed-off-looking baby, "I *can't.*" Even as he said it, he pictured that money. Pictured the scene—smelled it, felt it . . .

No. No fucking way.

A sigh came through the line. "You're breaking my heart, mister."

"I have to get out of that line of work sometime, Em. So do you, for that matter."

"Twenty grand says I can put off retirement for a few more weeks. And you—the Casey I know would have taken a job ten times trickier than this and for half the payout, just for the fun of it."

"Well, I guess I'm just not the—"

Mercy woke, squawking and angry.

"Is that a *baby*?"

"It's not mine. It's complicated. Anyhow, I have to go. Nice working with you, Em."

"I'm keeping you in my Rolodex. I know you—you can't quit that easy."

"Watch me." Casey hit END and tossed his phone on the couch.

"Shush," he told the baby. "Shush your beautiful face, please. Your mom hasn't slept in, like, three days . . ."

At four months, the infant book had said, both Abilene and her daughter might soon be getting eight hours a night, but this baby clearly had no designs on higher achievement. Casey had spent a lot of time in Vegas, and he'd known alcoholic insomniac gamblers who were more lovable at three a.m. than this baby was.

Above him, footsteps.

"Shit. Please be Christine, please be Christine."

There was a chance it was—he was in Christine Church's home, after all, and she often rose at ungodly hours. Christine and her husband, Don, and their son, Casey's good friend Miah, lived in this big old farmhouse at the western edge of their cattle ranch. Casey was here about every other night, checking in on Abilene, helping with the baby as best he could, when he really ought to be home, in bed, asleep.

Hell, I shouldn't be in Fortuity at all.

Or anyplace in Nevada, for that matter—not when he could be back in Texas, saying yes to that contract, looking forward to meeting Emily for a drink to go over the logistics, salivating to get the project going. He shouldn't be co-owner of a bar. In the light of day, he was glad he was, but just now, when he was sleep deprived and missing his old paydays, his old freedom . . .

Above, on the landing to the second-floor rooms, a door opened, spilling soft light. Shit, Abilene.

"What's the matter?"

"We're fine."

She padded down the steps and into the den in her sleep clothes—pajama pants with a pattern of stars and moons, an oversized and faded Dolly Parton concert tee. Her long, dark ponytail was all cockeyed, her normally wide eyes squinty and bleary. Cute as fuck, really.

"Sorry," Casey said, bouncing the angry baby. "I've got her. My phone rang. She'll be back to sleep in no time," he lied. He didn't know much about babies, but he was steadily coming to understand this one, and when Mercy was pissed, she stayed pissed.

"Give her here."

"No, go back upstairs."

"Try giving birth to a baby and then ignoring the sound of her crying," Abilene countered. "Sit."

He dropped back on the couch and Abilene sat beside him. He passed the squirming bundle into her arms.

Casey stretched his neck from side to side, feeling the hour. Feeling, as he often did these days, half-incompetent at most everything he was attempting to do—run a bar, help out with his family's issues, care for an infant. The one thing he was truly exceptional at was off the table. He'd grown used to feeling capable, used to knowing without a doubt that he was the only man for the job. But with that job shelved, and maybe for good, he couldn't say he much enjoyed the alternative. It roused an old, familiar restlessness in him, the same one that had driven him out of this town to begin with. His self-serving side wanted to run straight back to Texas, except he was all in now. For the first time in his life, he was neck-deep in responsibilities, with others seriously depending on him. Running wasn't an option . . .

Not unless he felt like turning into his old man, that was, which was about the only thing that scared him worse than commitment.

Warmth broke through his worries—the warmth of Abilene's thigh through his jeans, and her upper arm against his bare elbow. She was short, maybe five-two, small framed but . . . plump? Casey didn't know what the acceptable term was to use in front of a girl, but you could say she was a little chubby, and had been even before her pregnancy had begun to show. It didn't bother him one bit. Her skin looked crazy-soft. Soft like her heavy Texas accent. When his dick got the better of him, he'd imagine how his hands would look on that skin, how she'd feel like heaven under his palms. Casey didn't discriminate when it came to women's bodies, and Abilene's was everything essentially feminine to him. Petite and . . . and *lush*.

It did things to him, even now. Always had. Probably always would.

Though it really shouldn't. She was too young, for one, and she was his employee to boot—she tended bar at Benji's three afternoons a week. And on top of all that, she'd gone into labor nearly two weeks early, while they'd been closing up together, and had given birth in the back of Casey's car, halfway to the nearest decent hospital in Elko, in the dead of night.

He'd had a crush from the second he'd laid eyes on her and hit on her and asked her out a hundred times—fruitlessly—before he'd found out she was pregnant, but he'd never so much as kissed her. Never really even touched her in any meaningful way before he'd found himself kneeling between her legs, getting screamed at, trying not to hyperventilate as a squalling baby had been born into his shaking hands.

Still, that had been four months ago, give or take, and since then his old desire had crept back in—and worse than ever, if he wasn't mistaken. No matter that he knew Abilene was over whatever she'd once felt for him. Motherhood ate up all her energy, and it really ought to have desexualized her in Casey's eyes as well . . . but in truth, he was straight up in awe of her now. And protective, as well, a sensation that always wired straight between a man's legs, it seemed.

So for a half dozen excellent reasons, Casey pretended he felt for Abilene what she now did for him—a brother-sister-type affection, nothing more.

He'd always been a goddamned good liar.

"Sorry," he said again. "I was really hoping to give you a decent night's sleep for a change."

"Don't be sorry," Abilene murmured, soothing Mercy. "Phones ring. Babies cry. I got four whole hours in. That's more than I would have if I was on my own tonight."

"You're not on your own—you've got Christine, too."

Abilene and the baby had moved here to Three C a week ago. Trouble was on its way, in the form of Mercy's father getting paroled. Guy was a gunrunner with a quick temper, the story went, and their breakup hadn't been pretty.

"Yeah, Christine's great for a couple hours' babysitting in the afternoon, but that's all I can bear to ask of her."

True. Miah's mom put in sixteen-hour days around the ranch, same as the men. "She frigging loves Mercy, though," Casey said.

Abilene smirked. "Miah better get busy and make her some grandbabies before she steals one . . . Oh, I shouldn't have said that. That was mean."

"No, that's true. She's broody as fuck. Oh, shit—shoot. Sorry."

Abilene shook her head. "You and that mouth . . . Would you fix me a bottle? That might calm her down."

"Sure."

Casey went to the kitchen and turned on a burner under a pot of water. He mixed the formula with a few good shakes of the bottle, switched off the stove, set the bottle in the pot to heat. Mercy preferred it warm, especially at night. So weird that she could have preferences, and a personality, when at four months old she was still little more than a good-smelling fat loaf—alternately angelic and livid. So weird that he even had this skill set, when four months ago he'd never so much as held an infant. Not that he was much of a natural. He still wound up putting on her diapers backward half the time.

When the bottle's temp seemed about right, he emptied the pot down the sink and swirled the formula as he headed back into the den.

Abilene accepted it, giving it a feel. "Perfect, as always."

"I'm like a human thermometer."

"Between you and the human poop machine," she said, nodding to the baby, "I'm starting to feel left out of the superpowers club." The baby took the nipple and Abilene broke into a smile that Casey knew way too well—a quick grin, stifled by a shy bite of her lip. Relief.

"Tell me about the house," he whispered.

Abilene's dream house, that was, an ever-evolving vision

of the kind of home she'd like to move into with Mercy someday, if she could ever afford it.

"Nothing fancy," she murmured. That was how it always started. "One story is fine. With a little yard, at least, big enough to run around in. And a white fence."

"What color's the house?"

"Also white. With red shutters and a red mailbox. And a red door."

"How many bedrooms?" he asked, and absently reached out to squeeze Mercy's tiny foot in its yellow sock.

"Just two. Plus a living room, and a kitchen big enough to eat in. And a washer and dryer—I never want to step inside another Laundromat for the rest of my life."

Casey laughed, smiled to himself. He'd ask her this question again, the next time they found themselves side by side this way, late at night. Each time, something new—the shutters, the fence, the mailbox, now two rooms and a washer and dryer. Next time, maybe curtains. And someday, he imagined, a Mr. Right to fill out the scene. Something hot squirmed inside him at the thought. Something hot and deeply pointless, as Casey was about as wrong for such a gig as a man could get. Even if some hint of Abilene's old crush still lived inside her, he couldn't be what she needed. He had no business promising anything real to anyone, and a kid raised the stakes a hundredfold.

He gave the suckling baby's wispy hair a faint stroke. "She has my eyes, you know."

Abilene straightened and rolled her own blue eyes. "Now, that would be a miracle of genetics."

In more ways than one; Casey didn't expect he'd ever have kids of his own. He wasn't cut out for it, for starters, and he also didn't entirely trust his own DNA. His mother had gone crazy in her early forties, and he had good reason to suspect the same fate might be in store for him. Like her, he suffered from occasional spells, like seizures. What exactly was wrong with him, he wasn't certain, but he knew for damn sure he had no business making promises he couldn't keep, not to a woman, and certainly not to a child. It wouldn't be fair to them, and it wasn't fair to him, either. Why torture yourself with a taste of that stuff, if it was only going to get ripped away?

Still, there definitely was something to babies. He'd never thought about them much before meeting this one, but they were good. Squishy to hold, infinitely simple in their needs, entertaining, nice to look at.

"You remember when she was born," Casey asked, "the very first words she ever heard anybody say?"

"'Bleeping hell, Abilene,'" she quoted, laughing, "'I'm on a mother-bleeping lease.'"

"In retrospect, 'Welcome to the world' might've been nicer."

"At least your insurance covered new seats."

Casey nodded. "Good to know emergency birth counts as an act of God."

"It ought to, considering all the blasphemy involved."

They fell quiet, and Casey studied her once her eyes had shut. He'd known her since the previous summer, worked with her on and off at the bar, both before and after he'd become co-owner of the place. Granted, he'd known her mostly while she was pregnant and stressed-out, but he still couldn't say he'd ever seen her as calm as she'd been since the baby had been born. Exhausted, sure, but at peace, too, he could tell. Like someone who'd found what it was they were supposed to be doing. He knew that sensation himself—missed the shit out of it. But he was happy for her. It was only a shame this peace was about to get disrupted. It was technically Monday now, and that meant her ex was out on parole tomorrow.

Just looking at her, with those worries nagging . . . Goddamn, his body didn't even know what to do with it all. How did men even survive having wives and children, Casey had to wonder, when he felt this mixed-up and protective over a woman he could only really call a friend, and a child who wasn't even his? That shit must feel deep enough to drown in some days.

Though to a better man than me, he thought, *it might feel like a nice way to go.*

Chapter 3

The old farmhouse was chilly, winter finding Abilene's feet through the broad floorboards and her socks. She shuffled out of the guest bedroom around seven with Mercy strapped to her chest in the baby sling. She may have failed at breastfeeding, but the scoldy-mother brigade couldn't fault her efforts on the wearing-your-infant front. What the benefits were meant to be, she couldn't remember. It felt like there were a dozen differing ways to be a good mom, and a million ways to mess it up.

"A woman's highest calling is to be a good wife and mother," her father's cool voice echoed. She shivered. He'd be horrified to see her now, but no matter—she had no wish to see him ever again.

Am I a good mother? I couldn't breastfeed. But what was that shortcoming, really, compared to getting involved with Mercy's father to begin with? *I was a different person when we met.* She'd grown up a lot since finding out she was pregnant. She might not have everything figured out—not remotely—but she had her priorities in order, at least.

And she *was* a good mother, besides. Maybe she was unmarried, maybe she had no clue what she was doing half the time, but she loved her daughter, and she showed that love. It was more than her father could claim to have done for her. *And I'm protecting her.* Abilene's mama had never protected her—not from her father's judgment and suffocating beliefs, and not from the perils and temptations of the larger world, after she'd run away from home.

The guest bathroom was cold, the lightbulb seeming

grumpy as it flickered to life. She brushed her teeth, eyeing herself in the mirror. Eyeing Mercy, and only half comprehending how it was she was here.

Same as how everything happens to me—I screwed up.

At least this time, there was a gem to be found in the rubble of the fallout. She smoothed her baby's soft hair and watched her tiny lashes flutter. It seemed unreal that someone as messed up as Abilene could have created something so perfect.

It hadn't even been Abilene who'd told her ex about Mercy—it had been Casey's older brother, Vince. Vince had done time with James, a year before Abilene had moved to Nevada.

Well, not moved to. Not exactly. Abilene tended more often to simply *find* herself in new places, more a matter of mishap than intention.

That was the story of her life, right there, she thought as she headed downstairs. Flight following mistake, following flight, following mistake, again and again and again. She'd screwed up, getting involved with her ex, and been swept here to the Churches' ranch for her own safety. She entered the empty kitchen, finding coffee warming in the pot and a plate of muffins on the oversized trestle table. She helped herself to both, settling on the long wooden bench.

She wanted better for her daughter than all that aimless wandering. She wanted her to have dreams and to make plans, and to move through the world with intentional steps that led her toward her goals. To carry herself to the destinations she chose. She didn't want her to be a brittle, helpless leaf, blown from place to place, propelled only by a need to escape, and never by desire.

Freedom—that was what she wanted for her daughter. Freedom of choice, and freedom from the guilt and shame and repression Abilene had grown up shackled by, and from the oppressive environment that had driven her to such extremes in the name of rebellion.

She glanced down and found muffin crumbs on Mercy's head. Catching footsteps creaking from the direction of the den, she brushed them away.

"Casey?" She'd left him sleeping upright on the couch

and found him in the exact same position when she'd crept through the den this morning.

He strolled in, rubbing his face. "Morning. Again. When did you two ditch me?"

"A few minutes before four, I think. You passed out. So did Mercy."

"And you?" Casey asked, pulling a bowl from a cabinet. "You get any more sleep?"

"An hour or so."

"I don't know how you do it, man. I get less than six and I might as well be drunk."

Abilene checked him out while he was distracted, fixing himself a bowl of cornflakes. Her libido had begun to return, if tentatively, and she was starting to take note of certain things for the first time in months.

Case in point, she was discovering all over again how much she loved Casey's arms . . . and probably because that was the most of his skin she ever got to see. He wore button-ups and T-shirts, and while they fit nicely, they didn't give much away. A fine pair of normal-guy biceps—lean and muscular, but not beefy like his brother's or her ex's. His forearms were just as nice, with blond hair and about half as many freckles as he'd had back in the summer. The hair on his head was a bit darker than when they'd met, more strawberry than blond now, but his beard had stayed the same—a brazen shade of red. Where he got that from, she couldn't guess, nor those bright blue eyes. He looked nothing like his black-haired, hazel-eyed tower of an older brother. And that suited Abilene just fine.

Casey was a nice, normal-sized man, with better things to do, she imagined, than spend his spare time lifting weights.

What those things might be, however, she couldn't guess. He was awfully cagey about what he'd done for a living before he'd returned to his hometown last August. But she could handle that. She had plenty of secrets of her own she didn't plan on sharing.

Heck, Casey didn't even know her real name.

There was something about him, though . . . something that set him apart from all her exes. It was in the way he stood and the way he talked. It was in the easy way he held himself, and in the old Chuck Taylors he wore when he wasn't in motorcycle boots. He'd be thirty-four on April fifth, more than a decade her senior . . . though he believed she was a couple years older than she was.

He had more than ten years on her, yet in some ways Casey seemed like a teenager. Normally that wasn't a plus for a woman, but Abilene's own teenage years had been forfeited. She'd never experienced young love as she should have, never been with a guy and had it be about fun, about exploring like dumb, eager kids. She was always the student, with men. An innocent in need of teaching, or saving, or corrupting. She'd fantasized a thousand times about how sex with Casey would be, and not even in a horny way—not since her hormones had banished her sex drive, at least.

He'd be eager, she bet. Silly, and energetic, and shameless. Up for anything, and every emotion he felt would be right there on his face. She loved his voice, too—not deep like his brother's, but soft, and sexy when he spoke low, late at night. What would he say, in bed? She swallowed, unable to guess but knowing it'd be brash. His ears and throat and cheeks would be bright pink, like they got when he was embarrassed. No guile, just proof that he wanted her. Lust bloomed at the thought, chased by a different heat—shame. The two were as married inside her as bees and their stingers, a product of the strict breed of Christianity she'd been raised in and formed by. The lust, she knew now, was wholly natural, a force from deep in her body. The shame was all in her head. Though knowing that didn't keep her from feeling it.

Where Casey was concerned, though, fantasies were all she got. Good as he'd been to her, as both a boss and a friend, she knew it shouldn't ever be more than that. She knew he'd been to prison, but for what crime, she wasn't sure and frankly didn't want to know. For her, it was enough to know that he'd done time. Enough to tell her that letting this crush grow any deeper would just be history repeating itself yet again. For her daughter's sake, she had to pick with her head the next time she fell hard for somebody.

And though she and Casey weren't meant to be, she welcomed the what-if daydreams. She'd missed being sexual these past months, and feeling the surge of power that came with it.

She might not be the most obvious sex object, but the whole petite-girl-with-big-eyes thing worked on some guys, and she'd always gotten a rush from seeing that glint in a man's eye. The power she felt, feeling wanted like that . . .

Sure, she'd been led astray, but never all that unwillingly, she could admit.

"Refill?" Casey asked, tipping the coffeepot to his own mug.

"No, thanks. One's probably plenty. Hoping I might steal a nap, if Mercy goes down at ten like she has been."

"Good thinking." He took a seat across from her, eyeing the baby. "You spill anything on her?"

"Not yet," she fibbed, spreading butter on the second half of her muffin. You didn't *spill* crumbs, she reasoned. You *dropped* them. No one told you crap like that about motherhood—how you'd accidentally drip oatmeal on your poor baby's head, or sneeze on her, or otherwise undermine your dignity on an hourly basis.

"What are you up to today?" she asked.

"Meeting my brother and Duncan, before Benji's opens," Casey said. Duncan was his co-owner at the bar, her other boss. "To finalize plans."

She knew what he meant—plans to do with what might happen once her ex was released tomorrow morning. After her shift tonight, Abilene would be hanging up her bar towel until further notice, and Vince would probably be arranging to meet with James, to take the temperature of the situation. She was afraid of the details. As long as Casey or Miah was nearby, she felt safe.

Though what am I really afraid of? she had to wonder. *James's anger, or everyone finding out the truth about me?*

False names aside, she'd been two very different girls in her short life. One sweet and lost, one thoroughly ugly. Neither quite what they seemed to be.

If the truth came out, everything was at risk.

Duncan might want to fire her. The Churches might not be so keen to have Abilene staying under their roof. Casey might quit seeing her as a scared young mother in need of protection, and people could start wondering if maybe she shouldn't be trusted with Mercy.

Because Abilene wasn't what she appeared to be. She

wasn't even Abilene, technically. She wasn't twenty-four, and while she might be in danger, she wasn't a complete victim in any of this.

She wasn't anywhere near as innocent as she seemed.

Casey got to Benji's at eleven and let himself in through the front door.

He and Duncan were having a kitchen installed, its space cannibalized from the former stockroom and an adjoining corner of the bar. It was going to be a boon to the business, and hopefully keep the drinkers from vanishing each night at dinnertime, keep the place relevant once the Eclipse—the massive and controversial resort casino just resuming construction in the foothills—arrived, along with its attendant competition. Casey had waged an epic battle with his new partner over the future menu, and won—they'd be specializing in roadside-style barbecue. Nice and simple, tough to fuck up. Duncan probably wished they could serve kale and quinoa and artisanal mulch or whatever he'd eat if given his snooty druthers, but Casey had stood firm. Ribs, chops, steak. That was the recipe for success, fitting their existing clientele and the vibe of the joint.

"I want to choose the sides, then," Duncan had insisted, cowing to the greater logic. "You can cook more than just meat on a grill. Even bikers and ranch hands eat vegetables, surely."

"Course. Corn on the cob and, um . . . Are baked beans a vegetable?"

"I'm not rebranding this place 'Benji's Coronary Artery Disease Depot.'"

"We can argue about this later, darling." And no doubt they would. They were mismatched, as partners—and indeed friends—went, but it worked, somehow. Casey and commitments were mismatched as well, but this place meant a lot to him. It was his own first watering hole, and a business that embodied the soul of Fortuity in every floorboard, every beam. If nobody stepped in, invested their money and time and energy in keeping it viable, it'd go the way of the local mining industry in no time, a quaint footnote in a struggling town's bleak history.

Kitchen construction had kicked off a little more than a week ago, with a three-man crew working daily before the bar opened, six a.m. to two. The project was due to wrap in early March, just a few weeks away.

To judge by the racket, the contractors were busy sanding something this morning. As if to confirm, Duncan strode out from behind the temporary partition covered in dust. He spotted Casey and raised a hand.

Casey waited until Duncan took his ear protectors off, then called out, "No doubt you'll be changing before you open this afternoon."

"No doubt at all." Duncan moved his safety goggles to the top of his head and glanced down at his beige-dusted clothes—jeans and a T-shirt, not his typical style. He looked naked in anything less than a suit. He was a British expat, a disillusioned former lawyer for the casino's development company, and pretty much nothing about him made any sense whatsoever in Fortuity. Casey supposed love did that to people. Changed their priorities, changed their assumptions about who they were and what they wanted.

"You look like a normal person, man. What're you doing back there anyhow, aside from getting in the way?"

"Micromanaging. It's been my experience that people work quicker and do a better job with some annoying prick hovering over their every move. When's your brother due?"

"Any minute. We should probably talk upstairs, away from the noise. Raina home?"

"Yes, but she's with a client." Duncan was dating the bar's former owner, and Casey's good friend, Raina. Her dad had been Benji Harper, the bar's namesake. She made no more sense paired with Duncan than Fortuity itself did, but the sex had to be off the fucking wall, because the two of them seemed to be as tangled up as ever, five months in. They lived together in the apartment above the bar, where Raina also did tattooing.

Out front, the rumble of Vince's arrival cut through the contractors' din, then died as he killed his bike's engine. Casey met him at the door.

Vince gave him a half hug around the neck with his beefy arm. "What's up, motherfucker?"

"Nothing good," Casey said, and locked up behind him.

Vince had inherited their dad's enviable height and build along with his black hair, while Casey was five-eleven, much leaner, with their mom's fair skin and hair. The latter was overdue for a trim. Any stranger seeing Casey standing beside Vince, with his clean shave and military-style haircut, would be surprised to learn that Casey and he were brothers. Hell, even Casey had his doubts about whether or not they shared a father. Unlike Vince, he didn't look a thing like the shit who'd run out on them when they were little, and if that doubt ever got corroborated, he'd throw himself a fucking party. He didn't want that deadbeat's blood in his veins, didn't want a thing to do with him. The feeling had been mutual, after all.

"Upstairs," he said, nodding to the rear of the bar, where Duncan was waiting.

Vince nodded at Duncan. "Welch."

"Grossier."

The two were perfectly civil, maybe even secretly fond of each other, but aside from being tall and owning old BMW motorcycles, they had nothing in common. Duncan was fair, fussy, and high-strung and appreciated opera, while Vince was more into tattoos and fistfights. The three of them headed through the back and up the stairwell, into Raina and Duncan's kitchen. A buzzing was coming from the adjoining room, telling them Raina was hard at work.

"So when'd you talk to him?" Casey asked his brother.

"Just this morning."

"And?"

Vince pulled out a chair and sat, planting his forearms on the dining table. "And he's a man of few words. And none of them were very encouraging."

Casey swore and sat.

Duncan filled a teakettle, looking grave. "What precisely did he say?"

"He said that nothing I could say was going to stop him from seeing his kid. I mean, I doubt he'd hurt the baby. But his ex . . . ? I dunno. I've only ever known the guy in the company of men, and he was no teddy bear."

"Violent?" Duncan asked.

"Fights, yeah. Which is just what you do on the inside, but he enjoyed 'em, same as me."

"You'd never hurt Kim, though," Casey said, meaning Vince's girlfriend. "Or any woman. Or a kid."

"Course not. And maybe Ware wouldn't, either—prison's not exactly the best place to get a handle on a guy. But we're not taking any chances. Can't discount female intuition, and the girl's fucking terrified."

"Did you tell him where Abilene's staying?"

Vince shook his head. "But I had to say how I knew her—that she came to me after he'd given her my name, and that I'd helped her get a job here at the bar."

"You tell him she *doesn't* work here anymore? Last thing I need is him showing up and getting pushy."

"I did, but I have no doubt he'll come by, demanding to know where she's at."

"And what's our answer to that question?" Duncan asked.

"None of his fucking business," Casey said.

Vince shook his head. "We tell him she's someplace safe, that the baby's fine, and they've got support. But we don't say where. Not until he proves he's willing to approach the situation calmly. And Case, you've got to convince her to talk to him."

"Personally I don't want him anywhere near her. But I see what you mean."

"Keeping her in hiding's not exactly sustainable," Duncan agreed. "Plus the longer we put off brokering some sort of meeting, the more upset he could get. We don't need a frustrated ex-convict roughing up the customers."

"Unless it's me," Vince said, smirking. He got excited about fights like a kid gunning for a trip to the waterpark.

Casey knew they were both right—Abilene had to face the guy sometime. "I'll talk to her, but don't hold your breath." She'd been putting up a brave front as her ex's release loomed closer, but he could sense the fear behind it.

"Has to happen. Even assholes deserve to meet their children," Vince said, "until they prove otherwise."

Casey felt his insides sour, thinking of their own dad. It burned him something nasty to know Mercy might have that kind of disappointment in store for her—a deadbeat, or maybe even worse, if Ware was the hothead Vince and Abilene had both made him out to be.

Duncan's striped cat came strolling through, bashing itself bodily into Casey's shins. He nudged it away. "Back off. I'm allergic to you."

"Talk to her," Duncan said, pouring steaming water into a cup and bobbing a tea bag. "It would be helpful for us to be able to tell this man that she's willing to talk, in time, if that's true."

"Yeah, fine."

"And I'll make it a point to be a regular downstairs until he shows up," Vince said.

Duncan nodded. "That sounds wise. I can't imagine anyone would take me seriously as a bouncer." He turned to Casey. "Is Abilene on tonight?"

"Yeah, her last shift. I told her I could handle it by myself, but she's desperate for the money."

Vince rubbed his chin like he wasn't happy about this plan, but held his tongue.

"You can try to talk her out of it, but I don't recommend it," Casey said. "Plus the poor girl's basically in witness protection as of tomorrow morning. Three C's roomy but it'd still feel like a prison if you weren't allowed to leave."

"Make sure Miah talks to all his ranch hands again—they're in the bar often enough, and we don't need one of them running into Ware and spilling the beans."

Casey nodded.

"Right," Vince said, standing. "I'm supposed to be at Petroch for a half day. See you fuckers later."

Duncan inclined his head and Casey said, "Bye." As Vince thumped down the steps, he asked Duncan, "What are you up to now?"

"I'm trying to have a late lunch with Raina before I open, so I thought I might get the delights of sweeping and mopping and toilet scrubbing out of the way now."

"Glamorous. Guess I'll be on my way, then."

They headed downstairs together and Casey snagged Raina's motorcycle helmet off the coatrack. "Tell your better half I'm stealing this. Just for the night."

"I doubt she'll notice. She's got two more appointments after lunch. I daresay no joyriding will be happening today."

Not for you, Casey thought. But he intended to give Abilene everything she had coming to her, on her final night of freedom.

Chapter 4

From down in the Churches' den came Casey's shout. "You about ready?"

Abilene checked the clock—twenty minutes of seven. *Oops.*

"Almost!"

Mercy was already fed and dozing in her car seat in the office where Christine was working, but Abilene herself was a mess. She dashed into the guest bathroom and dried her hair, hunted down two shoes that matched, and realized too late she hadn't shaved her legs. So much for the skirt she'd pulled on, and too bad—she always made better tips when she showed her legs. Men really didn't care if your legs were all tanned and svelte like a gazelle's, or plump and pale like her own, as long as they were bare. Oh well. She dug out some jeans and named herself presentable. She didn't much care what she wore, only where she'd be spending her night. Behind the bar, with Casey, for the last time until she didn't know when. It took her back to a simpler time—before he'd known she was pregnant, before he'd been her boss or watched her become a mother. Back when he'd still hit on her, and still looked at her with fire in those blue eyes.

"Ready," she called as she shut her door and shouldered her purse. The second-floor landing on this side of the house overlooked the big den, and she could see Casey leaning on the back of the couch, checking his phone.

He glanced up as she hurried down the steps. "Grab your coat, why don't you?"

"I'll be okay. Your car warms up quick." She didn't have a ride of her own just now, which sucked. Her little crapbox '94 Colt was in the shop, needing a whole new engine. She couldn't really afford the repair, but as it was Vince who'd gotten it towed into town for her last week, she had a sneaking suspicion the bill would never arrive.

The Grossiers and Raina, and even Miah to a lesser extent—he was by far the most upstanding of their tight little group—had all made her nervous, once upon a time. She was no stranger to shady company, but the lot of them were all so much more . . . *something*, than she was used to. Like they knew and trusted their own places in their dusty, scrappy hometown.

Abilene, on the other hand, felt lost most of the time, and more insecure than ever now, with Mercy to worry about.

"We're not taking my car," Casey said as she met him downstairs.

"Whose, then?"

"It's your last night of freedom until this all blows over. Thought we might brave the cold and ride into town in style."

"What, on your bike?" Jeez, she'd never ridden on a motorcycle before. "I dunno."

"Bundle up. Bring gloves, too—it'll be real cold by the time we close up."

She weighed her anxiety against Casey's confidence. Maybe he was right. Maybe she ought to relish the wind in her hair one more time, icy though it undoubtedly would be.

"Fine." She grabbed her winter coat off its hook in the front hall and pulled on her mittens. "What about a helmet?"

"Got you covered." Casey led the way outside, down the porch steps to the big front lot. As she eyed his Harley, the last of her hesitance waned. This machine no longer looked like a frigid threat to her life, but rather a perfect excuse to wrap her arms around the man she was otherwise in no position to embrace. Twenty socially acceptable minutes, each way, to spend with her body hugged close to his . . .

Sign me up.

Casey handed her a black helmet and clipped his own silver one on.

"I've never seen you bother with one of these before," she said, fiddling with the strap.

He helped her tighten it, seeming tall and exciting. "Got to start setting a better example, if you're gonna keep letting me hang around your kid."

Her goofy smile went blessedly unseen as he swung his leg over the seat.

"Thank goodness I didn't wear a skirt." And thank goodness Casey was busy digging in his pockets for his keys and didn't see her graceless first attempt at getting her leg up and over the back.

"Little help?"

Without a word, he hooked out his arm and she used it to haul herself into position.

"Thanks."

"Hold on tight."

She did, looping her arms around him. He was wearing a hoodie, and a sweater underneath, she could tell. And under that, she could just make out the shapes of his trunk. *Man, you smell nice.* Probably just his soap, she guessed, but sexy all the same.

The engine rumbled to life, puttering loudly as he cruised them toward the road.

"I've never done this before," she shouted.

"Bit more fun in the summer," he called back, once they were on the pavement.

"I'll bet." And would she still be in Fortuity come the summer, she wondered? She hoped so. It was tough, though. Once everything calmed down, she'd have to find her own place and pay for some kind of childcare so she could work more hours. In all honesty, the math just didn't add up, not without any family nearby to lean on . . .

I won't go back to Bloomville. Even if her pride somehow let her, even if things got that desperate, there was absolutely no guarantee her parents would talk to her, baby or no baby. She felt tears well as she imagined the worst—what they might say about Mercy, if they found out who her father was. *You haven't changed a bit, have you, Allison?*

You and these older men. When are you going to learn to keep your goddamned legs closed? That's what they'd say—what her father would say—and her mother would flinch at the cuss and start praying. Crying and praying.

So, no. No way in the darkest, hottest corner of heck was she ever going back.

She locked her arms up tight around Casey, shut her eyes, and tried to forget.

It wound up being a busy night at Benji's, and Abilene counted up two hundred and eleven dollars in the tip jar. "Wow, good haul for a Monday."

Casey was loading the washer with the final few last-call glasses and tumblers, and he shot a smile over his shoulder. "How much?"

"Over two hundred."

"Shit, that *is* a good haul. And it's all yours."

She frowned, clutching the bills in a fat, messy stack to her middle. "No way."

"Fuck yes way." He straightened and switched the washer on. "You think I earned even a quarter of those tips, anyhow? You're actually polite to people. Plus you're a girl. You keep it all. I'm your boss; I'm telling you to."

"Gosh. If you insist." She could certainly use it. "Thanks."

She eyed Casey as he went around the now-empty barroom, wiping tables down with a wet towel. They'd been busy, and the place had grown warm. He was down to his T-shirt, and she bit her lip as she watched his circling arm.

It wasn't merely a blush of lust she was feeling for her boss. There was that, but also more, something almost fiercer than sex—appreciation. He signed her paychecks and babysat for her, had been giving her rides for the past week, and got creepy customers to back off when necessary. He did so much, and she took so much.

Not forever. Someday she'd know security. Someday she'd be with a man who treated her as good as Casey did, for all the right reasons—go to bed with him for all the right reasons—and be the one contributing now and then, instead of the one always in need of bailing out.

She followed in his wake, stacking barstools on the

wiped tables, trying not to look at his butt. Failing. She could have had him, last summer. He'd wanted her, and she'd wanted him right back. But she'd been so mixed-up from the pregnancy and all the ugliness that had preceded it, she'd kept him at a distance. Now, though, a selfish bit of her wished she'd gone there. To know what he'd have been like in bed, if nothing else. For the memories.

All that left her with were theories. She watched his arm again, letting one hatch, feeling a flush creeping up her neck.

"Deposit ready?" he asked.

"Locked in the register." Duncan liked to review each night's receipts, then go to the bank himself. How had Casey put it? The man had a hard-on for accounting.

"Then let's get you home."

She pulled her jacket from the cubby under the counter. "Seems silly that you're bothering to crash at the ranch—you'll only be there for, like, four hours by the time the sun's up."

"Probably." He pulled his sweater over his head. "But tomorrow's a big deal. You think I'm leaving your side the first day your ex is loose?"

"He can't know I'm staying at the ranch yet."

"But why take chances?" Casey zipped his hoodie.

"Duncan's not working three to two all by himself tomorrow, is he?"

"No, Raina agreed to come down and close—almost every night this week, in fact."

Abilene's neck warmed at that, some weird mix of shame and gratitude. Her former boss was more than happy to have retired from bartending. "That's awful good of her."

"I bet part of her secretly misses it. Must get boring, busting only Duncan's balls all the time."

She laughed. "Still, it's insane how nice you've all been, bending over backwards to look after me and Mercy."

Casey shrugged as he headed for the fuse box, then switched all but the security lights off. "That's what you get for ever going to my brother for help in the first place, honey. Now you're stuck with the whole goddamn bunch of us . . . Though the irony of it is, he helped you to begin with because you were carrying his old prison buddy's baby. Now he's trying to help protect you from the guy. Kind of fucked-up, but hey, it's Fortuity."

"Effed up or not, I'm really grateful for everything. And I hope it doesn't go on for too long."

"Me neither. For your sake, that is." He headed for the back and she followed. They grabbed their helmets by the door.

The temperature had dropped, way down to freezing to judge by how their breath fogged the night air.

Having already survived one trip on the bike, Abilene clambered aboard behind Casey with passable confidence. She was pooped, looking forward to bed, and hoping the baby was having what Christine called a "merciful night." But the moment the engine started up between her legs, all that fatigue rattled away in the brisk February breeze. She squeezed Casey tight and had to remind herself not to confuse vibration with arousal.

It didn't help. The noise and the wind swallowed her, left her feeling alive and awake in a way unique to being on a motorcycle. Suddenly it made sense, why people would want to live their waking lives on these things. So much freedom, without any windows standing between you and the world. All those stars overhead, no roof to hide a single one.

And a warm, strong man in your arms, she thought, hugging Casey's middle. Did he get pleasure from feeling her at his back, as anything more than a reprieve from the winter air? She hoped so. She was a mom now, and his employee—thoroughly unsexy roles, but she hoped some shadow of his old crush had lingered.

Yeah, right. Not after he'd seen her give birth, seen her grouchy and frustrated at two a.m. She knew, from hearing Miah and Christine talk about him, Casey wasn't historically a guy who stuck around and did the right thing. He was kind of like Abilene in that way—always adrift—except it sounded like he'd been in control of where he wound up. In addition to his record, he'd been a card counter in Las Vegas for a while, which struck her as the shadiest thing you could probably do for a living without actually breaking the law.

The wind found her hands through her knitted mittens,

and she inched them into the pockets of his hoodie. He felt good against her. Warm, strong, and big. Big enough to make a girl feel feminine and protected, but not so big that it was intimidating.

As she held on to him, she wondered how it'd feel, being in his lap. Her thighs around his hips, his excitement right there, against hers. His hands on her waist. Just to feel a man like that again, right there against her . . .

Not just any man. Your boss.

What had James said to her, back when they'd been together? *If you'd ever gone to college, you'd have lost a good professor his tenure.* He'd been teasing, and at the time she'd laughed. She knew she had a type—you could only make the same mistake so many times before you had to admit it was more than a coincidence. But it wasn't funny anymore. Not now that she had Mercy to think about.

The scattered lights of Fortuity fell away behind them, the bike's headlamp the only glow to be seen until the lit gate of Three C appeared as the highway curved. This was her last night like this—closing up late, riding home out in the open, be it in a car or on this motorcycle. Tomorrow, she had to start watching her back. She tried to soak up every second that was left, but in a blink, Casey was parking by the fence.

He helped her down after he cut the engine. "Not so bad, right?"

"It was fun. Worth the frostbite." The automatic porch light came on when they neared. Abilene dug her keys out of her purse as they mounted the steps and let them both inside.

"Man, we missed some good dinner," Casey said, shutting the door behind them. "What do you think? Meat loaf? Pot roast?" The house was warm and smelled impossibly good, like gravy and rosemary. Someday Abilene would have a little home that offered Mercy this experience—comfort and hot meals and nice smells. A fireplace, holiday traditions.

"Bet you there's leftovers," she said, hanging up her coat.

"Bet you they'll taste real good around four o'clock, when your daughter decides to wake us up."

They walked to the den, where Casey would be making

his bed once more. It was a comfy enough couch—a big old tan leather behemoth, probably as old as Abilene—but he had to be missing his apartment. And his freedom. And his privacy.

"I better head up and check on Mercy," she said.

He nodded as he sat and unlaced his boots. "See you in the morning, hopefully. Though if you need any help, you know how to wake me."

She smiled. "One good poke to the forehead. Night."

"Night, Abilene."

"Thanks again for the ride," she said, and her smile felt shy when she offered it. She headed for the steps.

The door to her room was open, and she found Mercy sleeping peacefully in the crib. She switched off the baby monitor, officially relieving Christine of her duties. She changed into her pajamas and scrubbed her face in the guest bathroom, shut the door, climbed into bed.

Sleep while you can, she ordered herself. The peace could be over at any moment, shattered by that noise that filled her so wholly with both dread and maternal urgency—the first tentative coo that inevitably snowballed into a squall.

But sleep wasn't coming. She lay in the darkness, trying to deep breathe, trying to think relaxing thoughts. But with the chaos of the bar gone and the distraction of the ride over, all that passed through her head were the what-ifs that surrounded tomorrow.

Today, she corrected. James would be released around ten in the morning.

The prison was ninety miles away. He could be in Fortuity by noon if he wanted to be. If he had his truck waiting for him and enough money for gas. How long would he need to find her? How long would it take to run into somebody who said, yeah, they'd seen a young brunette around, didn't she just have a baby? Heard she was staying up at the ranch out east, they might say, and just like that . . .

Poof. Poof went her security. Poof went her secrets, if James saw fit to tell Vince or the Churches or Casey or anybody else about the way they'd met. Poof went custody of her child, maybe.

Maybe. Only maybe. She wasn't that girl James had first met. She was good now. Wasn't she? Better, at least. She was *trying* to be good. She worked hard, hadn't had so much as a sip of beer since the moment she'd found out she was pregnant. It was almost impossible for a mother to lose custody to a father.

He couldn't get her child taken away.

Could he?

Chapter 5

With sleep eluding her and lying in the dark producing nothing but waking nightmares, after twenty minutes, Abilene abandoned the covers and poked her head out the door.

A lamp was on in the den, and she crept onto the landing. Casey was lounging on the couch, tapping on his lit-up phone. He never failed to make her feel competent and secure when she needed those sensations most, and right now she craved reassurance like a fish craved water. She went back into her room and put on a bra and socks, left the door open in case Mercy woke, and padded to the steps.

Casey sat up as she reached his periphery. He glanced at his phone, then switched it off, screen going dark. "Thought you'd be out like a light in five minutes flat."

He spoke softly, as all the Churches were sleeping. She loved when he did that. Normally he was a loud, brash man, not strong on the volume control, but she adored how his voice sounded in late-night moments like these. So close to a whisper. Soft in every way.

She shook her head. "Can't sleep. Too much on my mind. Were you about to turn in?"

"Don't have to. Hey, how about I start a fire? It's kinda chilly down here."

A fire did sound nice. She got settled on one end of the couch and pulled an afghan over her lap, watching Casey assembling wood and balled-up newspaper pages in the big stone hearth. His back flexed where his sweater pulled tight across his shoulders, leaving her warmer by a degree.

His lighter snicked, and as yellow flames licked at the wood, he joined her, peeling off his sweater and tossing it over the couch arm.

"How you feeling about tomorrow?" He kept the lighter in hand, running his thumb along its smooth silver corners, worrying the lid. He toyed with the thing on boring nights at the bar, too, and when he was trapped with the sleeping baby on his lap.

"A little scared," she said. "To be honest, I'm trying not to think about it."

Studying this man's handsome face was certainly a welcome diversion. It was more than mere gratitude drawing her to him, she realized. There was a very real chance that once James was out, her past would follow suit. Everyone believed they were protecting her welfare—and they were. But James could hurt her worse by talking than by hitting her, and she bet he knew it.

Depending on how pissed James was, in a week or a month or who knew how long, Casey might know the truth about Abilene, and that would just about destroy her.

She knew she couldn't ever be with this man. But she still felt for him—worse than ever, in fact. Going forward, she'd make better choices. Find herself a man as sweet as this one, minus the criminal record and all the secrets. But she couldn't deny she still wanted him.

She eyed his mouth. *And I don't want much. Just a taste. Just a kiss.* A farewell kiss, to say good-bye to her old habits, once and for all.

He smirked, seeming to realize she was staring. "What?"

"Nothing. Just in my head."

"If we weren't on baby patrol, I'd take you out back and make you smoke a joint."

She smiled and shook her head. "I'm not much for drugs."

"Pot doesn't count."

"Pot also never solved anybody's problems."

"Nah, but it'll shut your brain up real good." He pocketed his lighter. "Damn, that sounds perfect, actually. Smoke a bowl, stare at the fireplace . . . Hardly anything better in the world than that. Not with your clothes on, anyhow."

She laughed. "Sounds fun, I'll admit." The exact kind of fun she'd missed out on in her teenage years.

"Being a grown-up is such a drag sometimes." Casey sighed.

"Tell me about it." Again, she couldn't help but imagine some different world, one in which she and Casey were the same age and had met in high school. Some world in which he'd maybe taken her virginity, been her date to prom, horrified her parents in ways that looked downright innocent, compared to reality . . .

Would he stop me, if I tried? Tried to kiss him? Tried to touch him? This felt like her last chance. Her last reckless mistake . . . Did that old crush still live inside him someplace, strong enough for him to maybe forget the baby and the danger and the fact that she was his employee, just for a little while? Make her feel like a sexual person again, remind her how good wanting someone could feel, and being wanted right back?

Heart pounding, she turned, bending her legs so her knees rested atop his thigh. She laid her arm along the couch, and her cheek on her shoulder, leaning a bit closer.

Casey seemed to take the move for exhaustion or vulnerability, and wrapped his own arm around her shoulders, giving her a little squeeze. It had been a long time since he'd touched her with this kind of casual ease. It reminded her of her final weeks of pregnancy, the nights they'd closed the bar together and he'd sometimes rub her aching back when there was a lull in orders. Not sexual, but friendly and familiar. Comforting.

Though tonight she wanted something more than comfort.

"Everything's going to turn out okay," he told her in that soft, fascinating, un-Casey-like voice. "Right now, this will probably be the worst of it. The waiting."

"I wasn't even thinking about tomorrow."

"No?"

"I was thinking about how much things have changed, since last summer. Since I first met you."

"No fucking kidding, huh?"

"You used to flirt with me," she said, making sure he'd hear the smile in her tone, and know it wasn't a complaint. "Shamelessly."

"And you must have turned me down, like, eighty times."

"I miss those days, sometimes."

He sat up straighter, took his arm back, and met her eyes. "I still think you're real pretty, you know. If things weren't so different, I'd still be hitting on you, every chance I got. Wait—did *that* count as hitting on you? Don't sue me for sexual harassment."

She poked him in the side and let her hand linger there. A tiny but bold move, and something spiked in her blood, something hot and nearly forgotten. Nostalgic, a touch dark. Innately natural.

Do what you always did best, a mischievous voice whispered. *And to heck with tomorrow.*

Casey swallowed and glanced at the fire, trying to blame it for how hot the room seemed to have grown. It couldn't be the contact, right? This was just friendly, innocent touching. Like friends might do, if they got along real good.

Like, real good, he thought, feeling the heat of Abilene's palm through his tee, warming his ribs. He couldn't seem to make sense of that hand.

"What do you want most, Casey?" She asked it quietly, but there was a strength in those words—a fierce and curious charge.

"What do I want?" He used to know the answer to that. He could've replied with a single word, without thought. *Money.* But things had changed since he'd moved back to Fortuity, and now the answer wasn't so obvious. He'd come home after that long, frivolous absence to find his mother a decade deeper into her mental illness, a childhood friend dead, and his hometown in the grips of scandal and tragedy. He'd agreed to stay as a promise to his brother, but more was holding him here now—he could feel it. Something stronger than his word, stronger than guilt. Duty. Pride, even. Foreign sensations, both. "I want . . . I want the bar to succeed, first and foremost. And for you to find your way through this messy situation with your ex."

"No, I mean, what do you want most in life? Like, some people want a family. Some people want to be successful. Some people want . . . I dunno, they want to be singers or actors, or to travel the world."

I want to be somebody, to the people I care about. That

was what came echoing back from his subconscious, though he couldn't say if that was exactly true. He wanted to *want* that. He wanted to be capable of it. But he also felt lost half the time, and his future was foggy in ways he couldn't begin to explain to her, and all of that made the wanting a dangerous luxury. The girl had enough worries. No need to burden her with the news that he was due to lose his marbles in five or ten years, like his mother.

"I guess I'm not sure anymore," he said. "What about you? What do you want? Aside from a white house with a white fence, red shutters, and a red mailbox?"

A long pause. "I think what I used to want was security. I was on my own, from the time I was pretty young, and that was what I wanted. What I missed. But that's more a need than a want. I think what I want most in the world now is to be a good mother."

"You're already that."

"I dunno. I mess stuff up every single day."

"So do all parents. You should meet mine."

"Maybe . . . But whether I'm there or not, that's what I want now. I want to be a good mama, and to make a safe, stable home for Mercy."

"Did you have that yourself, when you were a kid?"

"I thought I did," she said, sounding far away. "But it wasn't quite what it seemed."

"Sounds like life."

"I guess. But anyhow, I want better for her. I want to *be* a better person, for her. Make better choices."

And Casey wanted the same, he realized. To be better than he had been. He couldn't say he had what Abilene did, though—a singular, solid reason to get there. He had Duncan and the bar to consider now, and his brother and mom. But nothing so real and monumental as a child. He only knew it felt good. Knew he'd begun feeling like a grown man for the first time, these past few months.

Freedom felt good, too, but in a fleeting, empty sort of way. Freedom felt like the rush and the relief of playing hooky to avoid a test you hadn't studied for. But doing the work, making the grade . . . that felt way better, deep down, and it stuck with you way longer. Pride versus the brief, false pleasure of avoidance.

"I want to work hard," Abilene went on, "and find us the nicest home I can. I want to save up my money and get some kind of education."

"Oh yeah?"

She nodded. "I don't even have a GED."

"What do you want to study?"

"Nothing glamorous. Just a skill, so I can get a steady job. I mean, bartending is great. It's perfect, right now, more than I could ask for."

"But it's not a career."

"Career isn't even the word. It's just . . . I don't want to be doing that in ten years. I want something flexible, like being a hairstylist, maybe. Something I could do out of my home, make my own hours. I can't assume I'll ever have any help in raising Mercy. You know, from a guy. A boyfriend or a husband. But something like that would be nice. Just something I control, that pays the bills, and that I enjoy."

"Sure." He wondered how much it would cost—beauty school or whatever modern term there probably was for it, and the cost to get some little storefront set up . . . *Probably less than I'd make if I went in on one last job with Emily.*

Abilene spoke quietly, the words sweet and sad, detached from the current thread. "I hope somebody'll look at me again someday, the way you used to."

He frowned, sad himself. "Course they will. Plenty of guys will. And still do." Nightly, at the bar. In fact, Casey had fantasized about punching any number of those guys in the face.

"I'm just a mom now."

"For one, you're more than that. And guys'll come into Benji's, once you're back to work—guys with no idea you have a kid—and you'll see. Some guy might just fall for you, find out you've got a baby, and not even give a crap. Happens all the fucking time."

"You think?"

"Well, bear in mind they'll need to come in on nights when I'm not around; otherwise I'll run them out on a rail."

A pause. "Why would you?"

"Kinda hard to be charged with being somebody's bodyguard and not getting a little protective," he fudged.

"Am I like your little sister now or something?"

He shook his head. *Far from it. I wish I could be so*

saintly. "Nah. You're my friend, and my coworker and employee. You're a lot of things, but sister's not one of them. Then again, I've never had a sister, so what do I really . . ."

He trailed off, distracted by her hand. Her fingers were opening and closing, bunching the cotton of his shirt loosely, letting it go, again and again. It seemed wise to write it off as an absent, thoughtless sort of touch, but he couldn't. Not quite. There was something else in the contact. Something mischievous, or curious. Something that got his blood moving quicker, pulsing lower. Heading in dangerous directions. He swallowed, and felt her attention on his mouth or his beard or his neck. *Am I dreaming this?* No, he couldn't be. Everything was too real—the smell and the dry heat of the fire, the scent of her shampoo or lotion or whatever that was.

And in a breath, it became very real. Very bold.

Her restless hand slid lower, fingertips finding his belt. He sucked a breath. "What're you doing, honey?"

"Something I want to." Her fingers slipped under his shirt's bottom hem, tracing his buckle.

His brain screamed, *Stop her,* but his cock screamed, *Let her. Kiss her. Pull her onto your lap and show her what she does to you.* The rest of him was paralyzed, trapped between the two instincts. All it seemed he could do was watch. Watch as her hand freed his buckle with an easy, knowing motion.

Fuck, I'm hard. Whatever words his brain managed to bully his mouth into speaking were going to look monumentally out of line with his body's obvious vote.

He grunted as she slid his zipper down, then covered her hand. He'd meant to pull it away, but his fingers weren't complying.

At a loss for anything else, he said, "I'm your boss."

She seemed to sense how thoroughly toothless that argument was, and squeezed softly.

Tell her this is wrong. That you don't want it. Lie, quick. But the only sound his mouth offered was a ragged exhalation, a noiseless moan.

"I never stopped having a crush on you," she whispered. "But I don't expect this to turn into anything, I swear. I just like you. And I want you."

"This doesn't feel right," he said, but the lie came out breathy and weak, the limpest protest. Nothing felt as right as this. She had to know what he really wanted, as she stroked her palm up the ridge of his erection through his shorts and fly.

"Fuck." His eyes shut, and his hand grew limp atop hers. "It's late."

"I don't care."

And shit, he didn't either. "The baby might wake up."

"And she might not."

Become that better man you've been telling yourself you are right fucking now, asshole, and move her motherfucking hand away.

But that voice was so small, and her touch felt so god-damn good . . .

His own hand slipped to her hip, up her side, but she caught it before he could cup her breast.

"Don't," she whispered. "I'm not ready for that yet. I just want to touch you. Make you feel good." With that, she let his hand go, only to head for his waist once more. This time, at least, he halted it in a firm grip at his belly.

"Jesus, honey, slow down." He laughed, feeling drunk, and did his fly and buckle back up. "Can't we kiss, instead?" Do things in the right order, at least. He'd wanted this girl for too long to rush now.

"Yeah," she whispered, "we can do that."

His hands were on her again in a breath, but more innocent this time—that soft cheek against his palm, silky hair in his fingers. Every nerve was screaming for him to dive right in, but he slowed himself down before their lips touched. He'd savor this moment, even as everything about it screamed high school grope-fest, right down to it happening on a friend's parents' couch.

He held her gaze for breaths on end. Her eyes were bright in the sunshine, as blue as sapphires or robins' eggs or any other insanely blue thing. But here in the den, lit by only the fire and a reading lamp, they were dark and deep, full of secrets, it felt like. Her lips looked just as they did in every fantasy he'd ever had about her—her mouth small but her lips full, seeming as innocent as the rest of her. Deceptively so.

Did those lips come up to meet his? He couldn't say how it happened, but they were kissing, light and distracted, voices hushed, hers faint and sweet, his deeper and rough now. He heard her name on his breath, the sound coming from no conscious corner of his head. As the final syllable settled between them, he took it further.

She tasted minty. *Just like she ought to,* he thought, the notion nonsense. Like he really knew her at all, had any clue what to expect from her. Not anymore, not now that he'd felt her hand between his legs, more brazen than he'd ever have expected. She was everything, here on this couch, in this moment. Sweet and wicked, a seductress and an innocent. A temptation and a terrible idea, and a foregone conclusion.

Emphasis on the terrible idea, his higher brain interjected.

Fuck off.

Her hand was drifting once more, seeking him between their bodies, cupping his aching flesh through his jeans, then rubbing.

"Oh God." *Tell her to stop, for fuck's sake.* "Jesus, honey, don't stop."

Wow, well done.

Her mouth was at his throat, her hair a soft, heavenly weight draped over his wrist and knuckles. And her hand . . . Christ, her hand was everything. He hadn't been touched like this in six months or more. He'd almost forgotten how essential it was. His head dropped back, inviting her kisses.

For half a minute he let her spoil him, until he was hurting and crazed and needing to kiss her back. Needing to give back, instead of taking. He held her head, fingers in her long hair, and drew her face back so he could meet her eyes. He let her see the desire surely burning in his, and then he kissed her exactly as he'd always fantasized he might. He cupped her jaw in both hands and brought his mouth down. She roused hunger in him—always had—and he let her feel that with every deep sweep of his tongue, every soft grunt from his throat, every needy flex of his hips, pressing his erection to her palm—

The worst sound in the world. The rattle of his phone buzzing on the coffee table.

He wrenched his face from hers. "Oh, for fuck's sake."

Abilene went still. "It's late. It might be important—Vince or somebody."

Doubtful. But he knew exactly who'd just be sitting down to start on her evening's business. With Abilene's hand still on him, he leaned forward and snatched the phone, accepted the private call. "I told you no, now fuck off." Hit END, tossed the thing aside.

"Not Vince, I take it?"

"No, it was nothing."

"Didn't sound like nothing."

The intrusion had sobered him. It offered a chance to end this, do the smart and honorable thing—*the thing a better man would do*—and land himself with the blue balls he deserved for having succumbed in the first place. He put his hand over hers once more, coaxing it to the safety of his thigh. "We should stop."

Her lips pursed, expression changing in an instant. "That wasn't, like, your girlfriend or something, was it?"

"No, just an old colleague. I mean, hey, I'm not a great guy, but I'm not a *complete* shit."

She looked deflated for a breath, then smiled. "You don't think you're a great guy?"

"Oh, hell no."

"How come?"

"You don't want to know, trust me." She was a good, Christian girl. He hadn't heard her so much as swear in the past four months—not since the pregnancy mood swings and the throes of labor had passed. She didn't need to know about his old life. Best-case scenario, it'd disappoint her. Worst case, those pesky morals would have her phoning the fucking feds on him. The latter felt unlikely, but in any case, the truth of his past was a burden this girl needed like a hole in the head. *My past and my future both.* Man, was he ever a fucking catch.

"You've been good to me," she said. "And to Mercy."

"That's different." And it was new. He was a good boss, he supposed, and tried to be a good friend. But he'd not always been the best son or brother, and while Casey had never intentionally hurt anybody, he was far from an upstanding citizen.

As his body cooled, his thoughts turned to that little fantasy house of Abilene's.

There were lots of places around Fortuity that fit the bill—modest little ranches that you could buy for pretty cheap. For now. When the new casino was up and running, who knew what might happen to the property values, but until and if that all went through, you could get a decent place for as little as fifty grand.

Casey thought about that job Emily had called with. His own savings was all tied up in the bar, but right there was an easy twenty grand. A fat down payment, and with a couple more gigs like that, he could buy a place outright for Abilene and her daughter. She couldn't afford it herself, not on a part-time bartender's wages, but it sure would do her good, that kind of stability. Before she'd come to Three C she'd been living in a rented room in a cranky old lady's basement—not exactly home sweet home.

Maybe three final jobs, and I could be her goddamn hero.

Except she'd want to know how on earth he was able to afford it, and telling her wasn't an option.

Fucking shame, too. The thought of it excited him. For plenty of good reasons, he couldn't ever be her man. Chiefly because of his mental health, but he couldn't tell her about that. Or rather, he *wouldn't*. He was only now beginning to face it himself—not only the shame and embarrassment of feeling faulty and doomed and helpless, but the guilt over how he'd handled his mother's decline. The dread of wondering sometimes if maybe he'd earned this fate, maybe he deserved it, for failing her, for running away as he had. So no, he couldn't tell Abilene why, and no, he couldn't be her man. But being a benefactor wasn't a bad consolation prize.

They'd gone quiet, and Casey's heart felt all warm and mixed-up. The kiss needed acknowledging, that much was clear. Hot as it had been, right as it had felt, they needed to agree it could never be repeated. Last thing this girl needed in her life was another complication.

"What just happened," he said, trailing off. "That kiss, I mean. That was unexpected. Real nice, but . . ." *Tell her it can't ever happen again, dumb-ass.* "Unexpected," he repeated.

"I know. I wasn't thinking straight, exactly."

"Me neither." He rarely was, not when this woman's body was within ten feet of his.

"I don't regret it," she added.

"No, I don't either. But given everything you're dealing with right now, I think we ought to agree not to do that again." He laid his arm along the back of the couch. "Not to pretend it never happened, but just . . ."

"Yeah . . . But it was real nice, just like you said. Nicest thing I've felt in ages."

He smiled, and in a breath he felt sad. He wished this was last summer. Wished this was the ignorant and blissful world he'd lived in when he first met her, back when he'd had no clue she was pregnant, no clue about her ex, no ties to her aside from his attraction. No ties to Fortuity, so when he inevitably fucked it all up, he could just roll back out of town with his sights glued firmly on whatever came next.

Oops. Should've thought of that before you bought a bar and started bonding with her goddamn baby. Shit. He'd gone from a completely free agent to a business owner, boss, babysitter, and bodyguard in what felt like a breath.

Guess when I step up, I step all the fucking way up.

"Tell me about the house," he said, wanting a distraction, and something familiar and innocent, to settle his racing mind. "Where'd we leave off? Two bedrooms now. Washer and dryer."

"Tell me about your tattoo," Abilene countered, her voice spacey and quiet, barely louder than the crackle of the fire.

He glanced at his outstretched arm, his sleeve pushed up to expose the ink on his shoulder. "What about it?"

"Why a horseshoe, but then a thirteen in the middle of it? Doesn't that kind of cancel out any good luck you're gunning for?" She traced the simple black design—dark gray, really. He'd gotten it in Vegas during his gambling days, probably seven years ago, now. He shivered at the touch, chest and neck warming in its wake.

"Horseshoe's only lucky if its ends are pointing up," he told her. "Like above the entrance to the stables, out back. Like a cup, to catch the luck or something like that." His was the inverse.

"Oh. Then why on earth would you get an *unlucky* horseshoe?"

"Because fuck luck." He smiled at her. "Luck is for idiots. If you're smart enough, you operate above that bull."

She looked thoughtful a moment. "You used to count cards, didn't you?"

He nodded. "It's legal, even if it doesn't make you too popular with the pit bosses."

"Was it just you, on your own?"

"No. I worked with a team of about twelve to fifteen, and we moved around constantly, trying to stay forgettable. You never do, though. But anyhow, fuck luck. Only suckers gamble for real."

"Huh."

"What?" he asked. He eyed her hair, curling his fingers into a fist behind her to keep from touching it.

"I dunno. I believe in luck. I mean, it feels like the only thing propelling people through life, some days. I wouldn't be sitting in this beautiful old house now if it wasn't for having the good luck of meeting all of you. I wouldn't have a job, either. Though I wouldn't have wound up here to begin with if it hadn't been for a bunch of bad luck. And some good stuff mixed in too, I guess."

"That's bullshit," Casey said. "Bad luck is just what people who make shitty choices blame their problems on."

She sat up, frowning, looking hurt by that.

"I don't mean you, honey. Abilene," he corrected quickly. *Can't go calling the girl "honey," now, can I? Fucking dangerous territory to go wandering into.* Though which of them he was worried about getting attached, he couldn't say.

"Sometimes our circumstances are out of our control," he said. "And that's not bad luck, either—there's no such thing. That's just life."

"I guess," she said slowly, still frowning, but looking more curious than offended now. "I never thought about it like that. About choices. I always thought I was just getting shuttled around by these things that would happen to me, like a leaf in the wind. I'd end up someplace bad, or maybe someplace good, and I was either scared or thankful about it. I guess I never gave much thought to it being all my doing."

"Well, not everything is within a person's control. But it's not luck—that's for fucking sure. At the end of the day, there's always someone to blame. And in my experience, it's almost always your own self."

"Huh."

"Luck's just an excuse that dumb-asses use so they never have to smarten up."

She cracked a smile at that. "I'm probably at a point in my life where I'd better learn to quit being such a dumb-ass."

He shrugged. "I don't think you are one, but yeah, now's probably the time to steal a little control back from the world. Luck's for people who don't want to make choices. But there's always a choice, no matter how trapped you feel."

"Do you ever feel trapped?"

He had to think about that. What he felt now—tied to this town by the business and his commitment to Duncan, tied to his uncomfortable home life by his promise to Vince ... *Trapped* wasn't quite it. Tethered, maybe, but he'd secured every single one of those knots himself.

"I don't think I've felt trapped since I was about twenty," he decided aloud. "Since I started looking around Fortuity and realized I was on a track to wind up a nobody, in a no-place town, for the rest of my life. 'Til someday I woke up with a bad back from four decades working in the quarry, forced to retire and spend my days bitching with the other old-timers by the Benji's jukebox. Sounds fucking cocky, but ever since I was a kid I thought I was too big for this place. Had more exciting shit due to me. I feel like an ass-hole saying it now."

"You're not a nobody here, anyhow. You're a business owner. You're going to preserve an important part of Fortuity's past for when the casino changes everything."

"Yeah, I hope so. But I also know my fifteen-year-old self would've been fucking horrified to hear I never made it out of here."

"But you did. And like you said, it was your choices that brought you back."

"Yeah." And now, at thirty-three, a little older and more sentimental, a little more vulnerable to guilt and regrets, Casey could admit that if he *was* doomed to lose his marbles in the next ten years, that time was better spent doing right by his mom and building some kind of professional legacy that didn't have him flirting with a place on the ATF's dance card.

The fire was mellowing; crackling yellow flames turned quiet and orange, lapping lazily at the pink logs. Beside him, Abilene yawned, and in its wake her gaze went to his tattoo again.

"For what it's worth, I feel real lucky to have met your brother, and you and Raina and Duncan."

Again, that was choice, not chance—she'd gone to Vince for help. But it was a nice sentiment, so he didn't contradict her. "And I feel lucky that I'm in a position to be of use to you."

"That's real sweet."

He squeezed her around the shoulders, just for a second. "I know. Don't tell anybody I said it."

She laughed.

"You should get back to bed," Casey said. "You'll need whatever sleep you can get tonight."

And as if on cue, the dreaded noise drifted down from above—a soft, single coo, promising full-blown wailing to follow inside a minute.

"Spoke too soon," he said, just as Abilene stood.

She paused to look back at him as she slipped her feet into blue flip-flops, smiling shyly. "Thanks for the distraction."

"Don't know if I should say you're welcome, or apologize for letting it get as far as it did."

"Don't apologize."

He nodded.

She pursed her lips, then bent down and kissed his cheek. "Night."

"Sleep well."

She smiled a final time, then headed for the stairs, holding up the legs of her pajama bottoms like a kid, to keep the hems off the floor.

Like a kid. So *un*like the woman who'd just turned him inside out—and without ever crossing third base. He shoved the thought aside.

Get your head on straight. Tonight was a one-off. A slip of her good sense, probably a need to escape from whatever thoughts she had coursing through her mind regarding what might come once her ex was out.

A dangerous ex, Casey thought, *and that child's father.* Sometimes he caught himself nearly getting attached to that baby, and had to pull himself up short. *Just because I can change diapers now, and heat formula, and have puke stains on the shoulders of half my shirts, doesn't make me anything more than a babysitter to that kid.*

The only thing he'd earned for sure was James Ware's anger, should the man find out how close Casey had gotten with his ex and his daughter. He swallowed, collar feeling tight.

Just keep it to yourself. Hope maybe you get nicknamed Uncle Casey, but beyond that, leave it the fuck alone. Quit feeling shit you have no right to feel.

No right, because he was his mother's son, with a sad fate likely awaiting him. And because he was his father's son to boot. He wanted to think he'd never turn his back on a commitment as huge as a child, but then again, if he'd been a big enough shit to skip town when his mom had started getting bad . . .

And because sure, he'd done better in the past few months, but that didn't change one important fact—at the end of the day, Casey was every bit the criminal Abilene's arms-smuggler ex was.

The only difference is, I've been smart enough not to get caught.

And he'd better hope to hell that good, God-fearing girl never found out the truth about him.

Chapter 6

Client's paranoid, major boner for discretion.
Wants you. $30K in your stocking if you come out
of retirement. Fucking hurry, he's losing his nerve.

Casey rolled his eyes at the text. He'd forgotten about it
until six thirty, while he'd been brushing his teeth. He tossed
his cell in his duffel bag, resolving not to reply. "Fucking no
means no, Em," he muttered to the empty den, then pulled
on a clean tee and a sweater. He ought to just toss the pay-
as-you-go phone in the nearest wood chipper and cut the
fucking cord with his old life. All those contacts gone, and
no way for any of them to reach him, no temptation to go
back to that scene, lucrative or not . . .

Soon. Maybe not just yet, but soon, he thought, remembering that house of Abilene's, those beauty school classes.
No sense burning bridges just yet.

The smell of sausages had woken him, and he headed for
the kitchen, finding Jeremiah Church sitting alone at the
table, leafing through a newspaper.

"Hey, man." Casey passed by, reading the headline over
his friend's shoulder. " 'Canola Meal Prices Stagnate, Expected to Dip.' Wow, fucking riveting shit."

"I'd mock your business right back, if I had the first clue
what it is you do, Case."

"I'm a bar owner."

"And before that you were a youth minister, I'm sure."

Casey walked to the coffeemaker. "You seen Abilene yet?"

Miah shook his head. "Think she's sleeping in."

"Good." *And you didn't hear any weird noises coming from the den last night? Nothing that made you worry for the sanctity of your family's couch?* His body roused at the thought and he felt his face warm.

"Ware's out when, exactly?" Miah asked.

"Ten. High alert starts around noon—he couldn't get here any quicker than that, if he can even manage to find out where Abilene's staying. But she's driving out to Elko with my mom in a bit, anyhow. Baby's got a checkup."

"That's probably best. Keep the girl distracted."

The girl. Right. Abilene the girl, so impossible to parse with Abilene the woman who'd sexually assaulted Casey last night in the best way. He swallowed, trying to dismiss the memory of her mouth against his, her hand between his thighs. *Worst possible day to get distracted, Grossier.* He turned his thoughts to her ex and let the anxiety scare some slim measure of his excitement away.

He stirred milk and sugar into his coffee and took a seat opposite Miah, taking note of his friend's clothes. He was the ranch's foreman, but he wasn't dressed in his usual dirty jeans and boots and flannel, prepared to spend the day on horseback. Instead he was sporting gray corduroys and a black button-up—the equivalent of formal wear, around here.

"Way you're gussied up, I'm guessing you're stuck showing those environmental people around again."

Miah rolled his eyes. "Another survey, yeah. Meant I got to sleep in an extra hour, though."

"What are they after, exactly?" Casey knew only that they showed up wielding clipboards and hard hats, and that they'd been by twice since he'd moved Abilene in.

"Silver State, the casino's new contracting outfit," Miah said, "is requiring the town to conduct a geological survey. They say they're worried about run-off from the construction messing up our groundwater, things like that. Sounds all conscientious and admirable, but I've got my money on them just wanting to cover their asses against any potential lawsuits. After what happened with Virgin River, they've got to know the town's feeling skeptical about the entire project."

Virgin River Contracting had been the proposed Eclipse

resort casino's first construction company, but they'd turned out to be corrupt. Some higher-ups had tried to keep the accidental death of an illegal worker secret, so they wouldn't risk the bonuses promised to them by the casino's development company, for finishing on time. That crime had snowballed, resulting in the death of a sheriff's deputy—a good friend of Casey's, once upon a time, in fact—who'd seen too much, and then the sheriff himself, who'd been tangled up in the contractors' racket.

"In theory it's a good thing," Miah said, "regardless of the motivation. Though it kills me to be spending my morning chaperoning them around when the last thing I want is for that casino to even go through. How many people have lost their lives now, yet we're still willing to welcome the goddamn thing? Welcome it to come through and rip this whole town to pieces, and for what? Some tax breaks? A load of menial service jobs built on tricking people out of their hard-earned money? Jobs that probably won't pay well enough to even keep the struggling locals in town once the property values get bloated out of all reason."

Miah wasn't alone in his thinking there. Plenty of people in Fortuity hoped the casino wouldn't get built—Casey's brother being one of the louder voices in that camp. Casey was undecided. A part of him would always resent the casino; a childhood friend would still be alive if not for that project. But on an impersonal level, he wasn't afraid of change, and the competition to the bar didn't scare him. Bring on the tourists, in fact. He was alone in his ambivalence among his friends, though. The rest of them liked their town the way it was.

"A club meeting's been called for tomorrow, early," Miah said. "Six a.m."

Casey dropped out of his thoughts and back down onto the hard wooden bench. "Goddamn."

"I know. But it's the only time your brother and I can swing it. If you're gonna feel bad for someone, make it whoever's stuck closing the bar tonight."

"True." And what a fucking way to kick off the day, Casey thought, getting Miah in the same room with Raina and Duncan. Miah had dated Raina a while back, and the guy was still struggling to get over the fact that she was now in love with a man he took for an entitled, pompous prick. So they weren't the best of friends, no.

"Consolation is, my mom promised to make pancakes."

"What a butch-ass load of bikers we are," Casey said. "Fucking homemade pancakes and everything. What's the meeting about?"

"Scheduling, mainly, making sure there's always somebody here with Abilene while this Ware situation unfolds. Plus I got a couple agenda items of my own. Nothing dramatic, just stuff to keep an eye out for."

Casey grabbed a fork from a small pile of cutlery and stabbed himself a sausage link from a dwindling platter. "Well, I'm gonna open the bar this afternoon after Abilene heads to Elko, so I'll tell whoever's around about the early wake-up call." No doubt Miah would prefer to avoid calling his ex and her lover.

"Sounds good."

An urge tugged at Casey, an impulse to ask Miah if he thought that he and Abilene messing around had been just as bad an idea as he suspected it was.

Or do I secretly want to hear him tell me to go for it? He had to wonder. That was just his dick talking, surely.

In either case, Miah might not be the right man for the job. He still regarded Casey as his best friend's obnoxious little brother in some ways. Easy for him to judge, when he'd been born into a respectable business, his path all laid out in front of him. Casey tried to imagine Jeremiah Church, future Three C patriarch and Prince of Fortuity, ever messing around with one of his employees, and decided, no, this was not the friend to confide in.

Duncan, however . . . Perfect as the guy might look, he'd fucked up his fair share of stuff. Plus he was discreet. Casey resolved to ask him when he went into town later. One thing was for sure: He could use some perspective.

James Ware shifted from foot to foot, waiting for the official at the discharge desk to return with his bin, all the shit he'd had on him when he'd been incarcerated back in July.

Eight months sounded like nothing compared to his first stint—five years—yet he felt way out of practice at this whole free-man thing. His jeans felt weird on his legs, heavy and stiff after all this time in orange scrubs and sweats. His belt felt strange, like the contraband it would have been only two hours ago.

He was tired and amped up, punchy from sitting through the release spiel and listening to his PO tell him about all the fees he'd accrued and when exactly they were due. He just wanted to get outside and to know that if he started walking, he could just keep on going.

Within reason, anyhow. *Fucking parole.*

Still, he was lucky he'd only been given a year, and served the minimum in the end. Amazing what a half-decent lawyer could get you.

The female officer appeared with the beige Rubbermaid and dropped it unceremoniously before him on the desk. He gathered his wallet, his phone, pager, sunglasses, keys. A half-eaten Snickers bar. He held it up. "Really?"

The officer smiled. "Your property, Mr. Free Man. Enjoy it."

With that, James headed down the corridor and out the penitentiary's front door. One of the guards on duty gave him a curt nod. He didn't return it.

He followed a sign to the visitors' lot, where an old black Ram pickup awaited him—his own wheels. There was dust all over the paint and scrub grass in the wheel wells, which told him Angie's deadbeat boyfriend had probably taken the poor thing off road. No fucking shock.

The door swung out and his sister jumped down.

"Ange," James offered.

"Big brother," she countered, and tossed herself around his middle. The heartfelt act would last all of a minute before they both remembered they couldn't stand each other. Wasn't as though she'd visited, apart from Christmas. Neither had their mom, come to that.

She stepped away. "Welcome back."

"Thanks. You look good." She looked like hell—too skinny in baggy jeans that used to fit different, and her brassy blond hair had black roots all the way to her ears. She looked like she was using again, but that was a fight for another day. And besides, she hadn't sold his truck out from under him. That was good enough for the benefit of the doubt on such a day as this.

"Where'm I dropping you?" he asked, climbing into the driver's seat.

"Richie's."

Figures. Fucking waster lived forty miles away in the wrong direction, but hey, Angie had shown up, after all. On time, even. More than he'd expected of her.

"Same place? Down near Ely?"

"Yeah."

"Right." He adjusted the seat and mirror and started the engine. Goddamn but it felt good to have his hands around this wheel again.

"You staying to visit?" Angie asked.

"No. Got business to take care of."

"Your first day out?"

"Overdue."

"Whereabouts?"

"Up north."

"You'd better stop and see Mom, or she'll never fucking shut up about it."

"Soon. But not today," he said, turning them onto the bleached-out desert highway.

Not today. Because yeah, he had business to take care of. Serious fucking business.

A debt to collect.

And tomorrow, an old girlfriend to track down.

Chapter 7

Casey barely saw Abilene before it was time to head to the bar, to his mingled relief and disappointment. Relief, as he had no clue how to handle her, after last night. Disappointment, because he'd be lying if he said he didn't want to see her. Look at her. Study her, and try to parse the girl he'd thought he knew and the woman who'd turned him inside out on that couch.

She stayed in her room until nearly eleven—sleeping, he hoped, or avoiding him after last night's little collision, he suspected—and with Christine puttering around, they got no chance to acknowledge any of it. He watched the baby while she showered and got ready for her doctor's appointment, and then the women were off. Abilene took the baby and thanked him with a smile, and he watched her head out with something odd and uncomfortable tensing his chest.

When he got to the bar, Duncan was already downstairs, hovering around the contractors.

"Hey," Casey called, locking the dead bolt at his back.

"Ah, you're early."

"Yeah, I was just killing some time, actually."

"Killing time, on such an auspicious day as this?"

"Abilene's safely off to Elko for the afternoon, so I can put the worrying off for a while yet. Can we talk a minute?" Casey asked, planting his elbows on the counter.

"Sure." Duncan strolled behind the bar, grabbed a stack of papers off the register and came to stand opposite Casey, frowning at the pages.

"Dunc, something happened last night."

His gray eyes grew wide and he set the papers down. "Not Ware?"

Casey shook his head. "No, he's only been out a couple hours now."

"So what, then?"

He blew out a long breath. "Abilene came on to me."

Duncan's posture relaxed. "Christ, you had me worried. Were you drunk?"

"No, and that's the fucked-up thing about it."

"How does being sober make it worse, precisely?"

"Because now we can't blame it on alcohol."

Duncan crossed his arms and leaned into the post at the corner of the bar. "I take it you succumbed to this pass, then?"

"Pretty much. Dude, I messed up, right?"

Duncan made a noncommittal face. "Not necessarily. It's inappropriate, and ill-timed, and fairly irresponsible on your part, but it's also not at all surprising."

"No?"

Duncan smiled, as dry as unbuttered toast. "Have you forgotten the way you two used to circle each other?"

"No, but I mean, I didn't know she was pregnant back then. Plus I'm her boss now."

"And I don't relish the day this implodes and we need to find a new bartender. But as I said, I'm not surprised."

Casey felt his face turning pink. "In my defense, it wasn't sex or anything." Though Christ, it had felt like more than what it had been, hadn't it? More memorable than the last time he'd gotten laid, for sure.

"I wouldn't overthink it if I were you," Duncan said. "Your very under-rested, very overstressed employee came on to you. The girl's awash with hormones I don't care to attempt to fathom, and scared, and probably somewhat imprinted on you. Unlikely though it may seem, you're the most reliable male role model in her life at the moment. Don't rake yourself over the coals for whatever's happened, but for goodness' sake, don't encourage it if you don't see it going anywhere."

"It can't go anywhere. That much I know for sure." Though Christ, he wanted to feel that again, everything she'd brought out in him, last night. Everything that had burned between the two of them. Propriety could go fuck itself.

Duncan nodded. "Her life is complicated enough without all this."

"Exactly. Plus she doesn't know about my mental health shit, and I don't feel like heaping that on top of all her other worries. Even if I *wanted* to make promises I'm not sure I'm actually ready for, there's no guarantee I'll be lucid enough to keep them in a few years' time."

"A fair point." Duncan headed for the register, unlocked it, and took out the previous night's deposit bag. "How's the girl doing, otherwise?"

"Okay, I think. Scared, obviously, but the baby's got a checkup, and it's probably good that she's had to get off the Church family compound for a few hours."

"No doubt. Would you start on the floors while I take this to the bank?"

"Yeah, sure. Oh—tomorrow morning, Vince wants everybody out at Three C for a club meeting. Get our heads together over scheduling watches for the next week or so. Plus Miah has some unrelated business."

Duncan looked uncomfortable, and not without reason. "Please tell me you're only informing me so that I can pass this along to Raina."

"You wish. You're as tangled up in all this business as any of us are. Like it or not, you're officially a Desert Dog. So your presence is required at meetings."

"We ought to put it to a vote. I can tell you now, both Church and myself will vote nay."

"Miah's too fucking busy to care about that ancient history, man, and club business trumps hurt feelings. Anyhow, it's got to be a breakfast meeting—six a.m. tomorrow."

He sighed. "Fine. How long are you in, this afternoon?"

"I can probably hang 'til six."

"In that case I might disappear into the office while you're here. I could get on top of placing the help-wanted ads." They'd need cooks soon, and at least two bar-slash-waitstaff, and there was no telling when Abilene would be back on the job. "And I've got to chase down a vendor about the counters that are going in this week."

"Works for me." Running around filling orders and making change Casey could handle, but he was glad Duncan was taking over the bulk of the tasks that required organization and a clear head. "Leave opening 'til five to me, if you want," he told Duncan. "I'll be fine solo 'til the postwork rush."

"I may just do that. Can you handle Ware alone, if he turns up?"

"Guess I'll fucking find out." He paused, nagged by another thought. He'd been caught up in two impulsive decisions last night, and he wouldn't mind Duncan's opinion on this one, either. "Can I talk to you about one other thing, real quick?"

"Of course. What?"

"So I . . . I found this service," Casey said.

"Service?"

"This mail-order thing that does DNA testing, with cheek swabs and shit, like you'd mentioned last fall." He'd seen an ad for it in a magazine, and early this morning—to distract himself from the ache Abilene had left between his legs—he'd gone online to check it out. "You can get your medical markers analyzed, find out if you have a higher chance of getting diabetes or cancer or Alzheimer's—whole load of shit."

"Including dementia?" Duncan prompted gently.

"Yeah." As far as Casey knew, that was what had left his mom a vacant, spacey husk by age forty. These days her world consisted of whatever was on the TV, and Vince, his girlfriend, Kim, their neighbor Nita, and Casey all split the duties of caring for her. Casey couldn't lie—stressful or not, this past week had been an undeniable relief, with Abilene's situation leaving him too busy to pitch in much on the family front. Every visit to his mom's place was a reminder that her depressing fate might be his own, and not too far down the road. He shared those occasional seizurelike incidents of hers, after all. During his own episodes he went into another place, had weird vivid dreams, all while thrashing around on the ground. Duncan had witnessed one.

Weirder still, those dreams had a creepy way of coming true, though Duncan knew nothing about *that* fucked-up factoid. Vince knew, and now Miah did as well—if only because Casey's last little spell had shown him a vision of Miah dying in a fire, on a starless night. He hoped that dream was a dud, though, or that they'd somehow managed to prevent it—starless nights only happened to Fortuity during the region's minuscule rainy season, and that had come and gone with the holidays, tragedy-free.

Vince believed that the dreams were something to be taken seriously. He'd seen their mom's crazy ramblings come true too many times to ignore them. Miah, on the other hand . . . well, skeptical was an understatement. He didn't have a superstitious bone in his body, plus, to be fair, the guy hadn't suffered so much as pizza burn since Casey had envisioned that fire.

He himself was starting to doubt if any of the stuff he'd ever dreamed up had been anything more than hallucinations.

But if I'm not seeing the future, what does that make me? The answer was, plain old fucking crazy. Just like his mom.

Either way, Casey wanted some answers—about his brain health, if not all this psychic nonsense. *Needed* answers. If he was going to keep telling himself he was finally manning up, there was no excuse to quit being such a goddamn pussy about it.

He told Duncan, "You can pay extra and get a thirty-minute consultation with a DNA expert over the phone, to go over the results."

"And you're going to do it?"

Much as hearing the truth terrified him . . . "Yeah, I think it's fucking time."

"Why now?"

The million-dollar question, right there. Maybe because having his feelings for Abilene violently reignited had got his subconscious wondering if his chances at a real long-term thing with a woman were well and truly fucked. Not that he wanted such a thing with Abilene, of course. She came with way too much built-in responsibility for his comfort. But somebody, maybe. Someday. If he had any somedays coming to him.

To Duncan, though, he fibbed. "All this shit here, with you and the business . . . I gotta know. *You* deserve to know if I'm gonna be fucking incompetent in five or ten years. Plus it's only a couple hundred bucks. I got no excuse to keep putting it off."

"Good man," Duncan said, and clapped Casey on the shoulder.

"I'll ask Vince to do the old swab too. Something to compare my results against, since he's never had any problems."

"Sounds wise. Always best to go into things with your eyes wide-open."

"That's what I figured." If he was going to do more than just resolve to become a grown-ass man, and actually become one finally, he had to quit running from the truth. Until now, he'd told himself that not knowing was best. And operating under the assumption that the verdict was going to be bad had given him permission to live selfishly, day by day, chasing money and pleasure.

Plus, in a very real sense, finding out he was doomed to whatever it was his mom had was a death sentence, because Casey had no intention of carrying on long enough to become a burden to anybody.

Nope. If he had five, ten more lucid years left, he'd live the holy hell out of every single day, then go up in spectacular flames, on his own motherfucking terms.

"I ordered the kit," he admitted. "Should be here within the week."

Duncan turned back to the register, separated the bills and receipts into piles and began checking them against a tally sheet. "Will you even be able to get your mother's sample analyzed? Is she competent enough to sign whatever consent form must come with the test?"

"Yeah, she has her moments. I'll have to lie to her, though, tell her she's signing my report card or something—she still thinks I'm in high school half the time."

Duncan winced. "How awful."

"You get used to it."

"I suppose that's one upside to having no parents at all—I'll never have to watch them decline."

"Amen."

Duncan left for the bank shortly, and Casey got to work, sweeping and mopping, squaring up the tables, organizing the pool cues and chalks. The contractors tidied away the fresh dust they'd produced and headed out.

Man, there were moments when Casey missed his old life. Working 'til dawn, rolling out of bed at noon, living for weeks on a single payday. No responsibilities heavier than making the rent and fudging his taxes. No attachments.

And yet those moments were fleeting. Doing the right thing these past few months was exhausting, no doubt, and stressful, and anything but leisurely. But it was satisfying, too. He liked himself more, if he was honest. Probably in no small part because he was doing what his dad had failed at: stepping up.

After he unlocked the door and flicked on the lights, he wandered out into the empty front lot and looked up at the BENJI'S SALOON sign. Its neon glow was all but invisible in the bright afternoon sun.

I fucking own this place. The goddamn heart of the town; one of few things worth preserving when the casino and all its attendant change descended. Just as Abilene had said last night. Even in Casey's old life, amazing as he'd been at his job, as indispensible a member of the team as he'd become . . . it wasn't as though he could go telling anybody about it. For all the greater world to see, he'd been nobody back then. Just some thirtysomething guy living in Lubbock, in a decent apartment, driving a Corolla, occasionally getting laid. But here . . .

Abilene was right. In Fortuity, he was somebody. Somebody important, in a way. An employer, a partner to Duncan, an active son to his mom, finally. And whatever he was to Abilene and the baby—something kind of shapeless, but definitely *something.*

"Fucking Fortuity," he muttered, staring down Station Street toward the tracks. His hometown, the one he couldn't fucking wait to escape when he'd been twenty. The town he'd avoided coming back to for nearly a decade. The town he'd thought he left behind forever, and good riddance.

Last fucking place he'd ever expected to feel himself getting attached to.

Abilene woke early. For half a breath, she was lost in the memory of that kiss—just long enough for her body to go warm, her eyes to shut, long enough to feel his mouth on hers and his excitement in her hand . . .

But the heat was gone in a breath, as the larger, colder

reality intruded. James was out. He was out, and he might be in Fortuity by now, for all she knew.

She'd slept poorly, and for once she couldn't blame it on Mercy—Casey had set the crib up in the den, volunteering to be on baby duty. She'd taken him up on the offer, thinking her daughter could probably use his calm energy right about now, more than her mama's jitters. It seemed she'd been right, too. The sound of crying had roused her only once, and faded as quickly as it had started. At least one of them would face the day well rested.

She took a quick shower, then went downstairs, finding Mercy dozing in the crib, but no Casey. Voices drifted from the kitchen, and she moved to the threshold.

"It's good and it's bad," Casey was saying. He had his back to her, sitting at the table.

Christine was busy at the coffeemaker in her robe and sweatpants, long gray-streaked hair twirled up in a fat turquoise barrette. "How so?" she asked him.

"Good that he didn't come around looking for her at the bar," Casey said, and Abilene took a step back into the hallway, knowing they were talking about James. She was curious how they'd speak of him, not knowing she was listening. How they'd speak about *her*.

"But bad, too, since we're no closer to knowing what mood he's in."

"I see what you mean," Christine said. "You sleep okay?"

"Not too shabby." It was a lie, and Abilene knew it. She'd heard him downstairs, picking out chords on Don's old acoustic guitar well into the wee hours.

"You need any help?" he asked Christine.

"I could use loads, actually, with six of you about to descend. Would you fry up some bacon while I get the pancake batter mixed?"

"Sure."

"What's the meeting about, anyway? The Abilene situation?"

She heard the fridge door open and close. "Yeah. Mostly just hammering out a schedule, I think." There was a pause; then he asked Christine, "What?" as though she'd shot him some kind of meaningful look.

"I really wish she'd contact the Sheriff's Department."

Abilene flushed.

"She couldn't get a restraining order, though—it's not like he's outright threatened her," Casey said. "I doubt there's some box you can check for 'He's just a scary guy.'"

"I'd still feel better if they were aware of the situation. They could be on the lookout for him, alert us if he's seen around."

"I know, but she refused. I think she's worried about pissing him off any worse than he might be already. Plus it's hard enough for her, having all of us knowing her business, and you know Fortuity—if this shit makes it to the BCSD, the whole town'll be discussing it by sundown."

It was a lousy option for other reasons, too, ones she didn't want Casey knowing about. Forms meant using your legal name, and Abilene using *her* legal name could make for some uncomfortable questions. She didn't know what exactly counted as identity fraud, but she cashed checks issued to a fake name, using a fake ID.

"I don't see how that's a bad thing," Christine said. "Pride never got anybody anywhere worth going."

"Well, you try talking to her, then."

"Believe me—I did. She was trapped in a car with me for four hours yesterday. We made it to Elko and back but the topic went absolutely nowhere. She trusts you and your brother, though. I'd hoped one of you might change her mind."

Casey laughed. "Girl's got more problems than we realize if she thinks us Grossiers are the pillars of wisdom and reason."

With things taking a lighter turn, Abilene chose that moment to intrude. She stepped into the kitchen. "What's so funny, so early in the morning?"

"Just ripping on the family name," Casey said, opening a package of bacon. "Baby still asleep?"

"Out cold."

"Good. Sit down. You want coffee? It's almost ready."

"Maybe in a bit. Anything I can help with, for the meeting?"

"Well, if we've got three on the job, we may as well cook some eggs," Christine said. "Scrambled will do. Maybe fifteen?"

"Sure." Abilene headed to the fridge.

"Sleep okay?" Casey asked her.

"Not terrible, actually. Thanks to being off duty."

"She was pretty mellow." He waited until she was right beside him, searching the cabinets for a mixing bowl, then murmured, "I need to talk to you."

She eyed him, nervous. "Okay." *What about?* About James, or about the other night? What Casey felt about what had happened, she wasn't sure. She wasn't even sure what she felt about it herself, yet. Only that she didn't regret it. Not a single moment, not a single kiss.

"I've turned on the griddle to warm while I get dressed," Christine said. "Don't burn yourselves."

"Thanks." Casey waited until she'd disappeared to turn to Abilene. "It's about your ex," he said, pouring coffee into a mug.

"What about him?"

"About you considering sitting down and talking with him," Casey went on, stirring sugar into the cup, "provided he approaches the situation like a civilized adult and not a psychopath."

"Fat chance."

His shoulders slumped and he shot her a look she'd never seen on that handsome face before—weary frustration. He slid the mug before her on the counter. "Honey, you've got to face him sometime. And the sooner the better, if you don't want to give him any more reasons to be pissed with you. Tell me what exactly it is you're scared of."

"His anger." There was more, of course. But she couldn't say, *I'm afraid of what you'll think of me, once you hear his side of things.* Neither could she say she was afraid that James might feel justified in trying to take the baby away from her—by law or by force—because there was no way she was telling Casey what kind of a person she'd been before they'd met.

She expanded on that lesser but still real fear. "He's got a violent streak and a hot temper. We had a bumpy, volatile relationship. I never wanted him in the baby's life. I'd have been happy to never have told him, except your brother thought that was a really dangerous idea."

Casey nodded. "Leave the eggs a second. Sit down."

She moved to the table with him.

"I've asked you before, but tell me one more time—has he ever hit you?"

She shook her head. "But he's shaken me. And I've seen him get physical with other people, and the way he looked those times . . . I've seen that in his eyes, when he's been angry at me, and trying hard to keep it all in. Plus I've never done anything this bad before—keeping him in the dark about a child. I don't want to find out what he's capable of."

"I don't much relish finding that out, either, but it's something we do need to know. You can't spend the rest of your life in hiding, honey. And I know you're starting to build a life for yourself here. You're important to the bar, and I think you like that job."

She nodded. She made good tips at Benji's, and she liked feeling as if she had a place in this town—even if only as a bartender—after being adrift for five years. That was a long time to go, feeling like you didn't belong anywhere, especially to a girl who'd had a seeming idyllic small-town childhood. Fortuity might be a hundred times rougher than Bloomville, Texas, but the bar's customers knew her name and asked after her baby. Made her feel like somebody, nearly.

"I don't think you want the solution to be that we dream you up some fake identity and ship you off to Arkansas to start over, all alone."

Now, *that* chilled her. She was already living under a false identity, already neck-deep in her first fresh start. Already living in fear that Casey might one day glance at her health insurance paperwork and realize Abilene Price was not in fact her real name, and that she might have to spill about how it was she'd come to be here with him. Tell him things she'd never even told James . . . and he'd met her during the absolute pitch-black rock bottom of her life.

"I don't want to go away," she said quietly. "But I don't know if I'm ready to see him yet."

"I kinda figured you'd say that." Casey sighed, sipped his coffee. "So here's the plan, okay? We sit on this issue until Ware's turned up and made contact. Chances are, he'll go after my brother. If he doesn't try Vince first, it'll be Duncan or Raina or me who encounters him, at the bar. Whatever the case, we'll wait until he shows, and we'll go from there. Take his temperature. See what he has to say."

A great wave of guilt moved through her—a sour, sharp sensation that rose from her gut and flushed her face, stung her eyes. It must have shown, as Casey took her hand. "It'll be okay."

I'm not scared. Not just now, not for herself or the baby. Just now she felt terrible and selfish and worried that something bad might happen to whoever did see James first. That someone would get threatened or hurt if they refused to tell him where she was. Was living with that guilt truly better than living with Casey finding out her secrets?

Mustering a little bravery, a little hint of the spine she so wanted to one day possess for the sake of her daughter, she nodded. "Okay. I'll talk to him. Once he's made contact, like you said." As she heard those words in her own voice, she sat up a little straighter, felt a little different, a little stronger.

"Good." Casey gave her knuckles a rub and let her hand go. "Drink your coffee."

She took a sip.

"It's gonna be okay, in the end. It's the uncertainty and the waiting that sucks, is all."

"No kidding."

There was a silence, and they focused on their coffees until the suspense became unbearable. She looked at him pointedly.

"What?"

"Is that it?"

"Yeah, that's it. Were you expecting something else?"

She looked to the mug cupped in her palms. "I sort of assumed you wanted to talk about what happened. Between you and me."

"Oh." A canyon-deep pause. "I hadn't planned on it. We could, though, if you want."

Jeez, did she? "I dunno." She wanted to know how he felt about it—she knew that much. Wanted to hear that it had meant something, anything, to him, even as she was afraid to admit the same.

"I mean, we talked some already, after it happened," Casey said. He was acting blasé, like it hadn't mattered, but whether that was because he regretted it or because he assumed *she* did, Abilene couldn't guess. What she really wanted to hear was that it *had* meant something. Anything at all, even if it could never go anywhere.

Abilene wasn't brave at the best of times, and with all the worries now rushing through her head, she had no courage to speak of. "Yeah, I guess we talked plenty already," she agreed. "I mean, it was just a thing that happened."

But something in her expression must have shown how much she hurt just now. He reached across the table again and touched her wrist. "It was real nice, though. It was a real nice thing that happened."

Her heart buoyed at that. She flipped her hand over, clasped his in return. "You think?"

Another nod. "Not something we can keep doing, but I don't regret it. Not unless you do."

She shook her head. It was weird, talking to a guy this way. Openly, about sex or anything else. She wasn't like Kim or Raina—women with no issues sharing their opinions and feelings with a man, talking with one like they were equals. Abilene had never been the equal of any of the men she'd been with, or hadn't felt like she was. She did what voiceless women did—she manipulated. Through sex or tears, she could coerce a guy into not being angry with her, or into lending her money, into just about anything. It wasn't good, but she'd gotten good *at* it. Way better at it than speaking her mind and articulating her needs. She'd gone unheard her entire life, after all. The concept was foreign.

What would she say, if she could get her mouth to speak the absolute truth?

I do want that to happen again. And again, and again, until my body's ready for more, and then I want to do a hundred other things with you. And to hell with his past, and all her vows to quit falling for criminals. Her life was teeming with uncertainty and worry just now, the temptation to escape into good feelings all the more seductive. To hell with everything that didn't feel half as wonderful as that kiss had.

But wants weren't needs, and what she *needed* was exactly the opposite of all these reckless, selfish desires. She needed stability and security, for herself just as much as for her daughter. Another encounter with Casey offered none of that. Offered nothing except excitement and a fleeting imitation of comfort, and desires like those had brought her nothing but ruin, again and again.

"The flesh is weak," whispered a voice from her past. *"The flesh is weak so the resolve must be steadfast. To give in to our animal natures is to turn our backs on the Lord, to trade our very souls for a taste of the Devil's wares. And those wares do not nourish; no, they do not. The wants of the flesh lead us only to poison."*

It was all such bullshit—every fear-mongering, sex-shaming word she'd been fed, growing up.

Except was it, really, when her past mistakes really *had* poisoned her life?

It has to be bullshit. If Mercy came out of one of those mistakes, there's no way it can be true.

Unless Abilene lost her, somehow. Unless that was the real punishment she'd earned herself—

"Hey," Casey said, leaning in, catching her eye. "You all right?"

She blinked, escaping her thoughts. "Yeah. Sorry. I've got a lot on my mind."

"No doubt. But you don't need to worry about what happened between us, okay? You can set that one aside. We had a moment, it was a little fucked, but also nice, and that's all it has to be. Okay?"

"Okay." Abilene swallowed, forced herself to believe that he was right, that it had been nothing more than a little effed but also nice. He made it sound so easy to set aside.

"Effed, and nice," she agreed. "And it *was* nice—nice to feel that way again, if only for a few minutes." She'd forgotten how much her body could feel, with a man. For a year now, she'd set all that aside and turned her physical self over to the baby's needs, and undoubtedly for the best. Though now she'd tasted that again . . . the memory of it lingered on her tongue, deepening to a craving.

And how unfair that people's greatest cravings so often made them sick, gave them heart disease or cancer, or left them addicted. There was a lesson in that. One she'd been needing to learn for years. She heard the baby fussing from the den and went to fetch her, setting her up in her collapsible rocker beside the table.

She eyed the clock. "Better get to work on those eggs."

"I'll get a bottle going—she looks like she'll be wanting one soon. And I can help out some more once the meeting wraps. I don't have much on my plate today."

"Thanks. You're the best." *Way better than I deserve. Yet way more trouble than I need.*

But she wanted him all the same. More than just about anything.

Chapter 8

Good job, Grossier, Casey thought as he turned bacon rashers over on the griddle, pleased with how the first half of his talk had gone with Abilene. *You sounded like a stern-ass man there.* Not some stammering, horny mess, like Monday night, barely able to hit the brakes. That was what she needed in her life right now—a decisive, firm, reliable man.

She needed Miah, basically, but Casey could fake it for the sake of the situation.

Miah and his dad strolled in soon, both dressed for work, and Don lingered long enough to fill a thermos and eat a test pancake before heading out on ranch business. Vince and Kim were next to arrive. Christine excused herself, and Abilene stuck around until Kim seemed to have gotten her fill of baby ogling.

"Better be careful," Casey muttered to his brother, and nodded in his girlfriend's direction. "You might be next."

"Thanks to all the Mom-sitting she's been doing, I think I'm safe for a few years, still. All Kim seems to fantasize about is travel." His attention turned to the heaps of pancakes and eggs and bacon laid out on the table. "Goddamn. Tell your mom thanks, Miah."

"Hey, I helped," Casey said. "I did the bacon. And Abilene did the eggs."

Raina and Duncan arrived last, a few minutes past six. Had to be Raina's doing—Duncan would rather slam his dick in a door than be late for anything.

"Sorry," Raina said as she brushed past, making a bee-line for the coffee. "I forgot there was no gas in the truck."

"S'fine," Miah said evenly, refreshing his own mug. He cast Duncan a cool look, nodded once in acknowledgment. Duncan returned it.

Miah took a seat on one of the two long benches, grabbed a wooden pepper grinder, and thumped it on the tabletop. "Let's get this thing under way—I've got a feed delivery coming at seven. Item one, we need to get the security coverage worked out."

"I took the liberty of printing up a blank roster," Duncan said, pulling papers out of a leather dossier.

"You know," Casey said, sliding the pancake platter over, "on TV, when motorcycle clubs hold meetings, it's to discuss who gets to murder the rival drug lord."

Duncan ignored him, clicking out the tip of a mechanical pencil. "Raina and I can cover the bar, through this week and also next, if necessary. That frees Casey up to stay here for much of the time, with smaller windows of cover so that he can attend to his personal domestic matters."

He shot Duncan a funny look. "You've been to my apartment. I don't even have any plants." And he didn't intend to leave Abilene alone for a moment longer than was necessary. He was already mixed-up from his nascent attachments to her and the baby, and that awkward-hot couch incident had only crossed the wires further. He was all messed up in his body with protective instincts he'd never felt for a woman before. He supposed that must happen when sleeping with somebody was off the table. Your dick transferred all that aggression elsewhere.

"You'll want to at least escape to do laundry and check your mail now and then," Duncan countered. "Vince, do you have any evenings free?"

He nodded and glanced at Kim. "You could watch Mom by yourself a couple evenings, right? If Nita could take the afternoon?"

"Sure."

"And I can relieve Case for a few hours now and then," Miah said. "After dinnertime, at least, but only until about midnight."

They spent twenty minutes hammering out everyone's shifts, and eventually a schedule came together. Vince had even offered to take the overnight watch duty on Friday so

Casey could get an actual night's sleep in his own bed, but Casey had declined—he'd only spend every last minute lying awake, worrying. Miah left for a minute to make photocopies in the office. He passed them out, grabbed a scoop of eggs, and plowed onward.

"Item two—the Ware situation itself."

"Been working on that," Casey said. "I talked to Abilene this morning. She's promised to talk to him, if a meeting can get arranged. If anybody runs into him, give him my number. I'll set it up."

Everyone nodded except Duncan, who, with the admin portion of the meeting wrapped, had gone silent, clearly feeling out of place when it came to matters that couldn't be solved with a spreadsheet.

"Sounds good," Vince said. "Keeping her safe's priority number one, but it's not going to work as a long-term solution. We need to know ASAP if this is going to end in some awkward convo or if a restraining order's getting filed."

Casey winced. Neither outcome appealed to him. Of course the latter was the worst-case scenario, but there was also a petty, insecure bit of him that couldn't help but think that she'd liked the guy enough to be in a relationship with him. She might've loved him, even, provided she hadn't stuck around out of fear. While a civil reconciliation was undoubtedly the best result they could hope for, his coffee curdled in his gut as he imagined them getting so good with each other that maybe they'd try to get back together, to make things work for Mercy's sake.

His fingers curled up into fists underneath the table.

Chill out. What the fuck had happened to the old Casey, anyhow? Before last summer he'd have taken one look at this situation—seen an emotional girl, a baby, and some mysterious gunrunner ex—and booked it out of there quick enough to kick up dust. He should have left the Robin Hood scene to his brother; Vince was the one who *enjoyed* bleeding, after all. Casey liked his face and limbs just how they were.

"Let's see where that goes," Miah said, meaning the plan to get Ware in touch with Abilene, "and regroup from there."

"Meantime," Vince said, "we're still on high alert. Especially you guys at the bar—no doubt he'll be looking for her there."

"I brought these," Raina said, rooting through Duncan's dossier. "Mug shot, plus a picture from the paper when he was arrested." She handed out printouts with the two black-and-white photos on them.

Casey studied it, stomach dropping. He'd been avoiding this moment.

Ware looked about how he'd pictured. No face tattoos, but a mean mug, shaved head, scar through one eyebrow, glare like an angry dog. Guy must have some kind of winning-ass smile, he thought, if a sweet thing like Abilene had managed to fall for him, once upon a time.

Miah nodded, studying his copy. "Thanks. That's way better than the photos I was able to find. Okay, item three: I've got some security concerns of my own."

"That doesn't sound good," Vince said.

"It's nothing compared to Abilene's worries." Miah sipped his coffee. "But last fall we found some evidence that pointed to possible drug dealing, out on the range. Or maybe not drugs this time—could be weapons or any other thing. But pickups and drop-offs of some nature, likely. Strange vehicles seen turning off the access roads, late at night."

"Déjà vu," Vince said.

Miah nodded. "It's happened before—one of my hands once found a cooler full of weed just sitting at the junction of two of our private roads. Whoever was meant to pick it up must've gotten lost or detained or something. We filed a report but nothing ever came of it. In any case, the BCSD doesn't patrol out here, and there're no lights or any workers out after sundown. It's an obvious temptation."

"You want us to patrol?" Vince asked.

"No, I can do that myself—I have been for months, just a couple times a week. There haven't been any known thefts or property damage, so it's more a nuisance than anything. But also not a development anybody wants becoming a regular thing. But I was thinking maybe one of us could go sniffing around the shadier corners of Fortuity. Drop hints like they're looking for a distributor, that sort of thing. I think that probably means you, Case. Too many people know Vince and I are friends to buy it, but you're still a new face to any criminals who didn't grow up here."

Casey shrugged, game for it. He did enjoy a good con. "I can give it a shot. Not sure where to start—or when I'll have the time—but I'll give it a try."

Vince said, "Dancer," just as Duncan suggested, "Perhaps John Dancer."

"Fuck me, that psycho? Last time I saw him he chloroformed me." Ostensibly as anesthesia, when Casey had been taken to Dancer to get a bullet tweezed out of his thigh, but it wasn't as though he'd consented to it.

"Count yourself lucky you got to be unconscious for most of that morning," Kim said.

John Dancer was Fortuity's least reputable resident— and that was saying something. He attracted enemies like horseshit drew flies, and lived in a creepy orange camper van way out in the badlands by the creek.

"He'll know you and me are friends," Miah said, "so no need to pretend you're after something shady."

"Bribe him if you have to," Vince agreed. "I'll comp you out of the club's account." Meaning the many coffee cans full of cash Vince kept secreted around the auto garage— proceeds from his sideline as an unlicensed bookie and the sale of questionably acquired cars. "Ask Dancer if he's ever done business with Ware, while you're at it," Vince added. "He's been kicking around here for twelve years, probably, and I still got no clue what he does for money. But I wouldn't be shocked if illegal weapons factored, here and there."

"Fine, fine." Casey glanced at his photocopy of the roster. "It'll have to be an evening. I'll try tonight, actually, if Miah can be with Abilene for a couple hours . . . ?"

Miah nodded. "Sure." He sipped his coffee and glanced around the table. "Any other business?"

Everyone shook their heads, so he gave the peppermill another rap and stood. "Meeting's adjourned. Thanks for coming so early, everybody. Stick around for the grub. And load the washer if you want my mom to stay sweet on you."

"I got it," Casey said.

Raina filled herself a plate, as did Vince and Kim. Duncan seemed content to eat nothing, sitting stock-still until Miah bade everyone a good day and disappeared.

Vince grinned at Duncan. "Now, that wasn't so terrible, was it, Welch?"

"He promised to punch me once," Duncan said. "Forgive me for finding it difficult to relax."

"We've all wanted to punch you now and then," Vince replied. "Take comfort in the fact that none of us actually has, so far."

"Yes, how reassuring."

"I've never wanted to punch you," Kim offered.

"I have," Casey said. "Real bad."

"I'm the only one who's actually managed it," Raina added. "Though technically that was an elbow."

"You also slapped me once."

"And this from the woman you love," Casey said.

Duncan rolled his eyes and pulled a stray newspaper over.

Vince ate fast and downed a cup of coffee. "Gotta head to the quarry." He swung his legs over the long bench, kissed Kim good-bye, then said, "Case, walk me to my bike."

Ah shit, what now? He set down his fork. Please not some serious-ass talk about Casey's glaring absence around the old homestead. Not that he didn't deserve it, after nine years away. He'd done better since he'd been back, but lately, between the bar and Abilene, he might as well still be in Lubbock for all the use he'd been to his brother. He felt a burning sensation along the back of his neck. Guilt.

Once they were outside, he asked, "This isn't about Mom, is it? I can go back to watching her mornings when this is all over. Then Nita could take a couple nights, and you and Kim could—"

Vince waved his words aside. "Chill the fuck out. I know you're busy."

"What, then?"

They reached Vince's old R80 and he pulled on his gloves. "Just wanted to say, good job."

Casey blinked. "What with?"

"You know, everything. Watching Mom when you can. Kicking in for the bills. Taking the lead around here, for Abilene. You've been acting like a grown man for a change." He smiled, the gesture's snide quality taking some of the edge off all this brotherly earnestness. "You're doin' good, kid. Keep it up." He gave Casey a hard slap on the arm, then mounted his bike.

"I'm thirty-three, you know," Casey said. "Don't act so shocked."

As he stomped his engine to life, Vince shot Casey a look, one that said, *Bet you're just as surprised as me.* Or something to that effect. Something snarky and annoyingly accurate. Yeah, he was thirty-three now, but that only meant he'd given his brother three-plus decades' worth of reasons not to expect him to ever step up or stick around. Casey rolled his eyes and watched Vince ride away.

He wasn't really annoyed . . . or shouldn't be, at any rate. That little moment had actually been really kind and genuine, two qualities Vince didn't display without some personal discomfort. By Grossier standards, you could've slapped some touching music behind that conversation, cued an "I love you, Dad," and rolled the credits.

But Casey was rankled nonetheless. Irked. If it felt patronizing, it ought to—before returning to Fortuity, he hadn't ever given anybody reason to expect him to be reliable or responsible or do anything that didn't directly benefit him. Vince knew that better than anyone. And if he was a little pissed, it was only because he had witnesses to this transformation, a load of people who'd known Casey the self-interested opportunist before now, and had every right to be surprised.

So maybe it wasn't annoyance at all. Maybe it was a little bit of shame, a little bit of hard-earned humility.

He watched until Vince disappeared around the bend, and replayed that parting look his brother had shot at him. *Keep this up and maybe you won't turn into Dad after all.* Maybe that's what that expression had been saying.

Even if it hadn't been, the thought sent a shiver through him. He headed for the house, rubbing his arms against the morning chill.

James Ware found what he was looking for right around high noon.

Fucking Fortuity, he thought, slamming his door, eyeing the scrubby, desolate badlands, squinting against that relentless sun. The old camper van was right where he'd expected to find it, parked where the creek banged an angle from south to west. And if the van was here, its owner couldn't be far.

"Dancer," he called. No reply. He walked straight up to the van, rapped on the passenger door. "Dancer."

A shriek came from inside— Goddamn, that terrible fucking bird. Sure enough, a white parrot came clambering over the seat's headrest to stare at James, its black eye judging, head bobbing, feathered mohawk flaring.

He turned at the sound of the rear doors squeaking open, and circled around to the back.

The man of the house hopped out of the van in jeans and little else—no shoes, no shirt, a bent, hand-rolled cigarette smushed behind his ear, half-lost in his messy black hair. His eyebrows rose and he smiled blearily—just awoken or thoroughly stoned? James didn't care to guess.

"Well, well, well, look who's been released. You get good behavior or something?"

"No, I got a good lawyer."

"This calls for a toast." Dancer leaned into the van and straightened with a bottle of rum, his long, fatless body moving with a weird, tweaky grace.

James put his hand up. "Here strictly on business."

"Suit yourself." Dancer uncapped the fifth and took a swig, then tossed it back inside. "Our last transaction got lost in the shuffle. You want your shit?"

"Or the cash value. Frankly I could use the cash more."

"Well, that's real good, as I already sold that inventory to an interested party. Not exactly the sort of thing a man needs lying around under his bed, you understand."

"Perfectly."

Dancer cupped an elbow, stroked his little beard. "So lemme think. I found you, what? Twelve units?"

"Fourteen, you fucking prick."

"Right, of course. Fourteen. And you paid me what, to source them? One twenty-five each?"

"One seventy-five. Try to cheat me one more time, John. Just try. I gave you twenty-four fifty up front, and I want twenty-four fifty in my hand before I leave here."

"Let's call it fifteen hundred, taking the burden of handling and storage I assumed into the equation."

"Let's call it fuck you, I want my twenty-four fifty."

"Two grand."

"I'm not gonna fucking say it again," James warned. "I know you made yourself a nice profit; now, comp me or we never do business together again."

Dancer sighed. "You drive a hard goddamn bargain—you know that?"

"Most of your associates too high to keep track of their own math?"

Dancer grinned at that and climbed back inside his van. He returned a minute later with a thick stack of fifties and twenties. James counted them out, then tucked the wad into his front pocket. "Better. You're off my shit list, if barely. And you can get on my good side if you can tell me anything about Abilene Price."

"That a girl?"

James nodded. "Twentysomething brunette, looks about sixteen."

"Sounds just like my type. Go on."

"Big blue eyes, Texas accent."

"This gets better and better. I'll give you five hundred bucks."

"She was working at that shithole bar downtown, but I haven't seen her come or go yet, and I need to know where she's living."

"Ah. I do know who you mean, actually."

"You've seen her?"

"Benji's only has about three bartenders," Dancer said with a shrug. "Kinda tough to miss. Also tough to miss that you didn't list 'vastly pregnant' among her many physical charms. You got yourself a dependent, Jimmy?"

"You know where she lives or not?"

"I don't. But I know who would—Casey Grossier."

"Grossier? Some relation to Vince?"

"His little brother, though they don't look much alike. He's the girl's boss. Him and this British prick named Welch bought the bar off Benji's daughter last fall. I doubt Welch would tell you shit about his employee's whereabouts—he's a cagey motherfucker. But Grossier might. He never fucking shuts up, and he can be bought, if nothing else. He just moved in above the drugstore on the main drag."

"What's he look like?"

"Hard to miss. About your height, red hair, red beard. Drives a silver Corolla, or sometimes an older Harley-Davidson, also silver."

"He pack like his big brother?"

"Not sure. But he's not dangerous like his brother—not in any obvious way. Smart, though you'd never guess it. Smartest dumb-ass you'll ever meet. Rumor mill says he ran a bunch of cons downstate and in California and Texas, but exactly what, I'm not sure. But he's friendly with the girl, and chances are, her employers know where she lives. I can ask for you, if you want. Asshole owes me one—I took a bullet out of his leg last summer."

"No doubt that offer comes with a fucking price tag, so no, thanks, John. But I'll bear you in mind for future transactions."

Dancer smiled, smug. "Much obliged. Anything else you need? Just got a case of what I think are quaaludes. Haven't tried one yet. Yours for a song."

"Not my product." James offered a final nod, then turned to head back to his truck.

He locked the cash in his glove box and started the engine.

Next stop, Casey fucking Grossier.

Chapter 9

Casey parked his bike on Station Street in front of the drug-store just as the streetlights were blinking on. He un-strapped his duffel from the back of the seat and found his house keys, circled around, and let himself into the stairwell that led up to his apartment. Miah was on bodyguard duty for a couple hours, so Casey could run some errands.

On the floor beneath the mail flap sat a small mountain of envelopes, mostly junk with the previous tenants' names on it—catalogs for medical supplies, that kind of sketchy, DIY shit. But sitting on its side, up against the wall, was a small brown box. He stooped, heart pounding. Sure enough, it had his name on it, and the cheerful purple logo for Life-Map, the DNA testing company, above the return address.

"Goddamn."

He'd paid for expedited shipping but hadn't expected it to come overnight. He could've used a couple extra days to wrap his head around the possibility that this little box might just be better at predicting the future than him or his mom. It could tell him he was fine. Or it could tell him he'd be crazy by the time he hit forty.

"Fuck."

He'd been going the ignorance-is-bliss route for so long, the idea of knowing the truth was undeniably terrifying. It could open up an entirely new future—one worthy of get-ting into a serious relationship for, of starting a family someday. And while that would be good news, he thought as he climbed the stairs, duffel bag bonking the wall with every other step, it was also what scared him. He'd spent the last few years diligently avoiding commitments and personal connections, too afraid of losing them if he wound up like his mom.

If he found out he didn't share whatever breed of crazy she had, he might just have to grow the fuck up, once and for all.

But I have, already. A little. Even Vince had noticed. He unlocked the door to his apartment, found the light switch, and dropped his bag on the floor. But if it turned out he wasn't going nuts, well, that landed him at a major crossroads. Keep going as he always had, or step up completely. Become the sort of man who somebody might be proud to call their lover or partner or husband, or maybe even father, someday.

Hold your horses there, bucko.

Even if he dodged his mom's misfortune, he feared inheriting his dad's legacy nearly as much as the mental illness. At least if he went nuts, it wasn't his fault. If it turned out he was just a flighty, selfish deadbeat who took off the second things got ugly on the home front . . . ? Yeah, that was all on him.

But maybe, he thought, setting the box on the arm of the previous tenants' fugly plaid couch, *just maybe, the test'll tell me what I've suspected since I was ten. That that deadbeat was never my real father to begin with.* Man, that'd be the ultimate load off, knowing he wasn't Tom Grossier's kid after all. Didn't seem so far-fetched. Vince looked just like their father, so the guy had strong genes. But Casey, on the other hand . . .

His head was racing with too many questions, and the answers were still days away, even if he overnighted the test back, even if he shelled out for the expedited lab processing. He had plenty to worry about outside of a cheek swab in that time, and he'd be smart to keep his head screwed on.

He looked around the apartment.

Nothing special, but it was spacious. To judge by the state of the place when he'd moved in, the previous tenants who'd lived above the drugstore had been enthusiasts of a different breed of pharmaceuticals, but for three hundred a month he wasn't about to bitch. Taking it in now, the space was barely recognizable. Not because anything had changed—

just because he'd spent so little time in here since he'd signed the lease. That had been a week after Abilene had given birth, and he doubted there'd been a day when he hadn't seen her since then. Either they'd been working together or he was swinging by with something she needed—first at her old place and more recently at Three C. And when he hadn't been doing that, he was loitering at Duncan and Raina's or his mom's house. He'd abandoned his few bits of furniture in his apartment in Lubbock and had some more important items in a storage unit down there—a unit he paid the rent on religiously, under a fake name. At some point he needed to make a road trip and dispose of that shit.

He'd spent almost no time awake in this place, he realized as he scooped his dirty clothes out of his bag. He tossed them in the laundry basket in his bedroom and grabbed some clean ones from his open suitcase. A stranger might think he'd been burgled, or skipped town in a hurry. He owned so little, and half of what he did call his was still in boxes.

When he'd lived in Lubbock, he'd made some effort with his place. Made it nice enough so if he got in a position to get laid, it wouldn't scare any willing women away. But here, well, he was just too busy. For the first time in his life, he had shit to keep on top of, every single day of the week. Between the bar and Abilene and his mom, he really didn't get much chance to do more for himself than sleep and shower and eat.

And if Casey was completely honest, he was proud of that fact.

He zipped his clean clothes and the LifeMap box into his bag and locked up. He'd swing by Benji's, make sure there'd been no Ware sightings, then see if Duncan or Raina—whoever was behind the taps—needed anything. Then he'd go by his mom's house and maybe get her and Vince to swab their cheeks and sign their disclosure forms, do the same himself, and get the thing packed up and ready to ship out in the morning.

He bungeed his duffel to his seat. It'd be fine for a few minutes—Benji's was barely two blocks west.

The bar's lot was half-full, not bad for this hour on a Wednesday evening, Casey thought, his shoes crunching across the gravel. And soon enough, this place might just get *busier* at suppertime, once the kitchen was functional. Christ, he hoped so. He hoped they did a killing, and fuck all the corporate chains that came to town to bleed the casino tourists dry—

"Hey!"

Casey turned to the front corner of the lot, where the shout had come from. His guts were immediately bunched up around his throat like a scarf.

Fucking James Ware himself. Looked just like his mug shot. Same scowl, same scar through the eyebrow. The recognition trickled down his spine, cold as ice.

Ware had been leaning against an older black pickup, but now he was moving, marching toward Casey. There were no smokers out front, nobody coming or going. Just the two of them.

"You Grossier?"

"Who the fuck wants to know?" No sense being polite, when that was the greeting he'd been offered.

"I'm James Ware." He stopped maybe four paces from Casey. His hands were balled at his sides, face set in a stern glare. His shaved hair had grown in just a little, enough to reveal he had a receding hairline. But he wasn't a bad-looking guy—just scary. The same height as Casey, but built more like Vince behind the gray T-shirt he wore.

"I heard you're the one who can tell me where to find Abilene Price," the guy said.

Casey crossed his arms, faking toughness as he had his whole life. He wasn't afraid to fight—he'd certainly been in his fair share of scraps and probably come out on top in half of them, but that was Vince's scene, really. And this guy had just spent eight months in fistfight heaven, honing his skills, no doubt. Casey mimicked his brother's tough-guy posture and cocked his head. "Who told you that, exactly?"

"John Dancer told me that."

Anger flashed, hijacked his mouth. "Goddamn." All the more reason to pay that motherfucker a visit real soon.

"So you know?"

"I'm her boss, but I don't just go giving out my employees' addresses to whoever asks for 'em. What the fuck do you want with her?"

Ware's eyes narrowed. "I need to talk to her. About some business we have."

That how you think of your daughter? Some business? Casey rankled, something dangerous crackling through him as he pictured the baby. He'd been feeding and changing and rocking and bathing that so-called *business*, and all at once he could understand Abilene's fear and stubbornness. To imagine letting this guy near Mercy made his blood go cold and hot at once.

"I know who you are," Casey said.

"I know you, too. You're Vince's little brother. I'm sure you know all about me, including the fact that Abilene's been keeping my kid a secret from me."

"That girl's my employee, and my friend, and her safety means way more to me than your hurt feelings, so don't hold your fucking breath. You give me a compelling reason to trust that you won't hurt her, and she agrees to it, and sure, I'll get you two in the same room. But just now I can't say I'm too sure of your intentions."

"My intentions are my own goddamn business. Same as that kid's welfare."

"And your other business involves illegal guns, I hear. I can tell you that I got no problem being a narc if it means Abilene stays safe. So you ever pull something out and threaten me or anybody I know for information, I got precisely fuck-all qualms about reporting it to the Sheriff's Department and getting you shipped straight back downstate."

"I'm not here to start trouble," Ware said, though his tone and posture hadn't softened a jot. "I'm here to talk to my ex. Now, you might think you know Abilene, but you don't. Not like I do. She's fucking helpless at the best of times, and I need to see with my own eyes that my kid is in good hands."

"I can tell you they're both fine."

"I have no desire to turn this into some legal proceeding, Grossier. Or any other ugly scene. I just want to see my kid, like any father would. Though if I don't like what I see, I'm prepared to make this nasty, I promise you that."

Casey's temper flared at that, skin going hot, brows drawing tight. It was the threat that had him seething, but there was more to it. *And what do you know about being a father, precisely?* Unless this guy had other children out there in the world, Casey was the one who'd put in the hours, lost the sleep, surrendered little scraps of his heart, one tiny connection after the other.

"You want to see her, you propose a time and place, and you tell me what it is you plan to talk about, and I'll see if she's willing. And there *will* be witnesses."

"Who the fuck are you to tell me my rights, exactly?"

I don't know what she and I are to each other, apart from a whole fucking tangled lot of something intense. "I'm someone who cares about her safety."

"You fucking her? That what this is about?"

Casey's neck flushed hot, and he was glad it was too dark for Ware to see. Last thing he needed was this asshole knowing he'd struck a nerve.

"That all you know about men and women?" Casey asked. "That they fuck each other sometimes?"

"I'm that kid's *father*. Not you. It's my job to make sure she's in good hands, and I will fuck you up if you try to stop me."

"Talk all the shit you want, but I'm the one who's been there for them since your daughter was born, and I've got a sneaking suspicion I care more about both those girls' welfare than you do. So here's what's gonna happen. I'm gonna give you my number, and when you're ready to talk like a civilized person, we'll talk."

"I'll take your number," Ware said, "but don't believe for one second that I think what's going on here is right." He pulled out a phone, and Casey gave him his unlisted, pay-as-you-go number. So much for the wood chipper. And one more reason to dread that thing's chiming.

"And get this straight," Casey said slowly, precisely. "You want to see her, you go through me. Nobody else. Not my brother, not my business partner. I don't want to hear about you bullying my customers for information, and definitely not my motherfucking family, you got that?"

Ware smiled, the gesture all nails and rust. "Yeah. I got it, big man. I cool off. I call you. We work this shit out."

"Good." Inside, he was shaking, but on the outside his body felt hard and coiled and ready to snap. He'd never known what protectiveness could do to a man. He'd always made it a point not to get attached to anything—or anyone.

"We'll talk soon," Ware said evenly, and turned away.

Casey memorized the digits on Ware's plate while the guy climbed into his truck, and waited until he had disappeared completely down the road before he walked back to his bike, abandoning his plans to check on the bar. His body was humming, right down in his guts and bones; his nails had bitten red marks in his palms. He'd deal with Dancer later. That shit could wait, as could the DNA tests and everything else. Right now all he wanted was to see Abilene and the baby, to confirm they were safe and sound, maybe never leave their sides again.

And one thing seemed goddamn certain, he thought as he stomped on his starter.

That cocksucker isn't getting anywhere near them. Not while there's still blood pumping through this body.

Chapter 10

Abilene woke slowly, unsure at first where she was.

That happened a lot at Three C. That had happened a lot during a rather dark period of her short life, as well, though now as she blinked blearily at the walls and windows, the room that came into focus was pleasant and familiar. The same couldn't be said for some of the holes she'd come to in.

The guest room was dim—its two windows were west facing, and when she'd nodded off it had been from the heat of the dipping sun. Now it was dark, the sky nearly black, and just the one soft bulb in the reading lamp by the bed was on, casting the room in its weak glow. She sat up and eyed the clock on the dresser. Not even seven, thankfully. Dinner wasn't usually until eight, and she liked to help when she could, setting the table at the very least—

A soft knock sounded at the door. She smoothed her hair, rose, and tiptoed over, expecting Christine or Miah. She was surprised to find Casey there instead. He was in his socks, his shoes and jacket presumably abandoned in the Churches' front hall.

"Hey," she whispered, letting him know Mercy was asleep. "Thought you were out until after supper."

"Something came up, so I rushed back."

She went cold in a beat, right down to her bare toes. "What?"

He came inside and shut the door quietly. "Your ex came after me."

Her eyes made a frantic inventory of him, searching for scrapes or cuts or rips in his clothes. "Came after you?"

"Nothing violent. Here, sit down." He nodded to the bed.

She sat cross-legged, facing him squarely, expecting him to sit as well. Instead he strode to the crib, bracing his hands on the rail and staring down at the baby.

"Casey, you're scaring me."

He straightened, turned. "Sorry."

She patted the covers. "Sit."

He took a seat at the bed's edge, rubbing his thighs.

"Tell me."

"He was waiting in the lot when I stopped by the bar, barely a half hour ago. He knew who I was—Vince's brother, and your boss. He wanted to know where you and the baby were."

She hugged herself, the room feeling cold and too dark.

"I didn't tell him, of course. I said to call me when he cooled down and could talk like a reasonable person."

"He was angry, then."

"Very. He took the number and climbed in his truck and rode off, after we traded some words. I think he'll call. I hope he will, at least. Though I won't lie. Before, I thought getting the two of you together to hash shit out was the only sensible course of action. Now that I've met him . . ."

"He's intimidating," she offered. A trait she'd found both terrifying and reassuring, depending on who had most recently pissed James off.

"He's more than that," Casey said. "He's intense in a way I don't like one fucking bit."

She nodded to the baby, admonishing the swear. What a losing battle that was turning out to be.

"Sorry."

"So you've changed your mind? You *don't* think I should talk to him?"

"Man, I don't even know." He rubbed his face, worked his fingers through his beard, sighed. "On paper it's the smart way to go. But I won't lie, honey. He scares me. It scares me to imagine setting up some talk, and him hurting you or threatening you. But keeping you hidden's no solution either. I dunno. I need some time to digest it all."

"Sure." She'd never seen him so rattled, and it worried her in turn. Casey was usually the picture of laid-back, always prepared to downplay any seriousness with a joke or trash-talking. She crawled across the bed to sit close. Instinct told her to touch him, to circle a palm on his back as she might do to Mercy when the baby was upset, but she kept both hands clasped safely in her lap. "Did he say anything else?" *Anything about me, about my past?*

"No."

Inside, she heaved a sigh of relief. "He's a real nasty piece of work," she offered. "Sorry you had to run into him."

"Better me than you. And better for all of us that we know he's in town, and what he wants."

True. Not knowing had been worse, in a way. But now having him only miles from her and the baby . . .

"I'm real sorry you're even caught up in all this," she said.

He met her eyes squarely, the mere look rousing goose bumps. "I was about to say the same to you. Don't you be sorry at all. *I'm* not sorry for a second that you're not out there by yourself, with nobody to help you."

That alone had tears brewing. She blinked and a fat one fell to the covers. Casey offered a smile, but he had it wrong—she wasn't crying from fear or stress or anything bad, really. It was gratitude that had her cheeks burning and her throat tight. Relief that, just as he'd said, she wasn't in this by herself.

She knew what had to be done. She had to talk to James. If she refused, he'd get angry enough or desperate enough to punish her, perhaps tell Casey the truth about her. Moreover, she needed to break those old habits and be brave for a change. Running and hiding had always been her default, but that had to stop—now.

"When he calls," she said, "I'll speak with him. Not in person—but I'll talk on the phone." Just having said it, she felt a little stronger, not quite as helpless.

"When he calls," Casey echoed, "I'll tell him you're willing to talk. But I'll make him call back at a specified time—no need for him to know exactly how close you and I are. Proximity-wise, I mean," he added quickly.

She nodded.

Casey leaned closer, his shoulder bumping hers. "You okay?"

"I'm scared," she admitted. *And of so much more than you could guess.*

"I won't let him hurt you—you or Mercy. I promise you that."

"I know." *Promise me no matter what he might say to you, you won't turn your back on me.* Far too much to ask, though, and she knew it. She stretched out on the bed, and Casey did the same. She wondered how close their hands might be, and whether the body heat she sensed was a figment or not.

Casey cleared his throat, spoke to the ceiling. "Can I ask you something that's none of my business?"

"I guess so."

After a pause, "How did you wind up with him, to begin with?" He turned his head to catch her eye.

Fudge. "We met during a really . . . hard period of my life. I guess I needed somebody strong, when I was feeling so weak. And I mistook violence for strength."

"You swear to God he never hurt you?"

She shook her head, hair mussing against the pillow.

"Doesn't have to leave a mark on the outside to count as abuse, you know."

She bit her lip, then spoke a grain of truth. "I've never had the best instincts, when it comes to guys."

"How so?"

"I guess I'm just one of those stupid girls who's always falling for the bad boy or whatever."

"You're not stupid."

"I'm not all that wise, either. If I was, maybe I'd learn from my mistakes." Though she was learning, she reminded herself. She'd been weak the other night and let her old urges propel her into Casey's arms, but she was smart enough now to at least realize what a bad idea that had been.

"It's never too late to start." Casey fell silent for a long moment, then spoke softly. "I need to say something to you."

"What?"

He stared up at the beams. "I lied to you, yesterday morning. Sort of."

"What do you mean?"

"I can't remember what I said, about what happened between us. The kissing. Probably something about it not needing to be a big deal." He turned his face to hers once more. "But it did mean something. To me. Something more than just . . . you know. What it was."

Her heart was beating hard all at once, body warm, hopes rising. "Me, too."

"You and I can't—or shouldn't—date. For a dozen good reasons. Most importantly, because I don't have what it takes to be any kind of role model to your daughter."

"Oh." And here she'd been expecting the lame, most obvious argument about him being her boss. "You don't have to explain . . . even if I can't quite see why you think that. You've been wonderful with her, since the night she was born."

"It's complicated. But it boils down to the fact that I don't know where I'll be in a few years."

"Who does, really?" She kept her words casual, voice light, though inside she felt all coiled up with hope and desperation, aching to beg him to change his mind. To think they stood some kind of chance. In a blink, all that wanting was back. At least this time, with this man, it was real. A genuine, deeply physical attraction, and not some ploy to attach herself to a guy for the sake of having somewhere to stay and somebody to protect her. Casey had been looking out for her for weeks before they'd ever kissed, and any money she got from him, she earned. They couldn't be anything serious—on that they agreed, even if she didn't entirely understand his reasons.

Where exactly did that leave them, though?

He sighed heavily and turned onto his side, gaze dropping to the covers or her arm.

"You don't have to tell me," she said. "I'm only curious. Like, is this to do with whatever you used to do for money?" She doubted that whatever his old, shady dealings had been, they could be worse than gunrunning. If anything, she didn't want to know. Not if they were never going to be something real, anyhow.

"It's nothing to do with that," Casey said. "My future's just uncertain."

It was obvious there was something he wasn't telling her, something important. But there was plenty she wasn't saying, either—things she planned never to share with him. Maybe it was selfishness; maybe it was self-preservation. Maybe it was wrong and deceptive and toxic to do so, but it was also a survival instinct. Maybe it was because the opening up of closets was a ritual reserved for couples.

Whatever the case, Christ in heaven, she was tired of secrets. Keeping them was like lugging a hundred pounds of armor around with you. Secrets kept people apart, even as they might stand side by side . . . *Or lie in the same bed,* she thought, letting herself register just how close their bodies were. She remembered the taste of his kiss, the feel of his mouth. The heat and insistence of him when she'd touched him there. She flushed.

"So the other night meant something," Abilene whispered at length. "Was there more to that thought?"

He swallowed, gaze moving to her face.

"It meant something," she said. "But we can't ever be serious. So what does that leave?"

"Aside from sexual frustration?" he asked, then smiled, tempering all the seriousness.

"I was never after forever with you," she said, realizing it was the truth. "I know I come with more baggage than most men are willing to take on." She'd only wanted a taste of what romance could feel like, with someone who treated her as Casey did. Just a taste. She'd had that now, though her body still wanted more, wanted to take things further, feel it all.

"That's not—"

She shook her head, in no need of whatever he'd been about to offer—a contradiction, an excuse, an apology. None of them mattered. "I only wanted to know what it would feel like, with you. With somebody who makes me feel what you do. Even for just a little while. A week or a day, or a single night. Just for as long as that kiss lasted."

Even in the dimness, she could see him blushing. It made her bold. Here was the moment when her selective and self-serving bravery *did* kick in—when a man tipped his hand, offered a little peek at his cards. When she could sense that a woman's body just might trump a guy's best intentions.

And it always does, doesn't it?

"You can't make any promises," she murmured, turning onto her side to face him fully. "And I don't have any expectations. That makes us sound awful compatible just now—don't you think?"

He swallowed, gaze seeking her eyes, her mouth, her breasts.

"I liked everything that happened the other night," she said, meeting his eyes on the final word. "Everything except for when it stopped."

Again, he swallowed, lips parting and looking fuller. Surely this professional gambler had a poker face to be reckoned with, but just now he was an open book. "Did you?"

She nodded.

"So did I," he said. "More than I thought I should tell you."

"I'm not as delicate as you think I am." She might wind up with a broken heart at the end of this non-courtship, but she'd lived through far worse.

He edged nearer, and she thrilled when his knee nudged hers. She opened her legs, welcoming his warm, heavy thigh. The contact was more sweet than sexy, matching the caution on his handsome face. She scooted close. He cupped her cheek and studied her lips for a long moment before meeting them with his own.

Her eyes shut, and she felt his collar in her grip, the top button of his shirt, a soft tease of chest hair against her knuckles. She wanted his shirt gone, and a chance to touch the unknown planes of his body. Wanted him completely naked, and excited. Wanted him hard and hot and begging for her.

"You just fucking love *to feel wanted, don't you?"*

James had laid that on her, spat those words in the midst of the fight that had her leaving him for good. Nothing stung quite like the truth. Nothing cut with so jagged an edge. She did love to feel wanted. It went beyond vanity, went someplace darker and deeper and uglier, but she hungered for that. Craved that power that no girl with her unassuming smarts or charms or looks would ever be expected to possess.

"Never give a man everything he's after," her grand-mother had told her. *"There's far worse words for a girl to be called than 'tease.' Hold a little something back. Dogs are happiest when they're hunting, so don't get caught until it's on your terms."*

She tried to imagine explaining this philosophy to Raina, on one of those nights back when they'd worked together. While Raina intimidated the crap out of her, she was also a bit in awe of how her old boss managed to go through the world caring so little what others thought. Saying what she liked, needing nobody. What would Raina counter her grandma's wisdom with?

Hey, if you want to date dogs, by all means, knock your-self out. I'll just be over here, fucking a grown-ass man.

Yeah, that sounded about right. And was probably fair. But Raina had more leverage in this world than Abilene did—looks, means, confidence, an established role in the place she called home. Playing games with guys might be deceitful and manipulative, but when it was the only tool you had . . .

Still, Abilene had no desire to play those games with Casey. There was no future for them, nothing at stake. Nothing standing in the way.

She kissed him deeper, welcomed his tongue. Imagined that he was her first boyfriend, that everything was how it should be. A do-over to fix her entire sexual history, make it all right.

She touched his face and hair, fascinated. He was so much more than good-looking to her. This was the first man—the first *person*—who'd held her daughter, the first face Mercy ever saw, first voice she'd heard. Maybe those things were making her project more onto this attraction than was wise, but it felt so good, she just wanted to stay lost in the rush. Never come up for air.

His hand roamed down her side, then eased up beneath her sweater to rest at the middle of her back. Through her shirt she felt the warmth of his skin—he radiated heat like no one she'd ever met. Like a permanent fever. She touched him in turn, rubbing his chest, tugging at the snaps of his shirt one by one, until she had it spread open and his blazing bare skin was under her palm. His breaths quickened and his kisses grew stilted, distracted.

"Take your sweater off, honey," he murmured, pulling back.

She did, tugging her long-sleeved tee back down over her belly. He wrapped his arms around her, kneaded at her back, his mouth hot on her neck, beard tickling. She held his head and shut her eyes, replayed every moan and cuss he'd let her hear when they'd first messed around.

What's changed? she had to wonder. This man panting at her throat was different. While on Monday he'd been hesitant, even a little resistant, now he felt eager and possessive. Hungry.

She drew her fingers through his hair, mesmerized. "Tell me what you need."

"I don't even know." His words were all but lost against her neck. "Just you. Here."

Her own needs, exactly. Just to feel this, in the midst of everything else that was happening. Something simple, primal, to banish the chaos for a little while.

She slid lower along his body, leveling their hips. He kissed her while she admired him, her hands taking in the curve of his back, the firm muscle of his butt, the heat of his skin beneath his shirt. Her thigh was locked around his, and when he began to move, she felt him—excited and hard behind his jeans.

For a long moment, everything was friction and heat. Then all at once, Casey stilled, pulling away enough to meet her eyes.

"The baby," he murmured, nodding to the corner as he caught his breath.

"It's fine."

"It's weird. Isn't it?"

"Parents have been doing it for centuries. She can't even see." There was a blanket draped over the side of the crib to block the glow of the reading lamp. "Just try to stay quiet." Abilene was aching to see that, actually—the strain on Casey's face as he struggled to stifle his sounds, his excitement.

"It'll be dinner soon. Someone could knock."

"Christine almost never does—it's too likely me or the

baby are napping." And precisely who was this man, suddenly so concerned with propriety?

"But when she doesn't see either of us," Casey said, "she might get worried."

She sensed it was a different person's worries that had him hesitating—his own. She'd seen this look in too many men's eyes to mistake it. The look of a guy who didn't always do the right thing trying desperately to figure out just how out-of-bounds things were about to get. And whatever he might say on the matter, this man was better than most. But she couldn't bear it if he chose to be good tonight.

Bad always felt so damn much better.

"Please, don't make this stop." She was begging—it was in her voice, probably in her eyes as well. "It feels too nice." Too real and easy, while reality was so uncertain.

Casey hesitated. "I guess we have a little while, still . . ."

She took that as a green light, drawing his mouth back to hers. And no matter his concerns, he was still stiff when she cupped her hand between them. He moaned against her lips, and his hips pressed him harder along her palm.

She worried he'd halt her when she went for his belt, but he didn't. Once the buckle was freed and she was fussing with the button of his fly, he surprised her. Edged her hand away and did the job himself, then pushed his jeans low on his hips. He led her back to his cock, wrapping her fingers around him through his shorts. He made a sound, a pained little sigh, as she stroked him, then put his mouth to her neck once again, kissing roughly between hungry breaths.

"You feel good," she whispered.

"So do you. Just tell me where I can touch you. Please. I fucking love your body."

She blushed, hot with nerves and pleasure. "I'm not sure. I guess, wherever you like, and I'll just tell you if it's too much. Just . . . just through my clothes, for now." Only one other time in her life had she felt this insecure about being naked before a man, and that had been with James. Though the circumstances—and indeed her physical flaws—couldn't be more different.

"Your breasts?"

They weren't as oversensitive as they had been, though

the thought still gave her pause. "You can try, if you're gentle. I'll tell you if it's too much."

His hand slid from her collarbone to her breast, cupping, nothing more. The heat of him alone sent a shockwave through her, tensing her body atop the covers and her fingers around his cock.

"Too much?"

She shook her head, managed a nearly noiseless, "No."

He offered a soft squeeze, and pleasure bloomed, if shyly. "That's nice."

"Good. You feel nice." His touch echoed his words, full of reverence and care and curiosity. She settled into the caresses, letting the last of her worry melt away against him.

Her own hand had gone still on his cock, and she could feel his hips flexing, aching for more but not forcing it. She gave him a long, light stroke, reveling in his reaction. His entire body tensed, then softened, breath coming quicker. She offered a slow pull, squeezing him tighter and earning a moan.

"Fuck, it's hot." He stripped his shirt clean away. His skin was fair, flushed pink here and there, just as she'd imagined.

"Here," he breathed, and reached between them to push the front of his shorts down and release his bare cock into her hand. His skin was hot and smooth, flesh hard. Her body responded, hunger rousing deep in her belly. Everything intensified as he cupped her breast once more—his sounds, his caresses, every muscle. Those hips pushed him deep into each of her strokes, mimicking sex, setting her on fire.

"Casey."

"Too much?"

"No. Not at all."

"Can I take your pants off?"

She hesitated. "I feel a little weird about my body. It's so different, since the baby. I'm not saying no, just—"

"Would you feel better if we got under the covers, maybe?"

She considered it, nodded. "Yeah."

They wrestled their way beneath the blanket, and she did feel more secure, more protected, as they pulled it up to their armpits.

Casey got his jeans kicked away, and when his hands

went to her waistband, her fly, she didn't stop him. Let him ease her corduroys down her thighs, then pushed them the rest of the way off with her toes. She was okay with her legs, but the tee was staying on. Even in the dark, even under the covers, even with this man . . . she wasn't there yet. Maybe *especially* with this man. The stakes hadn't ever felt so high with a guy before.

You've never been with one who treats you like this one does. Who treated her like a grown woman, instead of some lost girl in need of rescue or exploitation.

He got above her, planting his knees between her legs. "Okay?"

All she could do was nod. It took her breath away, this feeling—shocked her, like a full-body memory. To be spread open like this, and to feel a man's excitement there, with the safety of their underwear still in place. She could handle this blunt and muted contact better than the explicit, focused attention of his fingers or mouth. She didn't want to be mastered or taught by a lover anymore. She wanted this. Exploring and experimenting, trying things out, seeing what felt good.

And this felt *wonderful.* A deeper desire was stirring, a first taste of that aggressive, almost angry sensation between her legs. The urgency of sexual need. But even more intoxicating than that was the promise of what it meant—that she could still feel these things, things she'd set aside for months. For nearly a year of her life, after having been a highly sexual person for so long.

He was braced on straight arms, and she stroked the muscles there, memorizing the shapes of his biceps and forearms and shoulders. She hugged his hips with her thighs and urged him to move. When he did, she shut her eyes and fantasized.

Images flashed, the sorts of thoughts she hadn't entertained so vividly in so long. How a man looked, during sex. The way his hips flexed and his chest muscles tightened, the way his arms and face strained as his cock rushed in and out, again and again. The way his lips parted, and the dark shadows that marked the joining of two bodies. Not romance—biology. More pornography than valentine, and so exactly what she'd been needing to take back, to reclaim.

Her softer feelings for Casey had never faded, but this . . .
All this, she'd missed. The ferocity of attraction. That thing
that castrated reason and had her wanting far more than
she'd planned on—their underwear shoved away and his
cock inside her, his body hammering. No thoughts of condoms or any other smart thing, just beastly need.

It was only her deepest self-conscious worries that held
her back. That, and the very real reminder of what consequences came with such recklessness—the biggest and most
life-changing consequence she'd ever weathered, asleep
only paces away. That held her back from pure abandon.
But it didn't quell the need to see this man, precisely this
way.

She urged his hips with her hands. "You feel amazing."

"And you're driving me fucking crazy," he whispered,
then took her mouth in a moment's messy, hungry kiss.

She spoke against his lips. "I wish I could give you more."

He straightened, shaking his head, eyes shut. "You're
perfect. This is perfect."

"I'm imagining more," she confessed.

"Yeah?"

"I've imagined everything, with you. Before the baby,
and now again. I forgot how good it feels, wanting someone
so much."

"Honey." He muttered it like an oath, like a dirty little
prayer, and his body seemed to speed of its own will. "We
can do anything you want. Anything you're up for."

"Tell me what *you* want. Even if I can't go there . . . I
want to hear you say it." Just like when he'd been merely a
boss and coworker to her, when the most contact they
shared was his hand on her back as he slipped behind her
to grab a glass or reach the register. She'd wondered then if
he still wanted her, ever. If he still thought of her that way,
and what he might want to do with her. "Tell me. Anything."

He lowered to his forearms, elbows tucked up tight beside her ribs, hips pumping fast. He was so hard, he had to
be aching.

"I want to fuck you. You have to know that."

She had, once upon a time, before he'd found out she
was pregnant. But he'd done so well to suppress it, since.

Yet it was still true, wasn't it? Even after everything they'd been through. She'd never have imagined any man short of a husband could muster the loyalty to go there.

Guess I didn't count on Casey Grossier.

"Bet you're soft," he whispered, lips barely an inch above hers, his breath sweet. "And warm. And wet."

Right now she was all three. But there were things she wasn't, anymore. That awful, loaded little word she'd both coveted and resented, formed by too many lovers' lips. *Tight.*

Such an ugly adjective, yet entrenched so deeply with what she represented to the men she attracted—innocence, some promise that her defiling was theirs alone to bestow. That word came part and parcel when you looked younger than your years, when you had a small frame and a sugary accent, when you were born with eyes that sent messages without your blessing, telling the world you were one way. James was the first man she'd been with who'd not treated her like some virginal cherub—and with good reason. The way they'd met, she hadn't exactly been the picture of purity.

"I'd die to be inside you," Casey murmured, voice low and strained.

It was with both bravery and fear that she spoke the truth. "I'm not ready for that yet. I'm sorry." Much as she wanted to see, even feel it, much as she wanted to please him, she couldn't. Not yet.

He smiled down at her, body stilling. "Don't be sorry. Last thing I want is to do something you're not into."

"Thanks." It wasn't as though she hadn't been with men who'd been content with the opposite. "I like making you feel good. It feels as good as sex to me, just now."

"Can I keep going?" he asked.

"Yeah."

He paused to get his shorts off, and when the blanket slipped away, she seized that moment to memorize his naked body in the low light. He pulled the covers back over them, surely for discretion and not warmth—the room felt about a hundred degrees now.

He stroked against her, and the motions of his body and

the friction through her underwear was as explicit as actual sex, after walling these feelings off for so long.

"Does it feel okay for you?" he whispered.

"It feels amazing." Truly amazing—she'd forgotten the way the desire gathered, spurred by every sense. Beyond the thrill of his rushing cock, there was the feel of his bare skin under her palms, the weight and heat of him above her, the sounds of his panting, the smell of him, the divine spectacle of his strained face. She drew that face close and kissed his mouth, needing to taste him. He groaned softly, hips speeding.

And all at once, she felt it—a rushing, building pressure, that warm wash of sensation.

Holy shit. She was going to come. She hugged his waist a little higher, seeking the friction that had the pleasure rushing low and hot and frantic.

"Casey."

She had no other words. She could only clasp the back of his neck and grip his arm, and hold on tight. He caught on in a blink—realized what was happening. His body tightened and the motions intensified, his pursuit going from pleasure-seeking to a focused mission. His every breath was a stifled moan now, desperate little seething huffs escaping in time with his racing hips. Her shirt had ridden up, and his head glanced her belly with every thrust. She could feel slickness there, evidence of how close he had to be himself. And that was what did her in, in the end.

"Casey." She held him tight and shut her eyes, lost to it—a rushing, rising force, as startling as it was pleasurable. It came to a head at the point where his hard cock stroked her seam, dropped her from the sky and back into her body. She came down breathing hard. Panting. Shocked and exhilarated and thrilled.

Her nails were dug into his skin and she let him go in an instant. "Sorry." Shame chased the pleasure as the dusk chased the day—inevitably, inextricably.

"Don't be sorry. Did you . . . ?"

"Yeah," she murmured, barely able to believe it. "Yeah, I did."

"Awesome."

She laughed, feeling tipsy now. Like the orgasm had been a shot of something strong, leaving a warm buzz in her muscles and her head. Even as a very young, deeply religious girl, she'd had a hard time believing God had made her body capable of feeling this good, only to proclaim it a sin. "I just need a minute." A minute for the burn of the shame to mellow, and a minute for her clit to recover enough for Casey to continue.

But for now . . . "Here." She reached between them, and Casey scooted up, straddling her thighs so she could clasp him. He groaned as her fingers closed around him, his hips jerking. She pumped him slowly in her fist.

"Fuck, that feels good. Little tighter."

She gave him that, trying to ignore an ugly pang as her brain fixated on that word once again. It didn't warrant dwelling on. She turned her focus to this moment, to watching his excitement mount.

"Could you . . ." He trailed off, looking lost to the pleasure.

"Anything," she prompted.

"Spit in your hand," he said. "I want to imagine it."

Imagine us actually having sex, she thought as she wet her palm. She slicked it along his shaft, then again. The rubbing became gliding, and she didn't know how anything could ever feel even half as intimate as this.

He put his hand over hers, speeding her touch. Showed her what he liked, curling her fingers around him just under his crown, working him in tight, short pulls. "Like that. Exactly like that."

She shivered at those words, excited all over again.

"Feels fucking amazing, honey. Don't stop."

"I could use my mouth . . ."

"No, no. Just like this. I'm so close."

"Good."

"Say my name," he murmured, eyes shut.

"Casey."

"Yeah."

She drew him down by the shoulder, said it again, and again, whispered it against his neck and kissed him there. She bet he was noisy in bed, normally—right now it seemed it was all he could do to keep his mouth shut. Every grunt and groan came out muffled and wild, a barrage of moans and hisses.

"Fuck," he whispered. "I'm gonna come. Don't stop."

"I won't."

"Say my name."

She raked his earlobe softly with her teeth, then said it, right there.

"Fuck."

His hips were bucking into her grip. He was there. She tugged her top up to her bust, held him against her belly as he came—a long, warm, body-wringing release. She could feel his cock throbbing in her grip, then softening, spent. He was panting like he'd just fled a burning building, pulse thumping a million miles a minute against her palm.

"Jesus."

She smiled. "Good?"

"Fucking unbelievable."

He took a long moment to come down, then moved to the side, seeming to scout for something to tidy her with.

"My towel," she said, and pointed to where it hung on the doorknob. She admired his naked back and butt and legs as he crossed the room, and hid a smile when he returned, holding the towel in front of him, wary eyes on the crib.

Abilene cleaned herself up and gratefully pulled her shirt back over her belly. Once Casey was under the covers, he urged her to face him, both on their sides.

"Hi," he whispered, smiling.

"Hi, yourself."

"You okay?"

Now, there was an understatement. "I didn't . . . I didn't know I could still do that. Get there." And so easily. Orgasms had never come easy to Abilene. She'd had sex well before she'd ever attempted to touch herself, and could never bring herself to give a man instructions. Casey, though . . . He hadn't needed any, but she also bet he'd take them, and eagerly. She could imagine finding the nerve to do that—to tell him faster, or slower, or harder, or deeper. Could imagine him taking the orders with pure excitement in his blue eyes.

"Well," he said, smiling, "you did. You got there."

"It's been a long time."

"Been a long time since I got to do that for a woman," he countered.

She studied his face. "Really?"

He nodded, the pillow scrunching his beard.

She narrowed her eyes, intrigued. "How long, exactly?"

He laughed. "Ages, it feels like. Since last spring."

"That's the last time you dated anybody?"

"Well, no. I was seeing someone right before I moved back here, but . . . Jesus, you don't want to hear about my exes."

She bit her lip, grinning, and poked his chest. "Of course I do."

"Liar. Chicks only say that to get you to talk; then they find something to hold against you for the rest of eternity."

"Casey, you're here because *my* ex is a violent gunrunner. You really think I'll be all that scandalized?"

He smiled at that. "Fair point."

"So tell me. Just about the last one."

"She was . . . She was a little weird. Actually, all my exes are at least half-crazy. This one never let me get her naked or even touch her, really. It was just, like, making out and blow jobs for two or three months."

"That *is* a little weird."

"Anyhow, that made it extra nice to get you off, just now. Feels like way too long since I've gotten to do that. Since I got to give something, after feeling like I was getting spoiled, never allowed to reciprocate."

She felt a blush blooming at that. "Felt real nice to me, too."

He scooted closer, close enough for the tips of their noses to touch. "You know I'd do more, if you wanted. Give you my mouth, if you like that."

Oh, *now* she was blushing. "Maybe. Sometime." She turned over, letting him spoon her. "Promise me something," she whispered, twining her fingers with his at her belly.

"Sure."

"Sleep here later, with me. Just for tonight."

A breath, and then, "Of course."

"It doesn't have to mean anything. I just need that. Just

this once." The orgasm had been a shock, not a need. A pleasant surprise, but not a primal craving, like the way she wanted his body pressed to hers through the night.

She felt his lips and the tip of his nose against the nape of her neck, his warm exhalation. "Whatever you need."

Just for one night, let her fall back on her old ways. Let her fall apart, need a man, use her body to keep his close. Just one night.

Tomorrow, she'd be stronger.

Tomorrow, she'd leave her old ways behind for good.

Chapter 11

Miah slid his rifle out from behind his driver's seat and strapped it across his back, slammed the truck's door in the icy night air.

"That'll do, King," he told his dog. She leapt from the bed, paused for a quick scratch behind the ears, then trotted off behind the farmhouse in search of a late dinner.

Miah's own stomach rumbled at the thought. His entire day had been thrown off by an unexpected visitor—a high-pressure rep from a large property management company, calling with an impressive buyout offer for the ranch. It wasn't the first they'd received since talk of the casino had begun, but it had by far been the largest, and its pitch the most aggressive.

Miah had been at the house grabbing lunch, and his dad had called him into the office, the impromptu meeting having just begun. It had been a hard sell, to say the least, and the prick had done his research. He knew the cattle market had been lousy, and the weather worse. He knew exactly what to say to get every last one of Miah's nerves up and humming, every last worry that kept him up late rising to the surface. *"If recent annual rainfall continues at its current trend, you'll be looking at a full-on, extended drought in the next three years. That really how your family wants to go out? The slow and painful way? Now, I've got an offer here that no sane man would be too proud to pass up. Get out while the getting's good, as they say."*

His offer had been obscene, but at the end of the day, the guy had wasted his own time. Generous figures or not, even in the midst of a nasty rough patch, the Churches would never sell. Three C had faced the Depression and the recent recession, a thousand fluctuations of the market, the encroaching threat of foreign-raised beef, dry season upon record dry season, and come out on top through it all. Granted, the last year had been brutal, and the books hadn't looked this grim in a decade or more. But that was the nature of the beast, and it'd take a real blow to ruin them. A multiyear drought, a sustained drop in the market. They might currently be one of the biggest businesses in Brush County, but they were still modest compared to the industrial operations. They weren't invincible, but they also weren't going anyplace, thanks very much. He and his dad had shared a good eye roll at the rep's expense after he'd been seen to the door.

Though his dad had seemed to shrug it off as bluster and brass, Miah didn't shake his own feelings so readily. He felt upended, if he was honest, and unsettled by the guy's pitch. There'd been something edgy behind the slick sales-speak, something jagged and a touch threatening. Then again, that could be fatigue making him paranoid. He hadn't been sleeping well lately, between the business worries and the Ware situation.

That little interruption had turned Miah's sit-down lunch plans into a hasty scarfing of leftovers at the kitchen sink. He'd meant to grab something between finishing up the day's work and going out on a patrol, but then one of the hands had hurt herself and been driven to the clinic by yet another worker, so he'd filled in, helping the others get the horses bedded down for the night. He still smelled like the stables now, in fact, and a hot shower was next on his priority list, after food.

He pocketed his keys and headed for the front steps. The porch light came on when he triggered the sensor, and he froze at the sound of scuffing, just around the edge of the house.

That was no animal. That noise was shoes on gravel, no mistaking it.

He slid his rifle around, perched it on his shoulder. No need to cock the thing just yet—could be a ranch hand or just his dad puttering. "Who's there?" he called, edging back down the steps.

No words answered him, but instead the thumping of feet on dirt.

He bellowed "King!" and took off running himself.

It was a man—already half-lost to the dark, but definitely a man—tallish, dressed in black, face obscured by a ski mask. He all but hurdled the low wooden fence that enclosed the front lot, boots pounding down the highway shoulder.

"Stop!"

If anything, the guy ran faster. He had a fifty-pace lead or more, and Miah wasn't gaining any ground, rifle banging him in the ribs.

"Stop or I sic my goddamn dog on you!"

The guy kept on running, and Miah couldn't risk slowing down long enough to fire a warning shot.

In the distance, taillights broke the darkness. Shit. There were no streetlights out here, but the glow from the lot was just strong enough to reach the bumper. Though son of a bitch—the license plate was nothing but flat gray. Fucking duct tape.

The truck peeled away and screamed off westward, back toward town. Miah scrabbled to a halt, shouldered the .22 again, but his dog shot out from behind him. He couldn't risk it. His entire body was heaving from the sprint, anyhow. He slung the rifle back around his body and swore, then whistled.

King came trotting over. "That'll do, girl. Bit too slow, sadly." They walked back toward the house.

"Miah?" It was his mother, calling from the porch.

"Yeah. Hang on." The winter air burned his rushing lungs, and the adrenaline was pulsing through his head, bringing an ache to his temples.

"What was all that yelling?" she asked as he hopped the fence.

"There was somebody skulking around the side of the house."

"What?"

"A man. I chased him, but he got away. Had a truck parked down the road."

Her eyes widened. "A truck? A black one?"

"Maybe. Tough to tell, but dark, in any case. Why?"

"Shit." She wasn't usually one to curse. "Abilene's ex—he drives a black truck. Casey had a run-in with him this evening. He just said."

Shit indeed.

"Guess he found out where she's staying." Miah mounted the front steps. His mom turned for the door, but he stopped her with a hand on her shoulder. She turned back around.

"You think we should tell her?" he asked.

She glanced down the road, worry creasing her brow. "Better she be scared than left in the dark."

He nodded. "Goddamn shame, though—she barely gets any sleep as it is."

"Tell your dad to turn the security cameras back on." Three C had about two dozen of them positioned around the house and stables and barns, as well as out on the range, for catching burglars and poachers alike. They rarely kept the ones near the buildings on. Waste of electricity and computer space; their threats usually came from four-legged predators, and more recently from those suspected drug dealers, two demographics who preferred the vast anonymity of the badlands.

"Good idea."

"Shall I talk to her?" his mom asked.

He shook his head. "Nah, I can. Ought to describe what I saw, anyhow. Ask Case if the truck sounds like Ware's."

She propped the door wide and he passed by, stepping inside. First things first, he stowed his rifle and got his dad up to speed, then went to the kitchen, where his mom was finishing loading the washer.

"You know where Abilene is?" he asked, shutting the fridge and twisting open a longneck. Christ knew he could stand a drink just now. He'd been hoping to cap off a long-ass day in front of the fire, put his feet up, nurse this beer with nothing on his mind except how good his bed would feel under his achy back. It was one drama after another today.

"Den," she said.

"Thanks."

He'd expected to find Casey there with her and to find the both of them on high alert from the shouting, but instead it was just Abilene, sitting cross-legged on the couch. The baby was nestled on a blanket between her thighs, nursing a bottle of its own. She looked up and smiled. "Hey."

"Hey, yourself." He sat on the coffee table, facing her. "You hear all that commotion just now?"

Her brow furrowed. "No. What happened?"

"Where's Case?"

"Upstairs bathroom."

The man appeared just then, on the landing above.

"We have a little situation," Miah told the both of them.

Casey's expression darkened and he jogged down the steps. "What do you mean?"

"Ware was just here."

His blue eyes widened, hands curling into fists at his sides. "What?"

"I didn't talk to him—didn't even see his face. But somebody was creeping around the side of the house when I pulled up. I chased the guy but couldn't catch him. He was white—I saw his hands when he jumped the fence. And he was driving a truck with the plate taped over."

"Black truck?" Casey asked. "A Ram, maybe? I ran into him this afternoon, but I was too busy memorizing his plate number to catch the make. Sounds like I shouldn't have bothered."

"It was dark, for sure. Older. Not a Ford—that's all I could tell you."

"I can't remember what brand it was," Abilene said. "But it wasn't new. And it wasn't big, not like your truck," she said to Miah.

"This was midsized. Probably mid-nineties."

"Who the fuck else is it going to be?" Casey asked grimly, then paused, glancing at the baby. "Sorry."

"He'd parked a hundred or more yards down the highway," Miah went on. "By the time I ran back to my truck and got it on the road, he'd have gotten far enough to disappear down the residential streets. I just wish I could've taken a shot at his tires, but my dog was in the way." He sighed, pissed and tired and frustrated, and took a drink deep enough to drain half his bottle.

"I can't believe he'd have the gall to come here," Casey said. "Not after I gave him a perfectly reasonable way to get in touch."

"Guess the man isn't the perfectly reasonable type," Miah offered, then looked to Abilene for confirmation.

"He is and he isn't," she said. "I mean, when things were good between us, he was pretty rational. But he can get mad, too, and when that happens I couldn't say where his head goes."

"One too many drinks wouldn't help matters, either."

"He was never a drinker."

"Maybe not, but the man's been stewing in prison," Casey said. "And I'm guessing he doesn't like doing things on another man's terms. What I fu—frigging want to know, though, is who told him where to find her. Who knew, and who'd tell? It was Dancer who told him to see me, but who would've told him Abilene was staying here?"

"Just about anybody might, if threatened," Miah said. "I'll ask all my hands tomorrow. They could've easily run into him at the bar. They were all told it was strictly confidential, her staying here, but threats are threats."

"Duncan wouldn't have told," Abilene said. "Or Raina."

Miah shook his head. Much as he loathed Welch, the guy was too stubborn and pompous to let anyone bully him into doing anything. And Raina would no doubt whip her shotgun out from under the counter the second somebody got pushy. No, one of the ranch hands was the most likely source. Miah just hoped if that was the case, the party in question would have the balls to own it. They were good kids, but they were young, most of them, still prone to self-preservation above most things.

"I guess in the end," he said through a sigh, "it doesn't really matter who told him. He knows now, and what we need to figure out is, do we need to move you two again?" He nodded to Abilene and the baby.

She looked stricken in a breath. "No."

Casey's expression was grim. "This is still the most secure place in town. I mean, I can't keep them at mine—I live on the main drag. Everybody would know inside an hour. Same as the motel. Plus she's got your parents' support here, not to mention there's cameras. The only other option might be to take her out of Fortuity."

Miah nodded, thinking maybe that would be best. Abilene's safety was paramount, no doubt, but he did have a business and his employees to think about, as well. Hell, the thought of Ware returning and threatening his *mom* had his blood boiling.

"Talking to Ware is still the most direct route to getting this shit resolved," Casey went on. "I sure wish I'd taken down his goddamn number when I gave him mine."

"Could he have the same one from before he went downstate?" Miah asked, looking to Abilene.

She shrugged. "Even if he did, I don't have it anymore."

"Vince might," Casey said.

"Maybe." But doubtful. The men had met in prison and spoken only during visiting hours these past few months. As unlikely as the prospect now seemed, they might just have to wait for Ware to call, or else go in search of him around town.

"One good thing," Casey offered, "is that he didn't appear armed, right? He ran. Didn't pull anything on you."

Miah nodded. "That's true." Maybe Ware hadn't come with entirely malicious intent; perhaps merely with a stalker's agenda, wanting to confirm that Abilene was indeed at the ranch. With her car in the shop, spotting her through a window would be the man's only chance to do so. Still, no rational person could look at this situation and tell himself that stalking was the best course of action. Hell, the psycho could've fucking *knocked*.

"My dad's going to get the security cameras turned back on tonight," Miah told Abilene. "They're hooked up to motion-sensor lights, but don't panic if it goes bright outside in the middle of the night—could easily be the barn cats or a coyote or any other thing. Just tell me or Case and we'll go out and investigate. Okay?"

"Sounds good." *Sounds terrifying,* her expression corrected.

"Anyhow, not much we can do for the moment."

"Except wait for him to call," Casey said.

Miah nodded. "Yeah. There's always that."

Casey eyed Miah's beer. "You done with work for the night?"

"Believe it or not."

"Would you do me a favor? Hang with these two for ten minutes while I grab a shower?"

"Sure. And I checked with my dad—I can handle things here in the morning while you run your errands." Casey had texted that afternoon to ask about it. "Only until about eight, though."

"That's fine—I just need to catch Vince before he goes to work, then swing by the post office. Thanks. And for this shower," he added. "It's in everybody's best interest, I promise." He grabbed his bag from beside the couch and headed back upstairs to the guest wing, leaving Miah alone with the ladies.

He couldn't help but notice the way Abilene's gaze followed Casey up the steps, and prayed it was innocent apprehension at watching her bodyguard disappearing out of sight. He loved his friend, but the last thing this girl needed was to develop feelings for Fortuity's prodigal son. Kid had come a long way since he'd skipped town, and he was a step up from James Ware, no doubt, but he wasn't exactly ready to take on the commitment this girl would require.

Still, far be it from Miah to tell anybody how to conduct their love lives.

I'll do my damnedest to keep her safe from one criminal, but if she's got it bad for Casey, that's straight-up above my pay grade.

At five thirty the next morning, Casey woke to the buzz of his cell in his jeans pocket.

He was in Abilene's bed, and he'd worn pants to sleep for two very good reasons—so his phone's alarm wouldn't wake anybody, and so he wouldn't get any more reckless ideas, pressed up against the girl in his shorts. And he *was* pressed up against her. Had been all night, except for when the opposite had been true, and she'd been hugging her warm body to his back, her breasts pressing gently with every breath. She'd dropped off the second they'd settled in, but Casey had probably lain there for two hours, caught in a calm persuasion of restlessness, pinned as always, lately, in some territory that lay between *protective* and *horny*. And since he'd run into Ware, the former seemed to have only ignited the latter. Still, no time to panic about what had gone down, this time—they'd both agreed, it was what it was, and nothing more. He'd made her absolutely zero promises, so he had no worries about breaking any. Plus overthinking it all was a luxury he didn't have this morning.

He eased the covers away, slid his arm out from under hers. February had never felt so damn cold as it did just now, leaving this bed.

Thirty minutes later, he was parking his bike a couple blocks down the street from his mom's house. Maybe it was naive, his hoping Ware didn't already know where his family lived, but why take the chance?

He didn't like this feeling. He'd experienced plenty of paranoia in his old line of work, but back then it had come bundled up with adrenaline. It had been pleasurable, in a way, that fear of getting caught. But there was too much at stake now, way more than just his own skin.

He grabbed the LifeMap package out of his cargo box and walked up the road.

Vince left for work at six thirty, so the kitchen light was on, predictably. Casey knocked at the side door and Vince pulled it in, nodding a greeting.

"Morning, cocksucker. Ready to get swabbed?" Casey heard the TV droning in the den, and no surprise—his mom was up at five and asleep by nine, every goddamn day like a rule of physics. Kim must've still been in bed.

Vince eyed the box as Casey opened it and set three clear cups on the kitchen table. Kind of like extra-narrow prescription bottles, with a plastic-sealed, one-ended Q-tip-looking thing inside, and a label printed with a barcode and each of their first names—*Casey, Vincent, Deirdre.*

"What's this going to entail, exactly?" Vince asked.

Casey pulled out the instructions and read them aloud. "Remove swab from sleeve. Rinse mouth with warm water before collecting sample. Swab the inside of one cheek with firm, up-and-down motions. Close swab inside provided cup immediately. *One sample per cup only*," he read aggressively, the final step set in all caps.

"Easy enough," Vince said, and the two of them swished their mouths out at the sink. The whole thing was done inside a minute.

"Cool. Now just sign this paper," Casey said, finding the form with Vince's name at the top.

He considered asking Vince to walk their mom through

the paperwork and the swab, but he knew deep down that was cowardly, so he gathered the form and the cup and a glass of water and headed for the den.

Sure as the sun rising, she was awake, glued to an infomercial. Or to the glow of the screen, anyhow—only God knew if she was actually retaining any of what was flashing by.

"Morning, Mom. You sleep okay?"

Her gaze moved slowly to his face. Here was where things turned either heartwarming or heartbreaking—fifty-fifty chance, lately.

"Good morning," she said slowly, and finally added, "Casey."

A wave of relief rolled through him at that. More and more, she recognized him. It was progress you couldn't discount, not when the first time she'd seen him after he'd come back to town, she'd shot him in the leg, thinking he was a burglar.

"Can you do me a favor, Mom? It'll only take a minute."

"Oh," she said spacily, slowly, attention drifting back to the screen, "I suppose I could."

"Great. Just take a drink from this," he said, handing her the glass. He let her drain it in a half dozen lethargic swallows. "Great. Now I just need you to open your mouth real wide so I can rub this Q-tip on your cheek, okay?"

"Q-tip?"

"It's for the dentist," he lied. What was he supposed to say? *You probably don't realize it, but you've gone completely batshit and now I need to figure out if I'm doomed to follow in your footsteps. Open wide.* "Won't take a second."

"If you say so."

She opened her mouth and he held her cheek, her skin cool and papery, a little eerie. Man, she'd been beautiful when she'd still been lucid. Prettiest woman in town, everybody had agreed. Now she was just a ghost, floating through the days with her brain half-gone, the rest of it lost to whatever was on the TV or outside the window, her once-red hair faded almost completely to white. Casey checked his own head for grays at least once a week, thinking they were as good an indicator of his chances at insanity as any. So far, none.

"Perfect," he said, sealing the swab. "And now I just need you to sign this paper, down here. To tell the dentist that he can check your Q-tip, okay?"

"The dentist?" She looked perplexed but took the pen willingly enough and signed her name, the signature a faint, loose shadow of its old self. How many times Casey had practiced and faked that signature, he cared not to guess. Probably as many times as he'd been sent home with detention slips.

"Thanks, Mom."

"Come and watch the news," she said in that unnerving ethereal voice, and patted the cushion beside hers. "There's so much happening in the world."

He eyed the screen, the logo of the shopping channel in the bottom corner. "Wish I could, but I have to get to the post office, then back to work. But Nita will be here soon. She likes the news." Or barring that, great deals on faux-sapphire jewelry.

"Yes. Nita."

He bent down and kissed her cheek, the sensation leaving him cautiously proud these days—not as unsettled as it had at first, when he'd come home. He was growing used to how her skin felt now, how she smelled. His mother was gone and she was never coming back, but he could do his duty, pay his respects to the living, walking effigy she'd become. "Bye."

In the kitchen, he sealed the cups and papers up in the padded plastic envelope that had come with the kit, pre-printed with express postage. Last step, drop them off in a mailbox. Last step until the time came to hear the results. He swallowed, stomach souring. Blamed it on two cups of black coffee and no food.

"So when do you hear?" Vince asked.

"Soon. They'll schedule a call after this makes it down to fucking Palo Alto." Casey tossed the instructions and the scraps of plastic wrap and the box in the trash, then made for the door. "Later, motherfucker. Say hi to Nita and Kim for me."

"Will do."

He pulled up at the post office, said a little prayer to a god he had zero right to be asking any favors of, and dropped the box into the slot. And with that, there was nothing more to be done on that front except wait.

As he hit the road once more and aimed himself east, he couldn't say if he'd expected to feel lighter or heavier with that package turned over to fate. What he did feel for sure, though, was surprise. Surprise that he'd just pulled the trigger like that, when he was pretty certain that even a week ago he'd have found a hundred reasons to procrastinate on the task and let that package collect dust on some shelf. Things had changed, in recent days. He'd changed, though in exactly what ways, he couldn't yet say.

He had two phones on him this morning—his relatively public one that the Desert Dogs and Abilene had the number for, then the shady untraceable one that Emily and his other bygone business contacts—and now James Ware— had. And he knew which was ringing now from the mere pitch of the buzzing at his hip. If it was Ware, the guy had one fucking massive nerve on him.

Casey swerved to a hairy stop at the shoulder of the quiet highway and killed his engine, whipped the phone out. Private, as always.

"Yeah?"

"It's Ware. I'm ready to talk."

Casey laughed into the bright morning light, steam rising. "Oh, are you? That's fucking hilarious, considering how shy you got last night."

"'Scuse me?"

"Who told you where she was staying?"

"Listen, Grossier, I got no idea what you're talking about. I'm just following your fucking orders here. You going to facilitate this shit or what?"

"You tell me which motherfucker told you where she's at, and maybe we'll find out."

"Listen," Ware said again, voice jabbing like a finger in the sternum. "I got fuck-all clue what you think I got up to last night, but whatever it is, you've got it wrong. Now, you tell me how this is going to work, and I'll play by your rules. Just let me talk to her. I'm way better at threats than begging, but hey, I'll pucker up and kiss your ass and say pretty please, if that's what it's going to goddamn take."

Casey frowned, a touch upended. *Stay cool. Don't fuck up. Don't mention the ranch.* "Fine. A phone call. You call this number at nine o'clock sharp, tonight, and I'll have her there." Arguing with the guy himself wasn't getting anybody any closer to figuring out his game, anyhow.

"Fine," Ware spat. "Nine o'clock."

"Fine," Casey echoed, and ended the call. He bellowed a cuss up into the blue sky, resisted the urge to slam that fucking phone down against the asphalt.

Chapter 12

The sky outside the guest room was bright blue as Abilene's eyes blinked open, the day already in full swing. Her stomach rumbled. Best to get herself fed before the baby got the same idea.

She dressed Mercy in a fleece onesie and lugged her out onto the landing, smelling bacon. No doubt any leftovers would be cold by now, any eggs already devoured, but a cup of coffee and some toast would be welcome. And some company.

Casey had woken her when he'd risen at five, but she'd pretended to be asleep. She'd strained for a muttered cuss, for any tiny sign that he might have regretted waking up in her bed, but nothing. He'd just slipped out quietly to take care of his errands, leaving an all-too-fleeting warm patch on his side of the mattress.

She smiled to herself as she came down the steps. Coffee was nice, toast was good, but neither held the skinniest little stump of a birthday candle to the feel of a warm man hugging you through the night. She wouldn't get attached to the sensation, but if ever in her life she'd needed to feel that, this week was the time.

"Hey." The voice made her jump as she passed through the den, and Casey sat up on the couch, revealing himself. Her shock must've shown. "Sorry. Morning."

"Morning. You done with all your stuff you had to do?"

He stood, nodded. Man, that body already looked different—already felt like *hers*, calling to her from these few paces away. He closed the distance, stroking his hand over the baby's head. Abilene knew exactly what that rough palm felt like, and yearned for a little taste of contact. Just a whisper of his fingertips across her cheek. Anything. *Junkie.*

"Glad you got to sleep in," he said. "You ready for breakfast?"

"Coffee, for sure."

He waved an arm to tell her to go ahead of him, and she did, feeling shy.

"Sit tight." He gestured toward the kitchen table. "I'll make it. Cream and three sugars."

She smiled at his back, chanced flirtation. "Can't resist a man who knows how I take my coffee."

"You think that now, but I'm about to wreck your day."

Her smile wilted. "What do you mean?"

He didn't reply. He came back with a mug and set it at her elbow. Then he sat himself, his cool expression casting that warm glow right out of her, like a blanket yanked from her shoulders.

A million awful scenarios rushed through her mind, the worst of them undoubtedly being that he was about to tell her she needed to go somewhere else. Far from this lovely old oasis of a house, maybe even far from Casey. Maybe into an actual safe house, into protective custody, where no doubt some authorities would be wanting to know more about her identity and her past than she was willing to share.

"What? Tell me."

Casey rapped the tabletop with his knuckles. Sighed. "He called."

"Oh." She hadn't expected that, not after last night. Talk about gall. "What did he have to say?"

"He denied coming by, no surprise. I wanted to tell him to forget it all. Forget getting to see you after that—" He caught whatever cuss would've followed just in time. "After what he pulled last night. But I had to calm myself down. Remember that nothing about this is going to get any better until we know where he stands. And the fact is, he's likely to be straight with you, not any of us."

"Probably."

"Maybe angry, maybe a little scary, but I'm willing to bet he'll tell you what's on his mind. You know him well enough to read between the lines? Sense if he's upset enough to try to hurt you?"

"I'd like to think so . . . But I've never given him this big a reason to be pissed before." She touched the baby's head fretfully, wondering how bad a swear "pissed" was. Probably small potatoes compared to the stuff Casey routinely let slip.

"I told him to call again at nine tonight, and that you'd speak to him. It's really the only option. You up for that?"

"No. But I'll get myself there, all the same." She didn't dare give James any more cause to spill his concerns to Casey or anybody else. The illusion of her innocence had never been so crucial as it was now. Being brave was the only option, lousy as she was at it. There was so much more riding on all this than her reputation, she thought, jiggling the baby when she fussed. There was the safety of everyone around her, of course, but beyond that . . . She owed it to her daughter to be stronger. Owed it to her to be the protective female role model Abilene hadn't had herself.

Casey swung his legs over the bench. "I'll get a bottle warmed up."

"Thanks."

"You want me with you, when you talk to him?" he asked as he measured the formula.

"No." No, definitely not.

She thought back to this morning and last night—to every time Casey had shifted in the night and roused her, every moment she'd gotten to spend next to him. She hadn't felt that secure in ages. Maybe not since before the great scandal of her teen years. Maybe not since she'd been a little girl, totally oblivious to sex. Even then there'd been the specter of an angry God hanging over her . . . But, man, had she ever come a long way from those original sins, from stealing mints from her grandma's purse or whispering newly gleaned swearwords to herself, trying on what it must feel like to be a bad kid. If only she'd known just how bad she'd turn out . . .

Casey heated the formula and passed it off, sitting close as Abilene coaxed the baby to suckle.

"You scared?" he asked her.

"Yeah. I am. But I can't put it off anymore." After she'd found out she was pregnant, she'd been so frightened of what James would say, of what he might threaten, she'd avoided him for far too long. It had been easy to, when he'd been locked up a hundred miles away. That wasn't an option now—he knew where to find her. And it wasn't an option going forward, not if she wanted to keep the promise she'd made to herself and be a better person for Mercy. The old Abilene ran and hid. The new one had to find the courage to keep her feet planted and face her mistakes.

"No matter what he says," Casey said, gaze on the nursing baby, "you'll feel better, after. Just having it done with."

"I hope so." Provided what he said wasn't, *I'm gonna get our child taken away from you.* She held Mercy a little tighter.

"You will," Casey said. "Uncertainty's always worse than whatever reality you're putting off facing." He looked thoughtful a moment, then spoke softly. "Just know that whatever happens, and no matter how bad it might be ... If he turns out to be a monster, like the worst possible scenario you could imagine, just know he'll be taken care of."

She studied his face, unsure. "You mean like ..." *You mean what? That you'd run him out of town? That you'd kill him?* Casey's shady reputation notwithstanding, she couldn't imagine him going *there.* Vince? Maybe. Just maybe. "What do you mean?"

"I mean if it comes down to your safety or the baby's safety ..." He shrugged, leaving her upended. Spending the night with him had been heaven, but this conversation was a stark reminder that this man who treated her so well was still far from a saint. She needed to keep that reality at the forefront of her mind, to combat the weakness of her body and her heart.

Unless James went psycho—which wasn't beyond possibility, if he'd stooped to stalking her—he didn't deserve a beat down. What he deserved, in fact, was answers. She steeled herself, trusting that everything would be better once she'd talked to him.

It was only too bad that the anticipation was such a bitch.

*   *   *

Abilene looked up as Casey squeezed her foot. They were sitting on the couch, her lying down, trying to breathe deep, and him sitting at one end with the dozy baby propped on his lap. She could hear Miah and his father talking in the ranch's office down the hall, two matching, distant baritones, and also the drone of the radio in the kitchen, where Christine was puttering.

"Almost time," Casey said. He was acting calm, though he had his silver lighter in one hand and was turning it around and around.

Abilene eyed the clock, heart thumping hard and quick. Five minutes to nine.

Casey shifted the baby's weight and dug in his pocket, handed her his phone. It was a chunky old thing, branded with the logo of a pay-as-you-go carrier. He had a smartphone, too, and she wondered anew why he needed both.

Bet I don't want to know.

"I think I'll—" She jumped as the thing buzzed in her hand, breath leaving her in a whoosh. "I'll go upstairs," she finished, and hurried out of the den. She ran up the steps, huffing and shaky as she hit TALK on the third ring and managed to say, "Hello?"

"Abilene?" That familiar voice, deep and cool and hard, like an echo from a grave.

"Yeah. Hang on." She slipped inside her room and shut the door. Once she was cross-legged on the bed, she said, "Okay."

There was a pause before he replied, the noise of a word nearly being spoken, then not. A long breath hissed through the line. "Well."

"I'm ready to talk." She hugged her middle with her free arm. Her back ached and she was shaking like she'd drunk ten coffees.

"Good. It's about goddamn time. What the fuck have you been playing me for, shutting me out? I find out from Vince Grossier that you're even pregnant to begin with; then you won't even do me the courtesy of a visit? Or a fucking *phone call*?"

"I know. But I was scared, after the way we ended things."

"Scared of what?"

"That you'd be mad."

"That I'd hurt you?"

"Maybe."

"If I was cold enough to hurt you, I'd have been cold enough to leave your ass exactly where I found it, now, wouldn't I?"

"I was scared of more than just that. I was scared you'd have wanted me to get rid of it. Or that once she was born you might try to take her away, because of . . . because of how I was. When we met."

"It crossed my mind, don't doubt it. But, sweetheart, you really think an ex-con stands a chance at getting custody of his kid?"

Sweetheart. She'd gotten so used to hearing a different man call her *honey*, that word sounded obscene coming from this one.

"I don't know," she admitted. If some social worker investigated her past, they wouldn't be impressed, and they'd also discover she was employed under a fake name, that she'd had no permanent address in six years, that she'd been a teenage runaway. Ex-con was bad, but was she really any less problematic, on paper?

"So why have you been hiding?" he asked.

"I have it real good now. Not perfect, but I have a job I like. Friends I like."

"Friends who don't know the *real* you?" James supplied, reading between the lines.

"I might not have all my crap together," she said, "but I'm working on it. And there's a lot I could lose, if you decided to tell people how I was, when you met me." Raina might've looked the other way about her lying to get her job at Benji's, but Duncan wasn't half as lax about legalities. As for Casey . . . She couldn't bear to have him find out who she really was.

"You think I'd try to fuck all that up for you?" James asked.

"Maybe I did. I mean, I saw how you can get, with folks who crossed you." He didn't just hold grudges—he went after people. He *hurt* people. She didn't think he enjoyed it, necessarily, but he could go there, and coldly. Easily. Like it was just part of the gig.

"You're not some shitbag who stiffed me on business.

You're the mother of my child ... Or at least that's what I've heard."

"She's yours," Abilene said in a small voice. "It could have only been you."

"I'm choosing to believe that. But it was fucked-up, you keeping me in the dark all this time. It was cruel, and it was selfish."

"I know. But I was scared. I had no idea how you'd react, what you'd do. And I doubted you'd want a child, especially with me, so I told myself it was a kindness, to not bother you about it. Plus I was sick of relying on men all the time. I thought it'd be easier, just dealing with it on my own."

"What changed your mind?"

"Vince said he had to tell you."

"And you would've just let me go on with my life, never knowing about it, if he hadn't?"

"Maybe."

"That's pretty fucking cold. You think that little of me, that I'd tell you to go fuck yourself, go and deal with our mistake, all on our own?"

"She's not a mistake," Abilene cut in sharply, her spine snapping smartly into place. Beat her down all you liked, but don't bring her baby into it.

"Fine—our little *miscalculation*. You think I'd just be like, 'Fuck you, bitch. Not my problem'?"

"I wanted to deal with it on my own. I had a job and a place to stay. I wanted to leave all that ugly stuff behind me and make something better for her."

"You heaping me in with all the ugly stuff?"

"You knew the old me. I didn't want that following me." No witnesses, no judgment.

"Guess maybe you fucked up, then, telling Vince Grossier."

"I didn't know what else to do. I didn't know anybody, only his name, and that he lived in Fortuity." James had called her when he'd been arrested and told her to find Vince if she ever needed a favor. Like an olive branch he'd held out after the way things ended, she'd thought in hindsight. "I had no choice. I had to see a doctor once I knew, and I needed money."

He sighed through the line. Abilene rubbed her foot; the thing felt like ice.

"I'm trying to make this right now," she said, firmly and without apology. It wasn't a voice he'd be used to hearing from her—the time they'd spent together had been typified by an erratic mix of honey and venom. But this was the new Abilene, ready or not. "What do you need to say, or to hear?"

"That you're safe and the kid's safe. Where's your head been at? You been tempted to use at all?"

"No. Not for a minute. Not even *coffee* until after she was born. I have it good now. Not much money, but my bosses treat me well." Back when she'd gotten caught up in the drugs, she'd had nothing in her life. No true friends, no job, nothing worth waking up for. Now she had more than plenty.

"Where you staying?"

Like you don't know. "With friends. But I'll find a new place soon. Just for me and the baby."

"What's her name?"

"Mercy."

A pause. "That's nice. What's her last name?"

"I didn't have much choice but to give her mine. My real one."

Another pause. "You never did tell me your real name."

No, she hadn't. Only that the one she used was fake. "I will soon. When you meet her, maybe."

"When'll that be?"

"Soon," she repeated, brooking no argument.

"You in Fortuity?" he asked.

Seeing as how he knew precisely where she was, it seemed pointless to lie. "Yeah." *Why did you run?* she wanted to ask. *How did you find me at the ranch?* But things felt like they'd taken a civil turn, and she didn't want to spark a fight.

"What's she look like?" James asked.

"She's real pretty. Blue eyes, more like yours than mine. She was a couple weeks early, so she's on the small side, but catching up quick."

"Tell me when I can see her."

"I need to talk to Casey and everyone, but maybe tomorrow."

"Why do you need to talk to them? And who's everyone?"

"Him and Vince, and some friends of theirs. Some friends of mine," she hazarded. "And they're protective. Nobody knew what to expect from you—including Vince, and he was the one who broke the news. You wouldn't tell him what your intentions were when you wanted to find me. And you were angry, he said."

"Because it was none of his goddamn business. I shouldn't *have* to explain myself to him."

"That's fair. But they'll want to be around, to make sure it goes okay. Leave me your number, and I'll talk to the people whose place I'm staying at and figure out a time. Okay? I'll call you tomorrow by noon at the latest."

"Fine."

She found a notebook and pen and wrote down his number. "Talk to you tomorrow."

"Hope to God you do," he said. "Good night."

"Night."

She stared at the phone until he ended the call and the screen went dark, then hauled her shaky butt off the bed and went downstairs.

Casey was on the couch, foot jittering a million miles a minute.

Across from him, Miah sat in an old rocker with the baby asleep on his lap. "Keep that up and your ankle's gonna catch fire."

"I—" Casey's head jerked up at the click of a doorknob overhead and he watched as Abilene emerged from the guest room. She smiled down at them as she headed for the stairs.

What did that smile mean? Relief? Maybe. Though with Abilene, a smile could just as easily precede her bursting into tears, so he wasn't banking on it. He stood and grabbed his beer off the coffee table, just for something to do with his hands.

She headed for the baby first, leaning down to touch her in some way Casey couldn't see.

"So?" he prompted, dying of impatience.

"You want me to take her?" she asked Miah.

"Nah, she's settled now," he said. "You two need to talk in private?"

She nodded and turned to Casey. "My room?"

He was already striding for the steps.

"Holler if she starts fussing," Abilene called back.

"Will do." Miah clicked on the TV, the drone of the news offering a little extra discretion as Casey and Abilene entered her room. Casey sat on the edge of the bed, clenching his hands so tight between his knees his knuckles went white.

She shut the door and turned to him, pulling his cell from her hoodie's pocket. "Thanks."

"Sure." He took it. "So what happened? How'd it go?"

"Could you hear anything?"

"Only that you were talking, not yelling."

She sat cross-legged at the end of the bed. Casey turned and did the same so he could face her.

"Tell me."

"He was angry. Frustrated."

"What'd he say to you?"

"That he wants to see her. Both of us. That I owe him that."

"He scare you?"

She took a moment to reply, staring thoughtfully at his feet. "Yes and no. I don't think he wants to hurt us. And I don't think he wants to try to take the baby away from me. He's mad, but mostly because I kept so much from him. He's an in-charge kind of guy, and I don't think he handles feeling helpless very well."

"Clearly not, if he came around here last night. What'd he have to say about that?"

"I didn't ask. I almost did, but by then he seemed way less angry, and I thought maybe it was best to keep him that way. Keep him talking."

Casey nodded. "I'm dying to know who told him where to find you." Perhaps he could make that information a condition of a face-to-face meeting. Casey still needed to have a little chat with John Dancer, and maybe a second, depending on whether the person who'd spilled about Abilene's location had done it for a payoff, or simply to keep all their bones unbroken.

"Miah's gonna have words for your ex," he said, thinking aloud. "Fuck with his property and his business, and that charming cowboy shtick falls away real fast. Maybe I'll leave that to him, and you and I can just focus on establishing some kind of civil discourse, or whatever, with Ware."

"I told him I'd see him. That I'd call him tomorrow to arrange a time, after I checked with the Churches."

His heart kicked back into third gear. "You sure you're ready?"

"I'm sick of hiding—I know that much. I'm sick of being afraid of him, and the unknown. And I want to be able to go back to work soon, get back to normal."

He nodded. "Course you do. Tomorrow, huh?"

"For the call, maybe the meeting, too. It's up to Miah and his folks, ultimately, if James is going to meet me here."

"And you're going to let him see the baby?"

"If it goes well, I said. If he keeps his cool."

"And you're *sure* you're ready?"

"Yeah." She curled up on her side, hair falling over the edge of the bed. "I'm ready."

"I'll stay close, and we'll make sure either Vince or Miah can be here, too."

"You going to eavesdrop?" she asked, something cagey in her expression.

Casey shook his head. "I'll stay close enough to hear if you call for us. We'll probably need to pat him down and hold his car keys, too. Hope he can handle the prisoner treatment."

"He's had enough practice," she muttered.

Casey sighed, sensing her weariness and registering it in his own bones. He lay down, too, body curled the opposite way as hers, so they were face-to-face, upside down. A small silent laugh hitched her shoulders, a gesture of exhaustion, not amusement.

"It's going to be okay."

"I hope so."

He reached up to take her hand, their fingers twining. "It's a shame he couldn't have explained himself to Vince, saved us all the trouble of putting you in lockdown."

"We were . . . We've got an intense history. He's mad about more than he must be comfortable sharing with anyone but me."

Casey nodded, ignoring the way his stomach soured.

In nearly no time, he'd grown possessive of this girl, and hearing her say those words—*history*, *intense*—made his insides squirm in a way he wasn't used to. His relationships had all been so frivolous, he'd rarely gotten close enough to a girlfriend to feel jealous this way. He'd been in love, or thought he had been. He'd said those words to a couple women over the years, and meant them. But could it really have been that deep, when he'd barely registered a fraction of this sting before, and when it had always been so easy to move on, once the fun faded and the expectations began to weigh him down?

By all accounts, Abilene should have him running for the hills. She was dependent, to say nothing of her child. She was a train wreck in ways he couldn't entirely pinpoint, and her baggage was big enough to cram an ex-con into. Whatever else was in there, he was afraid to know. And he didn't *need* to know. They weren't a couple, wouldn't ever be; plus nobody was a *completely* open book. There were always a couple pages glued to the cover. Always a few unknowns.

He chanced one last squeeze of her fingers before letting them go. "I'm real proud of you for talking to him."

She shrugged. "I'm real ashamed of how scared I was. How much worry I put everybody through, avoiding it for so long."

"You did your best in a fucked-up situation."

"Doesn't feel like I did."

"Honey, if you could see all the shitty decisions I've made in my life, or Vince, or Raina ... Anybody except Miah, basically. You'd think we were all the biggest dumbasses you ever met. Fucking things up is just part of life. The best you can hope for is that you get most of it done before you hit thirty."

"I have a child, though."

"Well, fine. Thirty or parenthood, whichever comes first."

And even thirty was pushing it—Casey hadn't begun to clean up his act until last summer, after all, and how old had Vince been the last time he'd been put away? Thirty-two, probably.

Way out of left field, Abilene whispered, "Do you believe in God?"

He shook his head against the covers. "No. You do, though."

"Yeah. I used to wear a cross, even. Constantly. In the shower, to bed, all the time. It was silver, on a silver chain. I lost it last winter, right around the time some things started going extra-wrong."

He smiled. "You think God was punishing you, for losing it?"

"No, more like maybe somebody upstairs decided I didn't deserve to wear it anymore."

"Now, that's just nonsense."

"It's how I feel . . . I think I'd like to start going to church again. Not a church like I grew up in, but something, I dunno, low-key."

"There's a Unitarian place downtown. Aren't they supposed to be pretty liberal?"

"Maybe I'll check it out. I don't think I've gone more than a dozen times since I left home. It used to be such a huge part of my life . . ." She trailed off, eyes unfocused, thoughts folded up deep inside. After a minute or more she said, "I think I might like to get another one. A cross, I mean. Save up a little money."

"Like a reminder to keep your shit together, when you look in the mirror?"

"Something like that."

He smiled. He'd wanted to be able to buy her something, something not too gift-y, but more meaningful than the diaper rash cream or hair elastics she might ask him to pick up at the drugstore. Was she thinking of the plain old cross kind, or a hard-core crucifix with the tiny suffering Jesus and all that . . . ?

"I'd better go relieve Miah," she said, pushing herself up to sitting.

"Okay." Casey rose to follow her. She was probably exhausted from all the stress, but he was wired. Maybe Miah felt like a movie or a game of cards.

Abilene turned with her hand on the doorknob, looking him up and down. "You don't need to go."

"I figured you must be wiped and that I'd give you some space."

She turned fully, leaning back against the door. "I feel

better with you than I do just by myself." Her tone was shy, maybe nervous. "I mean, if you felt like hanging out, that is."

Hanging out? What did that mean, exactly? A heart-to-heart, or another collision, like yesterday afternoon? He swallowed. "Whatever you need."

What the girl needed, of course, was more than he had to give—a future, for one, and security. Not security like he was offering, playing bodyguard this week, but the real stuff. That C-word he'd been running from his entire life— *commitment.* And yet . . .

Maybe it was the possessive caveman in him not wanting to imagine her with anybody else, but some selfish part of Casey refused to think there was anyone better for her. He knew what she deserved. A man who'd do anything, risk everything, to keep her safe and to make her smile.

He could do that much. But all the rest? The long-haul stuff? To commit not just to one woman, but to a child as well. If he even had a future to look forward to, was he really capable of offering all that? If he had any doubts, the choice was obvious. There was no way in the hottest corner of hell he'd get himself in a position to let Mercy down the way his own father had done to him and Vince. Some men just weren't built for that shit.

Make no promises, break no promises. That was the simple answer. Until those test results came back, it was the *only* answer. Once they did, if somehow, through some stroke of good karma he'd never earned, Casey found out he did have a future, then what? Then, he supposed, he'd have a choice to make.

Keep things simple and selfish, or finally man the fuck up.

Chapter 13

Casey used the guest bathroom while Abilene was downstairs. As he scrubbed his face with a cold washcloth, he had to wonder, did the Churches think there was something up between the two of them? Miah wasn't naive, and Christine was a bloodhound about that stuff. He returned to the bedroom and shut the door as silently as he could, cheeks warming.

Abilene had returned and was leaning over the crib. As she turned, she pressed a finger to her lips.

He nodded. They might talk all night or wind up fooling around again, but either way it would be going down in whispers. He didn't mind. And he honestly didn't mind either way, what sort of "hanging out" this might be. If all she was after was a warm body against hers and a decent night's sleep, he could be that.

He'd dedicated so many years to taking, he'd forgotten that it could feel this good, providing. Maybe he'd never even known it, before her.

I turned into my old man after all. The one vow he'd ever made to himself, he'd broken. He'd run off when things turned grim at home and called it freedom. In reality, it had been cowardice.

Well, fuck all that.

"How you feeling?" he asked softly.

Abilene shed her jacket and rooted through the dresser, pulling out pajama pants and a T-shirt. "Good, I think. Dazed, and still a little scared, but good. Could you turn around a sec?"

He went to stand over the crib, studying Mercy's peaceful, fat little face while Abilene changed.

Her shyness didn't bother him. He'd had lovers who liked to keep the lights off during sex, partly, he guessed, because he was attracted to girls who were a little bigger than average, and maybe a little more self-conscious than average. He'd been with brazen girls, too, skinny and curvy alike, but the shy ones prevailed, looking back. Opposites attracted, he supposed.

"All set," she said.

She was climbing under the covers when he turned around. Uncertain what she might be after, he sat on the other end of the bed, content to talk. He squeezed her foot where it tented the blanket. "Anything in particular you need?"

She shook her head. "It's just nice to have you here, with all this stuff running through my head."

"I can stick around until you fall asleep, if you want. Maybe talk about something super boring, to help you get there quicker . . . ?"

"You could maybe stick around for the night. If you want to."

Casey swallowed, his ever-hopeful dick growing curious about the invitation. "I could."

She sat up, hugging her knees. "If this drama with James calms down after the meeting, I guess everything might go back to normal. You can sleep in your own bed again. I can start looking for a place."

"You know the Churches don't mind if you stay on for a few more weeks."

"Yeah, Christine said so. It's awful nice of them."

"And I'm happy to help you move again." If you could even call it moving. They'd gotten everything, including the baby's stuff, from her old place to Three C in just one carload each. It had taken all of three hours from the time he'd showed up to help pack to when she'd folded the last of her clothes into the borrowed dresser.

"You get a place of your own," he said, "and we're going to need to hook you up with some things. Furniture, microwave, TV . . . Not that I'm one to talk. My apartment looks like a squat."

"We can go Dumpster diving together," she said.

"Deal."

Neither spoke for a long moment, though both gazes lingered until Abilene bit her lip, looking away.

"What?" he asked, and gave her toes another squeeze.

"Are we ... Did you want to do more than hang out, maybe?"

"I told myself yesterday was a one-off," he said, but when her face fell, he hurried to take it back. "Only so I wouldn't get my hopes up about it ever happening again. I mean, *I* don't see the harm in it. But if you thought it was a bad idea ..."

"Not if we both know where we stand. What do you ... What does it mean to you?" she asked. "Be honest."

"I like you," he told her, point-blank. "I've liked you from the second I saw you. I liked you when the hormones made you a psycho, and I like you at three a.m. with baby puke in your hair. I think you deserve better than me, and more than I can promise anybody, but I won't pretend like I don't want to be with you, in whatever way's on offer. What about you? What does us fooling around mean to you?"

"I've just missed feeling all those things, I guess. And in a selfish way, with everything as scary as it has been, I want it even more, if only to feel something nice for a change. Mercy's small now," she said, gaze drifting to the crib. "She won't remember any of what's been happening—not the moving around, not any of this business with James, not anything that's changed between you and me. In a couple years I'm going to have to be careful of how close I let men get, so it's not just me who'd be in danger of getting attached." She looked back to Casey. "But for right now, I think it's okay." She sounded different, since that phone call. Even tired and rattled, her voice was as strong as he'd ever heard it. "Right now," she said, "I think it's what I need. I don't need promises of forever; I'm up to my eyeballs in commitment already. But to feel like more than just a mom for a few nights, for however long it might last ... ?"

He felt his pulse spike.

"Can we be that way?" she asked softly. "Just make each

other feel good?" Her gaze moved down his body, lighting a fire in his belly.

"We can be whatever way you like."

"Come over here, then. Remind me what I've been missing out on."

Casey stood from the bed, peeled off his socks, ditched his hoodie. He kept his jeans on and climbed under the covers.

"Can I hold you?" he whispered.

Her reply had an edge to it that he'd never caught before. Mischief. "You can do anything you want."

Casey swallowed, blood pumping quicker. "I want to kiss you, then."

She shifted to lie on her side and he did the same. As his mouth met hers, he eased his knee between her legs and drew her close by the waist. He wouldn't rush her, wouldn't get pushy, but it felt nice, taking even these small liberties. Made it feel like she was his. His to touch as he desired, his to cater to. He cradled her head, thumb tracing her ear, and kissed her deeper. A surprised huff of a breath from her nose tickled his cheek, and he gave her more of his tongue. Let her feel his hunger. Let her know she stirred more than gentle feelings in him, more than affection and deference. Deeply, darkly primal urges.

She wanted him back. He felt it in the way her fingers gripped his shirt, and he could hear it in her breaths—tiny mewling noises now, helpless little notes of wonder. He slid his hand to her butt and tugged her closer as his hips began to move.

She broke their mouths apart, already panting.

"All right?"

"I can't believe how . . . how much you make me feel." She swallowed audibly. "Up until yesterday, I'd forgotten what it was even like, wanting somebody this way."

Casey felt something similar, something he couldn't quite articulate. He'd never set his entire sex drive aside, but this . . . *This,* he hadn't felt in ages. He'd wanted women, and badly, but not the way he wanted Abilene. This felt *big*. Felt huge to a man who'd gotten in the habit of settling for the best offer available.

There had been no yearning in his life in recent years. No wanting, aching, waiting, and finally tasting. Only stumbling into beds and lives. Until now.

"I know what you mean," he whispered, and kissed her lower lip. "You've gone a long time not wanting like this. I've gone a long time not *feeling* this."

"Feeling what?"

"Everything," he said, the answer meaning nothing, yet so much. He climbed on top of her. Her thighs hugged his waist, urging him to move, and with two short strokes, his jeans were a straitjacket.

He'd never pressure her to do anything she wasn't ready for, but he couldn't hide what he desired, either. "I want you," he whispered. "So bad."

"I want you, too."

"Tell me," he said, rubbing against her, slow and light, "that someday, we'll go there together. That I can touch you there. Or use my mouth. Or be inside you."

She softened beneath him, legs going slack. Those blue eyes were bright even in the near dark, and her stare stilled his hips. "Why not tonight?" she asked.

In a breath, Casey was overheated. "Tonight?"

"If you have condoms, that is." She looked shy at that, and he had to smile. He'd seen her give birth, yet she was still embarrassed to say *condom* in front of him.

"I think I do. Can you hang on a minute?"

She nodded.

Casey prayed the den would be empty as he slipped out the door. As he stepped onto the landing, he found he wasn't in luck—the TV was on, volume low, and Christine and Don were sitting together on the couch. He wondered how flushed his face must be as he started down the steps.

Christine looked over as he neared. "Needing the couch? Our show's nearly over."

"No, no. Just my shaving bag."

"Shaving bag?" Don asked, chuckling. "I was starting to think you'd forgotten what a razor was."

"Don't get excited—I just need my toothbrush." He crouched before his duffel and dug for the nylon pouch, thinking he might just escape without interrogation until—

"How's Abilene doing?" Christine asked.

He got to his feet. "Pretty good. Relieved, I think." And let *them* assume he was sequestered in her room for moral support, please and thanks. "The baby's taking it easy on her tonight, at least."

"That's good to hear."

"Yeah. Anyhow, see you tomorrow." And with that, he hurried to the steps. He stopped in the guest bathroom, thinking he might as well brush his teeth, swerve and avoid the lie. As he did, he poked through the inside pockets of his shaving bag and found precisely one condom. He couldn't even remember whom he might've been seeing when he'd bothered to pack it, but it wasn't expired so he beamed a little thank-you to that forgotten woman. He spat and rinsed and stole back into Abilene's room with the plastic square clinging to his sweaty palm.

She sat up as he entered, expression expectant.

He flipped the condom up between two fingers like a playing card, a little sleight-of-hand trick he'd taught himself when he was ten.

"We don't have to use this," he said firmly, setting it on the side table, "if you think you're not ready. It'll just be here, in case you decide you are." He undid his belt and pushed his jeans down.

"I'm ready." She welcomed him back under the covers. "Just nervous."

He edged close, locking their legs together. "What about?"

"My body just doesn't feel the way it used to, before the baby."

"Ah. Well, I made you come yesterday, right?"

She nodded.

Casey got back on top, bracing his arms at her sides and his knees astride hers, hovering. Smiling. "You hadn't expected you would," he prompted.

"No."

"Did it make you feel like you got your body back, just a little?"

She thought about it. "Yeah, I guess it did."

"And maybe whatever happens tonight will get a little more of it back."

"Maybe."

"Abilene," he said, his face so close to hers, their noses

touched. "There's nothing I want more right now than to make you feel good. Whatever that looks like, I want to do that. Be that for you. You willing to let me try?"

Another nod.

"Can I touch you?"

"Okay."

He kissed her, lightly at first, deeper, then pulled away to settle between her legs on his knees. She let him undo the bow of her drawstring and ease her pajamas away. His breath grew shallow at a moment's peek between her legs. No panties, just her, obscured by the shadows. He could smell her, as well, if faintly. Christ, he'd forgotten that scent. His cock went from pulsing to pounding in a single heart-beat. He stroked her from her calves to her thighs, loving the feel of her. Soft skin, soft flesh, everything perfect, right down to the little Band-Aid on her knee. When she twitched, he made the touch firmer.

"Better?"

"Yeah. Sorry, I don't know why I'm so—"

"Don't apologize to me again."

She bit her lip, as though she'd nearly apologized for apologizing. "Or else what?"

"Or else something mean," he said softly, still stroking her legs. "I dunno what yet, but something awful. Maybe I'll sing to you."

She smiled. "I like your singing."

"When have— Oh, to the baby."

"And in the car. You sang along to 'My Sharona' last time you drove me to town. You didn't know half the words, but I like your voice."

"Well, I'll cook for you, then. I cook the worst eggs you've ever tasted," he promised, squeezing her ankles, calves, thighs, hips. "You want them burned and rubbery, or all snotty in the middle?"

"Gross." The word was barely a breath, as his thumbs ran along the creases of her uppermost thighs, close enough for him to feel the soft tease of her pubic hair. She sucked an inhalation as though shocked or tickled, and Casey made the touch firmer. He planted his knees wider, opening her legs in turn. Her calves were cool at his hips, telling him precisely how hot he was burning for her. His mouth felt dry, cock already hurting from neglect. He let his hand inch closer, closer, until his thumbs found the plump swells of her outer lips. Their collective breath came up short.

He laid the length of his thumb along one edge of her sex and slowly drew the other down the seam, then up. As he brushed her clit, she jolted, grasping his upper arms.

He went still. "You want me to stop?"

"No. It just . . . zapped me."

"Okay." He curled forward to kiss her belly through her shirt, hands still frozen. "If anything's too much, just say."

"I will."

He traced both thumbs along her outer folds this time, down and back up. A softer buck answered when he glanced her clit, chased by a sigh.

He smiled to himself. He knew there were men—men like his brother, he bet—who'd find all this waters testing too much work to bother with. Guys who didn't want to pick the lock, preferring to just go charging through like a battering ram. Casey, however, enjoyed picking locks, both figuratively and literally. Loved a challenge. He loved figuring a woman out, discovering what could melt her nerves away, what could leave her begging for more.

He bet most anybody who hadn't slept with him would assume he was the battering-ram type, which was fair—he was pretty blunt in most aspects of his life. But in his old line of work, and in bed, he was a perfectionist. An artist, as Emily had called him. He wasn't jacked like Vince, or freakishly good-looking like Duncan, or any kind of small-town royalty like Miah. He wasn't even a great person, he suspected, but he was a damn good lover. And he'd stay on his knees all night, taking it stroke by stroke like a painter, if that's what it would take to figure Abilene out.

"That feels nice," she whispered. Her eyes were shut, her lips parted.

He took the touch deeper, finding her wet. His breath hitched; his face warmed. His cock ached, dying to get inside her.

"Feels nice to me, too." Deeper still, until his thumb was slick from her. He rubbed her clit—small circles at first, then lighter flicks. He got his other thumb wet and touched her with both, in tiny symmetrical strokes like parentheses.

Her legs tensed and squeezed and a soft moan hummed in her throat.

Bingo.

He gave her exactly that, playing around until he knew how much pressure to use, exactly how slow she liked it. Slow was good—he loved when a woman needed it slow. Seemed like they came for ages when you coaxed it out, instead of a fast and frenzied rush.

Abilene was getting close—he could tell from how stiff her clit was, and how her lips had grown swollen. From the smell of her.

"Can I use my mouth?" he whispered.

"Yes."

He moved back, dropping onto his forearms. He slid one hand under her ass and eased her thigh wider with the other. He took her in with a long greedy breath, and sighed his satisfaction right there against her pussy.

There was a lot to be said for deprivation where sex was concerned, and aside from the odd glance of his nose, he ignored her clit to start. He pressed kisses along her seam, licked her lightly, then deeper. He hadn't tasted this in far too long. So long she could have been his first, for how exotic it felt.

He gave it to her like that for long minutes, until her fingers were in his hair and her belly was quivering with little gasps. When her legs tensed, he eased them wider. He didn't hide his own excitement—he moaned as loudly as he dared and let the odd sigh steam her skin.

"Casey." The hands on his head were growing plaintive or bossy, fingers tugging at his hair.

"What do you need?" He knew but wanted to make her say it.

"Higher," she murmured.

He had no doubt she was too shy to say "clit" but no matter. Maybe given time, she'd learn to get demanding. Casey liked few things more than getting ordered around in bed, especially by shy girls. He rewarded her with a long, slow lap of his tongue, all the way up and over her clitoris.

She gasped, grip tightening. He gave her another stroke, another, and crept that hand on her thigh up closer, closer. Close enough to run his thumb along her wet lips, then dip inside. Another gasp, and it was all he could do not to free a hand and touch himself. His dick was a screaming frustrated beast.

He closed his lips around her clit, working it with his tongue as he eased two fingers inside her. Was she thinking about what might come next? About his cock? Was she thinking of him at all, or of whatever mysterious fantasies hatched inside women's heads when they were inching toward orgasm? He didn't care, as long as he was the one getting her there. He worked his fingers in and out, reminding her of what she hadn't felt in over a year, teasing himself with what *he* hadn't done since last spring. Imagined how sweet it'd feel to sink inside her, right here, and slowly, torturously, edge himself to a body-wringing release.

Her hips told him when he'd found the right speed and pressure—they rolled subtly, seeking his tongue and the thrust, mimicking sex. He wanted to groan, to swear, to tell her how fucking hot she was; he didn't. He kept up the pleasure until her motions grew sharp and urgent, until her hands trembled, and he let her hear his desire in the moans rising up from his throat, humming against her pussy. He wished he could see her face as he had yesterday when he'd made her come, beautiful and wild and disbelieving.

He got her voice instead, whispering his name. That sound rang through his head as he brought her to orgasm, his hips pumping in time with hers, cock dying to be where his fingers were. As her body stilled, he did the same with his mouth and hand, and sat up. He rubbed her legs, memorizing her expression. The cheek lit by the weak light was pink, and her lids were half shut. She looked dozy and dazed.

"I do good?" he asked.

A smile broke through her stupor. She nodded. "You did real good. You did perfect."

Better than you've ever had it? A question whose answer was none of his business, though he hoped he could guess.

And he hoped for more than that.

He got his legs between hers, and tucked his forearms up against her ribs. Kissed her.

Excitement rolled through him, a fever sizzling in its wake. He kissed her neck, shifted so their bellies and hips pressed tight, so she could feel how bad he needed this. "Being inside you was all I could think about when I was doing that."

"Me, too."

Another flash of heat, and he groaned into her skin. His hips were already moving, stroking his cock along her pussy, his shorts dragging against her wetness, so fucking hot. "I can't wait."

"Then don't."

He pushed up on straight arms and looked to the table, but she already had the condom in hand. As she opened it, Casey got his shorts off, knelt, primed himself with a light stroke—no need. He was as hard as sin, already wet himself. Her gaze took it all in with a hunger he hadn't seen in those blue eyes before. Made him feel fucking huge.

He took the condom from her and rolled it on. Fuck if that didn't feel good in itself, after so long. The promise inherent in the cool caress of the latex.

His hand was shaking as he guided himself to her lips, every cell pulsing in time with his thumping heart. He eased into her with a single, slow push.

"Fuck, you feel incredible." He could only shut his eyes, sink down on his elbows and press his face to her neck. It had been so long since he'd felt this. So long since he'd been invited here. And he'd wanted her for ages. "You're so warm."

She tensed. "I'm not . . . I know I'm not as . . . since the baby."

He cut her off right there, propping himself up to hold her stare, and began to move, easing out, then back in a little deeper. "I'm not thinking about the things you're not, honey. You're warm," he told her again. "And wet. You're perfect. You're the best thing I've felt in my whole goddamn life."

She bit her lip, a smile dimpling her cheeks.

"And you're gorgeous. You just tell me if anything doesn't feel good."

"Nothing."

"Then tell me if anything feels amazing." Whatever that might be, he do it again, again, a hundred thousand times until he felt her quaking beneath him.

Of course in reality, he had to doubt if he could last that long. Already the pleasure was mounting, tight and low, spurring him to go faster, deeper, harder. He held back, not ready for it to be over. He focused on the subtler sensations, like Abilene's hands. They were soft, her palms cool on his ribs. Focused on her eyes and the way they moved up and down his body, curious and hot.

He groaned—louder than he meant to, then froze for a couple breaths, straining for a sign that he'd disturbed the baby. None came, and he eased back into the moment. Back into this beautiful woman.

"Can't tell you how bad I've wanted this. And for how long."

She stroked his arms with hungry hands. "Me, too."

"Here." He pulled out and moved to his side, urging her to do the same. He needed her face close, her mouth near enough to kiss. They scissored their legs and Casey got back inside her, shoving one arm beneath the pillow. God yes—that face, right here. He kissed her lightly as he found a good angle, held her thigh tight to his hip. Everything felt right. Nobody on top, the two of them on par. He slid his hand up her side beneath her shirt. As the top rode up, she seemed to curl in on herself, face pressing against his neck.

How she didn't realize her body was exactly perfect, Casey couldn't understand. All he could do was show her how he felt. "Take your shirt off. I've seen this," he added softly, rubbing her belly through her tee. "I've done more than just see it." He'd come on that soft skin yesterday.

After a moment's hesitation, she'd worked the shirt up and off. She still had her bra on, and as much as Casey was dying to see her breasts, he didn't press. He sealed their bodies close and drove deep, slowly, again and again. "You're so fucking soft," he whispered.

Her mouth was at the base of his throat, words warm and private. "You aren't."

Casey chuckled, kissed her forehead. "No, I'm not. That's what you do to me." He held her ass, tugging her tight to him, and he pushed as deep as he could go. It was so good, he felt a groan roaring up from his chest. It took everything he had to hold it in. "Fuck. Kiss me, honey."

The way he held her, she couldn't reach his mouth, but her lips teased his throat. Her tongue, a little rasp of her teeth. He shivered at that tiny taste of aggression from this sweet, hesitant girl, and let her hear how it excited him. She gave more, and his hips rushed. February was gone—their bellies and thighs were slick, the room like a sauna. He wanted to stay here tonight, sleep in this bed, keep the smell of their two bodies and this sex fogging his senses as he dropped off to sleep beside her.

He buried his face in her hair and moaned. "You're gonna make me come." It might be his body driving into hers, but that mouth on his neck was making him crazy. "Say my name."

She did, her breath hot on his skin. He could only moan in reply, and turn everything over to his dick. His hips were pounding, sloppy and fast, frantic, chasing relief.

She whispered it again. "Casey." Her hand was on his arm, gripping, thumb stroking. She was excited. Maybe not near the brink, but turned on—no mistaking it. He imagined next time, imagined her coming on his cock, saying his name, begging him not to stop. Or perhaps just her hands on him, her breath rushing, her eyes closed. He fantasized about all of it, until he felt that tether inside of him snapping, aggression and urgency going slack as the pleasure dropped him into free fall.

"Honey." He was half on top of her, hips racing him home, body slapping. He'd forgotten how it felt. How fucking good it was, losing it inside a woman, face-to-face. He crested from need to ecstasy and to marrow-deep relief in one long, wringing rush, then came down slowly, reeling.

Her hold on his arm softened, and he realized he might be squishing her. He eased out and rolled onto his back, folded the condom into the shorts he'd tossed on the floor. The sheets were cool on his shoulders and back, and he shoved the covers down to his waist, burning up.

"Goddamn."

Abilene turned over and laid an arm along his chest. He closed her hand in his, pressing it to his heart so she could feel it pounding. He side-eyed her. "You trying to kill me, honey?"

She smiled. "Never."

His laugh came out in a soft rush of breath. "Jesus, I guess I needed that."

"You deserved it."

He shook his head, thumped their hands atop his chest. "No. Nobody's entitled to sex. Nobody owes sex. You just have to be happy when it falls in your lap."

"And are you happy?"

"Fucking ecstatic." He squeezed her fingers, then drew them to his mouth and kissed them.

She snuggled closer, locking a leg over his. "Good."

"Tell me that'll happen again."

"I sure hope so."

Better add condoms to the shopping list.

"You sleeping in here again tonight?" she whispered.

"I want that if you do."

"Of course I do. But people are going to catch on soon."

"So let them. I don't care. Do you?"

She didn't answer right away.

"Abilene?"

"I don't know if I care or not. It's just that . . . We agreed this can't be anything serious, is all. I wouldn't know what to tell people, if they asked." She didn't sound fretful, merely puzzled. "What would you tell them?"

He considered it. Imagined Christine grilling him over morning coffee. "I think I'd probably say that you and I are getting close. Leave it at that."

"Oh." A pause. "That's nice. I like that."

"And it's true, right?" He turned back to his side, pulling the length of her body to his, splaying his fingers along her back, possessive.

"Yeah. It's true. This is as close as I've gotten to anybody in a long time."

Close as you were with Ware? James Ware was cut from a similar cloth as Casey's brother—he was like Vince with no sense of humor, and it was tough to imagine such men letting women turn them soft. But of course Vince had managed it with Kim. They'd been together for months, and weathered some pretty ugly stuff between the casino chaos and living with Vince and Casey's mom, yet Casey didn't see any cracks forming between them. So maybe Ware was capable of it, too. Though he preferred to imagine the man had never treated Abilene as he could. That *no* man had ever lain with her just this way, talked this way.

Such a fucking goner.

Abilene squeezed his hand, then let it go, rolling away. "I'll be right back."

"Where you off to?" He studied her naked body before it was swallowed up by her shirt and pajamas, memorizing the soft swells of her breasts, belly, butt, calves.

"Bathroom." She smiled at him as she smoothed her hair, then slipped out of the room.

Casey stared up at the beams ribbing the sloped ceiling, then shut his eyes. Breathed it all in. Felt the cool air on his chest, the warm covers around his waist and legs.

A thought struck him with such ferocious clarity, he got chills.

Please, don't let me go crazy.

A few months ago he'd walked through his life with that same prayer running on a loop in the back of his head, but his reasons for wishing it had been selfish. He hadn't wanted to be pitied, hadn't wanted to be dependent, hadn't wanted to lose his mind before he could enjoy the money he'd made, and more recently, before he had a chance to see the bar succeed. Now it felt different. It had begun feeling different ever since he'd kissed this woman, hadn't it? What else could explain his sudden, impulsive urge on that very same night, the one that'd finally had him ordering the genetic testing kit?

Don't let me go crazy. Don't take my life away when I've only just started making something worthwhile of it.

Don't make me have to leave her.

He sighed, eyes opening as the water ran in the next room. She'd be back in a minute. His to hold through the night. His, for now.

His, for as long as karma decided he deserved it.

Chapter 14

At two minutes to four the next afternoon, Abilene strained for sounds—the slam of a truck door outside, of knocking, voices rising.

This room was nearly as far as you could get from the front lot, and the window was shut. Didn't stop her imagination, though. A hundred times she could swear she'd caught a doorbell; talking or shouting or the sounds of a fight. All figments. The only actual noises were the occasional creak of the old house, the tick and whir of the heat coming on at odd intervals.

Four o'clock was the time she'd given James for their face-to-face meeting, and likely his first encounter with his daughter, provided things went well.

Mercy was downstairs, being looked after by Christine. Casey had offered to be in the room with Abilene when everything went down, but of course she'd declined. There was too much to be unpacked that she never wanted him to know about her. Too much at stake in the truths she'd omitted, the assumptions she'd let him make about her—

She sat up straight at the sounds of activity beyond her room. Real ones. Voices, then the heavy thumps of two sets of footsteps on the uncarpeted stairs.

She watched the door, heart clenched and pounding, temples throbbing, palms damp. Even as she hoped it would never open, every second that elapsed before it did lasted an hour.

Muffled words were exchanged outside the room, and then one set of steps faded back down the stairs.

"Come on," she murmured, staring at the knob, daring it to twist. "Come on, come—"

A knock.

"Yeah," she called.

The door swung in, and there he was.

James seemed shorter than she remembered, though perhaps that was merely a side effect of all her time spent around Vince and Duncan. He looked a little older, too, and she supposed prison must do that to a man. He was still handsome in his intimidating, fierce way, but weariness had etched fine lines across his brow and shadowed his blue eyes.

Mercy's eyes. Darker than her own. Moodier.

He kept his gaze on her as he shut the door, expression guarded. His lips were set, as were his shoulders. He looked like a man entering a ring with a spook-prone horse, exuding an aura of forced calm.

She'd brought a chair up from the kitchen and set it facing the bed. The noise of it scraping on the floor as he took a seat felt so loud she flinched.

"Abilene," he said evenly, planting his elbows on his thighs. She knew not to expect a cordial *Thanks for agreeing to meet me* or the like. Despite his psychotic move on Wednesday night, turning up and creeping around, she owed him whatever he was after—another apology, assurances, proof she had things under control. And she did have most of it under control, she thought. Beneath the jitters, she felt strong. She felt ready for this.

"You look good," James said. He didn't mean she looked pretty—he meant that she looked healthy. That she looked *clean*.

"I feel good. Just a little sleep deprived."

"Where's the baby?"

"She's asleep. Someone's with her."

"Tell me I get to see her."

She nodded. "Unless this all goes real badly, yeah, you'll get to see her."

That softened his jaw. And that jaw was coated in dark stubble—unusual for James, a man who rose each morning at the same hour, rarely drank, and never smoked, who thrived on routine and shaved daily. She remembered another time when she'd driven him to forsake his regimens and lose his focus. She remembered all the power she'd felt, seeing the strongest, hardest man she'd yet met reduced to a nervous wreck. Oddly, it made her curious to watch him when he held his daughter for the first time. Would that moment change him, soften him, as his worry and care for her had, once upon a time last winter?

"I know you must be impatient," she said. "But let's talk first. We both must have more things to say than we did on the phone."

A silent, mirthless little laugh curled his lips. "Yeah, I've got things to say."

She nodded to tell him to go ahead.

"You want to know why I needed to see you so goddamn badly?" he asked. "Why I'm so fucking *angry*? It's because I'm scared to death."

"I know. But the baby's fine. And I'm a good mother, believe it or not."

"You gotta understand, Abilene, you don't want me to see you both, and my mind goes right back to that shithole I found you in."

She felt her face turn hot. She didn't remember much about the place, that beige trailer she'd called home for days or maybe weeks, at the rock bottom of her heroin addiction. She remembered how it smelled. Like struck matches and incense, like unwashed sheets. Like stale sex. She had no memory of James finding her, only of waking up in his house, in his clothes, bleary and confused and wanting nothing except her next dose.

"*Who are you? Where am I?*" she'd asked.

"*My name is James. I found you in some hellhole of a double-wide in Lime. You're at my place.*"

"*Why?*"

"*Because I bought you for six hundred bucks off some junkie in a stupid hat.*" Her old dealer, and a buyer of James's illegal firearms.

"*Six hundred dollars? I'm not a whore.*"

"*I never said you were. You're here because you remind me of my little sister and because I'm a fucking idiot. I have absolutely zero interest in fucking you,*" he'd said. "*Not even if you took a shower—which you really fucking need to—*

and not if you gained ten pounds, and put on some lingerie, and did your hair real nice. The only reason you're here is because I couldn't not get you out of that place, but I don't have the first clue what I'm gonna do with you. Except maybe sober you up, and feed you, and make sure you get that goddamn shower. After that, your choices are up to you. I'm just doing the bare minimum I need to to get some fucking sleep tonight. You got that?"

For a criminal, James had proven a man of his word—he hadn't made a move on her. Hadn't put a hand on her except to usher her out of his little house, into his truck, through the entrance to a methadone clinic. A shake on the shoulder to wake her each morning . . . and a rougher, two-handed shake later, when she'd really pushed him.

She'd stayed with him for more than two months. Long enough to pass through the hell of withdrawal and get clean, to gain back the twenty pounds heroin had stripped from her bones. Long enough for her hesitation to grow to trust, for trust to become gratitude, and, in time, for gratitude to morph into a crush. He'd been thirty-seven, and she twenty-one, but age gaps had never given her much pause.

He'd resisted her flirtations admirably, for maybe two weeks. But in the end, no man was that saintly. James had tried to be, tried real hard, God help him, but it had been no use. Abilene had been helpless in many ways, but not without her leverage.

The sex had been good. Not amazing, but intense, and tender as well. With other guys she'd been in it for whatever benefits were to be gained—shelter or favors or money—but with James it had simply been the contact she'd wanted.

For him it had been sexual, too, almost purely. Sex and some affection, probably a touch of attachment. She'd made him feel strong and needed, she thought. He'd made her feel safe and desired. It had met their needs for as long as it had lasted, but it had always been doomed, and they'd both known it from the start.

Whatever they'd been had lasted just a few weeks. Long enough for them to mess up and for her to get pregnant, though she hadn't known that when she'd left him. She hadn't gotten her period in ages, hadn't felt normal in forever; the symptoms had been wasted on her until she'd been four months gone, and by then James had been out of her life for longer than they'd ever been together.

She studied his expression, all that skepticism, maybe even pity. It burned her. There was a time when she'd been only too happy for people to see her as helpless and in need of safeguarding. It had been her currency. But with Mercy now in the picture, the concern grated, as did the assumption that she always relied on other people to get what she needed—the assumption that she couldn't make it on her own.

"I'm not the same person I was when we met," she told him.

"I hope that's true. But you gotta understand, my imagination jumps straight to you using, not caring about anything except where your next fix is coming from. That girl I found in that trailer, she couldn't take care of a baby. She couldn't take care of *herself*. You're a goddamn professional victim, sweetheart. So sue me if I was worried you might need rescuing. Again."

"Well, *I don't*," she spat back. "And I'm not a victim. I never was."

His smile was pitying. Maddening. "You were sleeping with a stranger for heroin when I met you. What the fuck does that make you? A goddamn feminist?"

"Fuck you."

That gave him pause. His expression went from smug to uncertain in a blink.

She was shocked herself. She doubted she'd cussed since labor. And before that, only during flashes of hormonal insanity. And before that, heroin withdrawal.

"I was never a victim," she repeated. She thought back on what Casey had said about luck, about choices. "Every shitty situation I've wound up in, I got there myself. Because *I* made lousy decisions and trusted people I shouldn't have. For a dozen stupid reasons. To defy my parents, to escape from my hometown, for a place to stay. For attention. I may have woken up in some real nasty places, but I walked myself there on my own two feet. I chose all of that stuff, though I'm not proud to admit it." At first, for a taste of freedom, of what she'd mistaken for adulthood. Later, out of necessity.

"You only think I'm a victim because I'm the woman. But you take a long, hard look at our breakup, and tell me who felt used when it all turned to shit."

He blinked at her, eyes wide.

"I haven't been a good person," she went on, cooling her head. "Not for a long time. Not until I found out I was pregnant. But I've done better since then. I quit smoking; I worked hard. I asked for help when I truly needed it. And I'm a good mother. Mercy is healthy and she's loved, and has a whole house full of people who want her safe."

"A whole house full of people who think *I'm* the dangerous one," he countered. "And maybe I am. Maybe I'm a criminal, and maybe I've hurt people, but never my family. Never any woman, and never any kid. I'm not perfect, but I provide. But you . . . You always fall apart or you run, the second something goes wrong."

He sighed, rubbed his thighs, and seemed to calm himself. When he looked up, he met her eyes squarely. "Can't you understand how I'd worry—given the way we even *met*? And when you refused to see me, you have any idea what flashed through my mind? How am I not supposed to jump to the worst conclusions?"

"You never had any faith in me."

His stare was steady. "You never gave me any reason to."

She felt tears welling.

"Don't," he said. "That shit won't work on me anymore."

Now she was just *livid*. "I can cry without it being some kind of game, you know. You hurt my feelings. What the heck do you expect me to do?" She wiped at her cheeks, so pissed she could slap him. He was the only man she'd ever struck in her life—pointless little shoves and punches and scratches in the midst of withdrawal, when he'd basically held her captive. She'd been an animal then, though.

"Look," he said, hunkering down, clasping his hands between his knees. "That baby is my daughter. I have obligations to her—to make sure she's safe and being taken care of. So let's get down to fucking business, okay? You'll need money."

She sat up straighter, taken aback. "Money?"

"I know you, Abilene. Well enough to guess you probably never signed yourself up for health insurance. So how deep are you in the hole, exactly? Births ain't cheap. How much do you need? I've got eight hundred on me, and more coming, once I chase down some customers."

"Well, you can keep it. I got insurance. Eventually."

"How much?"

"*Nothing.* Vince gave me a few hundred dollars to cover my first doctor's appointment—give *him* your dirty money. I got on insurance. And I worked and paid my bills and my rent. And I got some of the medical expenses and some of the baby's things for cheap, because of my income."

"Well, you shouldn't have fucking had to. You should have come to me. Let me take care of it."

"You were in *prison*," she cut back.

"I've got ways."

"I don't want your shady money, James. I don't want to pay for Mercy's diapers with the proceeds from you selling stolen guns. Ever since I knew she was coming, I've done everything the right way. I've worked and I've lived cheap, and when I've needed help, people have helped me because they care."

"Grossier," he said, then clarified, "Casey."

"Everyone in this house. And my other boss at the bar. The lady who used to rent a room to me—she let me out of my lease early and even let me have my deposit back. I've had help, but because people *wanted* to help, not because I scammed them into it. I'm not who I used to be."

He nodded slowly, hesitantly. "I can see that. I can see enough to believe that—some of it, anyway. You look healthy," he allowed. "And this is a real nice place. But it's still my kid, Abilene. You two need somewhere permanent to live. Somewhere stable. It's my job to provide that. Where the money comes from shouldn't matter."

"Of course it does. James," she huffed, exasperated, "I'm not doing shit the wrong way anymore. Not ever again. I'd rather live in one crummy little room that I pay for with my tips than let you buy me a whole house with your filthy money."

"My filthy money got your ass clean."

"And I owe you for that. I might even owe you my life. But things are different now, and I don't ever want to have to tell my daughter that her dad's going back to prison for ten years—or worse. You've been busted twice. They catch you again, or if some weapon you sold winds up killing a cop or something, and they trace it back to you . . . All the money in the world doesn't mean crap if you get locked up for good. And I'm not being evil here. And I'm not telling you that you can't be a part of Mercy's life. But if you are, you better believe you're going straight."

His eyebrows rose. "You got any idea how much I can make in a year, doing what I do? And you got any clue how much I'd make if I went and found some job fit for an ex-con with a ninth-grade education?"

"I don't care how much you give us, only that it's clean."

He shook his head, heaved a deep breath. "You were so much easier to like when you were a mess—you know that?" Then his expression softened, telling her it was a joke.

She didn't smile back. "Easier in a lot of ways, I'm sure. But I'm serious. I'd take fifty bucks a month that you made as a fry cook over five thousand that came from guns. And you can find something—you're strong. And you must have learned some kind of skill in prison."

"The math doesn't work—"

"We'll make it work. We have to. I can't go back to how I used to be. Not anymore. My daughter's not growing up with a criminal for a father or a train wreck for a mama. You go to Vince, see if he can get you a job at the quarry or something. Get a trucking license. Anything, so long as it's honest."

He rubbed his thighs again, looking pale. "I'll think it over, okay?" From a man who didn't back down, ever, it felt as solid as a promise.

"Good."

"Now we need to talk about Grossier, though. You and him."

"Casey? What about him?"

"You two. What are you?"

"He's my boss. And my friend."

"Tell me straight—you fucking him?"

She bit her tongue to quell a reflexive lie. She nodded. "Yeah. What about it?"

"I just want to know who he is to you. Who's coming in and out of my daughter's life."

Who she thinks her daddy is, Abilene read between the

lines. "He's a good man." Or he was now, she trusted. What he might have been before . . .

"I know he wants you safe," James said. "But I also know he's been inside, and I don't know what for."

"Neither do I. And I don't want to." All she knew was that it had been during his time in Vegas, so probably something to do with gambling.

"He's coming around our daughter, so I goddamn do."

"You're one to talk."

"Yeah, I am. Because everybody knows exactly what it is I've been up to. And that I've done my time. But what do you really know about this guy? Really?"

"I know he treats me good. And that he cares about the baby."

James flinched at that. Had to sting, knowing a stranger had been filling those shoes in his absence. Sleeping with his ex, caring for his child. Whatever came next, and for however long the present situation was reality, those two men would have tension. Some real ugly, heavy tension.

"You'll just have to get good with him," Abilene said. "Because he seems determined to be there for me." As her lover, just for now, but as her boss and friend long after they quit sharing a bed, she hoped. Though would Casey still be so devoted, if James told him the truth about her?

"It's not about my feelings," James said evenly. "It's about what's best for the kid."

He'd cooled himself off, and she did the same. She'd owed him answers and handed them over. But in all fairness she owed him a little more.

"I'm sorry," she said. "For keeping you in the dark. And for how I was when we split."

"Not much to be done about it now."

"Except to apologize. So I'm sorry. You know, I stole from you, when we broke up."

"Three hundred dollars," he confirmed.

It was technically three hundred and thirty that she'd taken out of his wallet, and he knew that, no doubt. She'd heard him on the phone with his customers, and he quoted people their debts right down to the penny, with interest. That he wasn't hung up on the thirty bucks reassured her. It hinted that she was still a person to him, not a transaction.

"I'm sorry I took it," she said.

"Don't be, for fuck's sake. That's nothing. Just a final fuck-you, and I was happy to let you have the last word, if the payoff was me stitching my life back together in peace after you ripped it up."

"I'm sorry, all the same."

"You needed it more than me. Long as it went to groceries or rent and not dope, what the fuck do I care?"

"I bought a car with it," she said lamely. The same heap she drove now. Two hundred fifty she'd paid, and used the rest for gas and a few meals. Not much of an investment, but it had been her first taste of freedom in months and months. It had carried her as far as Fortuity before the gas ran out. Dead broke and hungry, she'd asked the waitress at the diner if she could maybe get some food and wash dishes in exchange. She'd been offered a job instead, and here she'd stayed.

"So what's next?" she asked him.

"What's next is that I meet my daughter. And after that we figure out where you two'll stay, and how to pay for it."

"I can worry about that. I'll be going back to work soon."

"You'd never have needed to stop if you'd been straight with me."

And here she stood, at the edge of what she feared most. Here she stood, ready to hand this man a knife and beg him not to use it on her. "James . . ."

"What?"

"I have a favor to ask you. A big one. One that matters way more than money to me."

"So ask it," he said, never one for a preamble.

"Please don't tell anyone about how things were, when we met."

He stared at her. "So you do get how fucked-up it was, then? You get *exactly* why I was so fucking eager to find you, make sure everything was okay over here?"

"I do, okay? Just promise me. Please."

"You don't want him to know how you were. He thinks you're some fucking innocent little girl who got mixed up with a big bad man, doesn't he?"

"Don't gloat. Just promise me you won't. If he finds out, it should be from me." And the only circumstance under which she could imagine telling Casey the truth was if they somehow fell in love, got serious with each other. But with his criminal past keeping Abilene at arm's length, and Casey's own mysterious misgivings, she trusted that was a conversation she could keep on avoiding, likely indefinitely.

"You're fucking right; you should tell him," James said. "You want to be good for our daughter, you practice what you're preaching. Be honest with a man for once in your life."

"You want our daughter to know why you missed her birth?" she countered.

"No, I don't. But I also know she's gonna find out someday. Because she's gonna ask, and I'm gonna tell her. Just like he's gonna find out about you. So yeah, you better tell him, unless you want somebody else painting that pretty little picture for you."

"I'll tell him. When the time's right." She didn't suspect any good could come of explaining to James that she and Casey were only lovers, only casual, not when he was feeling so vigilant about the stability of Mercy's situation. She let him infer it was more than it was, if only to skirt a lecture.

"We both fucked this all up real bad," James said at length, tone softer. "Parenthood, I mean. And I'm really goddamn pissed at you right now. For not telling me, then for trying to shut me out. For running to a load of strangers and making me out to be some kind of psycho. I did a lot for you, you know. I forgave a lot, overlooked a lot. You used me and I was happy to let you, and this is how you repay me?"

"You scared me, when we broke up. I thought you might even hurt me."

He shook his head, looking ancient. "I wish I could say you knew me better than that . . . But maybe that's too much to hope for."

"And you didn't handle this situation all that great, yourself. Coming around in the middle of the night, spying or whatever that was about."

He sat up straight. "What, now? This the same crazy bull Grossier was yelling at me about?"

"You came by. Miah saw you."

"Who the fuck is Miah?"

She sighed, exasperated. "The guy with the black hair. Your height. He and his parents own this ranch. And he saw your truck, chased you down the road. Don't deny it."

"I sure as fuck *will* deny it. I've never set foot on this property before today. I didn't know where you were. And even if I had, I wouldn't've been stupid enough to show up uninvited. Grossiers pack more guns than sense."

She wanted to believe him, only it didn't add up. Who else would show up in a black truck, the same week James had been released and was trying to get to her, and come snooping around the farmhouse?

Still, she trusted his expression, and she'd never known him to lie—lying was for cowards like the old Abilene, whereas James feared nothing.

But she couldn't accept the coincidence. Not a hundred percent.

"Now," he said, standing. "I want to meet my daughter."

Chapter 15

Casey was planted in the rocker, with a clear view of the second-floor landing and Abilene's door. His muscles were tensed, ears trained for the flare of voices. So far, nothing but a dull murmur, no discernible words. Then, after what felt like three hours but was probably closer to thirty minutes, the door opened above. He gripped the arms of the rocker, resisting the urge to jump to his feet.

Abilene emerged, followed by Ware. She looked calm; he looked stony. As they came down the steps, her eyes locked with Casey's and she smiled, giving his heart permission to slow.

Ware also looked his way, unreadable. The guy could have been pissed or relieved or frustrated or plain old tired, for all the emotion that glance gave away.

Look at Mercy with that expression and I'll break your face, Casey thought.

The two paused at the bottom of the steps, and Abilene said, "We're going to go and see Mercy."

Casey nodded. "Okay." The baby was in the office—Christine was keeping an eye on her while she did paperwork. Nobody had thought it would be a great idea for Ware to show up and find Casey holding his daughter.

They disappeared down the back hall, and Casey released the chair arms, fingers prickling as the blood rushed back to their tips. He took a deep breath, shoulders shaking as it drained back out. He wanted a beer. Wanted a shot, but his pride was interfering with the impulse—he didn't care to exchange any words with Ware and have the guy smell booze on him. Which was fucked, really, to care so much about the opinion of a criminal, only he wanted so badly to appear worthy of all the trust Abilene had put in him.

He listened to the office door open and close, caught soft voices. Christine appeared shortly wearing a cautious smile. She held up two sets of crossed fingers.

"She seem okay?" he asked.

"I'd say so. I think she looked relieved. Nervous, but relieved."

He nodded.

"Coffee?"

"No, thanks. I'm counting down the hours until it's socially acceptable to hit the bourbon."

"Don't blame you. It hasn't been this tense around here since the last property scout came knocking." Christine headed for the kitchen.

Casey focused on the clinking of dishes and the rush of running water, trying to distract himself. He wanted like hell to sneak down the hall and listen at the office door. He wanted to know what they were saying. He wanted to know if Ware was holding the baby, and whether or not she seemed to like him. The sharpest, fiercest bit of him bared teeth at the thought, a jealousy he'd never even conceived of before. He didn't consider himself Mercy's father by any stretch, but a part of him did identify—and with secret pride—as the primary man in her tiny life. His fingers curled up tight again, forming fists atop his thighs.

A clatter drifted from the front of the house, then a hiss—the screen door shutting, followed by the inner one. He heard Miah call a greeting to his mother; then the man himself entered the den. He looked funny. A touch pale and upended.

"Hey," Casey said, standing. "They're in the office now."

Miah kept his voice low. "That's not the truck."

"What's that?"

"The black truck parked in the lot—that's not the one I saw the other night. It's got a faded old bumper sticker on the tailgate, and I didn't notice that on Tuesday. And I took a look at the plate, to see if it looked like there'd been duct tape on there, any dust stuck to it—nothing. That's *not* the truck."

Casey frowned. "So what the fuck does that mean? That he was telling the truth? That he didn't come around here?"

Miah shrugged. "That, or he borrowed someone else's pickup. I dunno, man, but it seems strange. Something's not right."

Casey's mind raced, trying to turn this news into a threat he could wrap his head around. "You think Abilene's in trouble?"

"Not necessarily. Not unless she has some other shady character from her past who might've come sniffing around. I don't know *what* the fuck this means, aside from that maybe Ware isn't the only person we have to be worried about."

"Who else could it have been?"

Miah shrugged. "No clue. We get poachers, and whoever's involved in the drug dealing or whatever it is, but not here. Not at the house. Scratch what we said at the meeting, about you asking around town about somebody dealing out here. That's not what this is about."

"Burglar, maybe?"

"They'd have some fucking balls on them, with all those lights on, all those vehicles parked out front."

Casey nodded. "Doesn't add up."

Miah leveled him with a look. "You gotta tell me if you've got any enemies out there, Case. You don't have to tell me what you've been up to in Texas, but this is my business now. You owe anybody anything? You cross anyone who might come looking for you?"

He shook his head, stumped. And uneasy. None of Casey's former clients knew his name or even what he looked like. The only unexpected visitors who might worry him were feds. He and Em had been careful, real careful, but you could never know if your name was on some watch list someplace, some database. Plus if Emily fucked up and got busted, he couldn't honestly say he trusted her not to sell him out for a reduced sentence. Hell, he'd probably do the same to her.

But since when does the ATF skulk around in ski masks and shitty old trucks?

"I got no clue, man. Maybe we ought to give the whole

town a good cruise, see if we can't spot that pickup in some-body's driveway . . . ?"

Miah sighed, crossing his arms. "Maybe. If the alterna-tive's waiting for them to come back."

"Maybe it *was* just some dumb-ass burglar, casing the place. Maybe you scared him out of thinking he'd ever try that shit here again."

"We can hope. But I won't sleep easy until I know for sure."

Miah took a seat on the arm of the couch, posture weary. He was dressed in dirty jeans and there was dust in his black hair.

"Go shower," Casey said, waving him in the right direc-tion. "Once Ware is gone we'll have a beer, talk this over."

Miah nodded and hauled himself to standing. "Best idea I've heard all week."

Casey clapped Miah on the back as he passed, thinking his friend was becoming more like Don every season. More serious, and burdened by more pressure. The casino chaos couldn't be helping, nor the looming inevitability of Miah becoming the sole captain of this ship.

Regarding any other person on earth, Casey would've thought the notion was stupid, but he wondered if maybe Miah needed setting up, romantically. If he was stuck work-ing himself into the ground the way he was, he ought to at least get to tumble into bed with a warm female body every night. Shame that probably half the eligible women in town were his ranch hands. No doubt he'd have some ethical boundary about—

The click and squeak of the office door snapped Casey's head to the left. Ware appeared first from the hall, followed closely by Abilene, the baby in her arms. They were talking softly but trailed off as they reached the den.

Ware cast Casey a cool glance, then told Abilene, "I can see myself out."

"Okay."

"Tomorrow afternoon?" he asked.

She nodded. "Two o'clock."

He touched the baby—or her clothes, anyway, the collar of her tiny shirt—then turned and headed for the front. Abilene watched him go, and Casey watched Abilene.

"Tomorrow?" he prompted, once the front door had hissed shut.

"Yeah." She seemed to snap out of a trance, bouncing the baby. "It went well. I said he could see her again."

"Did you let him hold her?"

She'd been studying the baby's face but looked up at that, expression curious. "Just for a minute—he gave her back pretty quick. I'm not sure he's ever held a baby before. He looked a little freaked-out."

Casey bet that was a first in itself—James Ware showing fear. That novel and fierce jealousy burned the back of his neck, and in a petty way he was glad to hear that the guy wasn't a natural with the kid. That maybe fatherhood was earned by how many hours you put in, not just whose DNA went into the mix. That made him think of his own dad, and his mood darkened.

"Miah saw your ex's truck in the lot," Casey said. "And he said it's not the same one he saw on Wednesday night."

She blinked. "Really?"

"Doesn't absolutely mean it wasn't him . . . But I have my doubts now."

"I had some of my own. He told me it wasn't him, and I've never known him to lie."

What was to be done about it, though? Nearly nothing aside from hoping someone spotted that other truck . . . But there had to be dozens of dark, midsized, older pickups around town, to say nothing of the county at large. Not so much needle in a haystack as needle in a needle factory.

"You didn't eat lunch," Casey said, setting the mystery aside. She'd been too nervous, earlier.

"No, and I'm starving."

"Feel like a trip into town? Grab something at the diner?"

She considered it. "I guess I could, now."

"Course you can. Celebrate your freedom—no more reason for house arrest that I can see." Her ex knew where to find her now, and it seemed perhaps he wasn't, in fact, crazy enough to stalk her.

"Okay, then. Let me just get Mercy's stuff together."

"Great." He accepted the baby so Abilene could head upstairs. She returned with a diaper bag, and they swung by the kitchen and chatted with Christine, filling her in about the meeting while Abilene fixed a bottle.

"It'll feel nice to get yourself off the rez for an hour or two, I bet," Christine said.

"Maybe a little. No offense."

She smiled and waved the thought aside. "It's no fun feeling trapped, especially with a new baby. When Miah was tiny, I used to look forward to my sister visiting, so I could get a little time to myself. I remember driving into town and just wandering the aisles of the drugstore, elated just to be someplace else. *Anyplace* else. I'd offer to take her now, in fact, except the vet's coming in twenty minutes."

"No, it'll be good for her to get a change of scenery, too," Abilene said, and kissed the baby's head, with her palm on Casey's shoulder. His face went warm and he was glad everyone was focused on Mercy.

"Dinner's at eight," Christine said, turning back to the laptop open on the table.

"Would you tell Miah where we got to?" Casey asked. "I owe him a beer and a talk."

"No problem."

Abilene took the baby and they headed out.

"I wonder when my car will be fixed," she said as Casey was unlocking his Corolla.

"I'll ask my brother. Hopefully this weekend."

"And when do you think I could go back to work?" She got the baby strapped into her seat. Casey's car would look weird without it, he realized, once Abilene was driving again.

"Let's hold off until after a couple more meet-ups, okay? But if the next two or three go well, and we can get you some childcare sorted out, I'd say there's no point in waiting. But . . ."

"Yeah?" She buckled her seat belt, eyeing him.

"Maybe stick with babysitters you know really well, okay? Just to start. Just to be safe. Me, or maybe Kim." Raina had the time and was equally trustworthy, but he couldn't picture her taking care of a baby. He tried imagining Duncan's attempt as well, and nearly laughed aloud. Though perhaps the two of them together might be able to survive it, some night when Casey and Abilene were both closing. He'd be tempted to videotape it, just to see Duncan's expression when faced with a filthy diaper.

"I miss work," Abilene said, once they were moving.

"It misses you. Or Duncan and Raina miss the two of us, I'm sure. Though before you say it," he added, noting her darkening expression, "don't feel bad. It's only a week, and I'm sure they're more than happy to help while things settle down for you."

"Everyone's been so nice about it all."

He shrugged. "It's what friends do." And he was proud to count himself a part of that group, he realized, after all those years of only looking out for number one.

"You're a very generous motorcycle club."

He laughed. "And you're very generous, even applying that term to us. Bikes just happen to be the thing we all bonded over when we were kids. The bunch of us are well overdue for a nice, long group ride, too." Duncan made things tricky; he rode just fine, and being with Raina, he ought to be invited on such an outing. But if he went, Miah likely wouldn't. Church would come up with a million work-related excuses, no doubt, so maybe some weekend soon they'd just have to trick him into it. He seemed to be getting over his shit with Raina, at least.

"You could come," Casey added. "Ride with me."

"That'd be the most exciting thing I've done in ages, if I could find a sitter."

"Confronting your gunrunner ex not thrilling enough for you?" he teased.

"The most exciting *fun* thing."

The speed limit dropped to thirty as the town materialized around them, homes and businesses growing dense as the rural route morphed into Station Street. It gave Casey a funny feeling and made him nearly wish he was working that night. He was in the mood to listen to the gossip, to pour drinks and take in the smells and sounds of the bar, the same smells and sounds from his childhood. Lubbock had been hot, but not like here. Not dry like northern Nevada, not half as dusty. Even Vegas hadn't smelled quite like Brush County did, like clay and sage, and distant fires, come summer. No place felt quite like home, he thought, as familiar buildings slid into view on either side of the road.

"Hey, it's your shitbox," Casey said, nodding to the auto garage. Vince had both bay doors wide open and was standing by Abilene's Colt with a wrench in his hand. Casey honked. Vince waved. "You'll be back on the road before you know it."

"I hope I can make all of this up to you guys someday," Abilene said. "Especially your brother, for the money he gave me, and now my car. And you, of course, for a million things."

"You don't owe me crap."

"I beg to differ."

Casey assembled his feelings, trying to get his mouth to go someplace soft and sentimental here in this car, as he'd managed in bed with her.

"Everything I'm experiencing, because of you and the baby . . . It sounds stupid, but it means a lot. I've never been for anybody what I've been for you two. And it's hard and it's exhausting, and I don't know what I'm doing half the time, but I like it. I feel useful in a way I haven't before. So you don't owe me a thing. You've given me plenty, trust me."

He was relieved to turn into the diner's lot and cut this conversation short. Nice as those things were to say, they also made him feel insanely naked. Which was fine when you were under the covers with somebody, but something else entirely out here in the larger world.

He got the car seat out and lugged the baby into the diner while Abilene held the door. He registered a mix of pride and awkwardness, carrying her in, and was pleased not to recognize any faces as they entered and scanned for a booth. Having been away for nearly ten years, he was always getting grilled by old neighbors and classmates about what he'd been up to, and he never had enough answers. Now, to get spotted with a woman and a baby in tow . . . ? He didn't have the energy to explain.

Once they were settled, an older waitress came by. Abilene had worked here for a few months the previous year, and there was the requisite fawning over the baby before coffee was on the way.

Casey didn't need to see the menu; it hadn't changed since he'd been a kid. He ordered a cheeseburger and Abilene got soup and a sandwich.

He hunkered down on his elbows and smiled at her. "Your first taste of freedom in almost a week."

She nodded. "Feels good. Smells even better." She held his gaze, then looked to the window, her smile goofy. "What you said, in the car . . ."

"It's all true. That's all we need to discuss about it."

"It was sweet," she said, meeting his eyes once more. "That's all. I don't think anybody's ever said something that nice to me before."

"Their loss."

She smirked. It wasn't a gesture she made often—her smile was typically broad and sudden, like clouds breaking wide, sun streaming down. Her cheeks still dimpled, but there was something sly about those lips, something vaguely wicked. He liked it.

"Did I actually find something that makes Casey Grossier bashful?" she teased.

His gaze went to the window, and the back lot beyond. In a second his mood darkened, his attention catching on an ancient orange-trimmed camper van, just pulling across three spaces beside the Dumpster.

"Hang on one sec," he muttered, rising. "I need to talk to somebody."

"Sure you do." Her tone was chiding; she thought he was avoiding discussing his feelings.

"No, I really need to talk to somebody." The van's driver's-side door had popped open, and John Dancer emerged.

Abilene turned in her seat to look. "Not *that* guy?"

Casey snapped his head around. "You know him?"

"He came into the bar once when I was pregnant. He didn't even buy a drink—he just wanted to talk to Raina. He took a look at my belly and said, 'Guess this spot's taken.' Something gross like that."

"One more reason to break his fucking arm," Casey said, sidling out of the booth.

Her eyes widened. "Don't do that. Whoever he is, it's not worth it."

"Not who he is, honey. What he did. I'll be right back. Don't watch."

Casey strode down the diner's aisle and pushed the door

open, setting its bell jingling. As he rounded the building, he shifted his pistol from the small of his back to his front waistband, at his hip, obscured by his jacket. He didn't want to use it, and doubted he'd need to, but Dancer was about as predictable as a feral raccoon.

"Hey," he shouted, marching toward the van. It took a major effort not to glance to the diner's window, to see if Abilene's blue eyes were on the scene.

Dancer turned lazily, clearly no stranger to getting yelled at. He had a lit cigarette in his mouth and wore aviator sunglasses against the bright winter sun. Casey could see himself approaching in the mirrored lenses.

"Grossier. What can I do for you this time?"

"You can hold still while I kick the living shit out of you."

Dancer's eyebrow rose, a dry smile tweaking his lips. "Neither you or your brother ever thanked me for that little favor I did you last summer. Can't say I appreciate the hostility." He turned his back to shut the door, seeming not at all intimidated. The crazy were obnoxiously fearless, Casey thought.

"You tell an ex-con with a shaved head where he could find my bartender?" he demanded.

Dancer took the cigarette from his lips and blew a jet of clove-stinking smoke to the side. "Ah. Well, that's not exactly private information, now, is it? More like small-town gossip."

That was as good as a yes in Casey's book. "You get straight with me right now, or I swear to Christ I'll beat you senseless." Dancer had an inch or two on him but probably weighed twenty pounds less. Whether he could scrap or not, Casey couldn't say, but he was only happy to find out.

"Last time our paths crossed I picked a bullet out of you, Grossier. Patched you up nice. It'd be real ironic if this time you gave me a reason to put one back in you."

Casey eyed Dancer's jacket, one pocket filled with his hand and quite possibly more. He cooled some. In all honesty, he didn't want Abilene seeing a fight, and though he bet Dancer was bluffing, he sure as shit didn't want her seeing him get shot in the thigh, or anyplace worse.

"You got any clue who you were talking to?" Casey demanded.

"Name he gave me was Ware. We had a little business transaction to settle, now he's out. He wasn't a hundred percent pleased with my service, so it seemed prudent to placate the man with a little harmless intel. Customer service and all that." He took a long draw off the cigarette. "And as all your bones appear to be intact, I don't quite gather what your beef is with me."

"A gunrunner, fresh out of prison, comes to you and asks where to find a girl? And it doesn't occur to you to lie and say you got no fucking clue? You got any sense of human decency at all?"

Dancer shrugged and pushed the sunglasses up to his forehead. He exhaled more smoke in Casey's direction. "I don't know the girl. I got no loyalty to the girl. I got no loyalty to anyone who doesn't owe me something I'm hoping they'll live long enough to deliver, so what the fuck do I care about her?"

Casey's blood was pounding in his temples and throat and fists, but he held himself steady. Kept his hands at his sides, well away from the gun. What had he expected, anyhow? An apology? A show of fear? This motherfucker had about two emotions, and neither of them looked a thing like regret.

"I'm feeling real hurt, here, Grossier," Dancer said, brows drawn up in a false show. "I mean, I give you medical attention, out of the kindness of my heart—"

"So my brother would owe you," Casey corrected.

"And I help your little business partner find those pesky old bones and clear his good name." He meant Duncan. And true, Duncan had said he wouldn't have gotten to the bottom of last year's drama without John Dancer's advice. "Now this is my thanks? I share a bit of innocent information—about a girl I got no obligations to, to a man who'd pistol-whip me as soon as ask twice—and I get your ass up in my face, demanding what, exactly? An apology?"

"You got some fucking nerve on you."

"Your girl—your employee, or your fuck, or whatever she is to you—she okay? Did he hurt her?"

Casey didn't reply, fuming inside. Guy had a point. Had something bad happened to Abilene as a result of all this, he'd have more than adequate cause to break Dancer's teeth. But as things seemed to be turning out okay, he'd only look like a psycho if he got violent. He stepped back a pace.

"I'm fucking watching you," he said, jabbing a finger in Dancer's direction.

A smile. "I'll be sure to wear my good panties, then."

"Fuck yourself, Dancer."

"Somebody has to." He turned his attention to his cigarette, killing it with a long suck, then grinding the butt under his heel. That done, he turned his back on Casey and headed to the rear of his van.

Casey returned to the diner fuming. The bells jangled violently, pulling him up short. He cooled himself, hand seeking his lighter in his pocket, fingering the smooth corners, seeking calm. No doubt everyone in here had heard his shout and watched that interaction, and he felt their eyes on him now.

Casey rarely showed his anger. He didn't *feel* angry all that often, in fact, and didn't like the sensation. If an emotion was going to leave him feeling out of control, let it be euphoria or excitement or lust. Shame enveloped him in a breath. His dad had hit Casey and Vince when they'd been little. Not a lot, and never too hard, though there'd been a couple times when their old man's hand had risen, open palm, knuckles out, only to get lowered again with a slow, purposeful effort. Casey shoved his own anger down, resenting this sensation. Resenting anything he found inside himself that painted him as his father's son.

As he walked between the booths and counter, he heard somebody tell their friend, "I really thought he was gonna deck that pervert."

By the time Casey reached Abilene, he was calmer, though he knew his cheeks and nose were red and condemning. He slid in behind the table, shifting his gun around as discreetly as he could.

Abilene's lips were a flat, white line, and she watched him as he sat.

"It's fine," he said. "Just had some things to say." He

doubted she'd heard anything they'd said apart from the first shout.

"What'd he do to you?"

"He's the one who told your ex where to find you. Sort of. Who told him to come after me, anyhow."

"Oh." Her gaze went to the back lot, but Dancer was gone. "That's crummy, but I suppose plenty of people could have done the same. It's not exactly a secret that I work for you. Or that we're close," she added softly, turning to free the baby's head from her tiny hood. "Anybody from Benji's could've told him as much."

"That may be true, but trust me—that asshole still needed telling off."

She shot him a look for the swear.

"Sorry. I'm angry."

"I can tell . . . I've only seen you this angry once before."

He frowned. He didn't ever want her to see him this way. "When?"

"Last fall, when some of the rednecks were giving Duncan a hard time in the bar."

"Oh, right." Casey considered that, a tiny bit relieved. In that sense, he had his dad beat. Tom Grossier would snap if you annoyed him. Casey saved his rage up for when somebody disrespected or threatened his friends.

As that realization dawned, he felt the anger lift for good. And just in time—their food arrived then. He didn't want those emotions here with him. Didn't want them infecting the little bubble that he and Abilene inhabited here and now. He didn't want to be like his old man or like James Ware or any other hard, angry man. He didn't want to be how his brother had been, before Kim had shown up, so emotionally constipated he had to get into fistfights to vent himself. He didn't want to be the kind of man that Fortuity demanded its boys become.

But he also had to admit, it had been way easier this past decade. Way, way easier when you didn't have any commitments, nothing and no one you felt protective enough toward to tap into these macho bullshit lava rivers that flowed in men's bodies, just waiting to erupt when a big enough fissure formed.

Fucking feelings, he thought, registering a rare and uneasy kinship with his brother and father. He turned his focus to his French fries, feeling hard and soft and completely bare-ass naked. Unarmed, even with the barrel of his pistol warm at his back.

Chapter 16

Drama at the diner notwithstanding, that afternoon was the most pleasant and relaxed time Abilene had passed in ages. After a stop at the drugstore, they drove around the county for an hour, taking in the landscape.

Even after only a week of being sequestered, she'd managed to forget how vast this place was. The sky seemed endlessly high, the badlands infinite. Freedom was nearly hers once more—not from the obligations of work and motherhood, but in simple ways. The ability to move as she pleased through town, and soon, the convenience of her own car.

Not that she'd be all that glad for these little trips with Casey to end.

Still, she'd get to work with him at the bar again, the place where their flirtation had blossomed to begin with, and soon after, their friendship. She might look naive, but she wasn't dumb. She knew that every time they messed around, every time they spoke as they had in the car on the way to the diner, she was falling for him. It was dangerous, but so, so easy. More natural than any other crush she'd gotten tangled in. Her curiosity mounted by the day to know exactly what Casey had done to earn his record, and what he'd been up to since then, that he seemed unwilling to come clean about, even to his closest friends. If she was indeed falling, she ought to know. If you fell with your eyes wide-open, you at least knew what was waiting for you at the bottom. And who knew—maybe whatever he'd done hadn't even been all that bad. Something forgivable.

Though in this situation, with Casey having made it perfectly clear that he wasn't available for anything serious, it was more than she could ask of him. Even if she did uncover his past—whether it was nowhere near as bad as she feared, or unspeakably awful—it didn't matter. It wasn't down to her to decide to make this real. He'd told her straight up, it couldn't ever be.

And maybe that's a blessing in itself. It wasn't as though Abilene was eager to share her own secrets. She shivered, watching the sun sink low over the mountains.

"Let's head back," she said. "I'd like to help Christine with dinner."

"Sure." Casey eased them onto the quiet highway's shoulder, then swung east. "Nice to get out for a change?"

"It was perfect. The most relaxed I've felt in weeks."

He smiled, eyes on the road. "I can tell." He faltered on the final word, attention dropping to his lap for a second. Abilene caught it, then—the muffled hum of a buzzing phone.

"Pull over if you need to."

"Nah, it's okay. Your ex has your number now, so it's probably not him. And I'm expecting a call, but it can wait until we're back."

Her thoughts immediately flashed to that conversation he'd had the night they'd first messed around. If *"I told you no—now fuck off"* could be counted as conversation, that was.

"A call from who?" she asked.

"Duncan." Though his answer came just a beat too late for her to believe it, she let it go. But he surprised her.

"Sorry. That was a lie. I'm not waiting on a call from Duncan. But it's weird and personal and too much to explain just now."

"Okay. Thanks for being honest, at least."

He cast her a moment's glance. "Sure. I've been trying to be better about that."

"So have I." It could be way easier to choose lies over the truth, but in the long run, looking back at how she'd handled things with James . . . The truth was scarier in the moment, but that discomfort passed quicker than the anxiety that came with going the coward's route.

"No more lying, no more cussing," Casey said, as they reached downtown Fortuity.

"Pretty ambitious New Year's resolutions."

"More like new *life* resolutions ... You know, before I came home, I had it really good. Or maybe not *good*, but easy. I worked as much as I wanted to, spent all my money on myself, had loads of free time, virtually no obligations."

"Sounds like heaven."

"I thought it was."

She looked at him. "Thought?"

"Yeah. I mean, looking back, what did I really have? Who was I, to anybody? I had casual friendships—people I'd meet for drinks a few times a week, and poker nights and shit. I had girlfriends, but no relationships that were going anyplace. I was living like a twenty-year-old. Like a spoiled one, who didn't even have to work hard to get by. I thought I had it made. Had it all figured out, but then when I moved back, it was kind of a punch in the guts, realizing how easy it was to say good-bye."

"To friends?"

"To friends, and my ex, my apartment, the city. Everything. It's like that life had been one big hotel room, and all I had to do was leave my keys and check out, and it was already halfway forgotten by the time I crossed the state line."

"And so what's changed?"

"Commitments, I guess. Having any, and also realizing I'm capable of keeping them. Responsibilities to the bar, and Duncan. To my brother and my mom. To you, now."

"That's just about over, hopefully."

He answered after a pause, voice softer, a touch nervous. "I hope you don't think I'm just going to back away, now that things with your ex are getting ironed out." He glanced at her.

"I dunno. But you've put your life on hold for us this past week, and even before that, you helped out way more than you could probably afford to, time-wise." She shrugged. The entire conversation had her feeling upended, if pleasantly. She'd never heard him talk this way—so candidly, about such personal things, and for the second time that day.

Something had changed last night, with the sex. She'd felt it herself, and now she could tell it was true for Casey, as well. She worked hard to hide the confusing, warm glow it left her feeling. "I wouldn't blame you at all if we went back to mostly seeing each other at the bar," she said. "You have a new life, like you said. You can't spend all your time trying to help me get mine in order."

"I like helping you," he said with another, more nervous glance. "I like that you rely on me." He nearly mumbled it, then added, "I'm not used to people relying on me. It's how I should have been for my mom, when I was younger, but I was too scared. And it's still scary, but it feels good, too. I don't know that I'd trade it for anything I had in my old life, when I think about it."

"Not even a few hours' sleep?" she teased. Between the bar and his family and her and Mercy, it seemed a wonder he ever got a chance to shower or feed himself. "I bet you're working harder than Miah, these days. New mothers' hours, practically."

"I'll sleep in a week or two, once you and your ex have some kind of routine in place, and he goes a nice long time not fucking anything up."

She let the swear pass. "I'll sleep better myself, then."

The lights of the ranch appeared in the darkening distance. Before them, the first stars peppered the horizon; in the side mirror, the sun had fallen below the tip of the western peaks, painting the sky deep aqua and indigo. She was sad for this ride to end, but eager for the warmth and smells of the kitchen. For the fireplace, later, and for whatever might happen at bedtime. Whatever might happen in her bed, with Casey.

He was glancing at his phone the second he'd slammed his door, and she told him to go ahead and deal with it. Don and Christine were both around, and she felt infinitely safer now, two conversations into her revised relationship with James. She fed the baby, then joined Christine in getting dinner organized. It'd be an hour or more before they actually sat down and ate, and she joined the elder Churches in watching the evening news.

Dinner was pleasant, though Miah was missing, still out finishing his workday. He didn't turn up until late, after his parents had retired upstairs. Abilene and Casey and the snoozing baby were cluttering up the couch in the den, the TV on low.

"Hey. Just me," Miah called after the front door clicked shut.

Abilene returned the greeting as loudly as she dared.

Casey sat up straight, looking bleary, like he'd nodded off. "Miah's back," she told him.

"Oh. Good." He got to his feet with a groan, sounding beat. "Now he's here, I could stand a change of clothes." With James now in the picture and seeming harmless enough, Casey probably didn't need to stick as close to her as he did, but she wasn't complaining. She missed his nearness when he grabbed his duffel and headed for the bathroom.

She looked to the clock on the mantel as Miah appeared in the den. "Wow, it's after eleven. That was one long workday." And he was up by five most mornings. "I hope you get to sleep in tomorrow."

"I don't even know what that means." He gave the baby's head a soft sweep of his fingertips, then sank onto the love seat and propped his socked feet on the thick wooden slab of a coffee table. "And I finished work around seven, actually. I swung by the bar, after. Just for a beer. Where's Case?"

"Changing." And Miah wasn't going to get away with slipping in that little detail about the bar, undetected. Surely it would be Raina and Duncan on duty tonight. She was surprised he'd want to face the two of them, together. Plus he was doing something he rarely did—avoiding eye contact, staring blankly at the television.

"The bar, huh?" she said. "And you're acting kinda funny about it."

He smiled and met her gaze. "It was a funny night. Not funny ha-ha, just . . . weird."

"Because of Raina and Duncan?"

"Sure, a little. Not as bad as it used to be, though. Just weird being out like that."

She noticed his clothes now. Jeans with no holes, and no dust caking the thighs, and a button-up shirt. "Oh. Did you . . . Were you on a date or something?"

He laughed. "No, no. But I *am* a couple years overdue for one, so I figured I ought to start showing my face in town more often."

"Good for you." He wouldn't have much trouble. He was handsome and charming, and rich by local standards. The catch to beat all catches, in Fortuity. "It won't take long, I'm sure."

"You clearly don't know how rusty my flirting game is."

"Did you meet any—" She was cut off by a loud pounding coming from the front door.

Miah was on his feet in a breath, expression hard as he hurried from the room. Casey must have heard the knocking as well; he emerged barefoot from the bathroom, still buckling his belt, and disappeared after Miah.

Alarmed, she hefted the baby, holding her close and straining for clues. There was another knock, cut short by the sound of the door opening.

"Denny." Miah's voice. He sounded surprised.

A woman spoke, but Abilene couldn't hear. Still, if it was somebody Miah knew by name, it couldn't be bad, surely. Far more curious than alarmed now, she carried Mercy past the kitchen to the front hall and stood beside Casey. A young woman about her own age was just inside the door— pretty, with a deep tan and a dark braid. She was dressed oddly, in yoga pants and flip-flops, with a blanket draped around her shoulders.

"There were camera flashes," she said to Miah, with a glance at Abilene and the now-fussing baby.

"Through the bunkhouse window?" he asked, grabbing his boots from under the bench.

"No, a ways off, but bright enough to see. He was taking photos, over by the stables—"

In the distance, three pops—gunshots, unmistakably.

Footsteps came thumping down the front stairs, and a moment later Don Church joined them in the crowded hall, tucking his shirt into his pants like he'd just pulled them on.

"What on earth was that?"

"Gunshots," Miah said, and jogged back toward the kitchen.

"Could be Jason's," the girl named Denny told Don, her face ghostly white now, voice shaky. "Somebody was creeping around near the bunks and stables. Jason and I were in the kitchen. He grabbed his rifle and ran outside, but the guy bolted as soon as the door opened. He chased him, and I ran over here."

"You call the Sheriff's Department?" Don asked.

"No," she said, and let Miah brush past, rifle in hand. "My phone was in my bunk." She disappeared after him out the front door, followed by Don once he'd laced his shoes. Abilene could hear him talking to a 911 dispatcher as his voice faded away. That left her and Casey standing around, staring at each other.

She cut him off when his mouth opened. "Don't go."

His shoulders softened. After a beat he seemed to submit. "Okay."

"Someone's sneaking around again?"

"Yeah, that was one of the ranch hands."

"I figured . . . It isn't James."

Casey shook his head. "Doubtful. Not unless he's a peeping tom as well as an arms dealer. C'mon, let's get back where it's warm." He shut the door and they returned to the den. The fire had cooled to a pink glow and Casey fed the hearth a couple fat logs while Abilene settled once more on the couch. She kept the baby in her lap, feeling uneasy.

"I hope no one got hurt . . . I wonder what on earth it could be about." Not her, she prayed, though it seemed unlikely.

Casey sat on the end of the couch, facing her, hugging his knees. "Maybe a thief. Times are tough, and there's plenty of expensive equipment here. Or maybe some creep with designs on one of the girls."

"'Creep' is an understatement, if they came armed."

"True enough." His gaze softened, settling on the baby.

"I feel like we should be doing something." She bounced Mercy, more to soothe her own nerves than to calm the baby's. There hadn't been any more shots, at least. That was something.

"We stay put, keep the baby safe," he said. "Fill Christine in if she comes down. Fingers crossed she managed to sleep through it."

At that, they both fell quiet for a minute or more, the

crackle of the fire dominating the still room. Her heart slowed a little, as moments passed with no further shots.

"That phone call you got earlier," she said gently, wanting a distraction. "Was it what you'd thought it was?"

"Yeah. I've got a follow-up conversation tomorrow; then after that, it should be all cleared up."

She pursed her lips, then spoke the truth. "I wish you'd tell me what it was about."

Casey sighed, shoulders rising and falling. "I will, once it's all settled. Right now . . . Whatever comes of it, it's going to change things for me. Majorly. I'll tell you once I know if they're going to change for the better or the worse, but before then, I think I'll keep the worrying to myself."

"I'm worried all the same. You make it sound like you're waiting on a cancer diagnosis."

His smile was weak and he didn't meet her eyes, and that only made her fret more. It was crazy how attached she'd grown to this man since last summer, and then in earnest, just this past week. Not dependent, for a change—not attached out of survival, as she'd become with way too many guys. Rather, emotionally tied up.

It was a strange space to be in with a man, caught in the no-man's-land between friends and lovers. Serious lovers. If it weren't for the baby, all she'd need was some minuscule sign that this could be real, and she'd be head over heels for him at the snap of his fingers. In it deep and fast and reckless, as she hadn't been since she'd been fifteen, and mixed up with her very first love. She hadn't fallen for James this way, nor any of the other men between her first love and Casey. Those in-between guys . . . she'd needed them too badly to fall.

Real, giddy love required surrender and trust and a touch of wonder, and such things were luxuries she hadn't been able to afford during her toughest years. Now, though . . .

Even amid the recent drama and the upheaval of new motherhood, even unsure how she'd make ends meet or where she'd live, her heart felt treacherously ready to tumble for this man.

They'd both spaced out, and the sound of the front door opening made Abilene jump. Miah appeared shortly. He looked tired and annoyed. Footsteps followed and his dad stalked through the den, heading toward the office with his phone in his hand, looking too cross for chitchat.

"No luck?" Casey asked Miah.

He shook his head. "Nothing. Jason chased him, but the guy was armed."

Abilene's hand flew to her lips.

"Jason's fine—they were sky shots, he thinks, but he quit following all the same. Said he heard a vehicle start up down the road and take off due west, but that's about it."

"A dark pickup, no doubt," Casey said.

"Got my money on it." Miah sank into the rocker, tilting his head back and sighing his exasperation. "Man, this pisses me off. Got a whole bunkhouse full of spooked hands now, thinking we've got a poacher or a thief or a pervert on the loose."

"Well, you might."

"What about the security cameras?" Abilene asked.

"Dad's checking them now, and there's deputies on the way, to get Denny and Jason's statements, and cruisers headed downtown, to look for the truck. I'm not holding my breath, though."

Casey swore softly.

"Maybe it's personal," Abilene said. "Somebody who has a beef with one of your employees, maybe?"

"Personally, I bet it's a burglar. A bold one. If this asshole's spying on any of the girls, or stalking somebody, why would they be taking pictures of the stables?"

Abilene nodded, feeling a little calmed by that. Burglary was impersonal, at least.

Miah thumped the arms of the rocker with his fists, looking like a man who'd be too keyed up to sleep tonight. "I'm gonna go see if my dad's found anything on the security tapes."

Casey watched him go, looking agitated, then stood himself. "I'll be back. I want to see what the tapes might have to show."

She nodded. "I'll probably get ready for bed." Mercy was already out cold.

"Yeah, you might as well. I think we can safely let our guards down, if only for the night."

She hesitated, unsure if she needed to tell Casey he was welcome to join her, or if it was implied by now. She imagined it was the latter—the condoms he'd bought at the drugstore with her weren't exactly subtle, as signals went.

"You can, um . . . you can join me, if you want," she said. "When you're done down here."

He nodded once, gaze skimming her body in a thoughtless, restless way. "I will. Right after I make sure Miah gets a stiff drink."

"Good idea." She held Mercy to her chest and stood. "See you if I'm not asleep."

Casey stepped close, rested a hand on the baby's back, and leaned in to kiss Abilene. On the lips, not the cheek. She watched him disappear down the hall with a broad grin overtaking those same lips, and the smell of him lingering about her.

Mine, she thought, with a bolt of ferocity she'd forgotten she could feel for anyone other than Mercy. That man was too many things—reliable and mysterious and goofy and a little dangerous; cute one minute, then handsome, then so sexy it made her pulse spike. Loyal and wild, and just a touch sketchy.

A hundred mismatched things, she thought.

And mine. If only in my dreams.

Chapter 17

Upstairs, Abilene laid the dozing baby in her crib, changed into her pajama bottoms and a tee, and settled under the covers, waiting. Perhaps twenty minutes later she heard steps, then water running in the bathroom. She'd left the door ajar, and Casey slipped inside. Finding her awake, his expression changed from pensive to soft in a breath. He smiled faintly and came to sit on the edge of the bed.

"Anything?" she asked.

"Not a lot. It was the same guy Miah chased, though. He recognized his build and his jacket, from the tape. At least that narrows it down to one confirmed white male creeper, and not a whole team of them. After last year's casino drama, this town needs another criminal conspiracy like it needs a drought."

"You get a drink into Miah?"

He shook his head. "He went out to talk with the deputies and his workers."

"Should we be worried? For tonight, I mean?"

"I don't think so. Guy's a coward, and those shots were probably designed to scare Jason off, not to actually hit him."

"That's something, I suppose."

"I'm with Miah—a burglar seems like the most obvious explanation."

"And not a very good burglar," Abilene wagered. "He's been caught twice now."

"Say the word and we'll get you and Mercy out of here."

She considered it. "To where?"

"My place, maybe."

His place ... There was an appeal to that, a dangerous one. He'd begun feeling like more than a friend and boss these past few days, more than a lover, even. Her growing attachment made it unwise, and beyond that, she didn't want to uproot the baby any more than necessary, or give James any reason to doubt the stability of his daughter's situation.

"Let's wait and see what the Sheriff's Department has to say. Maybe they'll catch the guy. I'd hate to put us both through the trouble if it gets resolved."

He nodded. "Whatever you're comfortable with. You gonna be able to sleep tonight?"

With Casey beside her? "Yeah, I think so. If you're sticking around."

Another nod, and something in his expression shifted. It was more than glassy-eyed lust. Something fiercer, and every sweet thing he'd said to her in the car echoed in her memory, warming her through. *I've never been for anybody what I've been for you two.* And no man had ever been for Abilene quite what Casey was becoming.

No doubt she'd wanted this man, each and every time their bodies came together, but tonight felt different. Like a change in the atmosphere.

A change in me, she knew. She felt more for him than she'd felt for a man in years and years, and she hoped he'd feel it right back in the way she welcomed him inside her tonight.

She shivered at the thought, excited. It was chased by a little pang of residual guilt—a by-product of her upbringing— but then, as always, that pang transformed, charging her as Casey joined her under the blanket.

He studied her face and throat. "What do you need tonight?" he whispered. "Comfort, or distraction, or ... ?"

"Both." She drew him close by the collar, and in a breath he was up to speed, exactly the man she needed. His hands were warm on her ribs, and his eyes closed as he brought his mouth to hers. He felt restless and hungry, and in no time his hands were urging her, directing her. He sat up, cross-legged, drawing her onto his lap, hugging her legs around his waist.

It was the deepest kiss of Abilene's life. The hottest, and

the sweetest. She wrapped her arms around his shoulders, hugged their centers together, and still she needed him closer. Needed to feel his strong, warm body on hers, to hear him, smell him. She let her hands roam as they wished, exploring his arms and chest and back.

It had been ages since she'd wanted a man this way. With abandon and ferocity instead of cautious curiosity. Even when she'd seduced James, she'd managed to be passive about it. But she trusted Casey so implicitly, the old role no longer fit. Every other lover she'd had had been like a lion or a wolf or some other skittish beast to be approached with deference, won through submission. But this man . . .

She wanted to be on top of him, just like this. To rub her body against his in whatever ways felt good, and to hell with whether it made her look aggressive or impolite. Sick of playing the helpless little girl part, she wanted to feel like a grown woman for the first time. Wanted to take, instead of be taken.

Casey drew his mouth back, smiling broadly, eyes crinkling. "You're different tonight."

"I feel different."

"I like it," he whispered.

"So do I."

He held her face and kissed her hard.

Her hand found the headboard and she held his shoulder with the other, and began to move. He was hard, and she drew her own excitement against his in tight, needy motions, swallowing his moans as they kissed, until his head dropped back, eyes shut tight. He looked overwhelmed, and his breaths were coming in panting gasps. She'd known sexual power before—a cowardly, manipulative, roundabout sort of power. But nothing like this. She felt as if she were riding a wild animal instead of merely taming one.

"Fuck, honey." His palms held her waist, eyes still shut, lips parted. She traced the lower one with her fingertips, kissed his chin and jaw and throat, his ear.

"Where'd you come from?" he murmured, barely loud enough to hear.

"You make me want things. Want to do things." Not to merely let things happen to her. She didn't know how to tell him what a revelation this was, so she let her body do the talking.

After another minute's friction, he panted, "I'm gonna fucking catch fire. Let's get our clothes off."

She knelt between his legs, plucking at his shirt's snaps. In a few clumsy seconds they got that off, and Casey shed his tee while Abilene worked his belt buckle open. He finished the job, shoving his jeans and shorts away. Abilene ditched her bottoms and shirt and bra, sitting naked before him now. She didn't care about her belly or breasts or stretch marks or any other thing. All that mattered was the gleam in his eyes as he surveyed her bare body—pure awe and lust.

She studied him right back. She'd never *stared* at a man this way, so openly. It had seemed more feminine to steal shy glances. It had seemed more like her, in keeping with that persona she'd hidden behind for so long. But Casey knew better. He'd known she was pregnant by a violent criminal and maintained a crush on her through it all, so it wasn't her more obvious charms that had attracted him. Precisely what it was, she couldn't say, but ditching the shy-girl act was like stripping away more than her clothes. Like that tired old victim costume she'd relied on for way too long lay in tatters on the floor.

So she let her eyes feast, loving every detail of him. His skin was pale, freckles still lingering on his forearms and face, and tinted pink here and there, a blush that went far beyond his cheeks. The hair on his chest and between his legs was golden brown, and he had two moles on his left pec, one on his throat, each the color of toffee. A mauve smudge of a scar marred one thigh—a souvenir from a gunshot wound, though that was all she knew of its origin story.

His cock was hard, flushed dark, the skin of his head gleaming smooth and taut in the light of the reading lamp.

She saved his eyes for last, their blue looking dark, deep. Through all the scrutiny, he lay still, hands on his thighs. His lips were still parted, and his own curious eyes abandoned their exploration to meet hers.

"Thanks," she said.

"For what?"

"For letting me just . . . look at you."

"Thanks for the same. You're beautiful."

She smiled and looked down, shy in a grateful, authentic way. "Thanks."

"You're perfect."

She met his gaze. "So are you."

His hand drifted slowly to cup the base of his cock, caressing the underside in slow, faint strokes. "I want you."

"Anything."

"I want you on top. I like you like this," he added, focus dropping to her breasts, her legs, back up. "All shameless."

She smiled again, blushing. "I like me this way, too."

"Hang on one sec." He moved, sitting at the bed's edge to root through the side table drawer. He took out a box of condoms, drawing his nail along the lid to break the seal. He detached one from a strip and stowed the rest.

"You mind?" he asked, holding out the little square.

She shook her head. Casey got back to where he'd been, legs spread, back against the pillows and headboard. She rolled the rubber onto him slow and careful, the act feeling like foreplay for the first time ever, instead of some awkward, mood-killing necessity.

"I haven't been on top in ages," she whispered, straddling his legs.

"Are you ready? I got lube, too. Or I could use my mouth, whatever you need."

Lube? Did people actually use lube? Abilene never had, ever in her life. Her very first lover had made it clear, if a woman wasn't wet, it was about the worst insult you could deal to a man's ego. James had always done the job with his spit, and she'd found that scandalous—felt ashamed that she'd needed it, but also relieved that he'd bothered to care.

"What?" Casey asked, smiling at whatever upended expression she was wearing.

"That's not . . . Do people do that? Just use that stuff?"

He laughed. "Lube? Yeah, of course. How else do you have sex in a big messy rush?"

She wasn't sure. Sometimes it was just uncomfortable, she'd figured. She'd always blamed herself for those times.

"Have you seriously never used lube?"

"No. Doesn't it . . . I dunno. Hurt your feelings?"

He snorted. "What kind of an asshole has the nerve to get his feelings hurt when he's about to get laid?"

Most of my exes, probably. She supposed it stood to reason, when you played the apologetic, deferring vessel, you attracted men who were content to treat you that way.

"The bottle's in the drawer," Casey said, nodding to the table.

She found it, messed around with the safety seal, recapped it. "How much do you . . ."

Casey took it, squirted a small shining blob on his fingers. She watched with fascination and excitement as he slicked his cock. Crazy. All this time, she'd assumed this was the woman's responsibility.

"Here." He wetted his fingers again and reached down between her legs, gently stroking the cool gel along her lips. Her breath drew short, from both the sensation and the brazenness of it.

Casey laughed softly, capped the bottle and tossed it aside. "Hope you don't think we're cheating somehow," he teased.

Maybe a little, but really, that was her first lover's voice, echoing from the back of her mind. She'd much prefer to listen to Casey's, which seemed to be telling her this was completely normal.

"Lay down a sec," he whispered. She did, and he moved to kneeling, straddling her leg, fingers returning to her sex to trace her now-slick seam with slow, light motions. "Feel all right?"

She nodded, all at once flushed and breathless. She'd never been touched like this, with such patience and reverence and curiosity. Her pleasure wasn't lost on him. He lowered, coming closer, bracing himself on one arm and casting her in a thrilling shadow. She could feel the heat coming off him in waves and memorized the flex of his arm as he touched her, the expression on his face, the promise of his ready cock.

"Could you . . . You know, inside me," she mumbled. A clumsy sort of request, but the fact that she was directing at all was miraculous.

"With my fingers?"

"Yeah."

He gave her two, slow and smooth, and her mouth dropped open.

He studied her face as his fingers worked, lust blazing in those blue eyes. "Tell me what you're thinking about."

"Just about how good that feels."

He added his ring finger, the penetration changing, heightening. His name fell from her lips.

"You want me to make you come?"

And she knew he could. Knew it as a natural fact. But she wasn't ready for this hunger to be over. She wanted to still be feeling all of this as he sank inside her. "Not this way, not yet. I want to feel you, first."

His hand slowed, then withdrew, and he knelt beside her. "C'mon." He urged her to him by the waist. One of his hands was slippery, the detail feeling dirty and exciting and new. She came close to straddle his hips, lifted up, and he held his cock steady as she eased down.

"Oh." The sensation was potent, this way. Obscene and a little intimidating, with her on top, and the friction all smoothed away.

"All right?"

"Yeah." She found the right angle, and with a slow, steady push she was seated tight against him. She could feel him inside, thrumming faintly.

"Christ." He wrapped his arms around her, pulling her close. Her collarbone was at his mouth, and he kissed her there, humming a hungry breath.

"You feel good," she said, starting to move. Her hips felt stiff, out of practice, but the motions were exciting. Something in the way her muscles flexed deepened the sensations inside, doubled them. Casey held those hips. His gaze was nailed between them, right at that explicit point of contact.

"Do whatever feels good," he murmured, sounding hypnotized. "Whatever you want from me."

She'd never come on top, but was eager to experiment. In time she found an angle that brushed her clit against the base of his cock when she eased forward and back, taunting with a tease of hair and the lip of the condom. The friction flared, urged her with a hit of heat and a tightening of her sex. She kept at it, and with each roll of her hips, she felt the pleasure drawing deeper, warmer, more urgent.

Casey moaned. He seemed to have noticed her fixation, and she nearly abandoned it, feeling self-conscious. But he held her hips tighter, locking them into those short, taut little strokes. They couldn't feel like much to him, but her excitement must. And she couldn't deny how good it was, how wild it felt, chasing the mounting pleasure.

Inside her he felt sinful, thick and hard, yet somehow patient, like he could do this forever, just be what she needed. *And isn't he? Isn't he exactly what I need?* In too many ways to ponder without losing track of her emotions.

One of his hands drifted higher, tickling her belly, her ribs, then cupping her breast. It was rough, but not scratchy, and he eased her into the touch, merely holding her first, letting the shock of it dull. In time he drew his palm up and down softly, stiffening her nipple and leaving her breath short. Her eyes closed and she moaned, every ounce of simmering pleasure doubling. Next came his thumb. He didn't tweak—she'd never liked tweaking—but ran it back and forth, back and forth, such perfect friction she felt an orgasm solidifying, growing heavy and hot inside her.

"Casey."

"What do you need?"

"This. Just this." She needed nothing except to keep going, and inside a minute, it came—that scary-hot rush, the desperate crest, the quenching plunge on the other side.

He stroked her cheeks and her hair, smiling as she came down, looking what could only be described as besotted. His complexion gave away his own excitement, his flushed skin not matching his patient, bemused expression.

"Wow," she huffed, slumping bonelessly into him.

"Wow is good. I'll take wow."

"Now show me." She righted herself, energy kicking back up. "Show me what you want."

"Move like you were."

She did, taking him in those tight little motions, on now-achy hips.

"Good. Now make it a little longer."

She lengthened the strokes, claiming nearly the full length of him with each push. He groaned against her shoulder, kissed her there, bit softly, swore. "Just like that. Exactly like that."

She didn't think she'd ever felt this way, taking orders from a guy. She'd been eager to please, or intimidated, or plain old obedient, but never *this*. Never so ... powerful. Her muscles stiffened as she made the strokes a little quicker, a little rougher, and he was panting now, breath huffing like steam at her throat.

"Fuck, please." His hands were on her butt, riding the motions, not rushing them. Not forcing or even urging. He was taking what she gave, and excitedly. *She* excited him. That thought alone had her body racing with his.

His plea heated her skin. "Don't stop."

No chance. This was too thrilling. This moment, like the brightest, hottest current flashing between their bodies. It all built to a frenzied head in a breath, as he clasped her hips and began thrusting himself, driving his cock quick and deep and rough, then finally going utterly still, pinning her to him as his body clenched, released, clenched, and ultimately relaxed.

Their skin was slick, collective breath rushing in the otherwise silent space.

She could smell him, that ripe male smell that tricked her for a moment into thinking it was the height of summer. The height of summer vacation, perhaps, and this the perfect summer fling. All her responsibilities and all the questions surrounding her were gone for that moment, her world reduced to a realm no wider than this mattress.

At length, he coaxed her away. She climbed under the covers while he left the bed to dispose of the condom. She welcomed his body against hers when he returned, and though she was still panting and sweaty now, the chill would find them soon enough, and she held him close.

He kissed her forehead. All she could think was, *That was perfect. That was everything.* Everything, and far more than she'd ever imagined sex could be.

"Hey," he whispered, when neither had uttered a sound in some time. He said that a lot, and the word felt like theirs. A miniature tradition, like how Casey announced, "Red alert," when detecting a diaper situation.

"Hey." She snuggled closer, no matter that his leg hair sort of itched her sweaty thighs, or that her face was probably all flushed and shiny. Everything was perfect, the way it was. She couldn't remember feeling this content. Not in years and years.

Not without drugs, anyhow.

All in all, the sex had probably taken only ten minutes, fifteen at the most. And yet it had been the most intense and indelible encounter she'd ever had. No candles, no music; not even privacy, when you got down to it. She didn't need those things when she had Casey. All the romantic trappings in the world paled next to the feeling of being so free with a man. So accepted, and so cared for.

"You sleepy?" he asked.

"Only a little."

"Tell me about the house, then."

"I'd like a garden," she said. "Like my grandma and my mama had—beds all along the front of the house. Though the flowers here would be different. It's so dry. But red flowers, to match the door and the mailbox."

"Good. Now tell me something about you," he said.

Her nerves prickled, chasing away the peace her body had found in the sex. "What do you mean?"

"Nothing heavy. Something nice. Just tell me something I don't know about you, Abilene Price."

That's not my name, for one. "Like what?"

"Like, what were you like in high school?"

"Well," she said, tiptoeing into the shallow end of a deep, dark pool. "I didn't graduate, so that'll probably tell you something."

"No?"

"No. I only got through my sophomore year. Things got rough after that."

"Okay, but before the rough stuff. What was it like then?"

"I liked school," she said, realizing how true that was. She carried a lot of shame around how her education had concluded, and avoided thinking about it whenever possible. But that was true, she had liked school. And it had liked her.

"I got straight As. I had to try hard for them in algebra and during the physics parts of science class, but the rest was easy. I was on the junior varsity cheer team, too. And I sang in the school choir."

"You sound like the opposite of me," he said, a smile in his voice. "I aced all my math and science classes, but scraped out plenty of Ds in English and history. Mainly because I didn't give a shit, though. I probably could've done way better, but I had, like, fuck-all motivation to try if it wasn't something that interested me."

"Were you a nerd?" she teased.

Casey laughed. "No, probably not. Fortuity shared a school system with four other podunk little towns, and it was pretty bare-bones. No math team, no chess club, none of those Advanced Placement courses. Plus I probably thought I was too cool for that shit, anyhow."

"I was on the debate team for a semester."

"Were you any good?"

"I dunno. At the research part of it, maybe. But honestly, probably not. I didn't like standing up there, arguing with smart people. I mean, I used to think I was pretty smart myself, but I don't like conflict. Not even civilized conflict."

"Do you not think you're smart anymore?" he asked, sounding troubled by that throwaway comment.

"Well, no. Not really. I mean, I'm not dumb or anything, but I've got a tenth-grade education. I was smart for a fifteen-, sixteen-year-old, but mostly because I was a good student. I doubt I've read more than a dozen books in—" She caught herself, about to say, *in the past five years,* which, if Casey was as good at math as he claimed, would've told him she wasn't twenty-four, as most people believed. "Since then," she finished lamely. A dozen books in five years, and at least half of those had been since Mercy had been born. Babies were good for providing sleepless nights and restless brains.

"I could be smart again," she decided aloud. "If I ever had a chance to go back to school."

"Is that what you want?"

"It sounds like a luxury. Like I said, I'd rather have a skill, like hairstyling or something. Getting a bachelor's . . . I don't even know what I'd want to study. If it can't help me pay my rent, and quickly, it sounds too frivolous to imagine. But maybe in a few years, when Mercy is in school herself, I could take some classes. I'd like to learn Spanish again. I was good at Spanish, and it'd be useful around here. How, I'm not sure. Maybe if I ever got some job at the casino or something. Some kind of administrative job." Such a thing sounded pleasant—steady and air-conditioned, with benefits, if not a ton of mental stimulation.

"If you'd ever forgive me," she added, wondering what kind of a future Benji's had, once the Eclipse was up and running. The coming crowds could have them thriving, or the accompanying competition could choke them into oblivion. It was hard to guess.

"You do whatever you need to do," he said. "And pretending the casino's not coming won't make it so. I'm all about exploiting a given situation, so if you decide it's what you want, I'd never tell you not to."

"Your brother would probably say it's disloyal."

"My brother would also say that family comes first," Casey said. "And you have to do what's best for Mercy."

She nodded, mussing her already chaotic hair against the pillow. "I'm trying to, anyhow."

Casey shifted his legs, giving her own a little breathing room; their skin was clammy now, and she turned onto her back, freeing her arms and welcoming the cool, dry air on them. He did the same, and took her hand atop the covers, in the little hammock the blanket made between their hips. He yawned, the sound long and lazy, and telling her this pleasant chat was coming to an end. Before he could nod off, she shared a little more of that truth that had for so long eluded her.

"This was really nice, just now."

"The talking, or what came before it?"

"Both." She hesitated before going on, unsure if it had been exceptional to him or not. What if the best sex of her life was nothing more than a typical encounter for him? He didn't hold back the way she did, after all. Tonight had felt like a deep, dark surrender to her, whereas a man like Casey probably put everything on the table, every single time he went to bed with somebody.

Still, her cowardly days were done. She was sick of hesitating, sick of deferring, sick of holding back her opinions, for fear they were wrong or dumb.

"That was amazing," she whispered.

She heard his head turn on the pillow, felt his eyes on her face without even needing to glance at him.

"You mean that?" he asked.

"Yeah, I do. Not just because ... You know, because I came," she said shyly. "I just felt really connected, I guess. It was ... I don't know what the word is."

"Intense."

She nodded again. "Very." But more. She'd had intense sex before, and it wasn't always a great thing. Sometimes it could feel a little scary. But tonight ... "Intense, but kind of freeing, I guess. I don't think I've ever felt like that, with a guy. Wild, maybe. Not out-of-control wild, just ... Shit, I dunno."

He laughed, possibly to hear her swear, or possibly at the way she was dancing around an eloquent explanation but so completely failing to pin one down.

"Electric," he offered.

She nodded vigorously. "That's a good word." Maybe not precisely the one she was after, but close.

Casey sighed. "Someday, honey, I'm gonna get you alone, I swear to God. In my bed, where we can be as noisy as we want."

She smiled at that. Their hands were clasped limply, and she threaded her fingers with his, squeezing until it nearly hurt, then letting them fall slack.

He kissed her forehead, whispered, "Turn over."

She did, enveloped by his strong arms. Enveloped in so much, it seemed. In feelings so much deeper than she was used to, and so much deeper than she'd ever expected them to get with this man.

I'm falling for him. Falling quick, and hard, and knowing beyond a shadow of a doubt, he had no plans to fall in return. The thought should have had her nervous, had her pulling herself up short, hitting the brakes.

But hearts didn't work that way, did they? And even if this falling could only ever lead to a painful crash, after all this time it felt too good to care.

Chapter 18

Lazy winter light woke Casey a few minutes shy of seven. Beside him, Abilene was snoring faintly, a wheezy hum of a noise he knew well now. He sat up slowly, not wanting to rouse her. Soon enough, she'd wake and no doubt be proud to realize that for the first time, Mercy had slept through a full night. Casey was proud himself, come to think of it.

Neither of them had thought to switch the light off before they'd conked out, and he sat at the edge of the bed for a time, watching Abilene's face. Her mouth was slack, her expression a mix of angelic and drunk. She didn't look dignified, but she looked goddamn adorable.

Last night was different, he thought, remembering it all with a warm flush. Abilene had been different. Fiercer. Needier, in that way that made a man feel a hundred feet tall.

Knock it off with that shit. Whether he was ready for something serious with her, he couldn't say anymore. But one thing was set in stone — he had no business even fantasizing about it until he got those test results.

Saturday morning proved quiet, culminating in a late, drawn-out family breakfast around eleven, once Don and Miah had finished their morning tasks. It was a somber affair, cast in the shadows of the previous night's drama.

"One of the hands found two shell casings this morning," Don said. "Twenty-twos."

"No shortage of those in Fortuity," Casey said.

Miah nodded. "No sign of a dark truck on the roads last night, but the sheriff's going to station patrolmen along the highway for the next few evenings."

"That's something," Abilene offered.

Christine delivered a plate of toast to the center of the table and took a seat. "We've had more than enough excitement for one week. I won't sleep until they catch this jerk. Oh—speaking of jerks, that rep you told me about e-mailed this morning," she added to her husband and son. "You weren't exaggerating when you said it was a hard sell."

Casey tuned out as the topic shifted. He was seated next to Abilene, acutely aware of how close their legs were, and acutely aware of that awareness. He tried to blame his edginess on the stress of those looming DNA results, but some of this agitation had a distinctly pleasurable edge to it.

Ware came by that afternoon to see Abilene and the baby, and it went much like the first time, except they passed the hour in the den, not in privacy. Once he'd left and Casey had made sure Abilene was pleased with how the visit had gone, he shoved a sandwich in his face and headed out.

The sun disappeared behind the hills beside him as he drove toward the highway. Stop one this evening was the grocery store in the next town, and he hurried through the aisles with the cart. He imagined doing this with Mercy in the little seat someday. Would that be fun, or a total pain in the ass? Parenthood struck him as a muddy mix of both those things. Then he realized he'd better save such theorizing for an hour or two from now, once he knew if he had any business contemplating such a commitment. Too much to wrap his head around. Too much to hope for.

The sky was black by the time he got back to Fortuity, and he parked in front of his mom's house and headed up the driveway with a bag of groceries under each arm.

No sign of Vince's bike, but he passed Kim's orange Datsun in the driveway then jogged up the steps to the side door, knocking before he barged in. "It's just me," he called. "I brought food."

It was Nita who appeared from the den, not Kim. "Casey, this is a nice surprise."

"Kim texted me a list this morning." He set the bags on the counter and started unpacking them. "Christine offered to help Abilene so I could swing by."

"And get a break from diaper duty, no doubt." Nita grabbed the yogurt and cold cuts and took them to the fridge.

"I don't mind that stuff." Sure beat the heck out of straining at every little creak and crack in the old farmhouse, expecting imminent disaster. You'd have thought that crap would've ended with Ware now placated. "Where's Vince?"

"Garage. Finishing up Abilene's car, I think. Kim's with him."

"Cool. I need to take a phone call in a few minutes. Mind if I hole up in my old room?"

"Not at all. It's still your house, too, you know."

Maybe, Casey thought as he closed himself in his tiny childhood bedroom. But also not. It was still his single bed under the one window, still his faded Super Bowl XXXIII poster on the door. The walls were still painted bright blue, but he'd moved on. Kim had a load of her things in here now—random furniture and a bunch of photography equipment—and he welcomed the change. He had an uneasy relationship with his childhood. On the whole, it had been happy enough, he supposed, but he'd left it behind. And maybe it was the leaving it behind that he wasn't entirely comfortable with. His dad had taken off when the stress of family life had become too much for him. Casey had taken off when the reality of his mother's decline had become too disturbing to bear. And when he thought hard enough about that parallel, the shame burned, and deep.

He pulled out his phone. Four minutes to six. Four more minutes, and the question that had been haunting him for five years or more would finally be answered. One phone call, and he'd know with more certainty than any vision could offer what his future would look like. Funny how he'd been only too capable of ignoring this shit for all those years, but now that the truth was about to come out, four minutes felt like fucking forever—

Brrrzzzz. His cell vibrated; then the chime kicked in. It took him three full rings before he brought his shaking thumb down and accepted the call.

"Hello?"

"Am I speaking with Casey?" asked a cheerful female voice.

"Yeah, that's me."

"Casey, good evening. This is Carrie Albini, calling from LifeMap. Does this time still work for you?"

"Yeah. Lay it on me."

She laughed politely, and there was typing behind her voice. "Great. So I'm one of the analysts here at LifeMap, and it looks like we're going to be consulting this evening about three different tests—yours and also Deirdre and Vincent. Is that correct?"

"That's right. That's me, my mom, and my brother."

"Great. And I see we've got disclosure waivers all signed and ready to go, so let's dig in. Now, in the mail you're going to receive very, very detailed reports on all three tests, but when a client requests a personal consultation, it usually means they have some specific concerns they'd like to address. Is this correct, in your case?"

"Yeah, it is."

"Okay, great." Man, she sure liked the word *great*. "Where would you like to focus our thirty minutes together, then?"

"Well," he said, sitting on the edge of his old bed, "my mom's, um . . . Her mental health is declining. She's never been diagnosed by a doctor, though."

"Okay, let's take a look." More typing and clicking. "I see here in the APOE allele for her test that, yes, she does carry the gene for non-Alzheimer's dementia."

He nodded, no words coming. Luckily, the woman went on.

"Are you curious to know if you also have this gene?" she prodded gently, voice lilting upward.

"Yeah. I am."

More clicking—easily three hours' worth of clicking, it felt like.

"I have good news for you, Casey. You and your mother do not share that gene."

He froze, eyes glued to a dark patch on the carpet. "We don't?"

"No, you do not."

"How sure are you?"

She laughed. "Ninety-nine-point-many-nines sure. Genetic testing is extremely accurate."

"Dude," he said, and flopped back on his covers. "You have no fucking clue how much of a relief it is to hear that." Such a relief, he felt tears welling in his eyes, snot building in his sinuses. He sat up and wiped his lashes dry.

"I can only imagine," she said.

"And my brother—is he cool, too?"

More typing. "Yes, your brother also doesn't share it. Though of course your chances on that one were a bit less nerve-racking, I'm going to bet."

Casey frowned, confused. It wasn't as though she knew about him getting spells and Vince not. "Why do you say that?"

Silence—a pause deep enough to park a car in.

"Hello?"

"Sorry." *Click click click, tap tap tap.* "You *do* know that you and Vincent don't share a biological mother, correct?"

He stared at the carpet stain, blank. "'Scuse me?"

"Deirdre is not Vincent's mother. Not genetically speaking."

"The *fuck*?"

Another pause. "I take it this is news to you . . . You have the same father of course," she went on quickly, like that even fucking mattered.

Fucking *fuck*, but Casey had always known the two of them couldn't be full-blooded brothers. They didn't look a thing alike. But all this time he'd hoped it was because he must have a different dad, somebody way better than the asshole who'd left them . . .

"I'll be goddamned."

"Would you like to speak with an emotional counselor?" she offered.

"What? Fucking no, I just— Sorry. It's fine. What else can you tell me? Are there any other weird neurological things in my report?" Anything that might explain the visions, if his mother also shared them.

Apparently not. The woman went through a bunch of results with him, but aside from a predisposition for anxiety and depression, Casey's brain tested deceptively normal.

"And of course those are very, very common across the board," the data chick said. "And depression and anxiety are also strongly influenced by environmental factors."

"Sure."

A pause. "Are you all right, Casey?"

"Yeah, I'm cool."

"Well, our thirty minutes are just about up. Have I answered all of your questions?"

"Yeah, I think so."

"Great."

Yeah, fucking great. You just ripped a huge fucking hole through my goddamn family.

"Now, when your reports arrive in the mail, don't be surprised if you feel overwhelmed. A lot of it's very technical, but if you go to our website, we have tools to help you make sense of . . ." She launched into her closing spiel, and Casey tuned out, peering around his room. Staring at the wall he'd shared with Vince, and trying to conceive how it was that they didn't share the *one fucking thing* he'd always trusted they had in common. Their mom. The *one thing* that had bound them together enough to even lure Casey back here in the first place . . .

He mumbled a half-assed thanks and a good-bye when prompted, and ended the call.

"Fuck *me*."

Casey wandered out of his room, numb, and dropped onto one of the kitchen chairs. How in the *fuck* was he supposed to break this to Vince? Tell the guy that he'd spent the past decade watching the heartbreaking mental decline of a woman who wasn't even his real goddamn mother?

No matter how Casey tried to word it, all that came echoing back was a big fat tangle of confusion.

He looked up as Nita entered the kitchen. She'd always been like an aunt to him and Vince—their next-door neighbor and childhood babysitter. She'd also been a way sterner taskmaster than their mom, probably because she'd had the energy to be. Dee Grossier, on the other hand, had seemed forever on the verge of a nervous breakdown after their dad took off. To be fair, Casey and Vince hadn't exactly been the easiest boys to raise. She'd been on a first-name basis with half the nurses in the Elko ER, for Christ's sake.

But Nita Robles was made of sturdier stuff, physically and mentally. She was a deceptively warm, soft, stocky woman, and the glittery blouses she favored belied the thick skin hiding underneath. She'd been left by her husband a few years before Dee had, and they'd bonded over that. In time Casey had come to learn that if he fucked up anything especially bad, it was best to tell Nita first. She'd come down on you hard, but she wouldn't fall to pieces crying like his mom had. Plus she was way better at relaying the news that you'd, say, burned down the neighbor's shed, in a way that wouldn't throw Dee over the edge.

Casey's phone was still in his hand, and he couldn't guess how long he'd been sitting there, shell-shocked. He ought to be over the fucking moon—and he would be, in time. But that shit about his brother . . .

Half brother. Just like you always thought.

"You look like you've seen a ghost," Nita said, uncorking a bottle of red wine at the counter.

"I just talked to the DNA people. The company I sent that test off to."

She froze with a glass in her hand, gaze glued to his face. "Oh?"

He nodded.

She filled the glass nearly to the brim and carried it to the table.

He managed to crack a smile. "You gonna get drunk, Nita?"

"I was going to enjoy a little taste while I watched the news, but I think maybe you could use a bit more than that." She slid it over.

He shook his head and pushed it back. "I got too much to wrap my head around just now."

Nita took a sip, swiveling the glass around by the stem. "I take it the news wasn't good. About you having the dementia gene."

Hearing her say it aloud, Casey snapped out of his stupor, sitting up straight. Of course that was what mattered most. His entire perception of his childhood and his family was fucked way up, but it wasn't the most important news. He wasn't going to go crazy. He had a motherfucking *future*.

"Fuck it," he muttered, and stood. He grabbed a second glass from the cabinet and filled it for himself, sat back down across from her. "Fucking cheers," he said, holding it up.

Looking mystified, she clinked it with hers. "This some kind of gallows humor?"

He took a deep drink, wincing, and shook his head again. "No. No, it was good news. I don't have the markers for dementia. Mom does. I don't. Neither does Vince."

Her shoulders dropped in almighty relief. "Jesus, Casey." She crossed herself, then immediately reached across the table and slapped his arm. "Why didn't you say so? And why do you look so rattled? Actually, wait—let's let the good news sink in first."

A-fucking-men. He tried to absorb this new state of reality with every cell in his brain. *I'm not going crazy. In ten, twenty, thirty years, I'll be the same person I am now.*

What would he have done different, if he'd known this before? He'd first started getting those disturbing episodes when he'd been living in Vegas, counting cards. He'd assumed the visions must be the first indication that he was going nuts, as his mom had. That had been the first sign of her decline, after all—sudden spacey spells, mumbled nonsense.

After that, his priorities had shifted. To make money while having fun had always been his life's main focus, and while card counting had accomplished that on a small scale, there was one thing he found far, far more compelling than gambling, and indeed more compelling than money. And so he'd pursued it, and in the end banked himself more cash than he ever could have in the casinos, working on a team. And fuck that it was felony-level illegal, because if he got caught, he'd suffer, what? Five, ten years of a sentence, maybe, before his brain floated off into the ether. So fuck consequences, fuck the future. Fuck everything outside of doing what fascinated him, and enjoying every cent it brought in.

Except now . . .

Maybe he'd known all along, it was time to get out of that scene. Time to accept that the future did matter—a terrifying, exhilarating relief, nearly too much to process. He'd spent so long living his life as though it were about to end, the possibilities that this news had opened were overwhelming. He could make commitments now, sure, but he had fuck-all clue if he was capable of keeping them, of offering them.

He slowed his racing thoughts, pictured Abilene and the baby. If they were his future, he couldn't say, but he was free to find out. Free to fall in love and have a family, if he was ready for it. Big-ass *if*.

"Mother*fucker*." He couldn't even believe it. Best news of his life. News that he still *had* a life.

"I ought to smack you for the cussing," Nita said, "but I'm too relieved to care."

"Before we get carried away with the celebrating, there was some bad news, along with the good. Unexpected news, at any rate."

"So spill—" She paused when Dee's voice drifted in from the den, needing something or other—the channel changed, a glass of water, the ceiling fan switched on or off. When she wasn't predicting certain doom, her worries were pretty simple. Nita stood and cast Casey a look, one that told him this conversation wasn't over, merely paused.

He found his hand in his pocket, worrying the edges of his lighter. He took out the Zippo, flicked it open and closed. He'd been doing that since he was a kid. It soothed him when he had shit on his mind. The *clink* of the lid popping up, the *snick* of the wheel, the metallic *snap* as he flipped it shut again. Twice he'd had the thing taken to a jeweler to get the hinge replaced. It had seen a lot of worries in the past twenty-plus years.

Nita returned shortly. "Okay, where were we?" As she picked up her glass, her gaze caught on Casey's hand. She frowned. "Let me see that lighter."

Casey hesitated, and she stuck out her open palm. He felt his face heating but passed it to her anyway.

"I remember this. This was your dad's." She turned it around, studying the old-school Harley-Davidson badge on the front. There was a date etched above it by the manufacturer, the same year Casey had been born. "You miss him, still?"

He shrugged and took the lighter back. "I barely remember him—he left two days before my fifth birthday." He'd found that lighter a couple of weeks later, wedged between the cushion and arm of his old man's recliner. His mom hadn't even gotten angry when he'd killed one of the only trees in their yard, trying to set it on fire. She'd just looked at that lighter and held his face to her hip, and she'd cried. She'd said, "I'm mad at him, too." Casey had rediscovered the lighter in the junk drawer not long after, and kept it to himself ever since.

"For what it's worth, I was surprised when he left town," Nita said. "He loved you boys."

Casey frowned. "You think?"

"Oh yes. He bragged about you both. Never within your earshot, but he used to come by to fix my old Pacer—Tom Grossier was the best mechanic in this town," she added, and sipped her wine. "Was and still would be. Anyway, I'd bring him a coffee or a beer, and I'd mention whatever I'd seen you and your brother getting up to in the yard that day, and his face just lit up, every time."

"What'd he say?"

"He always told me exactly how tall Vince was, right down to the half inch—like I didn't see the boy every day with my own eyes. And he was *always* going on about how smart you were."

"Smart?"

"Oh yes. About how you'd invented a new game, or taken something apart to see how it worked."

"Jeez. All I remember is getting yelled at, for breaking stuff."

Her smile turned sad. "Well, fathers can be like that with their sons. They can equate praise with coddling, I think— my own father was like that with my brothers. And Fortuity's not the kind of town a man wants to subject a softhearted child to."

"No, I guess not."

"But come on, Casey. The suspense is killing me. What was the bad news?"

"I, um . . ." He lowered his voice, even knowing his mom would be tuned in one thousand percent to whatever crap was on the TV. "I found out that Vince and I . . . That we don't have the same mother. Our mom isn't *his* mom."

Nita's expression changed, but not as Casey might have expected. There was no puzzlement there, no shock. The realization hit him in an instant. "You *knew*?"

She nodded. "I did, yes."

"Jesus." He'd said it too loud, and she shot him a cautious look. He said it again, more quietly. "You fucking knew, all these years? Since when?"

"Since after I'd known Dee maybe a year or so. She and your dad moved here when Vince was tiny—just a few months old. No one had any reason to suspect she wasn't his natural mother. But then when she was pregnant with you, she told me. You were her first and only biological child, after all. I think she *needed* to tell someone. Everyone assumed she'd already been through childbirth once before. That couldn't have been much fun."

"So who in the fuck is Vince's real mom?"

She shrugged. "I honestly don't know. Dee never talked about her much, except to say she was your father's ex-girlfriend. And she didn't think too highly of her—that's for sure. Though how could she? She loved your brother like a son. He *was* her son. Imagining how another woman could ever give him up was beyond her."

"How the fuck am I supposed to break this to Vince?"

Nita looked cagey, fiddling with the stem of her glass. "Do you think it's even wise to?"

"You think I can just *know* this, just sit on this news, and not tell him?"

Nita studied the tabletop a moment, then met his eyes with her brown ones. "You have to understand a couple things, Casey. Firstly, that your mother loved you both— loved Vince as much as she does you, her own biological son, and even with Tom leaving her the way he did. And she still loves you both, in her way. But secondly you need to understand that Vince loves her, too, in spite of everything that's happened. He's sacrificed a lot to stay here, to take care of her, to provide for her."

Casey felt his legs go leaden at that, guilt catching like an anchor.

"Vince might talk big about how loyal he is to this town, especially with that casino coming down the pike," Nita said, "but he truly committed to Fortuity when he committed to your mom. He accepted that he was stuck here for as long as she lives, and at some point, he must have decided to make the most of it."

And sadly, "making the most of it" in Fortuity amounted to menial jobs or physical labor for most people.

"But that makes it even more fucking unfair," Casey said. And it made him feel like more of a world-class shit than ever, for not having been the one who'd stepped up and stuck around. "That Vince could've gone someplace else, been something more. But he chose to stay here, to take care of a woman who's not even his real mother?" *And if he hadn't, it would've been down to me.* And what scared Casey worst of all was trying to guess if he'd have done as his brother had. Manned up, been the good son. He honestly couldn't say.

"Think about it this way, Casey." Nita took a long drink from her now dwindling glass. "What do you think would've happened to Vince, if he hadn't had your mother tethering him to Fortuity?"

"I dunno. And none of us'll ever know, since he never got the chance to find out."

She smiled sadly. "Your brother's no saint, honey. Even with all these responsibilities, he's been to prison twice, and jail more times than I can count. And that's *with* your mom to worry about."

Casey considered that. "So, what? You think he'd be even worse off if he wasn't stuck caring for her?"

She made a noncommittal face. "No one can say for certain. But if he's been as careless as he has, with the fights and the drinking and the questionably come-by cars, all with a major responsibility on his shoulders . . . I'm just saying, it wouldn't have shocked me if Vince wound up serving a far longer sentence in his life, if it weren't for your mother's decline. I think that loyalty could quite easily have saved his life, in fact. Vince, more than most anyone I know, needs something to be loyal to. Take that away, and I don't care to guess where his life may have gone."

Casey felt sad at that—sad way deep down, enough to ache. He'd never thought too deeply about his brother's motivations. Vince was an open book in most ways, so unapologetic there seemed no reason for him to keep secrets. Casey, on the other hand . . . He was used to serving only his own interests, and he'd done things he wasn't proud of. He kept secrets not only because the truth could get him incarcerated for the rest of his life, but also because he knew in the back of his head, he didn't want decent people—people like Nita or Duncan and especially not Abilene—to know about them. *Though now I've got no choice but to do better.* All his excuses had been obliterated by that one phone call. And more even than he *needed* to start doing better; for the first time in his life, he *wanted* that.

"So you don't think I should tell Vince?" he asked Nita.

"Only you can decide that, Casey. But before you do, ask yourself what there is to be gained from him knowing the truth."

What there was to be gained . . .

It was so fucking tricky, trying to be a good man. He'd have thought that being honest was the simple answer. That the truth was always best. But she had a point.

The truth would bring Vince, what? Pain and confusion, maybe a full-on fucking identity crisis. The knowledge that he'd spent the past decade caring for a woman who wasn't his real mother.

But she cared for him, too. Raised them both the same, the best way she could manage.

And maybe . . . maybe, addled or not, she was entitled to her secrets, too. There was no dignity left to her anymore, no autonomy, no independence. Maybe she deserved to at least hold on to this—the myth that she'd raised a son good enough and loyal enough to stand by her, through every ugly turn her mental health had taken.

Why take that from her? Why taint Vince's own choices and sacrifices by telling him the truth? The truth would only hurt him. Keeping it buried only hurt Casey.

And don't I owe my brother just a little suffering, for how he stepped up when I wouldn't?

"There's a lot to be said for the family you choose," Nita said softly. "You and Vince, you're like my nephews. You're the closest I'll ever have to sons, and I know you know that."

He nodded.

"And the fact that I *chose* to make you two hooligans a part of my life, and to see your mom as my sister, hard as things have been . . . In a way, that means more than the family you're born to, obligated through your blood."

Casey nodded again, lost in thought. Lost in a singular thought—in the knowledge that there was a part of him that very much wanted to be able to point to Mercy, a year or two from now, and tell somebody, *That's my daughter.* Not by blood. By choice.

He took a deep breath, feeling too much. And nowhere near drunk enough, frankly. There was only one question nagging at him, before he could commit to his choice.

"Did she ever try to get in touch?" he asked Nita. "Vince's real mom?"

She shook her head. "I haven't got a clue what became of her. All I really know from your mother is that she was young. Young and unfit. How, I couldn't say, or even whether that was just your mother's opinion. But no, she's never made contact, far as I know."

He sighed, feeling a hundred. "Guess Vince and Raina have even more in common than I'd thought. Wait a second—Vince's real mother wasn't Mexican, was she?"

Nita smiled. "I don't think so."

"Okay. Just making sure Vince and Raina aren't, like, brother and sister or something. Though, thank God they never fucked."

Nita rolled her eyes. "How's Abilene doing, anyhow?"

Casey decided to spare her the finer details of the drama, saying simply, "Things are quieting down." No sense mentioning the other mystery now plaguing the ranch; Nita was probably on track to go to bed happy, knowing Casey wasn't crazy. Let her stay in that space.

"She and the baby are doing good," he added.

"Lucky girl that she's got you at her beck and call."

He blushed, and bright pink to judge by the fever creeping up his neck.

"Oh, Casey—you've not taken up with her, have you?"

"Why would you even think that?"

"Because you're red as a beet."

"We're not . . . anything." Now, there was one heck of a lie—they were about sixty things to each other. "I mean, we're not dating."

Nita blinked dryly. "Oh well, that doesn't leave anything out, now, does it?"

"We're not. And I wouldn't wish me on her, anyhow." If he'd been too selfish to step up for his own mother, what happened if he got serious with Abilene and the going got inevitably hard with insta-fatherhood? Well, then they'd all find out exactly how closely he took after his old man, wouldn't they? And that question scared him about as bad as those unknown test results had.

"What do you mean?" Nita demanded.

"You know me—my love life's always been a fucking

sideshow. Plus all the girls I date wind up being crazy, and Abilene's perfectly normal. So maybe it's just not in the cards."

Her eyebrows rose. "Are all these ex-girlfriends of yours in junior high?"

He frowned. "No, of course not."

"Then you've been dating women, Casey."

"Okay, fine—all the *women* I date wind up being crazy."

"Sounds like the common denominator might be you."

Casey rolled his eyes. Nita smirked, wrecking her snooty poker face. Though actually, when he thought about it . . .

"If I *am* the common denominator, then it stands to reason I'm probably the last thing that girl needs in her life."

"You're not used to being there for people, are you?" she asked. "Not used to being the man a woman sometimes needs, when she's struggling."

"No, and that's exactly my point."

Nita smiled kindly. "You're so unused to it, in fact, it seems you don't even realize that's exactly what you've become."

He blushed again, brain scrambling to figure out if that was true.

"I won't make a big deal of it," she said, "but I'd be remiss not to say I'm proud of you. And how much you've grown, these past few months." With that, Nita looked at her watch, then stood. "I'd better check on your mother."

He eyed the microwave clock. "You just don't want to miss *Wheel of Fortune*."

She laughed. "Well, maybe not." She paused halfway to the door, turned back to him. "Why don't you join us, Casey? If you can spare the time. Vince and Kim are due back any minute."

Seven thirty? He'd miss out on a hot dinner at Three C, but fuck it. Christine had freed him up until nine.

Plus, wonder of wonders, Casey kind of felt like hanging out with his family, just now.

Chapter 19

Miah dragged himself up the porch steps and through the front door close to eight, beat to the bone. His workday had started at six, after staying up until past two dealing with the previous evening's episode with the burglar. And while he'd thought a steer caught up in a length of barbwire fencing—in need of disentangling and a visit from a vet—had promised to be the headache of the day, he'd been wrong.

When the animals caused trouble, that was just the job. But when it was people who showed up, looking to lend you a headache . . .

He'd swung by the house around three, in search of something to appease his growling stomach, just as an unfamiliar luxury SUV had rolled under the arch and into the lot. He'd paused by the front door, already knowing what it would be about, but praying he was wrong.

He hadn't been.

The property scout—a different one than earlier in the week, though no less pushy—never made it past the porch, but he still managed to eat up twenty minutes of Miah's time, hinting at outrageous figures but not producing any until Miah was on the verge of kicking him back down the steps. The man hadn't matched his shiny wheels. He'd been well dressed but greatly overweight, and sweating in a way that no healthy person did, not in February, in one of the driest patches of the country. Miah spent too much time around animals to enjoy the interaction; he could sense nerves in a steer or a dog or a person, and they set him on edge himself. He'd wanted the man gone, and fast, but even forsaking the thinnest veil of courtesy, it hadn't come quick.

"Maybe we ought to take this inside," the man had suggested. Miah had suggested he was perfectly happy with his feet planted right where they were.

How many ways did you need to tell a person you weren't interested? In the end the scout *had* written a number down, all discreet and conspiring, like he was letting Miah in on the deal of the century. And in truth, the number had given him pause. More than Three C was worth—acreage and infrastructure and stock included—and the guy had claimed he worked for a hospitality outfit, interested in turning it into a dude ranch. They'd way overvalued the place, for their purposes. Miah didn't doubt that such a venture could do well, once the casino had tourists paying attention to this quietest corner of the state, but even so. The number had been ludicrous, if all they intended to do was throw up some imitation-rustic luxury cabins and hire horseback-riding instructors. Granted, eighty percent of the land in Nevada was owned by the government, but they could still find a decent chunk of property elsewhere in Brush County and build it all from scratch for a fraction of that price.

Ludicrous or not, no number scrawled on a business card could ever change Miah's answer, nor his dad's, nor his mom's. He didn't even need to consult them. The answer was no, and always would be, no matter how long they stood on the porch.

"That's a shame, Mr. Church. A real shame," the man had said, frustration finally cutting through his cheery magnanimity, reddening his already pink cheeks. "But you hang on to that card. How about that? Maybe run it by your folks?"

"Our answer won't change," Miah had assured him, but tucked the card in his pocket all the same. "Now, if you'll excuse me, I've got work to get on with."

"Of course, of course. But you talk it over with your parents—Donald and Christine, isn't it? And if you decide maybe you'd like to hear more, well my number's right on the card. Morning, noon, or—"

And Miah had stepped inside and closed the door. Not aggressively, but firmly. He half wondered if the guy wouldn't stand there talking to the wood for another twenty minutes. It was no less pointless an endeavor than trying to win any of the Churches over.

The rest of the afternoon had gone to plan, at least. He was behind and much of the day's tasks were physical, and by six he was exhausted and ready for a beer and a chance to put his feet up, except another wrench lobbed itself into the works.

One of the younger hands, Katrina, had found him in the stables. She was crying before he could even hang the coming week's roster on the clipboard's peg, and tears always stopped him in his tracks. Ranch workers weren't soft people, and this girl had never been an exception.

"I have to go away for a while," Kat had told him. "I'm going back to Layton to stay with my parents until somebody catches whoever's been sneaking around at night. I mean, I hope you'd still want me back, after, but I can't stay."

He'd had to take Kat to the bunkhouse kitchen and sit her down with a cold drink and wait for her to calm—another fifteen minutes lost—but he'd gotten to the bottom of it. She'd been stalked by an ex when she was nineteen, and the entire situation with the camera flashes freaked her out, even if everyone thought it was a burglar. Miah couldn't fault that. He made sure it sounded unlikely that this ex could possibly be the one who'd been coming around Three C, and promised her that of course her job would be waiting for her once everything was cleared up. He'd even carried her suitcases out to her car and made sure she had cash for a coffee and gas.

He'd waved as cheerfully as he could manage as she turned out of the back lot, but inside he'd felt miserable. Everything around here was a fucking shambles. Property vultures circling, creeps skulking around. Why couldn't the chaos look like it usually did—brush fire, rustling, maybe a cougar sighting? Hell, he'd even take a listeriosis scare over all this human drama.

And so it wasn't until eight that he found himself done for the day. He normally liked to grab a shower before dinner, but when he stepped inside he could smell that his mother had been busy, and suddenly hygiene could wait. He headed for the kitchen, surprised to find Abilene flitting around, not his mom.

"Heya," he offered, and headed for the fridge, after a beer.

"Hey." She had a mixer in one hand and a big bowl of steaming, boiled potato chunks before her on the counter. The baby was in her rocker beside the table, those wide blue eyes gazing up at a menagerie of colorful, dangling animals.

"My mom put you to work?"

"Sort of. She seemed stressed-out, so I told her I could make dinner. Well, I mean, she'd already had the meat all seasoned and ready to go. I just put it in the oven and peeled some potatoes."

She'd done more than that. There was gravy simmering on the range, and when he peeked in the oven there was a pan of vegetables roasting on the shelf above the beef.

"Smells like heaven," he told her.

"I hope so. Should be ready in about twenty minutes." She glanced at the oven clock. "I hope Casey's back in time."

"Oh right, he's at his mom's place, huh?" Miah twisted his bottle open and took a long drink. Goddamn, beer never tasted so good as when you were ready to collapse.

"Yeah," Abilene said, her voice almost too casual, somehow. "And some other errands, I think."

"You been feeling okay, on your own?"

She nodded. "I'm not worried about James anymore. If I was on my own all night, I might be anxious, but not for any good reason, you know?"

"Wish I could say I did know." Miah took a seat. "But this bull with whoever's been sneaking around has me pretty keyed up myself. One of our hands had to go and stay with her folks until it's resolved. The whole thing's got her real uneasy."

Abilene frowned, dropping chunks of butter in with the potatoes. "I could see that. I mean, the guy was creeping around the bunks, right? And with a camera? Gross."

"No doubt."

"Pardon me," she said. "I'm gonna be noisy for a minute."

Miah scooted down to the end of the bench, watching the fidgeting baby and sipping his beer while Abilene whipped the potatoes. Man, did this kid have tiny feet. And fingers. And finger*nails*. Everything, miniature. He wondered how long it'd be before he found himself with a daughter or son of his own. A few years, at least, but he was starting to believe it would still happen, sooner or later. He was over his ex, finally. When he'd still been mired in that heartache, meeting someone new, someone he could love enough to start a family with ... It had seemed all but impossible.

But time healed all wounds, they said, and he felt ready to move on. *Best way to get over one girl is to get on top of another,* Vince had told him. That wasn't Miah's style. Simply to have a crush on somebody would be a welcome change to his daily life. If only that somebody would turn up. Fortuity didn't exactly draw the bachelorettes in with its promises of gainful employment and exotic nightlife. He might just be grateful for the casino after all, if that was what it took to bring some new blood to town.

His mom walked in just as Abilene finished with the mixer, followed shortly by his dad. No Casey, but around here dinner waited for no man.

Miah told his folks about Kat's departure, and about the property scout. The former was sad news all around, and inconvenient to boot, but the latter ... With a beer cooling his blood and good food in his belly, the whole thing struck him as a touch funny, in retrospect.

"That *much*?" His mom gaped when he passed her the card with the figure on it. "That's even more than the first guy's offer. What's he know about this place that we don't?"

"Sure he knows something," her husband said bitterly. "Probably has some tip about whatever new highway's bound to be coming through or some horse crap like that."

"Even if that was true," Miah said, "it's not like anybody's going to make us rich—not with whatever compensation a road would bring. Not enough to justify that number."

"Maybe somebody's found gold in the creek," Abilene joked.

"They're about a hundred and twenty years past the

trend," Don said, dismissing the idea with his fork. "All we're rich in here is land. Land that we haven't wrecked, unlike some of the so-called modern cattle operations I've seen."

He was getting het up, and his wife shot him a look. "Don."

"Mark my words—this is no dude ranch they want to put in. It's either some slimy insider deal, some highway scheme with a load of slot parlors and service stations and strip joints, or else it's some industrial outfit, after our range. MacPherson's, maybe. I've been hearing rumors that they want to go large-scale grass-fed for years now—"

Miah's mom butted in. "Don, not only is this all beside the point; it's incredibly boring for Abilene to listen to."

Abilene shrugged, seeming amused by the whole thing. "She's right, though. If you're never going to sell, who cares what they're after?"

"True enough," Don said sagely. "True enough. If we ever sell, it'll be from a natural disaster. A complete dry-up or a massive outbreak. A true catastrophe, not just because some sweaty shit from God knows where shows up, waving his boss's wallet around." Too late, he realized he'd sworn, and apologized to their guest.

"I'd love to know what the deal is, though," Miah said, and speared a wedge of carrot. "Can't say I'm not curious, the way they've come on so strong these past couple weeks."

"The casino's starting to look like it'll actually go through," his mom offered. "Have you driven by the foothills lately? The heavy equipment's all come back, plus we got a notice in the mail with a blasting schedule from the Silver State people."

Miah smiled dryly. "I'll hand it to the new contractors— they're more courteous than Virgin River ever was."

His mom nodded. "Or gun-shy, anyhow. And either way—whether they're ethical or just trying to cover their butts—you won't catch me complaining. If there's got to be a casino, this is looking like a vast improvement, so far. No one can argue that."

Miah smiled grimly. "No, I guess not. Though it sure would be nice to wake up and realize the whole damn project was just an awful dream."

*   *   *

Once dinner was over, Christine ushered Abilene from the kitchen, telling her she'd done plenty for one night and to go take it easy while the rest of them dealt with the dishes.

She was only too happy to comply. Mercy had been suspiciously calm all evening, and was now due to boil over at any minute. Sure enough, she went into a fit no sooner than Abilene had started up the steps to the guest wing. It took a good hour to meet all her needs and settle her back down, but at long last she seemed to have wailed herself into exhaustion. Maybe she'd even make it two for two, and sleep through the night again.

Abilene got settled in bed, though she wouldn't sleep herself, yet, not until Casey was back. A glance at the clock beside the reading lamp told her it was ten of ten. If he didn't show by eleven, she'd text him. She didn't want to appear too needy, but at a certain point, worry would kick in. Worry for him, and worry at the prospect of facing a night without him nearby, in case there was another prowler incident.

For now she'd read and try to not fret too much about what could be keeping him out for so long, when all he'd said was that he needed to take a phone call and check on his mother—

She turned at a soft rap on the door.

"Come in."

Casey's voice. "It's only me."

Only. Only the person she wanted to see most in the entire world. "Come in."

She sat up straight, flinging the magazine she'd been browsing under the bed. It was an old copy of *Glamour* that she'd "borrowed" from the pediatrician's office more than a month ago. She'd bring it back next time Mercy had a checkup, but for now, it felt like a lifeline to the outside world. Or actually, no—to the past. To simpler times. She'd had subscriptions to about five of those dumb magazines when she'd been fourteen, fifteen—sent to her grandma's house, since her dad would never have approved of all that makeup and such short skirts. She'd pored over them the way she once had her *Picture Bible*, fantasizing that someday she'd be skinny and fashionable and have a cell phone and kiss boys.

Casey closed the door softly behind him and walked to the crib to peek over the edge. "Hello, beautiful."

"Little Miss Beautiful had a huge meltdown, so now she's out cold. You don't need to whisper."

"You about to steal some sleep yourself?"

She tried to read his expression. There was intensity there, but not lust, she didn't think. "I don't have to."

"Cool if I hang out?"

"Of course." If Abilene had her way, his sleeping in her bed would be the default.

"I heard I missed your home cooking tonight."

"No big deal."

"I would've liked to have been there. You Texas girls can cook."

"The trick is to never drain the fat out of anything," she teased. "Did any of the deputies down the road give you grief on your way back here?"

"I got stopped, but they just checked my ID and called Don, got the go-ahead. Small price to pay for a little peace of mind."

That gave Abilene pause, and she hoped she wouldn't find herself in a similar position. She had no clue if her fake license was good enough to fool an actual cop, and to boot it didn't match the name on her registration. She'd have little choice but to show them her real one, and that name wouldn't ring any bells if they called Don. *Allison Beeman? Never heard of her.*

"Did you have that call you'd mentioned?" She asked it casually, though Casey had implied that whatever the conversation was about, it was miles from trivial.

"Yeah." He joined her on the bed, sitting beside her with his back to the headboard and spreading his legs. He patted the space between them. "C'mere."

She relocated, smiling broadly and glad he couldn't see how goofy she must look. He wasn't wearing a jacket, and his chest warmed her back through their T-shirts.

"So what happened?"

He wrapped his arms around her middle, linking his fingers at her belly. A few days ago, such a thing would've made her self-conscious, but he liked her body, just as it was. She trusted that much.

"This'll be between you and me," he said. "A few people know, but not many."

She laughed, nervous now. "You'd better tell me before I start jumping to wild conclusions."

After a deep breath, he did. "When I was about twenty, my mom started going crazy."

"Okay." She knew the gist of the situation, but not much. She covered his hands with hers, rubbing his knuckles. "Is this to do with her? Like a diagnosis or something?"

"Not exactly. But the backstory is she has some kind of early-onset dementia. She was just starting to get spacey and forgetful around the time I moved away. Now she's pretty much checked out of reality, twenty-four-seven. Spends all her waking hours watching TV."

"That happened to my great-grandma, but not until she was almost ninety. I'm sorry. I know how sad it is."

"Yeah, it is . . . But so a few years ago, I started getting these funny spells myself. I thought they were seizures. Maybe they are; I'm not sure. Anyway. I was worried maybe those episodes were the first sign that I was going to lose my mind, like my mom did."

In a breath, Abilene was worried. Terrified. She held his hands tight, bracing herself.

"She started declining when she was in her early forties," he went on. "The, um . . . One of the reasons I told you I didn't think you and I could be anything serious is because I didn't know if that was happening to me, too. My mom has spells—not as violent as mine, but similar. It seemed likely it was related to her other issues. I was afraid to know for sure what it was all about, because me going crazy seemed like the most obvious explanation. And if I was, it didn't seem fair to get into something with you. Like I'd be making a promise I might not be able to keep, if things ever turned serious."

Jesus, she'd never have guessed his hesitation was down to something so intense. "So what was the phone call about?"

Another deep breath. "I sent DNA samples to a company that does genetic analysis. Mine and my mom's and Vince's. They can look at your genes and tell you if you have the markers for a load of diseases and mental disorders."

She nodded. "I've seen the ads on TV." She'd always thought it sounded like a terrible idea—she worried enough as it was, without knowing what latent illnesses might be scribbled all over her DNA. But in Casey's situation, she could appreciate needing answers.

"The call I had was with an analyst from there," he said.

"And?"

"And my mom has the markers for dementia. No shock."

"And *you*?"

A long, ragged, quaking sigh, and his arms trembled around her waist. Her heart broke in an instant.

"Oh, Casey." She wrapped her hands around his wrists and held on tight, as though that could fix it somehow. "I'm so sorry." For him, and for herself. This was nothing like the theories she'd cooked up, for why he was being cautious about the two of them. So much worse. So much more—

"No," he said through a hitching breath. "No, honey, I'm all right. I don't have what she does."

"What?"

"I'm not going to lose my mind."

"You're not? You're sure?"

"As sure as science can make me. And Vince is fine, too."

"Jesus," she huffed, short of breath, heart racing. She craned her neck to meet his blue eyes and found tears glossing them, a sight she'd never seen before. "You scared the shit out of me."

"Sorry."

"I thought you were upset."

"No, no. I'm just . . . I'm rattled. Relieved, but a little messed up. I've been operating either out of denial, or under the assumption that I was going to go crazy for so long . . . I think I'm in shock."

"It's good news, though. It's all good news, right?"

He nodded—she felt the gesture and heard his relief in the next exhalation he let go. "It's the best fucking news ever."

"I wish you'd told me before, what it was all about."

"No, you don't. You've had enough to worry about."

That was probably fair. But what did all of this mean for them?

"How long have you been worrying about this?"

"For a few years, now—that's when the episodes started. But I blocked it out for most of that time. I can be real good at denial, when it serves me."

Can't we all?

"It was after I came home and saw how bad my mom had gotten . . . Then I was fucking scared to death. Too scared to get the testing done, even. It seemed better to just live in the moment and ignore what might be coming."

"Why'd you change your mind?"

"Partly Duncan. He suggested the testing, last fall. And once we'd gone into business together, it started weighing on me more. I mean, before, my future was nobody's concern except mine. But now I have him counting on me. And my brother, since I've started pitching in, helping with our mom. And . . . and you. You and the baby. You depend on me."

"Well, yeah, I have. But you shouldn't feel like—"

"No. No, I like that you do. Maybe a year ago, the thought of it would've sent me running for the hills, but now, here, actually being that for the two of you . . ." He unlaced his fingers and turned his hands around to take hers. He balled them into fists and squeezed them. "I meant what I said in the car. I like how it feels. Being useful. Or needed."

A hopeful and possibly naive thought occurred to her. "Do you think this is going to change things for you? I mean, do you think that whatever it is you used to do—the shady stuff—do you think maybe you chose that because you figured you had nothing to lose? No future ahead of you, so fewer worries about doing something to mess that future up?"

"No doubt. I've always operated thinking, well, if I'm fucked no matter what I do, I may as well make a load of easy money and enjoy it while I can."

"And this changes that philosophy?" She wanted to hear him say yes. Without knowing what he'd done and how bad it might have been, there was no telling if she'd change her mind about being with him. But hearing him say he'd do things differently now, that his priorities were changing . . . She'd be a liar if she said that wouldn't weaken her hold on her feelings for this man.

"Course it does," Casey said. "The things I've done ... Well, let's just say that the threat of a life sentence is a lot more scary when you know your lucid years could go on for another five decades."

"Life sentence?" she echoed, all at once unnerved. She turned around to face him.

He smiled and smoothed her hair. "I promise you it wasn't anything violent."

"That's something ..." That was a whole heck of a lot, but ... "But that's still scary."

"Never scarier than now that I have a real life ahead of me. Trust me. I'm changing."

What about your feelings for me? Does this change them at all? She'd grown bolder these past few days, more demanding, but she didn't yet dare ask that question aloud.

She wanted to cling to him in the wake of this talk, in any way she could manage. Sex seemed the context least likely to give away exactly how darn attached she'd grown.

"You said you like feeling needed by me," she said.

"More than I'd ever expected I would."

"I'm glad. And I do need you. In more ways than you know." As she stroked her hand down his chest, his eyes widened and his lips parted. She felt a rush at those changes, excitement to watch him transform, the relief on his face tensing to something darker. "It's meant a lot to me, being with you this week. I've gotten back a part of myself I'd almost forgotten about; it's been so long since I've felt these things. Been this way."

He swallowed, looking hazy. "You have no idea how goddamn good that makes me feel, honey."

"You just found out you've got your whole future ahead of you," she whispered. "We should celebrate that. Celebrate life."

"Amen."

And she welcomed his warm weight on her, his knees between hers, his mouth when he kissed her, deep. And when the time came to welcome his cock, she reached for the lube herself, no longer intimidated.

He sank inside with a breathless shudder, looking overcome. She stroked the goose bumps that rose along his arms, marveled at him. She marveled at herself, even, at the hunger in her motions, the abandon she felt with this man. She marveled that sex could be so freeing, so intuitive and natural.

So many times, he'd asked her what she needed, here in this bed. Tonight he wouldn't have to ask. She'd show him with her body, tell him with her words, unbidden.

She stroked his hair, his face, his arms. "You feel good."

He moaned, hips speeding.

"I like that," she whispered. "When you go faster."

"Yeah?"

She smiled, nodded. "I like seeing what I do to you." And someday she wanted to hear it, too, just like he'd said. The two of them, alone, and that voice she loved so much, unbridled.

So tell him so. "I want to know how you'd sound, if we were alone."

"And I wish I could let you hear it."

"Give me a taste. Just quiet, in my ear."

He shifted lower, weight on his forearms, and put his mouth to her temple. His breath alone was enough to tighten her sex around his.

"Wouldn't be quiet at all, if I had my way." He was so close, she could hear his lips and tongue shaping each word.

"Just a taste."

His hips slowed, and that voice dropped as low as she'd ever known it. A dark moan rose and peaked each time he drove deep. Her fingers curled against his back, nails digging, and she hugged her legs tight to his waist.

"You like it fast, though," he whispered, and nipped at her ear, took her a little quicker. He gave her the sound of his breaths, raw and tight, until she was pawing, panting, squirming beneath him.

"You ever touch yourself, honey?"

"Sometimes." She felt that familiar trickle of shame cool her body, melted in a beat by the fire raging between them.

"Do that now," he said. "Let me see. Let me feel you come, with me inside you, just like this."

She'd never done that—never dared to, never imagined it was an option. She'd have thought such a measure would hurt a man's ego, though once again, she'd not counted on Casey Grossier.

"I'll let you see, if you let me watch you," she told him. "Lean back a little."

He gave more than that, planting his knees wide, sitting upright, holding her hips. He let her see everything happening between them, and she feasted her eyes. When her hand slid down her belly to tease her sex, she felt no shame, no embarrassment. Watching his hips roll, his muscles clench, watching his skin, flushed and gleaming in the lamplight . . . she was too full up with lust to leave room for anything else. Too full up with lust to just lie there, in fact.

"I want to be on top."

His parted lips curved to a smile. "Oh, do you?"

"Yeah."

He gathered her in his arms, hauled her up so she was in his lap, then lowered himself, head at the foot of the bed. He bent his knees, seating her tight against him. His hands urged her hips, his gaze locked to her breasts, and she found that same sweet spot as the last time, that friction that made her feel like an animal. She took her pleasure with no self-consciousness, only naked aggression. When she came, she let him see it—whatever was written across her face—let him hear. *Hell, let the whole damn town hear it, and the heavens above.* Nothing that felt this good could possibly be wrong.

He came mere moments after she did, holding her hips still, pumping his own until his back arched and his eyes shut, his teeth clenched. She watched with wonder, drunk off him. When his pleasure finally let him go, he urged her to lie with him, pulling her tight to his panting body, back to chest.

"Jesus," he huffed into her hair.

She grinned, giggled, clasped his wrist at her waist and sighed.

"Good?" he asked, and kissed her shoulder.

"Better than just good. *Fun.*" Not an adjective she was used to assigning to sex.

"Yeah. Yeah, it was. And different. Every time, you're different."

"You make me different," she whispered. "I like it."

They fell silent, and she felt his breath grow slow and steady against her nape, felt his heaving ribs settle into a lulling pulse against her back.

He's right. That was different. Different, even, than it had felt yesterday.

A lot's changed since yesterday. He'd shared something big with her, and his whole life was opened up wide before him.

And there was more, of course. She was falling for him, undeniably. She wanted more than he'd been prepared to offer, and more than she even knew if she was prepared to admit. Not without knowing the darker details of the past he seemed ready to leave behind.

And I have to tell him, before my heart wanders too far off to ever call back. Before Mercy, none of it would have mattered. But before Mercy, Abilene's own best interests had never much mattered to her.

"I have something I need to say to you," she said as their bodies cooled. Neither had spoken in ten minutes or more, and already her voice had gone a little shaky.

He must have noticed, as he moved immediately, sitting up cross-legged beside her. Abilene did the same, pulling the blanket over their laps.

"What is it?"

"I'm nervous," she admitted.

He smiled. "So am I now, but that's okay. You can tell me anything."

She looked to her hands, took a final, deep breath, and leapt. "Well, I, um . . . I like you. You have to know that by now, the way things have been. But what we both decided before, about how it can't be anything serious . . ."

She couldn't read his face, but she knew he was hanging on her every word.

"I don't know if that's still what I want," she admitted. "I think maybe I'm in danger of wanting more. And I think if we keep going like we have been, and sleeping together, I'm going to get myself into a position where I might get my heart broken."

After a long pause, he finally spoke. "Wow. Okay." Was that shock in his voice? Awe? Sheer terror?

"Tell me what you're thinking," she said.

"I'm thinking nobody's ever made me feel half as flattered as you just did," he said, smiling still but looking nervous, too. "But if you're going to be that honest, I better be, too. I don't know what I want. Wait—no, that's not entirely true. I don't know what I'm *capable of*, I guess. Even knowing my mental health is stable, I'm afraid to promise more than I'm used to delivering on. Because it's different, with a baby in the picture."

She nodded. "It is. And I'm not exactly sure what I want, either." She drew her spine up straight and did something she wasn't accustomed to—she made a demand of the man she was sleeping with. "Before I could ever know if what I want from you is a future, I'd have to know what it is you've been up to, since you left Fortuity. What you were doing in Texas."

He swallowed. "I'm not sure I could tell you that."

That brought a frown to her lips. "It was illegal; that much is obvious. And if you don't think you want anything serious, of course you don't need to say. But if you ever thought maybe you did, I'd have to know. I've gotten real good at ignoring red flags, but I can't do that, now that Mercy's here. I thought at first, I just couldn't fall for another man with a criminal record. But you seem like you've changed, like you said, and I'm starting to wonder if maybe I could get past that."

"I have changed. Or I'm starting to. Trying to."

Abilene nodded, feeling hopeful. She'd forgiven James a lot, and he'd hurt people. For all she knew, he may have *killed* people, and if not, she had little doubt that the weapons he ran would have managed the crime by proxy. There was no way Casey was a hit man or a rapist or a sex trafficker or anything truly heinous. He used to care about money, a lot. So a thief, maybe? A counterfeiter? A criminal of some sort, she imagined, but not a violent one. She trusted that. Sensed it. And he couldn't scare her off. Not unless . . .

"It's not about drugs, is it?"

He shook his head. "Nothing to do with drugs."

She sighed inside, relieved beyond measure. That was the only deal breaker she could think of. Anything else he might've been in his old life—scam artist, bank robber, porn star—she assured herself that she could take in stride.

"Okay. Good."

"But it's tricky, honey. If I told you what I've done, you'd have all the information you'd need to get me put away for the rest of my life."

Her bubble promptly burst.

"I can't have you knowing those things."

"You think I'd tell someone?" She couldn't say which hurt worse now, that or the fear of hearing the details. *Do I even know who I've been sleeping with? Who I've let into my life, and my daughter's?*

She did know who Casey was, in some ways. Knew he was kind, funny, patient, caring, passionate. She'd finally done it, it seemed. After years and years of falling for bad boys, she'd found a good man—good in the here and now, if not in his past. A good man who lit her up, and who seemed lit right back. She refused to give up on that dream, not until she knew the ugly truth.

"It's not that I don't trust you," he said. "Not at all. But if you knew, and somebody came investigating me in a few weeks or months or years, that could make you complicit."

"Jesus, Casey. What on earth did you do?"

He smiled his apology, the gesture tired and sad.

"You promised me you didn't hurt anyone."

He shook his head. "Not physically, no. I was a thief, but in exactly what way, I can't tell you. Not yet, anyway."

"Okay." A thief, just as she'd suspected. Her chest loosened, if not completely. "Would you at least tell me what it is you served time for?" She could probably go online and find out, or ask one of his friends, but she wanted to hear it from Casey.

"I did six months, when I was twenty-two," he said, then smirked. "The charge was impersonating an officer."

She blinked. "What?"

"It's a long, ridiculous, blurry story. I was pretty new to Vegas. There was a lot of alcohol involved, and a girl, and me agreeing to pass myself off as a cop to try to keep her friend from getting the real police called on him by a pit boss. I was young and dumb—it didn't occur to me that she was asking me to commit a *felony*. But anyhow, I did my time, and the friend I got busted trying to help, he wound up being my in with all those card-counting folks, so there was that, at least."

Her nerves unknotted. "That doesn't sound *so* terrible."

"Nah, it was just stupid as shit. My first attempted con, you might say. I learned a valuable lesson at least—don't drink on the job."

"Thanks for telling me that much, anyhow . . . I can't pretend I'm not curious if whatever we are to each other goes deeper than I was ready to admit. And if you decide you agree, I want to hear about you. And I have skeletons in my own closet that you'd deserve to know about." She couldn't say whose past should give the other more cause for misgiving, but she was sick of hiding. She was ready to find out, if being with this man was the prize up for grabs.

"I think I'd better head downstairs," Casey said lightly.

Her heart went still between her ribs. "Oh. Okay."

"Miah and his dad are still up," he added, a little too quickly, and stood from the bed. "No need to start rumors."

She sat up and watched as he dressed. "No, I guess not." But she knew Casey well enough to guess that under normal circumstances, the comfort of a warm bed and the haze that followed sex would easily trump any worries about seeming improper. No, he was leaving because he needed distance, space. He was leaving because she'd spooked him. She'd told him she cared; she'd made the beginnings of demands. She'd pried, and she'd scared him away.

"If I wind up on the couch," he said, buckling his belt, "I'll see you tomorrow, okay?"

She nodded. "Sounds good."

With a final, tight smile, he added, "Sleep well," and shut the door behind him.

But she knew already, she'd sleep like absolute shit.

Chapter 20

Casey stirred early—just after five, the DVD player's clock told him. He was wide awake in a breath, like he'd blinked last night and then found himself lying here on the couch, never having slept a wink.

I'm sane. The thought struck with such a bolt that he could've jammed his tongue in a socket. In an instant, every muscle was taught. His vision in the dark room felt more keen, each cell in his body alert. Getting the news had left him shell-shocked—vaguely pleased and relieved, but also reeling. Overnight the disbelief seemed to have burned away, and in its wake he felt alive beyond comprehension.

I'm sane.

And I think maybe I fucked everything up.

He couldn't say how long he'd lain awake after leaving Abilene's room last night, how long he'd stared blankly at that stuffed antelope head, worrying his lighter, feeling lost. Feeling like—no, *knowing*—that he'd messed things up. That what Abilene had had to offer was exactly what he wanted most, deep down, but he'd let the old Casey fuck it up, reverting to outgrown priorities when faced with something that demanded more than he was used to giving. Being with her required commitment and honesty, and trust. And it required him to come clean about how he'd spent the past three or four years of his life, and to admit, even to himself, that he wasn't entirely proud of it.

But the second he'd left those covers, he felt it in his gut—he'd made a mistake. She'd handed him a chance to become that man he'd been wanting to be, and he'd chosen instead to be a fucking coward.

Sure, she scared him a little. So did the baby, and so did airing his dirty laundry. The entire goddamn situation terrified him, but deep down, he didn't fear all that commitment and honesty half as badly as he craved it.

And I can have it.

The test results made those things possible, and maybe that had him scared, too. He'd spent so many years imagining he had no future, finding out he did was an unexpectedly frightening reality. Like his life was the widest, longest expanse, with too many paths, too much possibility. Way too many ways for him to fuck it all up.

He looked to the landing, to the guest bedroom door. *I already did fuck it up.* Two steps into a thousand-mile journey into the unknown, and he'd already made a wrong turn. His heart knew what was best for him, but his fears had led him down the coward's path last night.

I can fix this, still. He wanted her—he couldn't deny it. It'd mean growing up, and real fucking fast, but he'd been working on that for months already. It'd mean telling her about his past, and risk her telling him she'd been wrong, that there was no place for him in her and Mercy's lives.

He shivered at that, pinpointing exactly why he'd run.

Because of what he'd told her, the other night. What he wanted most. To be better than he had been, and to be worthy of people's trust and love. She had the power to grant that wish, and the power to destroy it. He'd never handed a woman such a weapon before. He stared at that door and imagined saying the words.

Be mine. It felt like a prayer. *Listen to my sins, and find it in your heart to forgive them.* A big ask, but their entire connection felt *big*. Rare. Right.

Whether he'd find the balls to say those things aloud, he couldn't guess, and he wouldn't be able to find out for a while yet. He had to head to the bar this morning—he'd offered to take the weekly inventory and let the contractors in for the day, so Duncan could have a morning to himself. Maybe that was best. Maybe he'd find a little courage on the ride.

He parked his bike in front of Benji's right around six thirty, the town feeling quiet aside from the few cars on the road, their drivers surely heading to the quarry or a construction site—guys like Vince, with backbreaking jobs and large thermoses of coffee.

Casey didn't mind a bit of dirty work, but as he unlocked the bar, he knew this was what he was built for. He might be able to do his brother's job, if not as well, but he also knew it was a waste of his skills. He was too social. And, no offense to Vince, too smart. Vince's power was in his body. Casey's was between his ears, even if it might surprise some people to hear that. Working for somebody else, and at a job that provided zero mental stimulation, would turn him bitter inside six months.

He smiled at the vinyl banner strung along the awning that ran above the bar's front door, the one telling passing carnivores that this place was going to be ready to meet their lunch and dinner needs soon. It read GRAND OPENING, EARLY SPRING, and provided the staff fell into place, they were on track to keep that promise.

He flipped the bolt closed behind himself and eyed the jukebox, considering it. Music might make taking stock a little less boring, but the silence was nice, in its own way. He liked the way his footsteps sounded on the floorboards, the random little creaks and groans of the old building as he strode to the office to fetch the inventory list. The front of the bar faced east and the morning light was nice this time of year, silvery and calming. Plus, Sunday or not, the contractors would be in soon enough, filling the place with their sanding or sawing or who knew what else, so he might as well enjoy the peace while he had it.

The workers did indeed arrive shortly, a few minutes after seven. Casey let them in the back door, then returned to his clipboard duties, tallying up every bottle and every bag of chips, every keg in the dusty basement, every lemon, every box of straws. When he next glanced at the clock, it read ten forty—ten twenty in bar time. He grabbed the laptop Duncan had bought for them to handle their accounts on from the office and set himself up at a high top before the windows, enjoying the last few rays before the sun rose to hide beyond the—

He frowned as a truck pulled into the front lot. A black truck. He slid off the stool, waiting with his hands on his hips, watching Ware park in the middle of the near empty lot, climb out, regard Casey's bike for a moment, then aim himself at the door. Casey met him there, already wearing his sternest face. He flipped the bolt and opened the inside door as Ware tugged the screened one open. The both of them stood there for a breath, taking up roughly the same real estate on either side of the threshold.

"Grossier," Ware said, with a little nod.

"You need something?" He wouldn't be rude—this was still his lover's ex, after all, and the father of a child whose history he felt bound to respect. But he wasn't feeling all that friendly yet.

"Saw your bike out front. Can I have a word?" Ware asked. "Ten minutes, maybe?"

Casey stepped aside, holding the door. Letting this guy know whose territory he was entering. He nodded to the table with the computer on it, shutting the thing as they sat down.

"This about Abilene?" Casey asked.

"Not exactly. This is about me. And about business."

Wary, Casey kept his expression stony.

"Sign out front says this place is going to be a barbecue joint in a few weeks' time."

"That's the plan." And the wailing tools and the radio drone coming from beyond the plywood partition ought to confirm it.

"You hire all your cooks yet?"

Casey blinked, surprised. "Why? You looking to be one of them?"

The man shrugged. "I've been all over this fucking county, looking for honest work—Abilene's told me, I don't earn clean money, I don't get to pass any along to her and the kid. There's not a ton of options for guys who're straight out of the pen."

"There's Petroch."

Ware laughed silently, not looking especially amused. "I'm pushing forty. I've got a working back for now, and I'd prefer to keep it working for a couple more decades. And if somebody wants to start me off at fifteen bucks an hour, they sure as shit better not cripple me for it."

Fair enough, Casey thought.

"Don't get me wrong—I'll take it if that's all there is to take. But I want to know all my options."

"You cooked before?"

Ware nodded. "Downstate I did. Both stints."

"I did six months there myself, but I don't remember being treated to any blue-ribbon barbecue."

He shook his head. "No, but I'm a red-blooded American man. I know how to fucking grill. Prison taught me how to cook everything else."

Casey considered it. Prison wasn't known for its cuisine, but what Benji's would be serving—steamed corn, baked beans, potatoes, coleslaw, and the rest of it—wasn't exactly gourmet. It just had to taste good and turn a profit.

"So you need cooks or what?"

They did. They'd been planning on hiring two full-timers and a couple of preps, in addition to two or three waitstaff, but hadn't had a chance to start the search, what with all the drama that had been afoot, partly courtesy of the man currently holding Casey's eye contact from across the table.

"We will. And maybe you're the man for the job. But I got other things to consider here. Like, why Benji's? Why not the diner?"

"They're staffed. So's the truck stop by the off-ramp."

"And it really has nothing to do with the fact that your ex also happens to work here?"

Ware crossed his arms on the tabletop, leaned in, spoke plainly. "I'm not looking to make anybody uncomfortable. I'm not looking to keep an eye on her, or get into her life any deeper than I have to for her to let me see my kid. I just need work, so I can help her take care of that baby, and you're just about the only place in town that's hiring. Trust me—you're not my favorite man in this county. I got no beef with you—you've been good to her, and to the baby, far as I can tell. But I still don't like you."

"I'll live."

"I was hoping it'd be your fancy-pants partner who'd be here when I came knocking, trust me. But I need money, and I need a job. An honest one. If you paid me a fair wage, I'd work hard until I could find something else. All I want is an application. If Abilene's okay with it, and your partner's okay with it, and you're okay with it, great. If not, no big deal."

"That's a lot of ifs." But the guy was being undeniably rational, and calm and civil, and motherfucking humble to boot, and Casey couldn't say the idea was *terrible*. Abilene could use the child support, no doubt, and a fair-minded biological father in Mercy's life. Treat him decent, he might be more inclined to do the same for the girls.

Plus that keeping-an-eye-on-people shit—that went both ways, didn't it? *The enemy you know*, and all that.

"I'll talk to Abilene," Casey said, "and if she's okay with it, I'll talk to my partner. And if he's okay with it, you and me will talk again. Why don't you give me your number?" Casey took out his phone and saved the digits Ware gave him.

"Thanks," the guy said, a touch gruff. Not rude, but a little annoyed. And understandably. Who wanted to come asking after a job from a man he'd only just last week nearly gotten into a fistfight with? Plus, depending on how much Abilene had shared about her current situation, he might already know, or could guess, that she and Casey were sleeping together. That lowered his own hackles some, and he felt a little bad for the guy. After all, Casey knew exactly what Ware was missing out on. A great woman and a great child. At the moment, he was closer to both of them than Ware had been allowed.

"Whatever happens with this place, and a possible job," Casey said, "good luck."

Ware shrugged. "Can't say short-order cook is topping my list of career aspirations, but I'll take whatever comes. Especially around here."

Casey nodded. Had to sting. In Ware's apparently now former field, it sounded like he was a respected and feared commodity, and probably had done well for himself, financially. Before the feds seized whatever they may have. Now, to be looking for a gig slinging barbecue just to make child support happen . . . ? Yeah, he didn't envy that.

Ware stood and slid the chair back under the high top. "Thanks for your time."

"Sure." He walked him to the door.

"Give her my best," Ware added gruffly, his back to Casey, expression surely stony as always.

"I will. Later."

He locked up behind Ware, feeling confused but calm. Hell, he'd been feeling confused about him ever since Miah had said that the old pickup now swinging out onto the street wasn't the one from the night of the first creeper incident.

Ware seemed okay. Cold, maybe, but not sneaky. He might be a criminal, or a recovering one, but at least he was an open book about it. More than Casey could claim to be. Plus, the guy was broke, had found out he had a child out there in the world and an ex who'd been more than happy to avoid him, yet he was determined to see the both of them, determined to pitch in. He could easily have disappeared from Abilene's rearview for good, saved himself the stress and the money, but he hadn't. That was something. That was a lot. He might not be Father of the Year, but that baby could do way worse, all things considered.

He could have just taken off. Taken off, as Casey had last night, the moment things got serious. Could have taken off like Tom Grossier did, only he hadn't. Hell, he was fighting to make himself a place in his child's life, *humbling* himself for the chance, changing. Going straight, because he knew the payoff was worth it.

Last night was my chance to do the same. Casey's chance to finally prove to himself he could set his precious freedom aside for once and embrace something worth committing to. It wasn't as though freedom had ever made him happy, after all. It had lined his wallet, perhaps, but what was that worth, when you had nobody you loved to share the money with? Nobody to support or help out or treat? And he wanted to do all those things for Abilene, yet the moment she'd opened that door, he'd slinked off in the other direction.

Ware humbled himself, he thought. And he admired the man for it.

I could do the same. It wasn't too late. He could admit he'd messed up, try to make this right. He had a chance to be the man he'd been wanting to become these last few months, quit running away from chances to grow up, and finally go running toward one.

He could, and he would.

He wasn't going to fuck it up twice.

Chapter 21

Abilene passed a listless morning, nearly grateful that Mercy was fussing up a storm at every turn. It took her mind off her own discontent, whenever she had a spare second to remember how she and Casey had parted last night.

I told him how I felt, and he bolted. The old Abilene would have beat herself up over that, blamed herself for scaring a man away. The new Abilene would count it as a blessing, she imagined, because she had no room in her life for a guy who wasn't ready to be what she needed. She couldn't say that was much consolation, given how disappointed she felt, but she made it a goal to try to get there, mentally, in time.

It was nearly one before Casey got back to the farmhouse—and nearly the end of Abilene's patience, which had been fraying steadily under the weight of her hurt feelings.

"There you are," she said when he found her in the den, bouncing a red-faced and deeply annoyed infant.

"Here I am. And yikes. Somebody woke up on the wrong side, huh?"

She's not the only one.

"Want me to try anything?" he asked.

"Knock yourself out. She's clean and fed and burped, and she slept almost nine hours straight through."

"Well, that's probably the issue, now, isn't it?" Casey asked the sputtering, seething baby as he lifted her from Abilene's arms. "You're much too well balanced, aren't you? No outlet for your tiny well of rage."

"Something like that." Abilene watched with mingled

frustration and awe as Mercy quieted in seconds, face going placid, blue eyes glued to Casey's.

"Show off," she grumbled, though she was grateful for the quiet.

"That's better, huh? How about I put you in your rocker?" He laid the baby in her seat, and Abilene held her breath, waiting to see if she started up again. Wonder of wonders, she looked as calm as could be.

"Hallelujah." She dropped her head against the couch's back.

"Your ex came by the bar while I was taking stock," Casey said, sitting on the next cushion.

Her head snapped right back up. "He did?"

"Don't worry—it was fine. He was after a job, actually."

She blinked. "Really? What, bartending?"

"No, cooking, once the restaurant opens."

"Oh. He did a lot of that in prison."

"Said he valued his spinal health over a paycheck from the quarry, and I can't say I blame him."

"So you said yes?"

"No, no. I told him I'd talk to Duncan and to you. If all three of us are comfortable with the idea, we'll consider him."

"I don't think I'd mind," she said, mulling. "It might be awkward, is all." But probably not terribly. James wasn't possessive or jealous. Not once an affair was over. You were either all in with him, or else you got the typical frosty reception he reserved for strangers and acquaintances. Only if you were his lover—or his enemy, or indeed his child, she imagined—did he bother getting wound up about you.

"It wouldn't be for a few weeks still," Casey said, "if it did even happen. Plenty of time to see how the two of you are getting along."

She nodded. "It's good to hear he's looking for legal work, at any rate." He seemed to be respecting her rule.

"I'll talk to Duncan then, see what he thinks." He rubbed his thighs, then met her eyes with caution in his own. "So, what are you doing this afternoon?"

"Just this," she said, nodding to the baby.

His lips thinned to a pensive line. "Hang on a sec." He stood and strode off in the direction of the office, and

Abilene heard knocking, then faint talking. He was back inside a minute and lifting the rocker.

"What are you up to?"

"Christine's going to watch Mercy for an hour or two. You and I have something we need to do."

If not for last night's talk, she'd have assumed he meant sex—men rarely moved with such purpose if they weren't about to get lucky. "What?"

"We need to talk," he said simply, disappearing down the hall with the baby.

"About?"

Casey either didn't hear or didn't care to reply. When he returned he was patting his pockets, pulling out his keys. He eyed her clothes. "Grab a sweater and jacket and your mittens. We're going for a little ride."

She was tempted to resist, but in the end, the baby was fed and in good hands, and she was more curious about what he needed to say than she was stubborn about last night.

Once she'd changed, she met him by the front door and they got their shoes on.

"Safety first," Casey said, and handed her Raina's helmet. She strapped it on as they headed for his bike.

"Where are we going?"

"To the place I always went to when I needed to get my head on straight about shit."

"Which is?"

"You'll see." He mounted the Harley and she got on behind him.

He rode them west, toward town, and then straight through it—all the way down Station Street, across the train tracks. He took a left on Railroad Avenue, passing the motel, then onto the quiet route that ran beside the foothills. Maybe a mile out of town, he eased them to a stop on the shoulder and climbed off.

Abilene did the same, unsure why this spot was significant to him. All she saw was a load of scrub brush and sage, a whole lot of desolate badlands to the east, and rising red rock to the west.

"Follow me." Casey headed toward the hills.

"This is where you come to think?" she asked, following his path between the boulders and brush.

"Just trust me."

She did, even as this mystery excursion had her scratching her head. They hiked for five or ten minutes up into the hills, until she was short of breath and warm enough to unzip her jacket and fist her mittens.

"Just about there," he said, kicking his way through a tangle of brush.

At long last, they stopped, and she followed his lead when he turned and sat on a flat outcropping, facing east.

"Okay. I see it now." She took it in—the whole of Fortuity was laid out before them, all the way out to Three C and the open range beyond. She oriented herself by the church in the center of town, finding Benji's and the diner, even the house she'd rented a room at, a little ways south.

"I haven't been up here in over ten years," Casey said, squinting against the sun, studying the landscape. "This is where I'd go in high school to smoke weed and think deep, philosophical thoughts. It's where I was sitting when I decided to leave town."

"Oh."

"It's funny . . . When I made that decision, a decade ago, now, this view seemed like everything I needed to know. Like I was looking at the future—at my hometown, the place I'd get stuck in forever if I didn't escape. It looks different now."

"How?"

"Lots of ways. I think before, I looked at this place and I thought about what kind of a life I could have, and all I saw was my dad's legacy. Or lack thereof. I think I thought, if I don't get out of here, I'm gonna be nothing. I'm gonna wind up working at the quarry, like every other nobody." He waved his arm south. "I'm gonna live in some little house, a few blocks from where I grew up, and in fifty years I'm gonna die and wind up in that graveyard." He flicked a hand to the northeast.

"And what do you see now?"

"I see memories now. I see the garage, and all the streets I drove down, the creek where we used to swim. I see Big Rock, where I kissed a girl for the first time when I was fourteen. And the train tracks that I followed when I tried to run away and find my dad when I was six. And I see the future, too. I see the bar I was barely old enough to drink at when I left town, and now it's mine."

She nodded. "That's all very nice, but what did you bring me here to talk about?"

He took a deep breath, let it out slow, and laced his fingers between his knees. When he turned, she did the same.

What precisely was charging those blue eyes, she wondered? Something beyond nerves. Waiting as he assembled his thoughts was torture, the longest half a minute in her life. "Casey?"

He huffed a heavy breath.

"I messed up last night. You told me you were starting to feel something, starting to wonder if we might be something serious, maybe, someday. And I let you think I didn't want that."

"Oh." Her chest felt funny and she resisted an urge to rub at her heart.

"I got scared, and that was lame."

"Scared of what?"

"Of coming clean, partly. About my past. And scared of what it all meant—commitment, stepping up. Like, all the fucking way up, when a part of me is terrified if I tried, I'd only find out I was just like my dad. Like I'd let you guys down in the end. Like I'd realize I couldn't cut it, and run out on you and the baby, and on my family and on Duncan."

"I can't imagine you doing that."

"Well, you haven't known me all that long. I'm a better man now, since I've come home, a better man than I have been for a long, long time. Maybe ever."

She could say the same about herself, she realized. It had taken Mercy for her to get her act together. Now a year clean, she could look back and realize that the reason she'd gotten addicted to heroin was that she'd woken up each morning and felt nothing. She'd had no reason to get up, nothing in her life worth being awake for. The chemical blank had felt better than all those waking hours of pointlessness. But Mercy had changed all that. There was a focus to her life, a reason to do better, to be better.

"You remember when you asked me what it is I want most?" Casey murmured. "And how I said I didn't really know yet? Well, I still don't, but I'm starting to. And it's because of everything that's come into my life these past few months. All the responsibilities, even the ones that scare me. It's feeling like I'm finally becoming a man, and you guys are no small part of that. I want whatever this feeling is that it's been giving me. Worthiness, maybe."

"I know *exactly* what you mean."

"I want to be worthy of people's respect, and faith, and love, maybe. That's what I want most now."

"Those are wonderful things to want."

"Way fucking better than money—that's for sure . . . I don't have everything all figured out," he said softly, his breath finally coming smooth and even. "And I'm still scared. Fucking petrified. But I knew the second I shut your door behind me last night, I'd made a mistake. I'm so scared of becoming my dad, but that's exactly what I did. I left the second you asked something of me that I was afraid I couldn't give. But I want to take that back, if you'll let me."

And would she? She nearly could, but not yet. "There's a lot I don't know about you, and plenty you don't know about me, either." The former no longer frightened her, but what he might make of her own past still did.

"Of course. And I don't know if I can be what you need. If I can be something for you that I've never been able to be for anyone before, and even though I don't know if it's enough . . . I know I'm thirty-three so maybe this sounds really pathetic, but I feel like a man, for the first time," he said, speaking to her hands or her knees. "Like a grown-ass man who can protect somebody, and take care of them, and cheer them up and crap like that. No woman's ever made me feel like that. Like you look at me sometimes and suddenly I'm eight feet tall, and that you think I can do anything." He paused just long enough to take her hand in his. "It makes me want to be better. And to do good. Makes me feel about a thousand things, all stuffed inside my chest, and in my head, and hell, in my dick probably, too. Like, everything, everywhere. I can't promise forever, or even that I won't fuck everything up, but I'd like a chance to try. If you wanted to give me one, that is. If you're ready to swap some skeletons."

She was already crying, and she stole her hand back to wipe at her cheeks.

Her entire life, she was coming to realize, she'd only ever wanted to be wanted. She'd wanted a father's love and a mother's protection, and in the end she'd run off in search of those things in all the wrong places. And now she wanted Casey, so bad it nearly hurt. So, so much rode on how he took her confession.

Casey had never been into her because he'd thought she was some innocent—the whole knocked-up-by-a-felon thing ruled that out. At the end of the day, this man had surely made his share of reckless, dumb decisions. Drug addiction and a sex scandal . . . He could handle that, couldn't he? He'd heard and maybe seen worse in his life.

Abilene steeled herself, took his hand again, and committed anew to face up to the thing she'd been running from for years now. The truth. The truth about who she was, and how she'd come to be here, now, with this particular man holding her hand.

"I'll go first," he offered.

She nodded. "I'm ready. I want to hear." *And I'm ready to talk.*

"Guess I'll start at the beginning." He kept his gaze on their linked fingers. "I was pretty much a normal kid, growing up around here. I shoplifted, and probably drank too much in high school, but nothing that your average small-town punk kid doesn't get up to. It wasn't until I moved away that I went a bit more rotten."

"Rotten?" Something about that word filled her with sharp misgiving. *But he said already, he wasn't violent. He never hurt anybody.* She prayed for the best, forcing deep and steady breaths as he went on.

"You know I was a card counter," he said. "That's no secret. And I did some grifting shit, too, during that time. Con jobs with some of the people I counted with—tricking people into parting with a few thousand bucks here and there."

"What sorts of people? Not, like, the elderly or . . . ?"

He shook his head, and her heart unwound by a measure. "No, nothing like that. We made decent money, and the cons were strictly for sport. We targeted the most obnoxious blowhards we met at the blackjack tables, typically."

"Okay." While not admirable, it certainly beat preying on the desperate.

"I never loved those cons the way I did the counting. Like I said the other night, I've always been good at math. I like numbers; I like science. The conning was a rush, but it never clicked for me the way the counting had. Not until I found a way to make it about what excites me."

"And what excites you, then?"

His smile was shy, or maybe guilty, and his gaze moved to the far horizon. "Fire."

She frowned, confused. "Fire?"

"Yeah. I was a borderline pyro when I was a kid. I know lots of boys are, but that shit just *fascinated* me. Always has. Most kids, they grow out of it by puberty, but for me, the romance never stopped."

The romance. She knew what he meant, as he said it. His eyes changed when he stared at the hearth at night, transfixed, sometimes, the way somebody on drugs could fixate on a pattern or texture or a dripping tap for minutes and minutes and minutes. She shivered.

She'd thought she could handle this, but all at once, she wasn't so sure. She'd thought that as long as he hadn't hurt anybody, physically, she could forgive him. Hell, she'd forgiven James. Then again, the woman she was now, with a daughter in her life, a future to consider, would *never* take up with James Ware. She'd changed so much from that girl he'd met in that trailer last Christmas, she was unrecognizable. Literally, and in every other way. And she felt colder with every word that came out of Casey's mouth, her blood growing icy with dread and worry.

Conning people. Not hurting them physically, but still hurting them. And on purpose. Sitting down and thinking up ways to hurt strangers. Abilene had hurt her fair share of people over the years, good ones and bad ones, but never on purpose. Never without regret. And she didn't hear regret in Casey's voice.

Those deeper thoughts scared her, so she turned to logistical ones. "What's fire have to do with conning people?"

"Everything, in my old business. I've probably read every book there is about the physics and chemistry of it, anything and everything about friction and accelerants, explosives, how it all behaves—just for fun. Basically turned myself into an armchair fire forensics expert. When I was in Vegas, if any fire made the news that was suspected to be arson, if I could I'd try to sneak onto the scene, afterward. Study the burn patterns, all that stuff."

"Okay . . ."

"Anyhow, that's always been a part of me. Always the thing that got me juiced like nothing else could—" He paused, looking up, catching her expression. Worry and unease had to be written all over her face. "You all right?"

"You're not going to confess that you went to work for the FBI, using your powers for good, are you?"

His smile was pure apology. "Sorry, honey. I liked money back then, as much as fire. And good doesn't pay all that well."

She nodded, and, feeling cold, she took her hand back and locked her arms around her middle.

"This is my confession, remember?" he said gently. "It was never going to be a happy surprise."

"I know. Go on."

"So, over time, hanging with all those card-counters and dabbling in those con jobs, I got involved with some folks who were into insurance fraud."

Fraud. Okay, that didn't sound *too* terrible, she thought, trying to quell the nausea.

"There's this whole criminal sector," he said, "to do with insurance. Guy takes out a big policy on his house or his boat or his business; then the place burns to the ground, he gets his fat payout."

"On purpose. Like, he sets the fire himself."

"Exactly. The thing is, arson's real hard to do right. It leaves a million fingerprints—in the chemical residue, the burn patterns, loads of little tells. You can't just splash some gasoline, light a match, then tell the investigators it must've been some faulty wiring. Dumb-asses try that shit all the time, and all of them get busted."

Her heart had gone from racing to plodding at some point, and as the truth began to gel, her body went cold, cold, cold. "So you did that yourself? Bought places only to destroy them and get insurance money?"

He shook his head. "No, I contracted. People hired me to

start fires *for them*. Then in exchange, I got a hefty cut of the settlement."

"But . . . I mean, what people? And where are you setting fires? In houses?"

"Some, but mostly commercial spaces. Most of my clients—"

"Clients?" That word sounded so, so . . . businesslike. So prim, or something. Something vulgar in its propriety.

He nodded. "Most of my clients were business owners on the brink of bankruptcy, or else they'd cooked their books or otherwise fucked themselves into a corner, and needed quick cash and a way out. I go in, I set up a scene—finesse some wiring, or maybe it's a faulty space heater, left on too close to a trash can full of paper. Maybe it's industrial—the right rags soaked in the exact sorts of chemicals you'd expect to find in whatever place of business it was, too close to a heating duct that's got too much dust built up in it. Whatever accident fits the scene."

"Accident," she repeated.

"Seeming accident, yeah. The key is to design the fire to burn through quick." He sounded excited now, talking faster, gesturing like he was recounting a boxing match. "You leave the right windows open in the right sort of weather, keep others closed, control the spread. Make sure the building goes down quick, ideally before the authorities can even arrive."

"The firefighters."

Casey nodded.

Her stomach turned all the way over, three hundred sixty degrees. "My grampa was a firefighter, and my uncle."

Casey sat up straighter, snapping out of his animated state in a blink. "Oh, honey—don't worry. Nobody ever got hurt by any fire I set. I was careful."

"Because you didn't want to get caught," she inferred. Anger was simmering now, melting some of the ice in her veins. Anger was her least favorite emotion, the one she avoided at all costs. But just now, trying to square the look in Casey's eyes with the facts he was telling her . . . She was pissed, yeah. "Only because if you *did* get caught, and somebody *had* gotten hurt, you'd probably be in way more trouble."

"Yes, because of that. But because I didn't want to hurt

anybody, period. We were careful. We made sure no other buildings were in danger of going up. We made sure there were no people around, no pets in the buildings. Hell, I did industrial jobs where we had to make sure we weren't going to release a load of toxic smoke too close to a residential neighborhood. We were careful," he repeated. "If anybody suffered, it was the multibillion-dollar insurance industry, and they're a load of cons themselves."

"But somebody *could* have," she said. "A firefighter could've been hurt or killed, responding to what you did. They could've gotten trapped and died, had a ceiling collapse on them, or . . ." She was about panting now, feeling suffocated. "I can't help but imagine it was my grampa or my uncle Hal who was in there. What could've happened to them."

"Don't picture a fire like you see on TV. We accepted these jobs because they were ripe for it. Remote, or out in industrial areas, dead after dark."

"But you couldn't know that something wouldn't go wrong. That somebody wouldn't get hurt. This was in Texas. You could've started a wildfire."

His smile was weak, and definitely guilty now. "No, I suppose you can't ever know for sure. All I know is that it all worked out. Every single job."

She felt hot all over, agitated and verging on out of control. She hated this feeling. This feeling had made an addict out of her, made her want to feel nothing, rather than sit in the discomfort of her own emotions. She focused on other questions, to keep in control of herself.

"Who's we? Who did you work with?"

"Small teams. Very small. I did the research and all the planning and set the fires. I worked with one of two drivers, who got me and the materials in and out, and monitored the police scanner. And then another one of us was in charge of brokering the deals—finding the jobs, setting the terms, working with me to pick the right time for it to all go down. Three people per job, just four of us, total, that I ever worked with. Though the woman who did the brokering, she worked with more teams than just the one I was on."

"Woman?" Why was that so especially disconcerting? *Because we're raised to be kind. To care about people and want to keep them safe.* Raised to defer and be good and please others. Especially men. Though where exactly had those values landed Abilene, anyhow?

Casey nodded. "Yeah, she's a woman. My partner."

"How long did you work together?"

"A little over three years."

"When was the last . . . job you did?" *Job.* That word tasted sarcastic on her tongue. Sour.

"End of June, last year."

"And what was it? Where, and what kind of a building or whatever?"

Another apologetic smile. "I can't tell you that. That's beyond just my own business. But I can tell you that nobody got hurt, and the client got paid. So did we. I used a lot of that money to buy into Benji's with Duncan, and some I gave to Vince, to help with our mother."

She froze. So her wages were paid in dirty money. Jesus, she'd thought she'd moved past all this when she'd put her foot down with James, told him he had to go straight. But all this time, every bag of groceries Casey had brought her, every check she'd let him pay in the diner . . . Every single one of those dollars could've left somebody dead. Somebody who'd dedicated their own life to helping others, at their own risk.

Christ, she had fuck-all clue what to do with *any* of this.

"Say something," Casey prompted after a minute's silence. "You're making me nervous."

"You . . . But all of this is over, right?"

"Yeah, I'd say so."

Her eyes widened. "You'd *say so*?" She'd heard him on the phone with someone, that night when they'd first kissed. His so-called partner, maybe. He'd told that person to fuck off, in no uncertain terms.

"I'd been on the fence about one final job, but I never agreed to it. So yes, it's over."

"You said you'd gone straight." Hadn't he? Or had she merely assumed? "You said you wanted to be a better man, from now on." *Because of me. Because of us.*

"The bar's nearly cleaned me out. I can pay my rent, keep food in the fridge and gas in my car, but there's other things I need a little padding for. One night's work, thirty thousand bucks. There's a lot of good I can do with that kind of money."

"But the money itself is *bad*," she spat, catching how hysterical she now sounded, and not caring. "And the bar is full of that same bad money." How on earth could it possibly succeed, when it was built on a pile of dirty cash? "Does Duncan know about all this? About how you made the money you used to go into business with him?"

Casey shook his head. "He knows it was shady, but he never asked for the details."

She wished she didn't know those details herself . . . But she had to, didn't she? Without them, she'd been falling in love with a stranger. With a man as bad as James had been. Maybe the bad that James did left marks on people's bodies, and bullet holes, and maybe he didn't apologize for those things. But he'd never taken pleasure from his job, she didn't think. Whereas Casey . . .

"Did you enjoy it?" she asked. "Those jobs?"

"I'd be lying if I said I didn't."

She stared down at his hands for a long time, more than a minute. Hands that had held her baby—the hands that had held her before any other person in the world. Hands that had made Abilene feel wonderful in ways she'd all but forgotten about. And hands that had struck matches and started fires, counted money, but in all likelihood never come together to pray for forgiveness.

"Say something, honey." There was worry in his voice, the excitement she'd sensed all drained away.

"I don't really know what to say. I'm not even sure what I think just now." All she knew for sure was that this changed everything.

"Tell me what you're feeling, then."

"I feel . . . disappointed. And a little disgusted, to be honest." She looked up and met his eyes, finding more than worry there now. Pain. That might've been enough to have the old Abilene wanting to take it back, to soothe his hurt feelings, but fuck the old Abilene.

"Disgusted?"

"Yes," she said, sitting up straight. "That you don't sound, with hindsight, like . . . like, 'Holy crap, I'm so lucky I never hurt anybody. Thank goodness I stopped when I did.' Plus you didn't stop, not completely. You were still thinking about doing it again."

"I was, but I won't now."

She huffed, exasperated. "Because of how I'm taking it, you mean?"

He nodded. "I only wanted the money for you. To help you find a place, maybe take some classes. I can make a person's entire salary in one night. Tax-free. And I'm not bragging, I'm just saying, that's a *lot* of money, a lot of money that could do a lot of good. But it's pretty clear you wouldn't take it, knowing where it came from."

She shook her head. "No, I wouldn't. I *couldn't*. Even if I sent it to an orphanage, how could it ever feel right? Nothing feels right now, knowing that. Knowing that's where my wages are coming from. Knowing that's how you paid for the groceries you've brought us, for everything you've ever given Mercy . . ." She sighed, shoulders trembling faintly, tears stinging.

Casey's eyes were wide, his lips pursed. He looked scared, and she'd never seen such a thing before. Not like this. Scared with no ferocity behind it. Helpless.

"I still appreciate everything you've done," she said. "I'm still grateful. But if I'd known then what I do now, I don't think I could have accepted any of it. Not anymore."

After a long, tense pause, he asked, "And so what does that mean for us?"

She shook her head, the gesture pure despair and uncertainty. "I don't know."

"I won't do that last job. I promise you that."

"But not for the right reasons. You'd turn it down now, but you . . . You were still going to do it."

"I was thinking about it. And only to help you, like I said."

She laughed softly, sadly. "That doesn't make it okay. That doesn't make you Robin Hood, Casey. That only makes you a criminal."

He flinched as though she'd struck him.

"You're still a good man, in a lot of ways."

"But not good enough?"

She shook her head, her heart breaking to realize it was true. Here she was again, falling for a bad man.

"Could I ever be good enough?" His expression doubled all that hurt in her chest.

She sighed again, the sound venting every bit of confusion and frustration weighing on her. "You don't regret it," she said. "You don't feel bad for what you've done." It was James all over again, only hidden behind an easy smile, instead of a stern scowl. A con man, indeed.

"I do now," he said softly.

"But—"

"I know, I get it. Not for the right reasons."

"Why doesn't that *terrify* you?" she demanded, barely recognizing her own voice. "Thinking about how easily you could have cost someone their life, and all for some money?" Abilene was no angel, but she'd only ever gambled with her own safety. She refused to fall back on victimhood now, but she'd never been the villain, she didn't think. She may have used men, but not a one of them hadn't been anything less than willing to take the implicit trade-off. Well, none except James. He'd fought her. Failed in the end, but fought, and none of the others had.

"I guess I never thought about it that deeply," Casey said, seeming to tease the truth out as he spoke. "I suppose maybe I couldn't have thought that hard about it, not without second-guessing myself. Losing my nerve."

"You make it sound like a game."

"I can only be honest with you, and say that yeah, that's exactly what it felt like to me."

"Are you . . . Are you proud of that stuff?"

A long and loaded breath seemed to inflate then collapse his posture. "I was. Not so much recently—not since I met you, and wished I could tell you I'd been something better than a con artist for the past decade. But yeah, in the moment, I was proud of it. Not because I was getting away with something, and not because of the money, even. But I was proud I'd never been caught. Proud that not a single one of those fires had ever been deemed arson. Proud, because I'd never been so good at something in my entire life. Better than anybody else I knew, anybody else on the planet, I hoped."

He called it talent, perhaps, but it struck her as no better than blind luck.

Still, this wasn't a debate they were having, but an airing of secrets. *I'd always assumed it would have been mine that came between us.* She'd assumed she could have forgiven this man anything short of violence. But in the end, it wasn't even the recklessness of his crimes that disturbed her most. It was his lack of remorse.

He spoke. "You can't see me anymore." It was a statement, not a question.

"No, I can't." Her voice hitched and she couldn't meet his eyes. "Not like I have been, this past week."

"I hope you can still work for me and Duncan, at least."

For now, she had little choice. Fortuity wasn't rolling in jobs, and Mercy needed a roof, and heat, and food in her belly. "I'll keep working for you. I don't know how I feel about it all yet, but I still need to support myself."

He nodded. "Good."

"Will you tell Duncan now, where all that money came from?"

"If he asked, I might. If you told me it'd go some way to fixing this—us—then I would, yes."

"I can't say it would. But he seems like he respects the law. You might owe him that much."

Casey nodded. "Maybe."

They fell silent for a long time, and in those minutes their breath lengthened, as did the shadows as the sun dipped closer to the hills.

"I got you something," Casey said, shattering the stillness. "I didn't buy it with dirty money, either—I bought it after I cashed my paycheck. Can I give it to you?"

"I'm not sure."

"You don't ever have to open it, if you don't want to." He stood. He reached into his front pocket and took out a little wad of red tissue paper and set it in her palm. "You can open it now, or next week, or never. But I want you to have it, either way. It's just a tiny thing."

She tucked it in her own pocket.

"Should I take you back?"

She nodded again. "Yeah. I'd like to get back before Mercy needs feeding."

"Are we still friends?" he asked as they began the descent.

She considered it. She still wanted James in her life—strictly on her terms, but she valued him in significant ways. Like James, she valued Casey despite his mistakes. She couldn't be with him, knowing what she did now, but neither did she hope never to see him again.

"I think so," she finally said. "I need time to figure out how I feel about everything you've told me, but I hope we can be."

A frail ghost of a smile passed his lips. "Me, too."

And they didn't speak again, not on the hike down, not on the ride back east, not a word until Abilene climbed off the bike.

"I'm gonna go and check on my mom," Casey said. "But tell Miah I'll be back later, just in case any more weird shit decides to go down around here."

"I will."

He held a thought in, lips pursed.

"What?" she prompted gently.

"Thanks. For listening, I mean, even if it wasn't what you wanted to hear."

She nodded. "Thanks for being honest . . . I won't tell anybody, by the way. Rat you out, that is."

"I think I already knew you wouldn't, but thanks all the same."

Her turn to pause, caught on a thought. "I never did tell you my own secrets," she said at length. "If it's any consolation, they might've had you second-guessing us right back."

He smiled softly, looking sad. "I never needed to know those things, Abilene. Whatever it is you've done, it couldn't change how I feel."

Tears brimmed at that. "Even if we weren't meant to be," she offered, voice just on the edge of breaking, "it was real nice, for what it was, even just for those few days."

"It was."

"And even if we weren't meant to be, at least you've still got your mental health, right? Nice long life ahead of you?"

He nodded. "Yeah. I suppose so."

A nice long life, she thought, and in time, other chances at love. Other women, and eventually one for keeps, one who could either forgive his crimes or else live peacefully not knowing the details. The thought filled her up with sadness, and jealousy, too. But deep down she was proud of herself. She'd grown up today.

"It's cold," she said.

"Go inside. I'll see you soon, tonight or tomorrow. If you want to avoid me for a while, I won't be hurt." His eyes said otherwise.

"See you around, I guess."

And with another tight little smile, he backed his bike up, woke his engine, and rode away.

She watched until he was out of sight, nothing left but a settling cloud of dust lingering in the waning sunlight. She watched the best man she'd met in ages disappear before her eyes.

A good man in many ways, but still a criminal.

Chapter 22

Monday morning found Casey up early once again, though more for a lack of ever managing to fall asleep than anything else. He'd returned to the ranch around ten last night, knowing Abilene would likely be in bed and wanting to give her space. And yeah, to spare himself the sting of whatever he might see in her eyes—pity, or regret, or worst of all, disgust. That was what she'd thought of his past, after all, and in hindsight, he couldn't blame the girl. Though that didn't ease the ache in his chest any.

He'd hung out downstairs while Miah had gone out on a late-night patrol of the property, on the off chance any of the hands came rushing over with news of another creep sighting. Nothing on either count, and nothing from the deputies stationed along the highway, and he'd fallen into a restless sleep on the couch around one.

He'd heard Mercy wake an hour later, wailing, and his muscles had tensed, poised to get him up and moving toward the stairs. A reaction more instinctual than intentional, and he'd had to remind himself in that second to stay on his back, stay down here.

He'd gotten to a point where that baby's needs felt like they were half his to meet. And he'd be smart to knock that shit off and content himself to help only when asked.

If she ever asks again, that is.

He'd never purported to be a good guy, never told himself there was anything redeeming about what he did in order to sleep at night. He'd slept just fine, knowing he was one of the bad guys. Not a terrible person, but no Boy Scout. Not unless fire starting had its own badge.

He did regret it all now—how couldn't he, when just as he'd been poised to step up and become the man he'd been wanting to be, it all came around to bite him in the ass? In the deepest pit of his heart, he felt a little broken, a little sick, to realize he'd always reserve a fond, nostalgic place in his heart for those three years' work. He'd enjoyed every second of those jobs, from the promise of a new gig through the planning and the sweet, torturous anticipation of a thousand Christmases, the adrenaline of the nights themselves, the euphoria of success, the trophy of the payout.

He supposed, for that reason, there wasn't much arguing with Abilene.

Fuck, this shit burned. In the fashion of every lame metaphor he could think of, his heart hurt. Like a cut, a vise, a bruise, a hole. All of them.

He'd fucked up a lot of things in his life, but never anything this good, and never anything he regretted half as much. So there was her remorse, right there. If only it weren't such a selfish strain of the stuff.

He hauled himself off the couch, knowing these thoughts would be following him for days, maybe weeks, trailing after him like a bad smell, asserting themselves the second he stood still long enough to catch a whiff. *Keep busy,* he thought. *Keep your mind on other things.* More useless advice he'd never given himself.

Perspective was key. She'd be working with him again soon enough, and he intended to help her move out when she was ready. Beyond that, he'd meant what he'd said—he was her friend, whether he got to sleep with her or not. It would hurt like fuck for a while, but Casey consoled himself with the lie that it wasn't as though he'd been in love with her. He'd never said it aloud.

Of course in the back of his head he knew he'd intended to, had yesterday's talk gone according to plan. It had been scrawled between every single sentence in giant pink glitter letters when he'd told her how much he cared for her and Mercy.

At least he had plenty to keep himself busy. He'd collect

his crap from around the farmhouse and take it back home. Vince and Kim had dropped Abilene's car off in the front lot last night, so she wasn't stranded anymore. Casey's stomach dropped as he remembered that the baby's seat was currently set up in the Corolla. That thing was a pain in the ass to take in and out, but today the chore would unleash some pangs a little closer to his heart.

He went around the house, finding his shaving bag, toothbrush, his hoodie from the front hall, a few items of clothing that had made it into the last wash and been folded and left on the dryer for him. Man, his apartment was going to feel like a tomb after this place.

He waited until he heard the shower running upstairs, then crept into Abilene's room. He found a shirt and a pair of his shorts. The ball of red tissue he'd given her sat on the dresser, looking unopened.

Better there than in the trash, he consoled himself.

Before leaving, he crossed the room to stand over the empty crib, running his hands along its rail and the yellow fleece blanket draped there. At first he'd found that soft, sweet scent of baby things alien and a little unnerving, but lately he hardly noticed it. Until now, that was, knowing he'd be catching it less and less.

They're not dead, you sad sack.

Then how come this felt so much like mourning?

He went back downstairs to pack his duffel. By the time he'd stowed it in his car and gotten the baby's seat out, the lights were on in the kitchen and he could smell the coffeemaker doing its job. He left the seat in the front hall and headed for the light.

Both Christine and Miah were up. She was pulling butter and bread and jam out of the fridge, and he was stretching his back, arms overhead, tugging at each wrist in turn.

"Morning, old man," Casey said, passing to take a seat at the table.

Miah turned, looking surprised. "Was it you who's been creeping around since four thirty?"

"Didn't realize it was that early, but yeah."

"Baby wake you up?"

He lied. "Yeah."

Don appeared, heading straight for the old laptop he

kept on the hutch with a mumbled good morning. A radio farm report of some sort was streaming shortly at low volume, though Casey couldn't guess what the man got out of those. In Fortuity, it felt like the forecast was just about always the same. Dry and sunny.

Though today was different, it turned out. At the very end of the segment, the droning weather guy closed by saying, "And don't forget to look skyward just after one p.m. this afternoon."

"That's right—the eclipse is today," Christine piped in, toast in one hand, mug in the other. "We should all take our lunch breaks late and enjoy it."

"I plan to," Miah said. "The hands have organized some kind of picnic, so I should probably check on them anyhow. No doubt somebody will pack beer."

"Eclipse," Don muttered. He'd shut the laptop and was rooting through the hutch's drawers. "Can't stand that word since the goddamn casino referendum passed."

Steps came down the hall, setting Casey's pulse on edge. A moment later Abilene joined the assembly, baby strapped to her front. She returned the Churches' greetings, looking shy, eager to blend into the background. Casey had to work hard to keep his eyes off her and his ears focused on the conversation.

"You *have* to watch, Don," Christine said.

"Yeah," Miah added. "The paper said the next total solar eclipse Fortuity will see won't come for nearly seven years."

"Seven years is nothing at my age. But forty-two grand is—somebody wants to come and look at that ancient John Deere that's been collecting dust in the junk barn." He meant the biggest of all of Three C's barns, a drooping wooden behemoth, its flaky red paint faded nearly to pink. Casey and his friends had wasted long summer afternoons poking around in there, climbing all over the disused vehicles and otherwise trying their level best to break their necks.

Don straightened triumphantly with a set of keys. "I need to make sure the engine still starts before they come by."

Christine rolled her eyes. "You're no fun."

"You knew that when you married me. Right. I'm off."

"Me, too," she said to the room at large, setting her plate

in the sink. "Got business to tackle now if I want to enjoy the natural spectacle of the universe."

That left Casey, Miah, Abilene, and the baby. Casey couldn't decide whether he was eager or petrified for Miah to take off and leave him and Abilene alone. There was so much he still wanted to say . . . though he doubted a word of it would do much aside from make him feel more helpless.

Perhaps for the best, the baby began to cry, and Abilene excused herself to change a wet diaper before her toast even got a chance to pop up.

Miah watched her go, then looked to Casey. To the hall. Back to Casey.

"What?"

"Something's up with you two."

"What makes you say so?"

"Usually she's got stars in her eyes every time she looks your way, but just now, I don't think she glanced at you once." That stung. And Miah's brain was usually too crammed full of to-dos to notice stuff like that, so the cloud in the room must not be confined solely to Casey's head.

He shrugged. "I don't think she slept well."

Miah walked over with a fresh coffee and straddled the bench, facing him. "You fuck something up, Case?"

He heaved a heavy sigh. "In a way." In another way, he'd done the right thing. Been honest. But he'd fucked up what they'd had, that was true.

"You guys didn't . . ."

"We already had been."

Miah looked to the ceiling as though beseeching a higher power for strength.

"Like you're even surprised," Casey said.

"No, maybe not. For how long?"

"Only a few days."

"Jesus, Case—now, of all times? Must be the most chaotic week of her life. Tell me you didn't break it off last night. Because the last thing that girl needs is another man letting her down."

"No, no. She ended it."

"You give her a good reason to?"

"Yeah, but not like you're thinking. Things were at the edge of maybe getting serious. We needed to tell each other about what our lives have been like, before we both wound up in Fortuity last summer."

"And she didn't like what she heard?"

"No. No, she did not."

Miah frowned, looking more sympathetic than judgmental now, at least. After a sip of coffee he asked, "What *have* you been up to, Case?"

"I'd rather not say."

"Considering all the dumb-ass shit we got up to when we were kids, the fact that you don't want to tell *me* isn't a good sign."

"Trust me—it's better if you don't know."

Miah was an upstanding, law-abiding sort of man. He wouldn't rat Casey out to the feds if he knew the truth, but Casey would no doubt lose a chunk of the man's respect. And he had to admit, that shit mattered to him now.

"She gonna be okay?" Miah asked, getting to his feet.

"I think so. Neither of us had promised anything to the other."

"That's something . . . I probably don't need to tell you, that sucks all the same. She's a good girl. And she seemed good for you."

He nodded, feeling that faint, raw strain rising in his throat—the first warning sign that he just might cry. "Yeah, she was." And she always would be, even going forward. For as long as she was a part of Casey's life, she'd make him a better man. He'd always look at her and remind himself to do better, to be worthy of what they'd nearly had, to maybe stand a chance at getting her back someday.

Big maybe.

Miah gave him a hard clap on the arm. "Sorry, man. But I'd better go start the day. Maybe we can drink on it, later."

Casey nodded, happy to be left alone. He could already feel how pink he'd gone and didn't relish an audience. He'd spent a lot of years thinking solely of himself. Seemed only fitting that he was on his own now, stuck sitting amid the smoking rubble of his choices, neck-deep in regrets.

A man makes his own luck, he thought, filling his mug when Miah had gone.

Only took ten years for mine to finally turn as rotten as I deserve.

Chapter 23

Not ready to face Casey alone just yet, Abilene hid in her room for most of the morning, poking around on Craigslist for rentals and finding the results bleak. There was her old room in Mrs. Dennigan's basement, but it had been cramped after Mercy had arrived, and the whole idea stank of regression, of going backward.

Apart from that, there was a six-month sublet in a rough section of town—which was saying something in Fortuity—plus some houses for rent, but those were all beyond her budget. She couldn't help but picture Casey's roomy space above Wasco's, with its tall windows, spare bedroom, sunny kitchen, huge living room. She'd fantasized a lot in only the past few days about what she'd do to it if he ever invited her to stay with him. Where she'd put the crib, what color she'd paint the rooms, if his landlady would allow it . . .

Stupid girl. Since when had her luck changed enough to manifest that kind of happy little dream life?

My luck has changed, though. Or her choices, to go by Casey's philosophy. In either case, little by little, since she'd found herself in this town, things had begun looking up. She'd landed a decent job at the diner, and then an even better one at the bar. Made good friends who looked out for her and Mercy. She'd had a taste of romance—only a taste, but sweeter than she'd ever expected. It hurt to lose it, and to realize it wasn't as perfect as it had felt, but in time it would give her hope, she imagined. There were men out there who'd treat her right, her and Mercy both.

The one you loved just turned out to be more crooked

than you'd let yourself guess, is all. He'd still been good to her, for all his now-glaring faults. He'd seen something in her worth treating well, so maybe another guy would see the same, one day.

Would Casey have forgiven all the ugly things I've done? She might never know. But maybe some other man, some other time in her life, would be able to.

Just now, it was impossible to imagine anyone lighting her up the way Casey had.

Outside her room, the old stairs creaked. Her heart was thumping in an instant—as hard as it ever had back when she'd feared James's intrusion—this time imagining it might be Casey. Come back to—what? Beg for a second chance, and a prescription for penance? For forgiveness? For—

"Knock-knock," came Christine's voice, and Abilene deflated like a pricked balloon.

"Come in."

She poked her head and shoulders in and spoke quietly. "Is she asleep?"

Mercy had gone down for a nap more than an hour ago. "Not for long. She'll be hungry soon. You don't need to whisper."

"It's nearly one. I was going to see if you wanted to come out and watch the eclipse with me."

"Oh yes. I would. Let me just get her bundled up and a bottle ready. Ten minutes?"

Christine nodded. "I'll be in the kitchen."

She'd miss this family when she moved out, she realized as she roused Mercy and maneuvered her into her little fleece hooded getup. Abilene's own family had looked picture-perfect growing up, but fractured and broken behind closed doors. The Churches came off as harried and a touch short sometimes, thanks to how hard they worked, but on the inside they were the nicest people you'd want to meet.

She found Christine in the kitchen, dropping sandwiches into a canvas lunch bag. "Couldn't remember if you like mayo or mustard," she said, grabbing a thermos, "so I made one of each."

"More of a mayo girl. Texan, after all. We smother everything."

Christine laughed. "Suits me fine. I can go either way."

And as they locked up and strolled from the farmhouse out toward the bunks and stables and barns, they chatted about the various merits of condiments—such a simple, mundane topic that it felt quenching, comforting, on the heels of the recent drama.

"Where are all the ranch hands?" she asked. "Miah said they were throwing a picnic."

"In the western eight," Christine said, though Abilene didn't know what this meant. The westernmost eight acres, maybe? Not far, she imagined, as Three C's range stretched miles and miles and miles out to the east.

"We'll find them, no doubt," Christine added. "By the rabble, if nothing else."

And they did. It looked as though just about everyone had taken their lunch break in accordance with nature—everyone except Don, that was—and at least two dozen workers and half as many horses were scattered around a greenish brown expanse just past the outbuildings, its scrub grass mowed short. Miah's dog came trotting up to them as they neared, pausing for ear scratches and sniffing opportunities. She was slender, with pointed ears like a German shepherd, but far smaller, with a grayish, mottled coat, and a black patch over one eye.

"I've never seen her so friendly before," Abilene said. "Usually she's more robot than dog."

"When she's on duty, yeah," came a voice behind them—Miah. He was lugging a huge plastic jug with a spigot at the bottom, like sports teams kept their Gatorade in. "But she gets an hour off today, like everybody else."

"I've never met a dog so well-behaved. The ones I grew up with jumped on people and barked at the littlest things." Her mom had had two yappy little terriers, and she'd never been real fond of either of them. She'd resented them, in fact. They were annoying and poorly behaved, yet somehow they'd been exempt from all of her father's militaristic rules regarding manners. Her mom had shielded them from his perfectionism, somehow, in a way she'd never shielded her daughter.

"Takes a lot of work," Christine said, patting the dog's side. "And a good set of genes—heelers are bred to herd sheep and cattle. Miah trained this one, and his dad trained her father and grandfather. It's in her blood."

"Must be in yours, too," she said to the both of them, and Miah nodded.

"I was always more of a horse girl," Christine said. "But you fall in love with a rancher, you'd better fall in love with the ranch."

They reached the edge of the gregarious crowd, and Miah wended his way through to heft the jug onto a folding table covered in bags of chips and six-packs of soda cans. Christine had brought a blanket, and she spread it out on the crisp, dry grass. Despite the winter chill, Abilene felt a wash of nostalgia as she lowered her butt to the ground, remembering a hundred family picnics in Lindsay Park in Bloomville. Those summer memories came with clouds attached, but she reminded herself that she'd forge new ones, this time as a mother, not a child. A different landscape, different faces, different smells on the breeze, but the same sun overhead, the same wide blue sky. She unstrapped Mercy and propped her between her crossed legs. She was still waking, gawking wide-eyed at all the activity.

A few of the female hands came by to gawk right back. Though they were Abilene's age, they were probably years from motherhood themselves, and she registered a jab of jealousy. In another life—one she hadn't screwed up so badly—she might've found herself a passion, a trade, a career. A purpose. The pang was brief, though, and shallow. She had her purpose now, she thought, bouncing Mercy by her armpits. Not glamorous, but important. And she was good at it. Far from perfect, but pretty damn good, considering. She sat up a little straighter, proud for a change.

"Quite the party," someone called. She and Christine turned to find Casey striding down the slope.

"If I'd known you were coming I'd have packed another sandwich," Christine said, and scooted over to make more room on the blanket. She had no clue that he and Abilene had just broken up, of course. For all Abilene knew, Miah's hopelessly romantic mother was banking on the two of them getting together.

That ship's already sailed. And sunk.

"I hadn't planned to come back out," Casey said, "but I stopped by the bar and figured I'd bring Abilene the week's schedule. And your last paycheck," he added, meeting her eyes. "I left both on your dresser."

"Thanks."

There was hesitance tensing his smile, like he wasn't sure if he was welcome on this blanket, in her estimations.

For all the heartache, she didn't mind him joining them. It wasn't as though her feelings could be flipped on and off like a switch. Her feelings were messy and sticky, and she knew it. They clung like summer heat or winter's chill, slow to fade.

Mercy held her arms out to Casey, and a piece of Abilene's heart broke. Her body wanted that same thing still—to reach out to him, be close to him. Her body hadn't forgotten what his could do to hers, when they came together.

Uncertainty passed across Casey's face as he watched the squirming infant, blue eyes glancing to Abilene's.

He's not a monster, she reminded herself. He was a con man who'd made a lot of selfish decisions for the sake of money, but he wasn't evil. Reckless and lacking in empathy, perhaps, but not cruel or sadistic. She lifted Mercy and got to her knees, passing her over. Casey's smile was brief and vulnerable, and he spread his legs and propped the baby between them. He knew most of the ranch hands—many were regulars at the bar—and some came over to say hello, the guys razzing him about the baby, the girls looking more approving, intrigued by the scene.

The young woman who'd come by the house the other night wrapped in a blanket was among them. She was wearing the hands' unofficial uniform, boots and jeans and plaid flannel, and she dropped to a crouch next to Casey. Denny, Abilene thought her name was.

"Good look for you, Grossier," she said, and gave Mercy's outstretched, chubby hand a little squeeze. She'd know Mercy wasn't Casey's, of course—all of the hands had been given the broad strokes, back when James coming around had still been a danger. "Gonna make a few of these yourself someday?" she teased. "Only in red?"

"Time'll tell," he said. "I'm in no rush."

Casey wasn't flirting back, but Abilene felt her insides curdle all the same. That handsome, charming, funny man had been hers for not even a week. But it would hurt like hell to one day see him flirting with another woman for real. To one day hear that he was seeing someone. To spot him *kissing* that someone, maybe. The thought alone burned.

Abilene panned the crowd and found Miah joking with his employees, and felt a deep vein of sympathy open up in her heart for him. Few wounds healed so slowly as love interrupted.

"Two minutes!" somebody yelled from the crowd, and the milling ranch hands began to settle, shielding their eyes with their hands, figuring out which direction to face to best watch the eclipse. The sun was high overhead, just beginning its westward descent.

One of the hands came around, handing out paper plates with holes pricked in them, for people to watch through. Casey thanked her and took three, passing them around. He also passed Mercy back to Abilene, deciding he wanted no part in accidentally blinding her. Though he missed the warmth and smell of her, both whisked away on the breeze. He wished Christine hadn't grabbed him when he'd arrived. It was hard being this close to Abilene and knowing he couldn't touch her. He'd have much preferred to be hanging out with Miah, and for all he knew, she wished the same.

In a way, he got his wish shortly. Miah jogged over with a plate of his own in hand and plopped down on the blanket's edge beside his mother. "Here we go! Natural wonder commencing in three, two, one . . ."

More like half a minute, as it turned out. Abilene turned Mercy to face her middle and they held the plates up to their faces, finding the sun through the pinpricks. At first it was nothing more than a funny little clipping snipped off the lower edge of the sun, as the moon began its trespass. Then more of a bite mark, and the sky grew eerily, unmistakably darker.

"You think Dad's secretly watching this?" Miah asked his mom, muffled by the paper plate.

"If he isn't he's the silliest sort of stubborn."

"Oooh." This from Abilene, as the sky took on a reddish cast and the nibbled corner of the sun turned rusty black.

Casey felt twelve again, or however old he'd been the last time he'd seen a solar eclipse around here. Middle school, easily. All he remembered for sure was that it had been May or June, just a week or two before school let out for the summer. His blood felt restless at the memory, itchy for escape.

I've spent enough of my life running, he reminded himself. *And it never got me anyplace worth bragging about.*

As the moon swallowed the sun to the one-quarter mark, the sky went full-on dusky, and he conjured other memories. Like of his dad teaching him and Vince how to hold a magnifying glass on a sunny day, at just the right distance to burn the eyeballs out of the people on the cover of *TV Guide*. Your typically classy Tom Grossier wisdom, and Casey had to wonder how old he'd been. Four, surely, as his father had left when he was five. Too young, no doubt, though he couldn't blame any of his pyro crap on the guy's sketchy life lessons. That shit was in his blood. If there was a gene for it, no doubt that LifeMap analyst could've confirmed it for him. Just thinking about those old issues of *TV Guide*, he could fairly smell the burning paper and ink. Taste the inside of his mouth, as it began, unmistakably, to water.

Come to think of it, he *could* smell smoke. Someone must have hauled a grill down. Though what sort, he couldn't guess—not gas, for sure, and not charcoal either.

Through the hole, the sun was a white sickle hugging a black hole of nothing, and the sky in his periphery had gone warm gray. He cast his eyes downward and lowered the plate. The horizon glowed a golden white behind the distant eastern mountains, but all else was darkening by the second, eerie and magical.

But something wasn't right. The breeze was blowing from behind—from the direction of town, not the picnic. It wasn't a cookout he was smelling. It was wood, and more. Chemical smoke, like fire lapping at painted boards. A stink he knew well, hard to get out of your clothes. He looked to the northwest, and though the sky was nearing nighttime darkness, he could see it. A plume of thick, dark smoke, coming from the direction of the farmhouse. He shot to his feet.

"Fire," he said. Softly at first.

Only Miah heard it. "What?"

"Fire," he repeated, louder. "Fucking hell—*fire!*"

Miah was up, squinting into the darkness. It had been a bright day, and no one seemed to have left any lights on in any of the buildings. You could just see their outlines against the reddish sky to the west. "Holy shit."

"Oh no." Christine stood, and word was spreading—half the workers had dropped their plates and were getting to their feet. The smoke was growing thick, fast.

Christine was on her phone, no doubt calling 911.

"Everybody!" Miah bellowed. "Head south! Take the horses and walk south!" He arched his arms in that direction, ushering them away from the path of the smoke.

Christine also hurried away, glowing phone pressed to one ear, hand clapped over the other to block out the shouting.

Up the hill, a light grew in the darkness—orange light.

"Fuck. Which building is that?" Casey shouted to Miah as he helped Abilene to her feet. "Follow the hands," he told her. "Keep the baby away from the smoke."

Miah squinted. "The stables? Or the barn."

They'd better hope it was the barn. Nothing but junk in there, while surely the stables were full of horses, with so many of the hands taking their breaks.

Footsteps pounded up from behind them—one of the hands emerging from the throng now hurrying south. It was Denny, and her dark eyes were wide, legs pumping.

"Your dad is in there!" she shouted at Miah.

"What?"

"In the junk barn! I passed him earlier, when he was on his way over there."

The tractor, Casey thought. He'd said he was going to be working on—

Miah was already running, and Casey took off as fast as his legs could pump, screaming his friend's name. *He'll run straight in there if I don't pin him to the fucking dirt.*

He was fast, but Miah was faster. It was only by the grace of another ranch hand catching hold of Miah's arms, spinning him around, and onto the ground, that he didn't go charging straight into the blaze. Casey tackled him, and with the other man's help, they managed to drag Miah back a few yards. The air between them and the mammoth barn was like a waterfall now, a wavering yellow wall of heat. The only mercy was that it was a calm day, not windy, and that the breeze was headed for the range and not the other buildings. Still, it was dry country. Even a single scrap of airborne detritus could start a massive brush fire.

Miah was shouting for his father, and the sound cut straight to Casey's bones.

"He might be fine," Casey said, struggling to keep his thrashing friend pinned. "He might not be in there."

Sirens sounded in the distance. It'd be too little, too late—Fortuity was the county seat, but even they had only one fire truck, and it was manned by volunteers. It'd be a long wait before the next nearest departments could rush over from other towns. Too late to save the barn. And unless Denny had been mistaken, or Don had been able to get out, too late to save Miah's father. Casey's muscles went watery at the thought, dread and fear and disbelief jumbled together, suffocating.

Miah went slack after a minute's violent struggle, his swears giving way to hoarse, primal sounds, then dry sobs.

Casey's heart broke for him. He didn't know what it felt like to have a father you were proud of. One you loved and idolized and modeled your own manhood after. It had to feel like a piece of Miah himself was burning up.

"He might not be in there," he repeated, clinging to the possibility himself. "Denny could be wrong. He could've gotten out."

Miah wasn't hearing any of it. He'd curled in on himself, forehead on the dirt, and Casey could faintly hear him saying, "Dad, Dad, Dad," the sound swallowed by the rush of the flames, the choking of his sobs.

"We don't know he's in there," the male hand echoed.

"Let's get you up," Casey told Miah. "Let's get farther away. There's too much smoke. There's machinery in there, right? It might not be safe."

That was what Don had been in there for—to dick around with some piece of equipment. Maybe that had started the fire. Gasoline or diesel, hay, all that brittle old wood, or whatever else might be inside. Could've been an accident waiting to happen.

Could've, but probably wasn't. The Churches weren't foolish or careless people. And that fact combined with whoever had been stalking around the place this past week added up to a gnawing pit, deep in Casey's gut.

And something else hit him as he stood, holding Miah's arm tight to keep him from bolting, watching the orange flames licking up at the now-lightening sky. Hit him as hard as a hunk of flaming shrapnel, cut him to the core.

The fire. On the starless night.

Only he hadn't seen a starless night, after all—no overcast evening at the height of the rainy season. He'd seen the dark of the eclipse, an *artificial* night. And he hadn't seen Miah, but his father. Silhouetted by the raging fire in his vision, they were impossible to tell apart, just two slender, tall men in jeans and Stetsons. Matching postures, matching mannerisms.

"Fuck me," Casey murmured.

Miah was jerking, trying to get loose, and Casey held on tighter, steering him away, back down the hill with the other man's help.

Fuck me. The visions didn't lie, did they? They only misled. It was lucidity and logic that got it all wrong, time and time again.

And if a good man was dead now, from a tragedy Casey had stood some chance at preventing . . .

He couldn't imagine how he'd ever forgive himself.

Chapter 24

The fire departments arrived—at first just the skeleton crew of the Fortuity volunteer brigade, followed long minutes later by forces from the surrounding towns and counties.

The volunteers managed to keep the blaze contained, and probably helped stop it from spreading to the bunks and stables and the brush, but the barn itself was an utter loss. Razed to the ground, practically, with one wall left standing, precariously. The collapsed shingle roof drooped in against it, the thickest of the now-blackened beams jutting here and there like charred ribs.

There had been no sign of Don. And no sign was a bad sign indeed, Casey couldn't help but think.

By the time the water trucks had come and the firefighters had things under control, the sky was once again as bright and blue and cheerful as one could hope for in mid-February . . . save for the fading black ribbon of smoke drifting east, bound for Utah.

Miah's dog stood twenty yards or so from the action, gaze locked on the smoldering rubble, body taut, tail still. It was one of the saddest sights Casey had ever seen.

The ranch workers were organizing themselves, moving frightened horses from the stables out to the range, away from the lingering smoke and chaos. Helicopters passed overhead—wildfire crews, no doubt, scanning for signs of stray blazes out in the brush.

Casey still had Miah by the arm, though the fight had gone out of his friend.

"Let go of me," Miah said quietly, eyes still glued to the smoking, steaming remains of the barn.

"You need to stay back."

"I need to help my employees," he seethed through clenched teeth. "I need to help get the animals away from here." There were tears streaking his cheeks, drawing pale tracks down the dark soot dusting his face.

Casey reluctantly, cautiously, let him free. Miah snatched his arm away, rolled his shoulders, called for his dog, and trudged off toward the stables. What on earth was going through his head, Casey didn't care to guess. But let him hide in the work. Let him hide from the looming uncertainty of what might've become of his father.

Through the blackened mess of collapsed boards and flaps of fallen roof, Casey could see the shapes of a half dozen pieces of heavy equipment. Any one could've been the machine Don had been planning to tune up. And under any pile of charred wood and slate roofing tiles could be the body of one of the finest men this town had ever seen.

I saw this coming, was all Casey could think.

He was rooted to the spot, unable to move. He'd seen all of this, months ago. He'd gotten the clues wrong and ignored the ones that counted. If he'd had his head on straight, he might've stopped all this. Maybe saved a life.

God-fucking-damn it, why the fuck had he been given this so-called gift, of all people? Why some flighty, self-interested criminal, of all the decent—

"Case!"

He turned, finding Vince running toward him.

"Where's Miah?" his brother demanded.

"Helping move the horses."

Vince's shoulders dropped in obvious relief, though his face said it all—the circumstances of the fire hadn't been lost on him. He'd probably remembered those words the second he heard there was a fire at Three C, in the middle of the eclipse.

"All I could think was, fucking starless night," his brother panted, recovering from his sprint from the parking lot or the house.

"It wasn't Miah," Casey said quietly. "But it might've been Don."

Vince's heaving chest went still in an instant. "Don?"

"He was supposed to be in there this afternoon. He told us himself. I think I saw it wrong, Vince—I thought it was Miah, but—"

"Where's Christine?"

"I don't know. She was calling nine-one-one, last I saw her. She was with the hands. I'm sure she's fine."

Vince's head jerked to the side, and Casey looked in the same direction, to where Miah was being led toward the farmhouse by a couple officials. Vince made to follow his best friend, but Casey caught him by the elbow.

He spoke quickly, quietly. "I don't think this was an accident, Vince."

His brother eyed him. Casey took it for skepticism at first, until Vince said, "Tell me exactly why not." Those five words spoke volumes, their message loud and clear. *It sure as fuck doesn't feel like one, but tell me precisely how you know.*

Vince's body had softened and Casey let his arm go. "The place didn't just burst into a massive fireball," he said. "It was a steady burn, no sudden explosions, and if Don started it by accident, he'd have noticed. Seen it happen, smelled it. He knew that barn better than anyone, and he would've tried to get to an exit. He wouldn't have just fallen down right there. Even as smoky as it was, he'd have hit the ground and crawled for a door."

Vince nodded, jaw set. He knew Casey wasn't suggesting that Don had escaped.

"If he *is* in there . . ." Casey already knew, in his gut, he was. He'd seen it months ago, after all, and his intuition had no doubts. "An autopsy's gonna show that he died from something other than smoke inhalation. A blow, or a shot." He hoped so, anyhow. If the man had subsequently been hit by a falling beam or a piece of the roof, it'd take a world-class arson investigator to spot any injuries he'd sustained before the fire began. Unless there was a bullet, that was.

"An autopsy might say this was foul play, but it's not gonna tell us who did it." Vince paused, studying him. "Could you?"

"I dunno. Maybe. Depends on how sloppy the guy was."

"They're gonna send a forensics team, no doubt."

"No doubt," Casey agreed. "For the insurance, if nothing else. But the lab work'll take days, maybe weeks. And we don't need proof this was no accident. We need to know who did it, and soon. Forensics will only give them a week's head start."

"Exactly. So what do you need?"

He gave Vince the side eye, wary. "What d'you mean?"

"I'm not stupid, Case. After that shit that went down in the mines, back in August, I knew what flavor of shady you turned into." Casey had played no small part in uncovering some grisly corpse-disposal practices perpetrated by corrupt actors from the casino's original contracting outfit. "What's your scam, exactly? Arson?"

He looked away, but nodded. "Commercial shit. For a cut of the property owners' claim money."

"You ever get caught?"

"Not even close."

"You know more than a forensics expert?"

Casey shrugged. "As much as. Enough to know how to trick one."

"Well, let's hope you know enough to finger whoever pulled this."

"I can tell you how it started, where it was set, what accelerant they used, what temps it reached, and how it moved—but I'm not a detective. I don't have a lab, and even if I did, there's not going to be much left in the way of fingerprints and fibers in there."

"Maybe not, but you're what we've got."

"There's Miah and Christine, too—they might have some guess who could've done this . . . though it doesn't feel right to start grilling them anytime soon. Not if he's . . ."

Vince nodded. "But the second you get a chance, I want you in there. I want to know what cocksucker did this. And I want to be there when we find him."

Casey swallowed, nodded.

"I'm leaving it to you," Vince said, and he headed toward the farmhouse, no doubt to find his best friend. That left Casey on his own, staring at the rising steam and dwindling smoke, the plumes of water still dousing the razed husk of the barn. Every gallon washed away a little more evidence, a little more of any trail that might've been left. And under all that mess must lie the body of one of the best men Casey had ever known.

When it all became too much to look at, he turned away, and went in search of Abilene.

Abilene was in a daze.

She'd followed the hands, walking a half mile or more to the edge of a quiet service road, a dozen of them huddled in a confused group, watching the black smoke snaking up and sliding away over the range on the wind. Sirens had come in wave after wave, the only noise more piercing than Mercy's wails.

An errant thought visited her as she stood there, lost in a storm of murmuring, nervous voices.

Casey showed up just before that fire started. He'd come trotting over to them not twenty minutes before the smoke had begun to billow, a self-described pyromaniac arriving from the direction of a blaze, to the party that had conveniently cleared all the witnesses away from the scene.

Don't be ridiculous. And that was how the notion felt to her—ridiculous. Though the coincidence was impossible not to notice, not after everything he'd told her last night.

When the smoke began to thin, it was collectively decided that everyone should head closer and see if there was any way to help.

Saddled with an infant, Abilene veered toward the farmhouse while the hands continued on to their colleagues, who were leading horses away from the stables. Things looked safe enough at the house, and there were two sheriff's deputies on the porch, talking with a firefighter and Christine. Abilene couldn't have guessed her tanned face could ever look so pale, and dread dropped like an anchor into her gut. Something was wrong, something that went way beyond property damage. She didn't dare butt in and ask, but instead slowed as she climbed the steps, listening.

"When was that?" asked a young black woman dressed in bulky tan and neon yellow firefighter's coveralls, speaking gently to Christine. Too gently.

"Early," she replied, sounding shell-shocked. "Seven o'clock, maybe?"

"And did he expect the repairs to take several hours?"

"I couldn't say. It depends on how much work the thing needed. But I haven't seen him . . ." Her normally capable, athletic frame looked frail and breakable, arms hugged tight around her middle.

She's talking about Don. He'd been going to look at some John Deere thing or other. Could that have caused the fire? A mechanical issue?

Then she remembered the mystery creep, and all at once it felt much too convenient for comfort. She'd stopped on the porch, staring now, and Christine reached out to touch her arm, steer her gently in the direction of the front door. So she wouldn't overhear anything more? Or simple permission to get inside, away from all the chaos?

Either way, she obeyed.

The phone was ringing from its stand on the hutch as she entered the house, and she had no doubt it would continue to do so for the rest of the afternoon as the news spread far and wide. The second it quieted, she heard the electronic trill of the office phone beckoning from past the den.

She'd been holding Mercy to her hip for ages now, the sling just a canvas tangle around her arm, too much to bother with in the height of the panic. All at once, in the eerie calm and silence of the house, she felt the strain in her back and neck and elbows, and set the baby in the car seat Casey had left by the door. She lugged it into the kitchen, downed a glass of water, then another. She considered camping out in here, torn between curiosity about what could be going on and fear of the same.

What if Don . . . She shivered, unwilling to think it. *He would have gotten out, surely.* And that person who'd been creeping around, they'd just been some potential burglar, or a pervert after a glimpse at the ranch hands undressing or something gross like that, not . . .

The kitchen felt too cold. Too cavernous. She heated a bottle of formula for Mercy and carried her upstairs, though she left the bedroom door open, wanting updates even as she dreaded them.

Mercy managed half the bottle before conking out, no doubt exhausted from the crying and the rattled energy of all the grown-ups.

Abilene stood over the crib for long minutes, watching her daughter's face, feeling out-of-body. Sounds from down-stairs snapped her from the trance—men's voices.

She hurried to the door, thinking at first she'd heard Don speaking, but no, only Miah. She recognized the other voice as well. Vince. She couldn't catch more than the odd snatch of what they were saying, but Miah sounded frantic and shaky, Vince cool and somber. The voices faded, the men seeming to have gone into the kitchen. Sure enough, she could make out the faint sound of water running.

Poor Miah. Part of her wanted to go downstairs, to see if she could do anything, but it was in that moment that she realized that she really didn't know the man. Not well enough to try to comfort him at such an uncertain time, anyhow.

She turned away, and her gaze caught on a flash of red on the dresser—the wadded tissue that Casey had given her. A present she'd not dared to open last night. Just now, her heartache paled to nothing beside Miah and Christine's, and she could stand the distraction. She picked it up and took a seat on the bed.

It was so light she'd probably have tossed it in the trash if she'd come upon it, assuming it was empty. It was secured with a piece of tape, and she peeled that free, beginning to unwind the tissue. After four or five turns, the paper parted, and pooled in its center was silver—a box chain, shiny as only sterling silver could be, brand-new. Something else poked from the tiny pile of links—a slim and delicate shape. She knew what it was in an instant, and a smile caught some-where between affection and heartbreak twisted her lips.

The little cross was almost identical to the one she'd worn for more than ten years. A half-inch tall, plain, no body of Christ. The chain was different, shorter than the one she'd lost, and nicer as well. She eased a loose knot from it and centered the cross opposite the clasp, letting it swing from her fingers.

She didn't know quite what to make of it.

Had their soul-bearing conversation gone well, it would

have been a more than welcome gift. A gift that told her she'd found herself a man who paid attention, who listened, and who thought of her in moments when they weren't together. She couldn't guess where in Fortuity he'd found this, either, so he'd gone on a mission for it. For her.

She closed it in her hand, felt the metal warming there.

Can I keep this? It wasn't a locket or some other pointed token of romance. It was a symbol of her misplaced beliefs, of her lost faith once again returning to her in the wake of all those desperate, squandered years. It was a gift chosen by a lover . . . but bestowed by a friend.

I'll wear it, she decided. Not yet, but eventually. To put it on now would be too mixed a signal to send Casey, and too much to ask of her own heart, besides. But in time, once their brief but blazing romance had mellowed to a fond memory, their friendship hopefully planted on solid ground once again, she'd put it on. And she'd wear it gratefully, with humility and hope.

The house gave a rattle, the subtle clatter of doors resettling and telling her someone had just come in from outside. The murmur of conversation in the kitchen flared for a moment, then went sedate once again. She heard Christine now, and also Casey. She debated going down, pursing her lips, legs trying to commit to standing or not. But then footsteps froze her, growing louder as they reached the den, then the stairs. She knew the sound of those shoes well, and she hastily closed the necklace in its tissue and slid it under a pillow.

Casey approached the bedroom with one fist raised, poised to knock on the frame. He lowered it when their eyes met. "Hey."

"Hi. Come in. What's going on?"

He closed the door behind him and leaned on the dresser. If he noticed the red tissue was missing, he didn't show it. She doubted something so trivial was on his mind now, even as that tiny present weighed on her own.

"Has anyone seen Don yet?" she asked, heart knotting between her ribs.

Casey shook his head. "It doesn't look good. The barn was the last place anybody saw him."

"Do you think . . . ?"

He nodded, just the barest dip of his chin.

Tears were slipping down her cheeks in an instant, as she let that fearful thought become real. "That's . . . God, I don't even know." He'd been so good to her. Maybe not warm and paternal, but patient, welcoming, helpful. Caring, in his own practical, rational way. "How're Christine and Miah?"

"I'm not sure it's completely sunk in yet. I don't think either one of them is ready to jump to conclusions."

"I heard Miah talking to your brother."

He nodded, then came to sit on the far end of the bed. "Vince heard about the fire while he was at work. Came right here . . . He had a weird feeling about it, I guess."

"When will they know for sure? About Don?" Her body went cold, imagining people having to sift through all that smoke-stinking, dampened mess, looking for— She cut off the thought.

"Not long, I don't think. Once everything's cooled and the smoke's cleared."

"God, this is just *awful*." There was no adjective that fit, none that didn't sound monstrously inadequate. "Do you . . . You don't think it was on purpose, though, do you? Like anything to do with whoever's been sneaking around?"

Casey didn't reply right away, expression clouded.

"Do you?" she prompted.

"It's too soon to say. But I'd be lying if I said I'd be surprised."

"Oh my God."

"There's no point thinking about it just yet," he said gently.

"That's so . . . I mean, did someone want to hurt him on purpose, or were they only trying to destroy the barn, or—"

Casey quieted her with a wave of his hand, smiling weakly. "We'll have more answers soon. For now the most important thing is to be whatever it is Miah and his mom are going to need."

He was right, and she did her best to block out the nagging, frightening thoughts.

"How's she?" Casey nodded in the crib's direction.

"She screamed herself hoarse while I was out with all the workers, waiting for the fire to die down. I don't think she'll be waking up anytime too soon."

He heaved a loaded breath, slipped his hand under his open hoodie and rubbed at his chest. "I'm trying real hard to not work myself up about how close the two of you were to all that. How wrong it could've gone." As he said it, his voice broke. Any fleeting worry she'd had about the fire having been *anything* to do with Casey evaporated in that instant.

She wanted to be close to him. Wanted his arms around her body and his soft voice in her ear, telling her it was going to be okay. Comforting lies, something to believe in while the entire world seemed to be coming apart around them.

But if she felt lost now, surely she'd only lose further track of her heart, if she let herself get too close. Clarity was in short supply at the moment, and never more so than when she tried to make sense of how she felt about this man. She pictured the necklace now hiding beneath her pillow, and that knot in her chest eased, though the tangle was as big a mess as ever.

"I need to talk to my brother," Casey said, "but I wanted to check how you were doing."

"Thanks. Do you think I should go downstairs? To try to help, somehow?"

He considered it. "Knowing Miah, he'll be out of there the second he finds a decent excuse, looking for shit to tackle so he doesn't get to think too hard about it all. But Christine could probably use the company. She'd been saying something about making coffee, for all the officials who're taking statements and waiting for the investigation to get under way. I bet she could use some help with that."

Abilene nodded. She'd bring Mercy down in the car seat and pray the baby kept on napping as long as possible. It was going to be a long day, and she had a terrible feeling that the answers they were all waiting on weren't going to be good.

Chapter 25

Casey went downstairs with Abilene and the baby, the three of them joining the periphery of the scene in the kitchen. Vince, Miah, and Christine were seated at one end of the long table, talking quietly. Christine's expression was calm, but her eyes were red and her hands shaky. Miah had a hand on her back, circling slowly, thoughtlessly, as the three traded empty consolations and theories about how Don could be anyplace—way out at the other end of the range, maybe, or who knew where. But Casey had seen the man's truck in the front lot, as had they all, he bet. These weren't words of comfort, merely words·that gave the Churches permission to live in denial a little longer.

Casey kept quiet, standing by with his arms crossed, and Abilene set the baby in her rocker while she went to load dishes in the washer, her motions careful and quiet, respectful. Fragile.

Casey felt much the same. Felt too many things, and none of them good. Yesterday he'd felt remorse about his old life, because it had cost him what he'd found with Abilene. Less than a day later those sour feelings had turned downright poisonous. He felt as though he were standing on the other side of his own selfish choices. Standing in the kitchen that might've belonged to the family of some firefighter, maybe, had one of his arson jobs ever gone tragically wrong. The thought alone had his throat raw and his eyes hurting. He swallowed the feelings down. They had no place beside Miah and Christine's grief.

The phone had barely quit ringing since Casey had arrived, and when it trilled yet again, Christine stood with a weary sigh. "I can't ignore it forever, I suppose."

Miah got to his feet. "Let me."

She waved him away. "No, I could use something to do. I'll be in the office, if any of the Sheriff's Department folks want me. Or if your father turns up," she added, then hit the phone's TALK button. "Hello? Marian, hi. Hang on one second." She offered the room a distracted, lame smile, then disappeared into the hall.

Casey eyed Miah. He was usually the picture of casual confidence, but he was hunched in his seat, fingers drumming his opposite elbows, feet fidgeting beneath the bench. Casey couldn't think of a single decent thing to say, aside from, "Anybody need a drink?"

Vince shook his head, and Abilene didn't even turn from her task. Miah announced, "I'd better go and check on the animals. I've got my phone if anybody needs me."

Casey and Vince nodded and let him go. Abilene turned once he'd left the room, locking her watery, worried eyes on Casey's.

"Come outside a minute," Vince said to him, getting to his feet.

Casey followed his brother out the front door and down the steps. Vince paused when they neared a pair of stressed-looking ranch hands who were smoking at the edge of the parking lot.

"I'll give you a buck for two of those," Vince said to one of them, pointing at their smokes.

"It's nothing." The kid handed Vince the pack he'd had in his shirt pocket. Vince accepted it with a nod and led Casey away, to the quiet far corner of the lot, where he knocked a cigarette from the pack and slipped it between his lips. "Gimme your lighter."

Casey hesitated, wondering if his brother would recognize the thing. "You've been free of those things for almost a year. You sure?"

"It's a fucking exceptional day," he said, cigarette jumping at the edge of his lips. "Now, gimme a goddamn light."

Casey pulled the Zippo out, flicked it open, and lit it, letting his fingers hide the insignia. No point triggering memories of their father, not when Miah's was so conspicuously absent. Vince sucked the cigarette halfway to the filter inside a minute, looking like a man who'd just surfaced from a long dive and tasted fresh air.

"Fuck me, I missed that."

"I won't tell Nita."

"Or Kim," Vince added, and slowed down some. "This is only a one-off." He glanced inside the pack. "A three-off," he corrected, and knocked out the other two smokes, tucking one behind each ear.

"Miah said something to me," Vince said, ashing to the side.

"Oh?"

"That tractor Don was fucking around with this morning— Miah had put the ad out himself, a few weeks ago, looking to sell it."

"Okay."

"So some guy calls late last night, wanting to see it this afternoon. Short notice, and maybe they knew it was old and in rough shape and would need some looking over, first. Maybe the guy even knew it was in the barn."

Casey nodded, catching on. "Because he'd snooped around in there himself already."

"It's possible. Maybe he even fucked with it, to be sure Don would have a hell of a time getting it running. Maybe he never even set foot in there today, if he was smart enough to rig it to catch fire, somehow."

"Maybe." Though Casey knew for a fact that that was some hairy, precision shit right there. And it didn't explain why Don hadn't been able to escape once the fire had caught.

"You say all this to Miah?"

"You crazy? His fucking father's probably dead. Last thing he needs is conspiracy theories before the body's even found."

"True." But he was with Vince, brain skipping ahead past the ugly truth yet to come, chasing answers.

"What else is on your mind?"

"It's even possible this cocksucker picked today on purpose," Vince said, "figuring most of the workers would be away from the bunks and the stables, watching the eclipse."

Casey nodded, not liking how premeditated this was

now feeling. And not liking at all how uncomfortably it echoed his own recent past. His so-called career. That regret that Abilene had wished he'd felt . . . Well, it was creeping in now, too real for his comfort, nagging and pawing at him with ragged, catching nails.

"You think somebody wanted Don dead?" Casey asked his brother.

"Do you?"

"I can't think why. He had industry rivals, no doubt, but who the fuck would want to *kill* him?"

"Maybe they wanted something else," Vince said. "Wanted to corner him, demand something, and maybe he couldn't deliver it? I dunno. Though I do know Miah's been bitching about how cutthroat some of the property scouts have gotten lately." He finished the first cigarette, lit the next off the butt before crushing it beneath his boot.

"This is so fucking messed up," Casey muttered, feeling frustrated and hot.

"We need to get you in there," Vince said. "How soon can that happen?"

"Depends. They'll be digging through it all soon enough. If they find . . ." He trailed off. He'd nearly said "a body," but it felt far too cold. "If they find him," he said carefully, "everything will grind to a halt for a few hours. They'll investigate before they move the body," he said, flinching inside, "but then they'll take it away to be autopsied. They'll mill around documenting everything for a long time, but eventually they'll clear out."

"Will anybody be left to guard the scene?"

Casey shook his head. "Unlikely. They'll probably just put up tape, once the forensic people have made their sweep."

"Then you go in."

"Sure."

"But don't be a dumb-ass about it," Vince warned through a cloud of Camel. "Don't go leaving your shoe prints or a load of red hairs all over the place."

"You say that like this hasn't been my job for three years."

Vince nodded, gaze on the horizon.

"I got no clue what I'll find," Casey said. "This guy could

be a pro or a total hack. But I'll do my best." He didn't hold out much hope, however. Fires spoke volumes about the way they started but didn't tell you jack about who struck the match. Not unless the person in question happened to drop a business card on their way out. "I can tell you if it was started on purpose, but if anybody stands a chance at saying who by, it's Miah."

"I can't ask him now . . . But it'll have to be soon. I'll see if he can't find out who answered that ad about the John Deere."

"Good a lead as any." Better than some dark-colored truck, some tallish, vaguish description of a white guy in a ski mask and jeans.

"Not much, though," Vince said grimly. "It'd take an idiot to reply to the ad with their actual e-mail address or leave a real phone number."

Casey stole the final smoke from behind Vince's ear and lit it for himself. It tasted like a thousand ancient memories. It tasted like ass, in all honesty, but the nicotine wasn't unwelcome. He blew out a long jet of smoke and told his brother, "We better hope we're dealing with a world-class fuckwit, then."

The news everyone had been dreading came around dinnertime.

Casey heard it from Vince, who'd been in the kitchen with Miah and Christine when the mayor, of all people, had come by to break it to them, with Fortuity's acting sheriff in tow, who also served as the county coroner.

Casey had gone into town to fill in Kim and Nita, then Raina and Duncan, and had pulled in just behind the sheriff's cruiser. Freeman, he thought the new sheriff was called—Wes or Les Freeman. He was tanned and tall and lanky, far younger than Tremblay had been—may that motherfucker rot in hell. He wore the uniform's matching khaki hat that Tremblay never had, and it made him look like a cartoon. Especially when Mayor Dooley joined the tableau, the squat little Napoleon in seersucker climbing out of the sheriff's car, ivory bolo swinging. The mismatched men headed for the house, and Casey hung back, knowing it couldn't be good. The mayor didn't show up at the home of the most prominent family in town to hand out happy news.

Casey sat on his own hood for nearly half an hour before the men emerged. He nodded at Freeman, who'd come by the bar a couple times as a patron. Dooley he didn't know aside from seeing his pompous face in the papers, and he didn't offer him jack. That dick had brought the casino to town, after all. And the casino had gotten Alex killed. He couldn't say he was much of a fan of the mayor, no.

Sheriff Freeman tipped his hat but didn't smile, and then both men disappeared inside the cruiser. Casey waited until they'd hit the road, then headed to the farmhouse on legs made of lead.

The scene he found in the kitchen about tore him to shreds.

Miah was holding his mother. Her face was buried against his neck, her shoulders hitching uncontrollably. Miah was crying as well, his voice breaking as he spoke to her. Vince was standing by the sink with his arms crossed, and he motioned for Casey to follow him and strode for the door.

"They need space," he said, heading for the den.

"They found the body?" Casey whispered, sitting on the coffee table when Vince took the couch.

He nodded. "Beside the tractor he'd been working on. One of the investigators said it started from diesel, and maybe Don had got caught up in it, if he'd spilled some on his clothes, or had grease on him or something. Nothing conclusive. That's all they said about it."

Spilled? Doused, more like. "Autopsy?"

"Still going on. They only came to say he'd passed."

"Does anybody need to go downtown to ID him?"

"Thank fuck, no. I guess they had enough to go on."

Casey nodded, and in a breath, the heft of the news came down on him. "Fucking shit. This can't actually be happening, can it?"

Vince didn't say anything, just stared ahead and exhaled slowly. A deep and cutting pang of guilt sank between Casey's ribs, as he tried to imagine having been here when the news about Alex had broken. Fortuity had always been quiet. If somebody died, it was of old age or maybe cancer, or drunk driving, or some freak hunting accident. This place was no stranger to fights and domestic violence, but murder? Alex had been the first—or rather, technically the second, though the undocumented worker whose bones had caused so much trouble last year hadn't been uncovered until a few months later. Sheriff Tremblay had been killed in his cell after his involvement in Alex's death had come to light—number three. Now Don made four. Though Casey supposed this latest one couldn't be blamed on the casino.

He was poised to ruminate on the thought, but Vince spoke. "The fire crews have all cleared out. Once it's dark, we get to work. I'll keep watch; you do your thing."

Casey shook his head. Above them, he caught the far-off chime of Abilene's phone. "I'll go alone. It's less conspicuous that way."

Vince looked dubious, but nodded. "What will you need?"

"Not much." Maybe a tarp to cut up and tape around his feet, to keep his treads covered. There wasn't much he could do about clothing fibers on short notice, plus at least a dozen people had been tromping through the debris already. He'd draw his hood and don some gloves and call it good enough. His primary concern just now wasn't covering his own ass, but finding out how this had happened, and more importantly, by whose hand.

"I have to get home soon," Vince said, glancing at his phone. "I'll check on Miah one more time; then I'm off. But if you change your mind and decide you want a lookout, call me. I could come out after midnight."

"I won't, but thanks."

Vince frowned and pocketed his cell. "Lemme know if you find anything."

"I will. And you better stop at the gas station and buy yourself some mints or something. You smell like an ashtray."

"Call me," Vince reiterated as he got up and headed for the kitchen. Casey listened as the voices there rose and mellowed, then to the footsteps, then the click and hush of the front doors as Vince saw himself out.

He glanced at the ceiling, wondering what Abilene was up to. Who had called her. But just then the guest room door popped open, and she emerged. She peered down into the den, eyebrows rising as their gazes met. He watched her make her way down the steps silently in her socks, the baby apparently left in her crib.

"Hey," he said.

"Hey. I have a favor to ask."

"Okay." Yes, please—any goddamn thing to keep him busy until late tonight.

"Raina called. She tried you first, but you didn't answer."

"I think my phone's in my car. What's going on?"

"She wanted to see if one of us could bartend with Duncan, so she could come see Miah."

Of course. They might be exes, but they'd been friends far longer. "I can go in," he offered. "I couldn't stay until close, but until midnight or so."

"She was just hoping for a couple hours. I could go, too. I'd like to, actually, if you could watch Mercy. Until ten, maybe?"

He nodded. "Sure." The bar might be good for her, just now.

"She ate a half hour ago, and I just changed her, so she should be fine, apart from maybe wanting some attention."

"I'm on it."

"Thanks. And I'm sure Raina would say the same."

He tailed her upstairs, hefting the baby from the crib while Abilene got her shoes on, then followed her back down to the den.

"Thanks again," she said, finding her keys in her purse.

"Anytime. Have fun," he added, though the sentiment sounded awful stupid the moment it left his lips.

She offered a weak smile and left him alone with Mercy. He struggled to imagine how on earth so many things could have happened in the past thirty hours. Two confessions—one of feelings, one of past crimes—then a breakup, an awkward breakfast, the eclipse, the fire. Soon, a night spent prowling around a dark murder scene.

He took a seat on the couch and got the baby comfortable, then switched on the TV and turned the volume down.

"You're awful lucky you won't remember any of this," he

told Mercy, passing over the news stations until he found a channel playing an old western.

She also won't remember Don, he thought. He'd held her only once or twice, and somewhat reluctantly, but he'd also given her a home for a time, and the protection of his family.

"You missed out on knowing a real good man," Casey told her. "As good as they come." He felt tears welling then, and blinked them away.

Chapter 26

Casey passed a quiet evening. Raina arrived about an hour after Abilene had departed, accompanied by the smell of pizza. That drew him off the couch, and he carried Mercy to the kitchen to join the world's most miserable dinner party.

"I didn't think any of you would feel like cooking," Raina was saying, setting three large white boxes on the counter as Casey entered. She cast him a lame smile. There were a lot of those going around today.

The meal was somber, and after perhaps forty minutes, Miah asked to be left alone with his mom. Casey and Raina excused themselves, finished their beers in the den, then bid each other a heavy good night. Abilene returned not long after and retired upstairs with the baby.

Casey waited until midnight, until he couldn't sit still any longer. He had a Maglite in his trunk, and he fetched it, stowed it in his pocket. With an idle thought about criminals returning to the scene, he got his pistol as well. He couldn't think where to find a tarp without looking suspicious himself, creeping around in the dark, but he did nab some extra-thick trash bags from under the sink and took two of those and a roll of duct tape with him, plus a pair of rubber dish gloves.

It was a dark night, the moon out of sight. Darker than it had been during the eclipse. A million times quieter, with a million stars now glittering above. He gave the bunks and stables a wide berth, hugging the fence that bordered the road. If anybody asked what he was doing . . . Shit, he had no fucking plan. Pretend he was drunk, maybe. He'd spent years caring about nothing more than covering his own ass, but just now, it was way too hard to give a shit.

The barn was in near darkness, with just the weakest trickle of light making it over from the bunkhouse windows. There was yellow tape up, but nothing more. To most people this looked like the scene of a tragic accident.

Lucky them, Casey thought, weary to the marrow with all the death that had begun skulking around his hometown.

He sat on the dirt, taped two layers of heavy plastic around each foot, and donned the gloves. Switched the flashlight on but kept it trained low, mere centimeters from the ground.

It had been a huge barn, but a secondary circle of caution tape narrowed ground zero—the spot where Don's body had been uncovered beside a small industrial tractor, black now, but surely the telltale green and yellow not twelve hours earlier. The floor was covered in junk. Charred wood, fat old nails, slate tile scraps everywhere. Casey turned his attention to the tractor first, to its engine, exposed where one panel had been propped up. He couldn't make much sense of anything with just one beam. Couldn't say where the fire had started, which way it had spread, how hot it had gotten. Only daylight could tell him those things. But tonight, he wasn't after the how. He was after the who.

He swept the light around the mess underfoot, shifting debris, looking for anything unusual and wishing he owned one of those doohickeys his father had had when he'd been little—a strong magnet on a long rod, for fishing dropped bolts and screws from underneath cars or behind workbenches. There might be a single tiny staple somewhere in this mess—the only clue left behind from a pack of matches. Even if there was, though, talk about a needle in a hay—

His hand froze, locking the beam on something square, just where his rustling, plastic-booted foot had pushed aside some litter. Square and black and familiar. He moved the Maglite to his left hand and picked it up.

A cigarette lighter.

It wasn't unlike his own—a chrome deal, though a gas station knock-off, not a real Zippo. He didn't dare wipe at the soot, on the off chance any fingerprints had survived, but instead peered at it by the beam of the flashlight. Like his, it, too, had an emblem on one side. Faux enamel, it looked like, and the plastic once coloring it had melted away, leaving only the metal relief of a cheesy skull-and-daggers motif.

Don didn't smoke, far as Casey knew, and even if he'd had a secret habit, he sure as shit wasn't dumb enough to have lit up while working on a greasy old tractor engine.

It could have already been here. Just another forgotten bit of junk cluttering up this disused barn. But Casey doubted it. Doubted it as surely as he could picture the amateur arsonist who'd started this fire—picture him flicking it open, striking the wheel, perhaps dropping it in surprise or pain when those flames lashed back at his hand, more aggressive than expected, startling him.

He set the lighter on the hood of the tractor and resumed the search.

Casey couldn't say how long he was there, scrabbling around on his hands and knees, peering at blackened scraps and bits of junk by the beam of the Maglite. He only knew that when his back began to ache and his head to throb that it must've been hours.

He checked his phone. Hours indeed. It was pushing six, and though he wasn't sure when dawn was due, precisely, he knew he'd be stupid to still be here once the sky grew light.

One cheap lighter wasn't much, but it was something. He slipped it into a sandwich bag from his pocket and picked his way through the rubble, the scorched earth, and eventually found grass and gravel beneath his feet once more. He ditched the taped-up plastic and the gloves, wadding them up and stashing them in his trunk for the time being. Sloppy, but time was of the essence.

He found his front door key and let himself into the farmhouse, relieved to find it dark and silent. Normally Christine would be up by this hour, but he had no doubt she needed to sleep in . . . if she'd dropped off at all. He fucked around until he found the right light switch, then crept up the front stairway to the Churches' wing of the house, hoping Miah's room was where he remembered, the last door on the left.

Casey knocked firmly. No answer. He turned the knob and eased the door in on a dark room. "Miah?"

"Yeah."

He pushed inside, letting the light from the hall reveal Miah, who was sitting on his bed, fully clothed, with his back against the wall and his hands linked atop his belly, staring at the far window.

"I got no doubt you don't feel like talking just now," Casey said quietly, "but I found something that I could really use your opinion on."

"What?"

"Turn on that light." He nodded to the lamp on Miah's deep windowsill, and he turned it on. He looked about fifty by its mellow glow.

"I found a lighter in the barn, beside the John Deere. Any chance you recognize it?"

He handed Miah the baggie, and the man's eyes were wide in an instant.

"You know it?"

"Yes, I fucking know it."

"Whose?"

Miah spoke so quietly—a simmering growl of a sound—Casey could only just make out the name.

"Bean?" he echoed.

"Chris Bean." Miah sat up, still staring at the bag. "He used to work for us."

"When?"

"Must've hired him five, six years ago. Fired him two winters back."

"Why?"

"Drugs. He was one of our best hands, until he got mixed up with amphetamines. I was the one who caught him at it. I'd know that lighter anyplace—I found him camped out in one of the outbuildings, and I saw it on the floor beside a couple of folded-up sheets of aluminum foil, with tweaker streaks burned all over them."

"You think this is revenge, for your dad firing him? That's pretty fucking extreme."

Miah shook his head. "Dad didn't fire him. I did. Dad gave him more second chances than he deserved, even paid for him to go to rehab. I'm the one who got sick of it and kicked him out." His head jerked to the side, facing the open door like he might jump to his feet and stride out into the predawn darkness at any moment.

"There any chance he could've dropped that in the barn back when he was still working for you?"

"None. I hustled him out that night. Stood there watching while he packed."

"He drive a dark truck back then?"

"No, but that doesn't mean shit."

Well said. "You know where he is these days?" Casey asked.

"I know where he used to stay, after he left."

"Has he been in touch since? Started anything, with any of you?"

"Nothing. But I'm only happy to start something with him right fucking now."

"It's six a.m.," Casey said, but Miah was already swinging his legs over the edge of the mattress and reaching for his boots.

"I'm coming with you." Casey didn't trust the hate blazing in Miah's eyes and wouldn't put it past the man to do something rash.

He followed his friend out of the room, down the stairs, and they grabbed their coats in the front hall. Miah didn't hold the door for Casey, just flung it wide and went striding into the dark. "We need answers, Miah, okay? Answers first, justice later."

"If you come, you stay the fuck out of my way."

"I can't promise that."

Miah stopped short. "That cocksucker *murdered* my father. You have any fucking clue what he has coming to him?"

"Miah—"

He began walking again. "Come with me and you'll find out."

"Just don't get yourself shot or thrown in prison for the rest of your life, man. Your mom needs you." Hell, fucking

Fortuity needed him. Needed the ranch. Vince needed him. "You got too much riding on your shoulders to fuck this up, Miah."

"You come, you better keep out of my way," he said again.

And what choice did Casey have, really?

Chapter 27

It wasn't a long drive—just to the other end of Fortuity, barely twenty minutes at the clip Miah was going. He turned them off the main road just before the railroad tracks and down a cracked and faded residential road, all the way to its end. It was one of the town's more depressing corners, dotted with small houses and trailers, a good quarter of them looking abandoned or at the very least terminally neglected.

The sun was just rising and Miah squinted at the various shitboxes they passed.

"What number?" Casey asked.

"Can't remember, but it was a single-wide, with an old-school laundry line beside it. Dad insisted on cutting him a final paycheck. I insisted on delivering it, so Bean wouldn't get a chance to play the pity card and try to win himself any more chances. I remember there were about six cars parked out front. Just what you'd expect from a load of—"

He went silent and eased them to a halt along the roadside, approaching a trailer. There were two cars and three trucks sprawled half on the patchy front lawn like beached whales.

"Motherfucker," Casey breathed. The far pickup was navy blue, and a good fifteen, twenty years old to judge by the headlights' glaucoma. "Could that be the truck?"

"One way to know for sure." Miah got out and pulled the rifle from behind his seat. Fuck, that wasn't a good sign. Still, Casey secured the pistol at his own back and followed, jogging to keep up.

Miah wasn't discreet. He circled the truck, boots crunching on the gravel shoulder. The bed was loaded with crap—a shitty old chair and cardboard boxes, trash bags that looked to be maybe stuffed with clothes, like somebody was planning on moving out, and in a hurry. Crouching, Miah inspected the plate, and Casey did the same. Though he couldn't say it was a shock, he still got chills when he saw the dirt clinging to it, in the perfect outline to mark where a sticky length of duct tape had once been pressed.

Miah stared at it for a long breath, then murmured, "I'm gonna fucking kill him."

"Dude—"

He was up, striding toward the house. Casey dashed behind to catch up, just as the door to the trailer popped open.

A slender pale man of thirty or so stood on the threshold, keys dangling from one hand, an army green frame pack in the other. He had a narrow face and stood about Casey's height. Bundled up and wearing a balaclava, he could easily have been taken for James Ware, if that was who you'd been expecting. He got one foot on the cinder block standing in for a front step and froze, eyes growing wide.

Miah kept on marching, the rifle swinging right along like an extension of his arm. "And just where the fuck do you think you're off to?" he shouted.

"Fuck," was all Chris Bean said before dropping his pack and hitting the dirt, running at full-tilt for Christ knew where, aimed at the badlands.

Miah was a dozen paces behind him and gaining. "You stop or I will fucking shoot you in the back!"

Casey got his own weapon drawn but kept the safety on. He hoped to hell Miah had the sense to have done the same.

He found out only seconds later that the answer was no.

The shot rang out in the still morning air, and an instant later Bean went loping off on long, splayed steps, one leg seeming to give out on him as he tumbled headlong into the scrub grass. Miah tackled him as he tried to stand, the impact of his body snapping through Bean's and knocking his face against the earth.

Casey skidded to a halt beside them on pebbles and rocks. Miah fisted Bean's jacket at the shoulders, flipped him over, and slammed him against the ground so hard his head bounced back like whiplash. *"Why?"*

"I had to," the guy gasped. His nose was bleeding from his first collision with the dirt, making his words gurgle. He looked about a breath from passing out, and not only on account of the flesh wound and the impact—his eyes were glazed and unfocused, chest rising and falling like mad, words slurred from more than a head injury, Casey bet. The guy was as fucking high as a kite.

"I had to," Bean sputtered again. "They would've hurt my wife if I didn't."

"Who?"

"I don't know, man. I don't even know. They never gave me names. They gave—" His chest jerked and he coughed, eyes growing hazy, drool slicking his lips.

"They gave you what?" Casey demanded. They needed answers before this cocksucker went into shock.

"Gave me money," he wheezed. "First just to tell them—tell them where to start a fire. Which building. What time. Then they—then they made me do it."

"Who?" Miah gave him another violent shake.

"Calm the fuck down," Casey said. "You're gonna knock him out."

"I don't know," Bean said, sobbing now. "I don't know. Just some guy, who worked for somebody else. No names."

"And you said yes?" Miah hissed. "After every goddamn thing my father did for you? Every fucking chance he gave you to clean your ass up?"

"I didn't—I didn't know it was him."

Miah's expression sharpened, tense body stilling by a degree. "What?"

"I didn't know, until it was already burning. I thought—I thought it was you. When he came in, he had his back to me. It was dark. He was wearing a black hat—he always wore a white one, before."

Miah sank back on his heels slowly, eyes wide, tanned skin going pale.

"It was you they wanted," the man wailed, then turned over, curling up on his side, racked by sobs. "I thought it was you I talked to when I called about the tractor. It was your name on the ad." But not Miah's number, apparently—

probably just the office line. "By the time I realized, it was too late."

Casey could only stare at his friend, feeling struck.

"Why me?" Miah asked, the rage gone from his voice.

"They said you were in the way. That's all they told me, I swear. They said, 'We need him out of the way.'"

"Out of the way of what?"

"I don't know, I don't know. They just told me, 'Get rid of him.'"

"What'd they give you? Fucking *money*?"

"I got busted for selling. They paid my bail. I was gonna get ten years, but they told me they'd get me off if I helped them out."

That gave Casey pause. Who the fuck would have the power to make that promise? A crooked judge, a lawyer? Whoever'd brought the charges? What reason would anybody in such a position have to want Miah dead? Unless it had simply been an empty promise, used to manipulate this addled burnout . . .

"When they told me what they wanted in return," Bean went on, "I said I couldn't. I couldn't do that. But then they threatened to hurt my wife." He began gasping, the sounds of a panic attack closing in.

"Who? Fucking *who*?" Miah shouted.

When the man didn't answer, Miah shot to his feet and kicked him square in the ribs. Casey scrambled to standing and pulled him back while Bean wheezed and clutched his middle. "You can't kill him."

"Why the *fuck* not?" Miah bellowed, his entire body thrashing in Casey's arms. "He meant to do the same to me! He fucking killed my dad!"

Casey managed to wrestle Miah to the dirt, pinning him on his belly as he swore and bucked. Bean was whimpering now, maybe even crying, voice growing fainter by the second, words sounding wet from more than tears, as though he were choking on something.

"You kill him," Casey told Miah, right in his ear, "and we never find out who hired him, you got that? You kill him and the person who wanted you fucking *dead* walks away from all this. Now this motherfucker's fucking choking or some shit, so I'm gonna let you up, and I'm gonna call nine-one-one, and you're not gonna touch him, you got that? We're gonna let the authorities take him, and they'll get you some answers. But you do *not* fucking touch him, you understand me? Your mom needs you too fucking bad right now for you to mess this shit up."

Miah went still. His face was jammed to one side, flushed red from the rage and the dust, equally. He didn't reply, but Casey had no choice but to take his body language as a truce. He stood, eyeing Miah as he pulled his phone out and dialed the digits. Miah sat up, facing away from Casey and the man on the ground, and hugged his knees.

"Nine-one-one, what's your emergency?"

"I need an ambulance, and the police. There's a guy on the ground—he's been shot and I think he's on drugs. He tried to kill my friend," Casey said, realizing with a chill that it wasn't merely a fib to imply self-defense. It was true.

The operator demanded the location and Casey gave it, staying on the line, answering questions until he was told that the authorities were on the way. He checked on Bean and found him breathing, if faintly, sounding as though he had a reed in his throat.

"Don't you dare fucking die, asshole. You've got too much shit to answer for." Casey didn't know a ton about first aid, but decided to leave him on his side, thinking it'd keep him from choking to death on all the shit leaking from his lips. There was more blood on the ground—a small pool of it, but not enough to equal a major artery, he imagined.

"Miah, gimme your knife."

Miah didn't respond, so Casey got up and forcibly took the thing, unclipping it from Miah's belt. He ripped Bean's pant leg open, wincing at the wound. It didn't look deep, but it was bleeding pretty bad, soaking his jeans.

Casey got his own hoodie off and tied it twice around Bean's thigh, tight. His pistol was probably evident through his shirt, but the thing was registered and he had a concealed-carry permit. He didn't relish the cops finding it, but at least he wouldn't get charged.

As the waiting commenced and his role as the cool-headed party ebbed, Casey felt his own rage rising inside.

Don Church was dead.

The man who'd taught Casey how to ride a horse and shoot a rifle. Who'd given him little tastes now and then of what a father was supposed to be like—calling him a dumbass and slapping him upside the head once when he'd been about twelve, penance for riling one of the stock horses. The animal could have kicked him, could've broken his skull, but you didn't consider that shit at that age. Casey had been hit by his own dad a few times before the guy had taken off, but this had been different. More startling, coming from a friend's father. Way more humbling, knowing he'd been called out for a stupid move, that he'd been traded a smack in place of a potentially fatal hoof to the head. More humiliating, too, because he'd always looked up to Don Church, thinking the guy was about as cool as dads came. As cool as a cowboy from a western. He'd grown up a little that day.

These past few months, Casey had been wanting to feel like someone important, like a man who mattered. He'd thought that his part in saving the bar was the way to achieve that, and it wasn't off the mark . . . but there was no more significant thing a man could be than a father, was there? Whether you were Don Church or Tom Grossier, the choices you made as a father could change people profoundly, for better or worse. Don had done so much good, for so many people.

Now he's gone.

He'd never meet Miah's future kids, or kiss his wife again, or see his land or his animals, or drive down Station Street with his tanned arm draped along the open window, raising his hand at every person he passed. He was ten times more recognizable than the mayor—a hundred times more respected.

Or he used to be. Past tense.

Casey glanced at Chris Bean, lying nearly still save for the faintest rise and fall of his ribs, silent except for that eerie whistling breath. *All because of you,* Casey thought, and felt his muscles tensing, wanting to kick and hit and strangle, to reach for his gun and finish the fucking job.

Not only because of him, he reminded himself. Bean was the bullet. You could curse the bullet all you wanted, but where would that get you, in the end? It was the hand around the grip and the finger on the trigger that mattered. The brain that gave the order to squeeze.

"You better fucking live," he muttered, squinting at Bean. "You just better hope you fucking live."

Bean did live, but not for long.

Long enough to die in the back of the ambulance from circulatory shock—a combination of stress and the drugs in his system, the news later reported—but not long enough to get questioned by the police or shed any more light on the tragedy now gripping Fortuity.

All told, Miah and Casey had spent about six hours being questioned by the authorities. Casey had confessed that he'd trespassed and shown them the lighter. He might get a fine for disturbing a crime scene, but both their firearms were legit. Miah had shot Bean, and from behind, so self-defense was no excuse. Still, the shot hadn't killed him—the drugs had—and Miah had ultimately been released. If he did face criminal charges, it'd be hard to make them stick, given the circumstances; Don Church had been a monumental figure in the county, and it was unlikely any jury of Miah's peers would want to see him punished for his part in turning his father's accidental death case into an arson investigation and possible homicide.

The autopsy had found two bullets in Don's back—one in his shoulder, one in his spine, both shot from medium range. They were 9mm, and their casings matched those from the warnings aimed at Jason on Friday night. Unusual marks on the slugs found in Don's body suggested a silencer.

If the circumstances were merciful, that shot to the spine meant maybe Don had died quickly, never having lived to suffer the fire.

It was Thursday morning, and Miah looked up from his laptop at the sound of the doorbell. He'd been wading through e-mails, business and personal alike, and trying not to drown in the process. This was the third morning he'd woken to realize his father was dead, and though the shock of it was fading, the pain hadn't ebbed a jot.

He shouted, "I got it," in case his mother had been poised to interrupt whatever she was doing in the office. He headed for the front door.

Not condolences, he prayed as he closed his hand around the knob. He couldn't take any more kind words, any more sad faces, any more goddamn *casseroles.* The funeral was set for Sunday, and he'd need all the stamina he could muster just to survive it.

He opened the door, finding his wish had been granted. But the visitor was still a touch troubling.

It was an official, dressed in the Sheriff's Department's khaki pants and jacket, a silver six-cornered star pinned above her left breast and a black leather messenger-type bag strapped across her modest chest. In light of Bean saying Miah had been the intended target of those bullets, he'd been offered a bodyguard, but declined. He felt suffocated as it was, and the authorities posted around the property felt like protection enough.

This officer was tallish, slim, with strikingly good posture. Her skin was dark brown, hair pulled into a ponytail and exploding at the back of her head in a thousand tight little curls. She looked about thirty, and Miah had seen her before—he was sure of it. But he hadn't known the BCSD to have anyone like her in their ranks. Hell, there was probably only a handful of African Americans in all of Brush County. Kind of tough to miss.

"Mr. Church, good morning. I'm Deputy Ritchey," she said, and he placed her by her firm, calm voice in an instant. The uniform had thrown him.

"You were here with the fire crew."

She nodded. "I'm a volunteer, when I'm off duty." She offered a cool hand, and Miah shook it.

"You probably know my name already," he said.

She nodded. "Jeremiah."

"Miah's fine."

"So is Nicki," she said with a little smile.

"Is this to do with the investigation?"

"No, that's in the detectives' hands. I'm just a patrol deputy."

"Oh." His shoulders sank. He'd kill for any hint that someone was making progress in figuring out who'd hired

Chris Bean. Wild, racing theories haunted him at night when he tried to sleep, but none felt right. Something was always missing—a motive big enough to warrant murder. Miah had given the names and contact details of the property vultures to the BCSD, on the off chance they might be linked. Still, it was all so muddy and desperate just now, and waiting was torture. If he didn't have a reeling business to keep afloat, he'd be out there himself, looking for answers. The inactivity left him feeling helpless, neutered.

"Can I help you with something?" he asked the deputy.

She slid her bag around to her front and opened its flap, pulling out a thick, quart-sized black plastic bag. "The forensics team has released some items from the arson investigation. Your dad's things, we guessed. I wanted to give them to you. If you'd like them, that is."

He stared at the bag, heart twisting, and he felt tears rising, contorting his face. "What sorts of things?"

"A pocketknife, and a belt buckle, and a watch."

His breath was gone, sucked from his chest. His legs felt funny and apt to give, and he sank awkwardly onto the bench. The deputy did the same, looking concerned.

He reached for the bag with a shaking hand, and the weight of it struck like a battering ram, knocking him hard in the heart, doubling him over. He felt a kind hand on his back, between his shoulder blades. It scrunched his shirt softly a few times, then rubbed.

"I'm so sorry for your loss," the deputy said. She sounded like she meant it, too, not like she was simply reading from the script.

Miah looked up enough to meet her eyes and give her permission to take her hand back. She scooted an inch or two farther down the bench, linking her fingers between her knees.

"I asked to come, to bring you his things," she said. "I lost my dad, too. He was a cop, back in Chicago."

"When?" Miah asked. "When did you lose him, I mean?" He was breathing quick, feeling like so much hinged on her answer.

"I was twenty-five, so almost six years ago."

"Oh. I'm sorry to hear that. You're a long way from Chicago," he added.

"Sometimes people need a change of scenery," she said with a smile.

"Your dad . . . Was he . . ." He trailed off, but she read his mind.

She nodded. "He was shot."

"How do . . . Does it ever stop feeling like this?" he asked, voice breaking. "How did you ever even manage to keep going, after?"

"I had to," she said. "For my son."

"Oh."

Her gaze was soft, her eyes dark brown and looking infinitely patient. A small comfort. "You must have people who still need you, Miah. Your mother?"

He nodded, a little bit of the steel returning to his spine. "My mother."

"Nobody's saying you need to be strong right now," she told him, and for some reason those words cut straight down to the bone. He started crying—loud and ugly and out of control—hugging his own arms, hurting like his heart was about to rip in two.

The deputy put her hand on his knee, squeezing. "You don't have to be strong," she repeated. "You just have to *be*. Just have to get up every morning, be with your mom, and take turns with her day to day, being the one with their shit together, you know?"

He didn't know, not yet. But it seemed he'd find out soon.

"It *will* stop feeling like this," she told him. "It won't ever stop hurting, but it won't always feel like this. You'll always have the memory. A scar. But the wound will heal."

He looked to the bag, which had fallen to the floor between his feet. He picked it up, held it out. "I'm not ready for this."

She accepted it. "Tell me where I can leave it, for when you decide you are ready."

He thought about it. "In the kitchen, just around the corner. On top of the hutch."

She disappeared for a few moments, then returned and took her seat once more. "Now, is there anything I can do? For you or your mother?"

He shook his head. "No, we'll be okay."

Another gentle smile. "It's okay if you're not, for a little while."

Tears stung anew, but he wiped them away with the back of his hand.

"I'll give you my card," she said, reaching into her breast pocket. "In case you think of anything."

He took it. "Thanks."

"I can see myself out," she said, poised to stand.

"Wait."

She met his eyes, settled back down with her hands clasped patiently on her thighs.

"Did you know Alex?" he asked her. "Alex Dunn?"

She shook her head. "That was before my time. I was transferred shortly after he passed."

Something cold dropped into Miah's stomach. "Oh. Were you his replacement?"

"It's not that simple. A lot of people got shifted around after your sheriff was arrested. But I suppose I was, in a way. You knew him?" she asked. "Alex?"

"Since we were kids."

"His colleagues have only good things to say about him," she offered.

Miah nodded. For all Alex's flaws, he'd been an excellent deputy. He looked down, feeling exhausted and strange and a little high. "What the fuck's happening to this town?" he asked the hallway at large.

"Change," the deputy—Nicki—said.

"Not for the better," he muttered.

She didn't reply. Miah glanced up, finding a sad smile on her face.

"Thanks," he said, and tried to let the bitterness go.

"My job," she said, standing. Miah did the same. "You take care of yourself. And your mother. She'll try to do all the healing for the both of you. But you step in and take over when you're up to it, okay? Us mamas, sometimes we need our sons to fill their father's shoes. But only when you're up for it."

He nodded, though filling his father's shoes ... He doubted he could ever fit in them. His dad's steps had felt as long and wide as canyons since he'd been a tiny kid.

Looking like the man didn't make Miah his equal. "How old is your son?" he asked the deputy.

"Nine."

"He ever have to be the man of the house?"

She smiled deeper, eyes crinkling. "More often than I care to admit. But he does me proud, same as you'll do for your own mother."

He tried to smile back, not feeling so sure.

"Take care, Miah." And she turned once more and opened the door, closed it softly behind her.

Chapter 28

Casey, Vince, and Miah were in the Churches' den watching the noon KBCN broadcast later that day, Don's death still dominating the headlines, no shock. Vince clicked off the TV as yet another uninformative report wrapped, tossing the remote to the next couch cushion and rubbing his face. The gesture said exactly what Casey was feeling. *It's another fucking murder mystery in Fortuity, then, is it?* But of course now was a time to keep one's frustration and anger to oneself. The tone of the room was Miah's to set, after all.

The man was quiet, sitting in the rocker, leaning forward with his forearms on his knees, staring at the now-dark screen. His expression was stony. He looked ancient, with circles under his eyes and the drawn cheeks of a man who hadn't eaten or drunk anything in days. But there was life in those eyes again, Casey thought. Determination or strength or at least *anger*, whereas last night there'd been nothing but blankness.

The floorboards overhead creaked now and then, the sounds of Abilene gathering up her and the baby's things. She was going to move out. She'd told Casey the previous morning. Rightly, she wanted to give Miah and Christine the space to deal with the brewing investigation, as well as their grief.

She'd talked to Raina and Duncan and would be staying in the guest room of their apartment above the bar until she found her own place.

She was treating Casey kindly. Being friendly, even, though there was sadness weighing down the edges of their conversations. Regret. Maybe a little taste of the mourning now suffusing the farmhouse, though for the death of their romance as well as that of a good man.

Vince broke the heavy silence. "Beer?" he asked the room at large.

Miah shook his head, gaze on the floor.

Casey shook his, too. "I'm helping Abilene move any minute." At least she'd agreed to let him help. She didn't hate him—she just couldn't love him. Last night she'd let him watch Mercy again while she went in for a short shift at Benji's, and he hoped she'd keep relying on him. He cared about that baby, more than he'd ever have guessed he might, and to hear Abilene say she wasn't comfortable with that anymore . . .

He sighed and stood.

"Grab me a bottle while you're up," Vince said. "Looks like I'm drinking for everybody." And given that it was noon on a Thursday, he'd told his bosses at the quarry to go fuck themselves. Certainly not the first time.

Casey fetched him the beer, then headed up to check on Abilene's progress. He knocked softly on the door.

"Come in."

He found the room nearly stripped. The bed where they'd come together was bare to the mattress, the bedding rolled up in a tangle at its foot. "Wow, that was quick."

She smiled and shrugged. "I never had much to begin with. Was that the news you guys were watching?" He'd filled her in on the previous morning's events yesterday afternoon.

"Yeah. Bean died of shock in the back of the ambulance. From the drugs as much as anything, it sounds like. Not from Miah shooting him." And it seemed the man had spilled enough to implicate himself before he'd gone under for good, if not to name any of his alleged bosses. "If anything, Miah's going to wind up a folk hero," Casey said. "People around here loved his dad, and they love justice."

"I guess that's something. That he won't be in trouble, I mean."

"It's a lot. Last thing the ranch can handle right now is to lose two of its owners."

Christ knew poor Christine was in no shape to handle it

all on her own. Some of her family had arrived from out of state, at least—two sisters and one of their husbands. They were downstairs now, cooking and handling the endless incoming calls with stern efficiency. The phone seemed to ring ten times an hour, but never with any insight into who'd wanted Miah dead, or why.

Abilene didn't ask Casey anything more about the news, and he didn't blame her. Everyone had information overload, and that combined with the grieving was enough to fatigue anybody. It reminded him way too much of the aftermath that had followed Vince's exposure of the now-late Sheriff Tremblay's involvement in Alex's death.

"Can I help with anything?" Casey asked.

"You could break down the crib," Abilene offered. "If you can find the right screwdriver." She paused, gaze catching on his left hand, its first fingers wrapped in a bandage. "What happened to you?"

"Nothing, just a little nick." Just a nasty little flesh wound from a pair of wire cutters, from when he'd been furiously snipping his old cell phone's SIM card into tiny slivers that morning. He'd lost himself in a frantic fit of anger, and his finger had paid the price. The rest of the phone had met its maker courtesy of a hammer, and he'd enjoyed every seething, righteous moment of it. He knew what that phone had been, with hindsight—an escape hatch. He'd hung on to Emily's number, kept himself accessible in case he ever needed an out, an exit ramp straight back to easy street for when the going got tough around here. In the wake of Don's death, he hated what that phone represented. He hated himself for having hung on to it for so long, and had felt better once those plastic shards had disappeared into their shallow grave . . . if only a little.

He held up his hand, pressing his finger and thumb together and pretending the pain didn't scream like an unholy bitch. "It's nothing, plus I'm right-handed. I can handle the crib." *Anything for you.* Anything she needed, anything she asked for. As for himself, he'd never needed to collapse into somebody's arms as badly as he did hers, right now. Except he couldn't. And he knew better than to even wish it.

He wasn't a fool. He wasn't going to play the same part he had since the fall, Mr. Useful, Mr. Reliable, and expect that, given time, she'd get over his past. Because it hadn't been completely in his past, just like she'd called it. He'd been considering that last job. He squeezed his hand into a fist, just to make his finger shriek.

He carried the bedclothes down and left them on the washing machine, found a couple screwdrivers in the Churches' junk drawer.

"Success," he told Abilene when he joined her back in the room.

She smiled politely, checking the caps on her toiletry bottles before tossing them in a suitcase. Something flashed at her throat.

The cross, he realized, taken aback.

"You're wearing it," he blurted.

She blushed and put her hand to the pendant, nodded.

"I wasn't sure if you would."

"I wasn't, either. But these last few days . . . Let's just say I've needed it, more than ever." She pressed it to her skin with her fingertips, like a tiny prayer, maybe. "Thanks."

He nodded and decided to let it rest at that. It was too dangerous to read anything into it. Dangerously hopeful.

The baby was in the crib, and she stared up at Casey with those wide blue eyes. Then she smiled at him. He smiled back, remembering the couple weeks before she could do that, back when he and Abilene had debated every little expression on her face. *Happy or gassy?* He straightened to look at Abilene.

"Okay if I take her out?"

She laughed, the sound like bells, cheering him some. "I didn't expect you to take it apart with her still in there."

"No, I just . . . I wasn't sure if you wanted me doing that now. Touching her or whatever. I know when I'm babysitting, it's different, I didn't want to assume. Or seem too familiar, I guess."

Her smile faded and her brows drew together, unmistakable hurt. She crossed the floor to stand beside him by the crib. She spoke to him but looked at her daughter.

"Of course you can still touch her. I don't hate you, Casey. I just can't be with you, how we were. You do understand why, don't you?"

"Yeah, of course." And better now than ever, after everything that had happened.

She sighed, shoulders looking heavy. Finally she straightened and met his eyes with those startling ones. "I promised myself when I found out I was pregnant, I wasn't going to make the same mistakes I had been. One of those mistakes was falling for the wrong guys, again and again. And believe me when I tell you, you're wonderful. You've treated me better than any other guy I've been with, and you're way nicer than any of them. Better in every way. But you're still . . . The things you did, and that you were thinking of still doing. It's illegal, and it's dangerous. For you and for other people. I can't let that kind of thing slide anymore."

"I'm never taking another one of those jobs ever again," he said.

She looked away, shaking her head. "I want to believe that. But even if I knew it was a hundred percent true . . ."

He nodded. "You don't need to explain." Never had he been so crystal clear on his own shortcomings, and how they must seem to an outsider. He'd had to fill Miah in some, to explain why he'd been poking around in the ruined barn to begin with when he'd found the lighter. It had curdled his guts to spill it all, knowing that the man had just lost his father to arson. Miah had taken it in stride, but Casey had felt dirty, deep down in his heart. Ashamed.

But it was too late for those feelings now, where Abilene was concerned. He'd had his chance to say the right things—to *feel* the right way about his own past—and he'd fucked it, thoroughly.

He half wished he *was* doomed to lose his mind, now and then. It seemed like the only thing that might spare him suffering the burden of this regret for the rest of his life.

Chapter 29

You don't need to explain. Those words echoed in Abilene's head as she got the baby into her sling and hefted her bag.

If only I could. She knew she couldn't be with him. She'd known it with perfect clarity just a few days earlier, but her sense of the reasons was growing fuzzy. Catastrophes had a way of putting things in perspective, of making minor horrors seem less atrocious by comparison. She couldn't be with him because . . . because . . .

Because he was selfish, and dangerous.

But what was selfish about risking his own skin, helping Miah hunt down the man who'd killed Don? He'd willingly told the authorities he'd snooped in a closed crime scene. He could've been investigated, maybe even gotten busted for all those jobs he'd pulled in Texas. He could have gotten killed going after Bean with Miah, had the man been carrying his own gun that morning. A selfish person wouldn't have done either of those things.

A selfish man wouldn't be helping a woman move, once he knew he had no chance of getting in her pants again.

And a selfish man wouldn't have sunk his life savings—shadily earned or not—into a foundering business in a last-ditch attempt to preserve something authentic in a community soon to be beset by outsiders.

He *had* been selfish. There was no escaping that fact, yet since he'd come home he'd been anything but. Even that dumb-ass move, considering taking one last job . . . Even that, he'd wanted to do for her. She believed that. For all his faults, all his crimes, he wasn't a liar, she thought, watching as he sandwiched the crib's mattress between its sides, screwdriver tucked into his back pocket.

"Be careful." She held her breath as they headed downstairs, worried he might trip and break his neck trying to carry it all at once, but they reached the ground floor without injury.

They found Miah alone in the den.

"Did Vince head out?" Casey asked him.

"Yeah. I told him to after he'd finished his beer. I need to get outside, check on how the hands are getting on with everything." He eyed their loaded arms. "Need help?"

"Nah," Casey said. "It's only a couple trips."

Miah got up all the same, no doubt eager for a distraction. "I can at least take her off your hands while you get the convoy organized," he said, gesturing at the baby.

"Oh yeah. That would be helpful." She set down her suitcase and got the sling off, and handed Mercy over. "Thanks. We'll be quick."

The two cars were loaded inside ten minutes, and Casey stayed outside, trying to get the Colt's trunk to shut around the crib's cumbersome corners. Abilene went back in to give the guest bathroom a final sweep, then downstairs, where Miah was settled back in the rocker with the baby propped against his chest.

"We're fixing to head out . . . I'm sad I won't be able to say good-bye to your mom," she told him. "And tell her thanks for everything. All of you. I can't say how much it's meant."

He opened his mouth. Closed it. She waited patiently, and at length he looked her in the eye and said, "Sit for a sec."

She perched on the couch arm. "Yes?"

"Casey said you guys are . . . Well, that you had been something, but now you're not."

She flushed, but nodded. "Yeah. That kinda sums it up."

"That's all I know about it, that and the fact that he said he f—that he messed something up," Miah corrected.

"It's not quite that. There were just some things in his past that I couldn't get on board with."

Miah nodded. "He sorta filled me in, too, after the fire. It's fucked up—I won't lie." He shot the baby an apologetic look for the cuss. "Sorry. But anyway . . . I mean, maybe my opinions about it are skewed, given how shady my best friend is, but I hope that if you two were something special to each other, that you'll be able to forgive him, sometime. That's completely your choice, obviously, but I just wanted to say, he's changed."

She nodded, hoping that was true. He'd been a bad man before he'd come home, but he was trying to be better now. Maybe not quite nailing it, but *trying*.

"More changed than you could possibly know," Miah went on. "I grew up with the kid, and sure, he's changed a lot since he was twenty, but he's also changed a ton in just the past few months. Since he met you."

Unsure what to say, she simply held his gaze, wondering what was next.

Miah sighed. "I'm such a wreck just now, I'm probably not even making any sense. But just know that . . . that he's different, because of you. The Casey who came back to Fortuity would never have bought that bar, or agreed to stick around for his mom, or done everything he has for you and the baby. Something's changed in him, and while I can't say exactly what did it, I have no doubt you're part of it. He's gone from self-serving to damn near selfless in the last six months. He's far from perfect. We all are. But he really *is* trying."

"I know. But it's still a lot to process."

"I'm not saying he's right for you or anything, and I won't pretend I know exactly why you had to end things. But if it was good, and it was real, and all you need is to forgive him . . . I don't know what I'm saying, except that good things don't come along every day. And sometimes the ones that do are worth working for. None of my business, obviously. But for the first time since I've known that man, he deserves some credit."

She felt her throat tightening, tears brewing, and found her fingers reaching for her cross. She was half-surprised to find something there to clasp once more.

She nodded. "He does. He's been amazing to me, and I don't want him out of my life. Or hers," she added, nodding to Mercy. "But he can't be the one for me, I don't think. It's too much to explain, but it's as much about me as it is about him. I've made the same mistakes, again and again and again in my life. And it's time to quit making them."

Miah looked sad to hear that. "I think he feels the same way."

That had the tears officially threatening to fall, so she rose and started getting the sling back on.

Miah sighed. "I'm sorry. That was none of my business."

"He's your friend. It's fine." Just hard, *so* hard to hear, when she was already having such a difficult time committing to the decision she'd made. She took the baby back and settled her in the cotton straps.

Miah's face was so full of pain, she thought. She and Casey not working out was trivial compared to what his family had just suffered, but it must hurt all the same, knowing yet another good thing had been lost.

"Give your mom my best," she offered, feeling lame. "Take good care of her, like she did for me and Mercy."

He nodded. "Always. It was nice having you guys here."

"Good luck with everything."

"You, too."

And with a quavering smile, she turned and headed for the front.

Casey was leaning on the hood of his car, looking at his phone. He tucked it in his pocket when the clatter of the closing door announced her arrival.

"Got everything?"

"I think so. Sorry to dawdle—I had to say good-bye to Miah. Say thanks and all that."

"Course."

He helped get Mercy into her car seat, and they each climbed behind their wheels and headed for town.

She eyed the farmhouse in her rearview. She'd been here just over two weeks, yet it had felt like a major, formative phase of her new life. Saying good-bye to Miah had been hard, but it was the next good-bye that she truly dreaded. Saying good-bye to Casey, this afternoon. He'd still be her boss, and hopefully her friend, but he'd so very nearly been so much more. She'd be saying good-bye for now, but also good-bye to everything they'd been for each other, this past week.

Will I greet him in a few months, when I come in for my

shift, and still feel all this? All the longing and the sadness, the regret that they couldn't have been more?

Miah's words echoed. *He's different, because of you.*

And she was different because of him. She had more faith in men than she had before, maybe ever. Faith that she could attract a guy who'd treat her well, respect her, worry about her, and be kind without expecting a thing in return. Maybe she'd managed to fall for yet another criminal, but she'd picked a good one, for a change.

For a change. She'd changed.

And he wants to change. He *had* changed, to hear Miah tell it.

She tried to imagine how this would've felt, if he hadn't been involved in all those dangerous things. If he'd been the good one, and she'd been the one whose confession had put an end to all of this. If she'd sat down and bared her soul and her past, and he'd told her, *Sorry, but I can't be with you. You're too damaged.* What had she told him, with her decision? *Sorry—you're too bad. Too crooked. Too selfish.*

Yet he'd never been any of those things with her. So much the opposite, in fact, that she'd been shocked to hear about the things he'd done.

She nearly wished they'd never decided to share their pasts. Things could have continued, all blissful and ignorant. Blissful and passionate and fun and affectionate, and she could have discovered what the tiny bud of their nascent family unit might've grown into.

Would things have been different, if they were in love? If they'd said those words aloud, made some kind of commitment before that conversation had happened?

I think I was already in love with him, so what does it matter?

It did matter, though. It would have mattered if she knew for sure he felt the same. Would have been so much harder if he'd ever told her, *I want that baby to call me "Dad" someday.* Oh Christ, that would've made it a million times harder to end it. And not because of the security offered by such a statement, just because . . . because . . .

Because it would've been real.

She stared at the silver of his bumper as they stopped at

the only light in town, a block from Benji's. And it struck, like a slap.

It was real. He has told me those things. A hundred times in the last few months. Never in words, but in action after action after action. Every time he'd shown up with groceries, unbidden. Every time he'd offered to babysit. Every sleepless night he'd suffered, every bottle he'd warmed, every time he'd driven her to town, every cross word he'd had for her ex. Every dollar he'd considered earning and giving to her, no matter how terrible that idea had been.

He had told her those things, hadn't he?

And actions don't lie. People could. Words could. But not months and months of kindness. And not the things his body had told hers, any of the times they'd come together in her bed.

She tailed him into the bar's back lot, heart feeling like a jumbled heap of too many questions.

"Home sweet home," Casey called as she stepped out of her car.

"For now, anyhow." She glanced up at the windows of the second floor, wondering what it would be like, staying with her boss and former boss. Casey was her boss as well, of course, but it had never really felt that way. Raina had been fair, but a hard-ass. And Duncan was . . . Duncan. Nice enough, but also stiff and stuffy and a touch overbearing when it came to rules and order. *Nothing compared to my dad, though.* Still, she'd be very mindful of keeping her and Mercy's stuff from cluttering up the common rooms.

"You'll find your own place soon," Casey said, reading her mind. The back door was unlocked, as promised, and he picked up a cinder block from beside the Dumpster to prop it open wide. Abilene got the baby out, seat and all, carrying her up behind Casey, who had a suitcase in each hand.

They found Duncan in the kitchen, finishing what looked like a plate of salad. "Oh good, it's not burglars, then."

"Nope, just your new tenants," Casey said dropping the bags. "Here, watch this." He took the car seat from Abilene, setting it on the table.

Duncan's eyes widened. "I'm due to open the bar in—"

"We'll be quick," Casey said, halfway to the door.

"Does it . . ." He eyed the baby, then Abilene. "Does she need anything?"

"No, she's fine. If she starts crying, I'll be back up in a minute."

"Right. So I just . . . let her cry?"

She smiled. "She'll be fine. I'll be right back."

She passed Casey on the stairs, flattening herself against the wall as he slipped by with the crib panels under his arms.

"He's completely terrified," she whispered.

"Excellent."

She headed back out into the sunshine, smiling genuinely for the first time in days, it felt.

They had the cars empty in no time, and back upstairs, Abilene told Duncan, "Thank you. And good job—you've officially babysat now."

"You're welcome." He stood, seeming eager to escape, as though she'd left him alone with a wolverine.

"Gosh," she said, carrying Mercy into the spare bedroom, where Casey was reassembling the crib. "I think he's, like, literally afraid of babies."

"Perfect for Raina, then."

She set the seat down and sat on the edge of yet another temporary bed. "Thanks again. For helping me move."

"Anytime."

Anytime, indeed. Anytime she'd needed him these past few months, he'd been there.

"Don't hesitate to ask," he added, crouching with the screwdriver in hand. "Just because you and I couldn't be . . . you know. That doesn't mean I'm any less fond of you. Either of you," he said, nodding to Mercy.

"That's awful nice."

He shrugged, eyes on the task. "Apart from the bar, and my mom, what else have I got to do with my time? It's my pleasure."

"No," she said, smiling. "It's not."

He looked up.

"Your pleasure? All those nights when she kept you awake, shrieking? All the nights you stayed up to stand guard, worried about my ex?"

"Well, it was my honor, anyhow."

His honor ... He did have that, in a way. And not long ago at all, he'd had her respect, her admiration.

And I still have his, if only because he never got to find out about my own mistakes.

She knew he was hurting, from how she'd rejected his past. Maybe he'd feel just a little better if she shared her own mistakes with him now. A little relieved, like maybe he'd dodged a bullet himself. It wasn't as though he was the only monster. She was far from perfect.

"Listen. Sit a minute." She patted the bed. "If you can spare it."

He sat and she did the same, facing him.

"You told me about your past," she said. "I still owe you mine. Maybe it'll help you understand why it is I need everything in my life going forward to be on the up-and-up."

"You don't owe me anything, but I'll listen all the same."

"It's ..." A ragged breath hijacked her chest, but she forced out a long exhalation, calming some. Damn, one word in and already she was a mess.

"You don't need to say it if it's only going to upset you."

"No, I do need to. Because I ... I've made *such* a train wreck of my life." She raked her hair behind her ears with her fingers, struggling for composure.

Casey moved closer and put a hand on her knee, rubbing. Such a familiar gesture. "Hey, it's okay. You're not the first girl who got knocked up by the wrong guy, you know. And you won't be the last."

"It's not that." She sniffed loudly and sat up straight, wiping her nose on her sleeve's cuff.

"Hang on." Casey got up and grabbed a box of tissues from the dresser. "Here."

"Thanks." She honked her nose and he waited patiently.

When her breathing had slowed some, he coaxed, "So if you're not talking about the pregnancy, what?"

She laughed miserably. "Where to begin? The baby's just about the only thing I've managed to do even half-right, these past few years."

"Start at the beginning."

"The beginning ... God. Okay. Well, I guess everything

first started going wrong when I was fifteen. I got into a relationship with ... with my preacher."

His eyes grew round, belying his calm voice. "All right." Between those two words were sandwiched a few others, to the tune of, *Okay, so that* is *a little fucked.*

"And I should tell you, my name wasn't Abilene back then—it's not even my legal name. My real name's Allison Beeman. And I'm twenty-two, not twenty-four."

He nodded, not looking completely surprised. "Raina said once she wondered if your ID was fake."

She met his eyes. "Really?"

"Yeah."

"Oh. Well, I got the fake one when I left home, and started lying about my name and birthdate. But if you ever saw my medical records, they have my real information on them."

"That why you wouldn't let me pick up your mail for you?"

She smiled her apology, feeling shady in an instant.

"And why you wouldn't let me come inside the hospital with you, after the baby was born?"

"That's why."

"You're not evading the law, are you?"

She shook her head. "I wouldn't even know how to, like, get a fake social security number or anything like that. I really only changed my name because I didn't want people plugging me into Google and finding out why I left my hometown—it made the papers, after all."

"What did, honey?"

Honey. She'd missed that name more than she'd realized.

"My preacher, he was about forty-five," she said. "And married. And I'm from, like, the quaintest little God-fearing town in Texas you ever saw. Church was everything, and everybody adored him. So did I."

"And he took advantage of that."

She offered another sad, sheepish smile, and Casey's expression changed—from concerned to surprised in a beat.

"You approached him?"

"Not exactly. But I wanted him, in a way, and he could probably tell. You have to know my family for it to make sense, maybe ... My dad was a retired colonel—I mean, he still is. My parents are still back there, alive and married and probably trying real hard to pretend I never existed. Anyhow, they're both hyperconservative Evangelicals, and it was just implied that I'd wait until I was married to have sex."

"Right."

"But I was always curious about that stuff. I was precocious, was how my grandma put it. Anyhow, my preacher seemed so . . . I dunno. He was handsome, and he was holy, so it felt like the attraction wasn't as sinful as it could have been, somehow. I got completely infatuated with him. And he must have known it."

"And eventually, he exploited that?"

She shrugged, not knowing the answer. "I couldn't say. It wasn't as though I didn't want it, and it wasn't like I ever told him no. Quite the opposite. I was fifteen, and so suppressed by my parents and the church . . . I know it seems like, oh, of course, it was the adult who's to blame."

"Well, yeah."

"He was only human. We both were. He was weak, and I was curious. I only wanted the attention, and to know what sex was like, and to feel wanted by a father figure, maybe, because my dad was so cold and strict."

"But he was still the adult," Casey said. "The one with enough years and sense to say no."

"You can make that argument, but I wasn't the innocent one in it, either. I have that energy that does something to certain men—makes them want to save me. And even at that age, I knew it."

He nodded grudgingly, letting her know he knew what she meant but didn't like it.

"It attracts both savior types and also some real creepers."

Casey smiled. "Which am I?"

She eyed him, curious. "I'm not sure. You tell me."

He replied after a long moment's consideration. "For me, it was never about that. It was partly about you being as pretty as you are, but I mean, when we met, you weren't exactly an easy target—you must've turned me down two dozen times. I think it was just your smile, or your eyes. Both. And how you laugh. Wanting to *make* you laugh. It was never about thinking you needed saving or protecting."

"Or corrupting."

He shook his head. "Nobody winds up in Fortuity because they're innocent. Well, almost nobody." He glanced at the baby. "But anyhow, what happened with you and the preacher?"

"We carried on for six months or more, and I got in real deep with him. I thought I was in love, and maybe I was. It's hard to know, at that age. I was so caught up in the feelings, I started losing track of my values—and I was a God-fearing girl, let me tell you. But I got this idea in my head that he'd leave his wife and we could run away and escape my stupid hometown and all those awful, small-minded people, but of course he told me that was impossible."

"So?"

"So I told his wife. In my imagination, I thought that would drive them apart, and he'd have no excuse not to be with me."

"But what actually happened?"

"She went a little crazy. I think she meant to just sweep it under the rug, but then she lost it in the middle of the Sunday service during a sermon he was giving about temptation. She stood up and screamed to the entire congregation what had been happening. The whole town was there."

"And you ran away because you were humiliated?"

"Not entirely. I ran away after . . . I ran away because a week later, his wife killed herself."

Casey's face fell. "Jesus."

She nodded, tears welling anew. "I'd felt awful after she told everyone—like everybody was either looking at me as a slut or a child-abuse victim. With pity or contempt. But after she committed suicide, I realized, in this massive, suffocating rush, how selfish I'd been. And reckless." She paused then, registering what she'd just said. *Selfish. Reckless.* Those unforgivable crimes she'd been holding against Casey. "I realized how blind I'd been, when all that time it had felt like some big romantic drama. She'd never been a real person to me. A real person trapped in the same oppressive community I'd grown up in, with a real life I was destroying." Her voice broke, shoulders beginning to shake.

"Hey." Casey touched her arm, rubbing it softly, up and

down. "It's okay. You were fifteen. We're all sociopaths at that age."

She shook her head. "Yes, but my actions killed somebody, Casey."

"If you want to blame yourself, you have to blame the whole goddamn town, too—the sort of culture you guys all lived in. People don't just end their lives because their marriages fall apart. She had problems of her own, I promise you."

"It's hard to see it that way."

"You can argue it all you want, but I could just as easily argue that your preacher seduced *you*. You have to cut yourself some slack. You were a kid, wrapped up with what sounds like some seriously messed-up adults. He was the one who should have known better. He was the authority figure, and three times your age, too."

She heaved a sigh, the noise catching on sobs.

"Anyhow, we *could* argue about it all afternoon, but I don't want to. Just tell me how you got from fifteen to twenty-two, and here."

"I was sixteen by then," she corrected, and blew her nose.

"Hey, you want a beer?"

She glanced up with raw eyes, frowning, unsure. Alcohol had never given her trouble like heroin had. She'd always hated the taste of it.

Casey didn't wait for her answer. He disappeared and she heard the noises in the kitchen, and when he returned, he had the necks of two bottles pinched between his fingers. But he stopped on the threshold, frowning, and promptly turned around like he'd changed his mind. When he next appeared he held two clinking glasses, whiskey on ice to judge by the amber color.

"Cheers," he said, forcing a tumbler into Abilene's hand.

"To what?"

"To everybody messing everything up, all the time. *Everybody.*" He tapped her glass with his. "Now, go on. You're sixteen."

"I was sixteen . . . My parents were talking about sending me away to a boarding school or maybe even this Christian place, a religious mental ward basically, because I hadn't stopped crying in days. I heard them talking about it. I'd just gotten my first car that summer, and I packed a load of clothes in the middle of the night, and I drove away. I had some money I'd saved from babysitting. I got the ID in Fort Worth, and I stayed there for a little while . . . I won't lie, the next few years weren't good."

"How so?"

"I had a tenth-grade education, and I didn't want to use my real name, since I didn't know if my parents were looking for me. I sort of doubted they were. There was never an Amber Alert or anything."

Casey frowned, heart twisting. "Really?"

She shook her head. "Knowing my dad, he would've been relieved to have me gone. When I say he was tough, and hard, I don't just mean strict. I mean, like, after that, I was dead to him. I'd humiliated them. I looked myself up once, a few months after I left. There were local news stories. They said that I'd gone to live with relatives, but nothing about where. There was even a quote of my mom saying how, like, their daughter felt terrible for what had happened and needed a chance at a fresh start, in a new community. Like they were respecting my privacy or something."

"That's so incredibly shitty."

She made a *tell me about it* face and sipped her drink, wincing at the sting. She hadn't tasted liquor in ages. Not since before she'd met James. Not since Lime. She set the glass on the edge of the dresser, done with it.

"So what was really happening?" Casey prompted.

"I was all over, crashing on people's couches. Working menial jobs sometimes. But . . ." She took a deep breath. "But it was easier for me to rely on men. And I don't mean I was selling my body. I mean I'd date older guys, the types who'd take care of me, let me stay with them, lend me money." *Sugar daddies* was the term, but she refused to speak it aloud.

"Some of them treated me fine. Maybe they were a little creepy, with me being so young, but they didn't exploit me any more than I was expecting or willing to be exploited, you know? Others weren't so good. I got smacked around a little."

Heat flared in Casey's eyes.

"I left those guys as quick as I could. I'd spent so much time feeling controlled by my father, I only wanted that stuff on my terms. With guys I felt like I had some control over."

"Sure," he said, looking a touch nauseous. "So how did you wind up in Nevada? And with Ware?"

"Things took a bad turn when I moved to Arizona with a guy. We fell apart, and I wound up dating a friend of his. That was a bad scene, and I was in a bad way. I felt like I didn't belong anywhere. Like there was no home for me to run back to. I even wrote to my mother one time, about two years after I'd left, and asked if I could come and see her—just her. She told me no. That my dad was having heart issues and he couldn't handle it if he found out. She also told me my grandma had passed away. I loved my grandma, *so* much. I took her last name—my mom's maiden name—when I ran away."

"Price."

She nodded. "And she lived in Abilene."

"Gotcha."

"It broke my heart, hearing she'd passed. And worrying maybe the stress I'd caused everyone might've had something to do with it. After that letter, I just had to accept, I had no home to go back to. Nobody. This was about three years ago. I went into a really dark place, and I started to just . . . drift. I worked on and off, and I . . . I tried heroin, then. For the first time. And not the last."

Casey's fist squeezed his glass—she could tell from the way his knuckles blanched. He'd not expected drugs, she thought. The possibility had never crossed his mind, and she wasn't surprised. Junkies weren't meant to be shy, or liable to blush at cuss words, or indeed chubby. She didn't fit the bill.

All he said was, "Jesus."

"It was bad. It was *really* bad. It started slow. I worked and used and mostly functioned for a year and a half. I wound up in Lime, through somebody who knew somebody, who knew somebody."

"That's where you met Ware?"

She nodded. "But not how you might be picturing. He

saved me, actually. He was probably the only man who ever saved me, without wanting anything out of it for himself—sex or some hero complex or any other thing."

"Oh."

"He was tough. He got me sober, and we did wind up sleeping together, obviously, but it was different from before. I wanted him—out of gratitude, I think. For what he'd done for me, not for what I could get from him, going forward. He wanted me back, even if he was never truly comfortable with it. He broke it off before I knew I was pregnant, and I took it real bad. I made it ugly, and he made it ugly right back. I tossed out some real low blows, and he dealt a few of his own. I'd never seen him that angry before, and it scared me. Enough to be too afraid to tell him about the baby. The way we left it, and the way he'd met me . . . I was afraid he'd try to get her taken away, or take her himself. And once I was involved with all of you guys, I was *terrified* he'd tell you about me. About the kind of person I was." She looked to the car seat and her daughter.

"So it was more than just fearing for your safety."

She nodded, gaze falling to her hands. "It was self-preservation. Which makes me feel all the more awful. I'm . . ." She looked up, met his eyes with tears stinging her own. "I'm so sorry. I let you get so close, to me and to her. I never should have, not with so many secrets. You deserved to know who you were getting involved with, but I was too scared of losing you to say."

"You deserved to know things about me, as well."

After a pause, she said, "I've been thinking a lot about what you told me, these past couple days. About who you used to be." She paused when the baby fussed, and rose to free her from the seat in the hopes of settling her. She sat back down, bouncing her gently.

"After everything I've just said, it might sound ridiculous, me saying that I'm trying to do good now. That since I found out I was pregnant, the worst thing I've done is lie—which for me is an improvement, sadly. But I really am trying. I just want to work, and make enough to support myself and the baby. No more secrets, no more dependence. I want a fresh start, more than anything. To believe that whatever new life I make for myself is an honest one. A genuine one . . ." Thoughts were forming. Solidifying, and she spoke them as they came. "And I think you want that, too. To put your old life behind you."

"I do want that," he said softly. "A fresh start. A respectable life. It took me way too long to regret what I've done. It took what you said for it to register . . . and it took the fire at the ranch, and losing Don, for it to really hit home. Now that it has, I . . . Christ, I feel sick. I think about what I used to do and I feel like I could throw up."

She believed him. There was pain on his face, so real and so sharp it stabbed her in the heart.

"We want the same thing," she said, realizing it as she heard herself speak. "But when you were honest with me, I turned my back on you."

"Not without good cause."

She shook her head. Something had come loose in her chest, like a clog finally washing free, letting things flow. She could breathe for the first time in days. She could feel air in her lungs, and blood moving through her body, as though her decision had shut her system down, protested by every cell in her body.

"Neither of us can fix what we've done in our pasts," she said. "But neither of us gets to move on, either, not until somebody knows what we've done and chooses to forgive us. Chooses to believe we're capable of doing better, going forward."

He nodded, and now his own eyes were welling. He sipped his drink, sniffed softly, held his tongue. There was fear in those shining blue eyes, and hope as well.

"I forgive you," she said, and leaned close to put her hand to his face—on his soft skin and scratchy beard. "Whatever you did before you met me, that was another life. And I don't want to punish you for it. I only want to see what comes next. What you make of *this* life."

He covered her hand with his. "That means a lot." Other thoughts hid behind his lips, and he seemed poised to share them, mouth opening and closing. When he did speak, it was only to say, "For what it's worth, I forgive you, too."

She felt her chin crumple, and tears rolled fat and heavy down her cheeks to land on the baby's leg. She choked out, "It's worth way more than you know."

"Put the baby down a second."

She moved Mercy back to her seat, and as she sat once more, Casey set his glass on the windowsill and pulled her against him, cradling her head, rubbing her back. He let her cry for long minutes, until her bucking shoulders went still and her breathing deepened. He seemed calmer himself. Stronger, if still uncertain.

"From now on," Casey said, sitting up straight to catch her gaze, "whatever we are—friends, or colleagues, or any other thing—we go forward accepting each other's mistakes with our eyes wide-open, okay?"

She nodded, dabbed at her nose.

"I won't ever hold anything you just told me against you."

"I won't, either."

"All I care about is what comes next. And if you need something from me, know that you can ask for it, and I'll give you whatever you need, because I care. Not because I think you need saving, and not because I want something from you. Just because I think you deserve a fair shot at this new life of yours, okay?"

"I've never doubted that."

"I want you to know," he said slowly, carefully, as though handpicking each word, "that nothing's different about how I feel for you. After hearing everything you've been through. I'm still crazy about you, no matter what you did when you were fifteen, no matter what happened to you in Lime or any other place."

Her chest felt funny. Light and . . . and porous. Like a sponge, thirsty to sop it all up. "Really?"

"Yeah, really."

Was that even possible? She'd never been able to forgive herself for her mistakes, or stop feeling dirty about her past. It had been impossible to imagine someone else managing it. Certainly not a guy. *The filth of your sins is a mark that will never wash off,* her father had told her. *No decent man will ever want you now.*

She'd ached so badly for him to be wrong, though for years her choices had fulfilled that prophecy. But looking at Casey now, in the wake of what he'd just said, and knowing how it had felt, every time they'd come together . . . A good man *had* wanted her, and still did, in spite of all those sins. Not a perfect man, but a good one. It seemed all but impossible. A miracle.

"I don't understand how you can know all that stuff and still see me the same."

"I can't see you the same, no. I can see way deeper than I did before, knowing all that. But I *feel* the same, I promise you. I got absolutely no attachment to a girl's innocence, or her being perfect, or ladylike, or any other thing. All I've ever cared about is how somebody makes me feel, and you make me feel like I want to do better. Be better. And I can honestly say, no woman's ever made me want those things before. You and Mercy," he said with a smile, hooking his thumb in the baby's direction, "you guys accomplished the impossible. Must be the blue eyes or something."

"Must be." She felt shy, but behind that, elated. And confused about where she stood, but also hopeful, and undeniably free of so much pain and guilt and—

"I still care about you," he said firmly. "I still *want* you. Now, you don't need to tell me tomorrow or next week or even next year that you know how you feel, where you stand, but if you ever decide that maybe you still feel that way for me . . ."

Her smile faltered, trembling under the weight of everything she felt. "I won't tell you tomorrow," she said.

"And that's fine. Like I said—"

"I can tell you right now."

He stared at her for a long moment, blinked once, twice. And then he exploded her brain.

"Marry me," he said.

"What?"

"Marry me, Abilene or Allison or whatever the fuck I should call you. Tomorrow or in five years—I don't care when, just say you will."

She couldn't say that. Couldn't say that or any other thing—she was too shocked.

"Nothing's going to change how I feel about you. Not your secrets or me going crazy, not anything. I'll ask you again one year from now, if you want."

"I think maybe you should." If only because she might need that long to be sure she wasn't dreaming.

"I will, then. In the meantime, keep thinking about that house. Imagine every last thing about it, because someday you and me are going to find that exact place and make it just how you want."

Her shock softened in a breath, so touched by those words, and to realize that this man knew her better than anyone else on the planet.

"I can tell you my answer now," she blurted. "It's yes."

He nodded, looking bewildered but pleased. "Okay, good. That'll take the edge off the suspense."

"Good," she agreed.

A pause. "What kind of a ring do you want?"

"God, I don't know. Something simple. Something silver. I don't need a diamond."

"How do you want me to propose?" he asked. "A year from now?"

"Exactly like this."

"You sure? Because this is pretty sloppy and messed up, and I'm starting to think I should have just kept my mouth shut."

"Nothing about you and me has ever looked quite like it was supposed to."

"That's true enough."

"So I don't care how you propose. I don't even care if you ever do. I only want to be with you again, for real. To see if this can work."

"C'mere."

She let him tip the both of them onto their sides, facing, legs locking. She toyed with the buttons of his shirt and his palm was warm on her waist. And his eyes were there, right there.

"Move in with me," he said.

She nodded. That much, she could promise. "Okay."

"My apartment's not your dream house, but we could make it into something special, something for now. Make a home out of it."

"You okay with curtains?"

"I fucking love curtains."

She laughed, rubbed his chest. "Good. It's not a home without curtains."

"It's not a home at all, yet. But it will be, if you'll show me what that looks like."

"Gladly." And she kissed him, slow and soft, watching a smile bloom on those lips as she pulled away.

"It's going to be a long, rough spring," he whispered. "With everything that's just happened, and with everything that's going to be changing around the bar. But let's make our place somewhere calm to escape to at the end of the day, okay?"

"I'd like that."

"And we'll throw ourselves a little party, just you and me and Mercy. It doesn't feel like a time to celebrate, but it seems like we ought to do *something* to mark the fact that I've got a future, and that you're in control of things with your ex. A lot's fucked-up right now, but those are two good things. Too good to just let go by."

"I'd like that, too."

He brought his face close, rubbing their noses together, brushing his mouth softly against hers. "Maybe it doesn't need saying, or maybe I should have said it before I fucking proposed, but I love you. You and the baby, both. You need to know that."

She pursed her quivering lips and nodded. "You didn't need to say. You've told me a hundred times, with your actions."

"Well, now I'm telling you out loud."

She swallowed, found her breath. "I love you, too." Every ounce of him. Every cuss, every awful mistake. People were made of both light and dark, and you didn't get to love the good without first forgiving the bad. She knew that now.

"How about we get the cars packed back up?" he asked. "Seeing as how you've decided to move, yet again."

She smiled, wide and pure and open. "We can do that."

"All right, then." He stood from the bed and offered a hand, pulling her to her feet. "Let's get you home, honey."

Start at the beginning of the scorching-hot
Desert Dogs series by Cara McKenna.

LAY IT DOWN

Available in print and e-book from Signet Eclipse.

The motel was on the so-called good side of the tracks, the western side, closer to the mountains. The bad side was where most of the locals lived, and it was also home to the grimier businesses—the quarry, some limping little retail operations, Benji's, a couple garages, the dump, the dueling liquor stores. The nice side boasted the tech company and its employees' homes, a half-decent grocery store, the Sheriff's Department, and the Volunteer Firefighters' headquarters. Alex had been a member of the latter, once upon a simpler time.

Vince was burning up inside as he and his impromptu date strolled down Station Street, headed for the tracks.

He was used to girls acting coy when he hit on them. Or scandalized. Or downright eager. He wasn't accustomed to this woman's reaction, though. He didn't even have the right word for it. A weary sort of . . . unimpressed. Goddamn if it didn't make his pulse throb.

She asked him questions about the businesses they passed, then let his arm go to snap a couple photos of the dilapidated Fortuity Depot station, and stare up into the night sky.

"Jesus, you guys get a lot of stars."

"Benefit of living in a one-traffic-light town." For now, anyhow. In a couple years, Fortuity would be twenty-four-hour neon pollution.

"You know there's going to be an eclipse around here in a few months?" she asked. "A full solar eclipse."

"I don't exactly keep current with astronomy."

"Someone on Sunnyside's marketing team mentioned it. I'm hoping they'll like my work and want to bring me back to photograph it for them. To use in promotional materials, since the casino's named the Eclipse." She messed with some setting on her camera, aimed it skyward, and set it beeping and whirring, capturing the stars.

Vince was distracted by other natural phenomena, such as the shape of her ass and the smell of that perfume. He wondered if she had a tripod and if that camera had a video setting. He wondered what he had to offer God to bargain his way into this woman's bed tonight. He'd been feeling way too much this week. Maybe he could at least wake up tomorrow clearheaded, with *sexual frustration* checked off the list.

They crossed the tracks, turned onto Railroad Avenue, and headed for the Gold Nugget Motor Lodge's well-lit lot. It was yet another local business that probably wouldn't survive to see the casino's ribbon-cutting. They were doing well now, most of the spaces filled with out-of-towners' cars—folks here on development business. But once the resort opened, economy chains would follow, to catch the workaday tourists' dollars. The Nugget would likely sell up, get turned into some name-brand outfit, get a major facelift. Good for the owners, maybe, but it made Vince's chest hurt, imagining everything anodyne, everything with a familiar logo slapped on it, the profits bound for someplace far from Fortuity.

Goddamn, since when had he turned so sentimental? He really did need to get laid.

Outside of room six, his companion's key jingled as she got the door unlocked.

Just that noise focused his energy, the fate of the world seeming to hang on whatever was going to happen between them now. He felt his blood pumping hot and saw that sensation echoed by the pulse ticking along her throat. He could just about smell the curiosity on her. Same as he could smell that perfume, those flowers that wouldn't last a day in this desert.

She turned in the threshold and Vince laid his forearm along the jamb, leaning close. She froze, but the interest coming off her was hot. She wasn't scared of him, but there was a hesitance there ... She was scared of what she felt. What she wanted. She wasn't used to putting impulse ahead of consequence, he bet. He could tell from how she spoke, how she dressed. *Impulsive* wasn't in her repertoire.

Welcome to Fortuity.

Vince stooped, bringing his lips to her hairline. Fuck, she smelled good.

"Thanks for the walk," she said softly.

"Ask me in."

He felt her exhalation on his neck, a tight, anxious huff. "I'm not sure."

"Bet you are," he breathed.

"It's been a really long, shitty day."

"All the more reason to end it on a high note."

She laughed, the sound winding him even tighter. "You're shameless."

"Shame's a useless emotion."

"I'm going to ask you one question; then I'll decide. Deal?"

"Shoot."

She looked up and held his stare. "What's my name?"

Fu-u-u-uck. "Uh ..."

Her brows rose. "You don't remember, do you?"

"No. No, I do not." But he'd memorized her backside, in that skirt. Ought to count for something. "Jog my memory?"

She shook her head with an irritated sigh and stepped inside. "Good night, *Vince.* Thanks for the company. Sorry it had to end here."

He grabbed her hand. "Oh, hey—come on, now. That's not fair."

"I was down for maybe being your random one-night stand, but not an anonymous one." Her fingers wriggled free. Her voice had risen, cool tones lost to something far hotter. "I wasn't feeling real choosy tonight myself, but I do have *some* standards."

"When you live in a town this small, you don't get much practice at memorizing new names."

"All the same, maybe work on that before you try to fuck me again. Sound like a plan?" She wasn't shouting, but every measured word hit him like a slap. He kinda liked it.

He nodded. "Sure. Sorry."

"Good." Her feathers were smoothing, but just this taste of her temper, just the pink staining her throat and cheeks . . . shit. The ache knotted deep in Vince's belly felt more urgent than ever.

"You still up for a ride, Sunday?"

She blew out a tired breath. "I don't know. Show up and find out, I guess."

"Will do." He took a couple steps back, paused with one foot still on the concrete. "Like I said—sorry."

She shut the door on him. A lock clicked and the lights came on, but the curtain swept shut before he could steal a peek at Kim's bed—

Kim. "Kim!" He went to the window, rapping the glass. "It's Kim, right?"

The curtain swished aside, framing her. She mouthed her muted reply clearly. "Too. Late."

"Shit."

She shut him out.

He knew when he'd fucked his chances, and he also knew the line between flirtation and harassment. But as he started across the lot, blood pumping so much mischief, he couldn't help himself. He turned on his heel and strode back toward room six, hopped onto the walkway and knocked.

Her shadow darkened the curtain as she passed, and when she opened the door, she kept the chain lock on. "What?"

"So, Kim." He hooked his finger around the chain, toying. "You'll tell me when it's time, right?"

She blinked wearily. "Time?"

"Whenever it's cool for me to try to fuck you again."

Her eyes rolled up. "Go away, Vince."

He smiled. "Whenever you're ready, just say the word. Can't wait for the chance. Till then . . ." He held his palms up, miming deference, and took a step backward.

"Yes, you'll be needing those," she returned. "It's going to be a long wait."

"See you Sunday. Five a.m."

"Five *a.m.*?"

"Sunrise, sweetheart. Dress in layers. No heels. I'll find

you a helmet. Oh and wear that perfume—that shit drives me up a goddamn wall."

And off he went, giving her no chance to argue. He felt the heat of her glare on his back. It felt as good as a curious hand on his dick, and he smiled to himself. The door thumped shut, and he could hear her voice through the thin wood.

"Son of a bitch."

The smile became a grin as he aimed himself downtown. "To be continued, sweetheart."

Kim fell asleep in a foul and frustrated mood, and awoke in a matching one. Vince's come-on echoed in her memory.

Ask me in.

The *nerve.* It hadn't even been a question, had it? More a command.

Fuck him.

And fuck the part of her that had been half a breath from doing just as he'd suggested.

She packed her camera bag gruffly, stuffing lens wipes and memory cards into the pockets as if they'd insulted her.

Had it been an incidental come-on? Maybe King Roughneck hit on anything with breasts if it stood still long enough, his attention as impersonal as buckshot sprayed in the general vicinity of animate females. Or had he read something in her body language or eye contact, some chemical invitation . . . ? Read the far-too-personal truth in signals lost even to her. That she wanted him. In her body, if not her logical brain.

Kim sighed, no clue which possibility annoyed her more.

She'd slept like crap, restless to the last cell. Coffee was needed. Stat.

At the energetically named Wild Horse Diner, kitty-corner from Benji's on Station Street, she climbed out of her rental car. The formerly silver Jetta was dusted to the finish of a cinnamon doughnut. It locked with an obedient bloop, and she carried her purse and camera bag through the open front door.

She had her pick of seats, snagging a booth at the end. When the waitress swung by, she ordered an omelet, and coffee was delivered as she was buffing her glasses on a napkin.

"Thank you. God knows I need this."

"Sightseeing?" the young brunette asked.

"Yeah, you could say that." Kim smiled, not feeling like soliciting yet another stranger's opinions about Sunnyside's casino project, nor indeed feeling as though she were somehow their representative. She'd been grilled not only by Vince, but by the motel's front desk woman, a drugstore clerk, the gas station attendant. People had questions about the development, probably good ones, but she had zero answers. Sunnyside was as tight-lipped as ... as ... as some gross, chauvinistic simile a man like Vince might come up with.

Damn. There she went again, remembering him. Vince ... Whoever. Gris ... Grim ... Grenier? *Grossier.* He'd probably forgotten her name already. Again. God help her if he actually showed up, the next morning. If he did, she'd go along for the photo ops, solely.

The company was paying her for five days' work and travel. In truth, way more time than she needed—she'd already have hundreds of usable shots by that evening. But she'd stay the full five, and not only for the money.

She wasn't in a rush to head home. Fortuity might be rough, the assignment not exactly a gold mine—she'd grossly underbid for it, desperate for a change of scenery, some breathing room—but at least here she didn't have to confront the awkwardness waiting back home. Her stuff still in Ryan's apartment, and the man himself. A man whom, on paper, she'd had no good reason to dump. But hearts weren't made of paper, were they?

Plus, when have I ever felt sure about a guy? She slumped at the thought. Maybe she was holding out for something that wasn't ever coming, waiting to feel that mythical lightning strike, that sizzle. What if that glittery expectation was all bull, cooked up by the same sickos who'd invented Valentine's Day and Brazilian waxing?

She opened her camera bag and propped the Nikon against her thigh, turning it on. She cycled backward past the black night sky, the train tracks and station ghostly in the streetlight. Then came a punch in the stomach.

That man. His flash-lit face was jarring and stark.

He'd turned his head slightly, and she could see the tip of that ridiculous neck tattoo curling from behind his ear like an evil sideburn, black like all the other work he'd had done on his arms. None of it scandalized her. Sleeves were as common as eyeglasses in Portland, though Vince was no skinny hipster. His bike was no doubt the kind that came with excessive horsepower and earsplitting, look-at-me decibel levels.

She clicked to the next image on the card. Studied that matchstick pinched between his full lips, the ones she'd managed to capture sans evil smirk, surely a rare sight. She'd surprised him on that first shot, his eyes still wide. The flash bleached his retinas pure white, hazel irises lit up—striated near-green, the color of lake water and rimmed in gray, a gold corona around his tight pupil. Nice lashes, dark as his hair and stubble. Nice brows, though one had a bald spot, the gully likely framing a scar the flash had blown out. The man probably had a hundred scars—and a dumb, macho story to explain each and every one.

When a man came built like Vince Grossier, it told you one of two things: Either his job was backbreaking, or he made violent love to his weight bench every morning. She had her money on the former, given the local economy and those dusty jeans of his. But no matter the cause, the effect was the same. All that muscle added up to a man who lived through his body.

The smart man will manipulate you, and the strong one will push you around. Either way, they knew where they wanted you. At least with the guileless, pushy ones, the Vince Grossiers of the world, you saw it coming. There was an honesty in that. It gave you a chance to put up a fight.

She toyed with the camera's DELETE button. One push of her thumb, and he'd be gone. She pressed and his image shrank, sucked off the screen forever. The second shot filled the void, those brows drawn in surprise and annoyance, eyes narrowed to match. Her thumb hovered.

She jumped as a steaming plate was set before her, stammered her thanks to the waitress, and shut off the camera. Shut it in its bag, like she'd stuffed down her attraction and shut that motel door on him.

Four more days, she reminded herself, spanking the ketchup bottle. Four days to do this job, four days to avoid heading home and facing the fallout with Ryan.

Four days in the desert of northernmost Nevada. In the New Wild West known as Fortuity.

She eyed her camera bag.

Four days to get real good at avoiding Vince Grossier. The rest of her life to get busy forgetting him.

ALSO AVAILABLE BY

Cara McKenna

After Hours

Erin Coffey starts a new position as a nurse at
Larkhaven Psychiatric Hospital where she finds she's
drawn to her co-worker...He embodies the bad-boy
type she's sworn never to get involved with, but when
he shows up at her door, Erin is shocked by his inde-
cent proposal and how much she enjoys submitting
to his every command.

Unbound

Merry's on a three-week hike through the Scottish
Highlands, but when disaster strikes, she's forced to
seek refuge in the remote home of a brooding,
handsome stranger. Rob exiled himself to the
Highlands years ago, but when Merry shows up on
his doorstep, he can't ignore the passion
between them...

Hard Time

When Annie Goodhouse steps into her new role as
outreach librarian for Cousins Correctional Facility,
no amount of good sense can keep her mind——or
eyes——off inmate Eric Collier. But when Eric begins
courting Annie through letters, they embark on a
reckless, secret romance...

Available wherever ebooks are sold or at
penguin.com

caramckenna.com